A PURPOSE TRUE

A Purpose TRUE

GAIL KITTLESON

WordCrafts

Published by WordCrafts Press
Buffalo, Wyoming 82834
www.wordcrafts.net

DEDICATION

To Mom, who always encouraged me in my writing, and to Dad, who served four years in the Army Air Force during World War II.

CONTENTS

PRELUDE

April 1976, a small Idaho town

Launching like a World War II V-2 rocket over the balcony of Faithful Shepherd Church was not in Kathryn's cleaning plan. She wasn't sure how she had slipped. She recalled the pews and organ appearing like dollhouse furniture from her high perch, and thinking she ought to haul in a ladder to dust all those niches and curves in the gorgeous hand-carved altar.

Had her hand slipped when she tackled some quarter-inch-thick dust in the neglected balcony, or was it her foot? Strange she couldn't remember, since her sense of equilibrium had distinguished her during parachute training thirty years ago outside of London.

But now, she sailed through the serene sanctuary air as she had way back then, jumping into the Nazi-occupied Auvergne. For a moment, floating over the staid pews as though time had halted, Kathryn could almost feel the cool French air whoosh around her. Seemed like any second, her silk chute would release and fill.

The towering ornate organ pipes along the north wall struck her as more beautiful than ever. Some gentle slant-eyed woman must have painted those oriental designs with great care.

But then a solid *thunk* on the hard, oak floor of the sanctuary ushered Kathryn back to Idaho. All she could see was the wooden lip of a hymnal holder a few inches above her face. Pain ricocheted through her mouth.

Her silk slip hiked up, so she tried to reach down and straighten things, but her arm refused to budge. She tried her left leg, then her right—no movement. Panic, like the volatile floor polish fumes, inundated her. A frantic "Help!" rent the quiet space. *Ah, that would be Darlene.*

Soon, a gravelly voice exuding meat-and-potatoes breath broke into Kathryn's awareness. "Nothing appears broken. Amazing, but then, I've never known a stronger woman."

She focused on the face, backed by embossed ceiling tiles swirling far away. The church board always chose the same color, as if the day-old biscuit hue were sacred.

Old Doc Randall's affectionate hazel eyes scrutinized her through lenses the thickness of her leaded bay window. "You all right?"

Kathryn's arched tongue failed to reach her teeth. "Yeh ... dus bappa."

"Just dapper, eh?" Doc's one-sided smirk reminded Kathryn he'd served in France, too, but in the Great War. She attempted to speak, but to no avail. What was with her tongue, anyhow?

"Follow my finger with your eyes." Right. Left. Down, up, and back to center. Doc pursed his lips. "Darlene's gone for a cold cloth. You'll need x-rays, so I'm calling an ambulance. Now, don't fight me." His brusque manner failed to hide a note of concern.

The somber lines of his face incited a giggle that revealed the sorry state of Kathryn's rib cage. A brief glance down revealed a mass burgeoning below her nose, a swelling blimp of a thing, and she eased a tentative fingertip toward her mouth. Her arm still worked.

Her fingertip seemed gigantic, otherworldly. Fiddling around with her tongue revealed the massive protrusion as her lip, already swelled to kingdom come. Mingling with the cleaning polish, the copper tang of blood nauseated her.

"Lie still, Kathryn. Your life could depend on it." Doc craned his neck back to observe the balcony. "That's a mighty long way for a person to fall. You took a pretty hard hit on this pew."

He pointed out a good-sized gouge in the golden oak, and an odd varnish taste registered in Kathryn's mouth. She wanted to smack him when he pried her lips apart, but a bloodied wood chip the diameter of her wedding ring emerged between his thumb and forefinger.

"A mercy you didn't swallow this ragged piece. Can you move your feet?"

Nothing but her arm cooperated. Darlene appeared, her eyes wild, and Doc exchanged places with her. His joints popped as he rose, and Darlene waddled closer on her knees. Unexpected coolness eased the pounding in Kathryn's head.

"Oh, how could this have happened? And the men just left for the mountains with the sheep—how on earth will we ever get ahold of them?"

The first question was intriguing, the second irrelevant. Everyone knew that once the herders left for the summer in their tidy portable wooden houses, reaching them was impossible.

So, how did she manage to fall? The last she remembered, the splendid stained-glass depiction of Jesus and the children had attracted her attention. She rarely noticed this highest window set behind the balcony pews, but with Darlene helping out today, the obscure niche came front and center.

Tackling the thick dust made her feel better, especially with her recent hard news about her dearest friend Addie. Somehow, tackling this long-delinquent dust lightened her heart. And then, Jesus caught Kathryn's eye. Blazing July sun radiated through his tawny hair and he welcomed several children with open arms.

A wave of something besides worry swept Kathryn. "Is that me there in your arms?" Her question hung like dust mites in sunlight, and a brief parade of all the times she'd experienced deliverance passed before her. Moments passed before the sensation coalesced... no matter what, a vast love held her close.

She closed her eyes for a second to contemplate, but her practical nature resisted sinking down on a pew. Instead, she thrust her dust rag at a filmy gray layer on the clock's far edge, highlighted by a narrow beam of sunshine—oh the richness of those rays finding an entrance to this shadowy corner!

"Kate." A voice from the top of the balcony stairs stopped her short. She breathed in her childhood name—years had passed since anyone called her that, and twisted toward the sound. But silence reigned.

Down below, Darlene swished her rag steadily over the pews—no, it wouldn't do to dawdle. Mara, Kathryn's first grandchild, would be coming over after school, since Gabby had a late meeting today.

On Kathryn's second swipe at the clock, an even brighter shaft of sunlight hit—wonderful rays that bespoke the high-country beauty just beyond this building. She shook off that voice calling her Kate—surely her imagination.

But was that a slight shuffle over near the stairs? She turned to look, and the next second, propelled headlong over the railing. Then that excruciating *thunk*, and now, a draft of air as the main sanctuary doors swished open. Timeworn floorboards vibrated toward her in a regular rhythm.

Darlene had slipped off somewhere, but something warned Kathryn to pretend sleep. The rhythm halted inches away. A painful slit in her eyelids revealed nubby brown wool tweed slouched over scuffed oxfords, and the headline of a folded Chronicle under a slender man's arm: *First Flight of Concorde Supersonic Jet*—a month behind the times.

The intruder leaned close. "I never meant to ..." His whisper left an unforgettable odor—Gauloise cigarettes. Short, wide, and unfiltered, their intense aroma instantly transported her to Turkey or Syria—or back to the South of France, where Resistance partisans smoked Gauloise as a matter of patriotism.

Scruffy and starving, they cried, *"Liberté toujours!* They've killed nearly a thousand at the Fort in Paris, and that butcher in Lyon executes even more, but we fight for freedom forever!" Prior to D-Day, that objective had infused Kathryn's every move.

The tweed man departed in silence. Moments later, Darlene squeezed Kathryn's fingers. "Stay with me now."

Watch out for Mara, she wanted to say. *Stop at Gabby's office and let her know about this.* Hopefully her eyes communicated what her tongue could not.

Darlene scrunched up her nose. "Oohf—where did that awful smell come from?"

Kathryn faded again, but a familiar tender tone replayed inwardly, the same almost unbearable divine love that had burned the backs of her eyes up in the balcony when she'd stared at Jesus and the children.

"Yes, it's you here in my arms, always. And remember, you can never really lose a friend like Addie."

Kathryn's unintentional groan deepened Darlene's puzzled look. "Oh, I wish there were something I could do. But you'll be all right, hon. I'm sure you will."

People surrounded them then, and someone took Darlene's place. "Careful now—her neck may be broken. One … two … three."

Canvas supported her, then a harder substance, like wood. A warm spring breeze touched Kathryn's cheeks, followed by an antiseptic smell. Narrow walls closed in, but just before the doors clicked shut, a small gust of air grazed Kathryn's ear, along with that same strong tobacco scent.

"Never forget Barbie—do you hear me?"

Her gut clenched, but something jostled her left shoulder, and searing pain engulfed her. Her cry emerged only as a whimper. Klaus Barbie, the Butcher of Lyon. How could she forget?

ONE

Intermittent snorts issued from the pigpen. The heady odor already permeated Kate's borrowed chore clothes. At her best imitation of Domingo's whistle, Le Chien bounded over to her, and Mrs. Ibarra glanced up from pouring potato peelings into the swill.

"You have learned quickly. See how the dog obeys." At least that's how Kate interpreted the petite woman's Euskara-tainted French.

A cold nose grazed Kate's palm, so she bent to pet the scruffy sheepdog's grizzled muzzle. The V-shaped patch on his left ear flopped awkwardly, evidence of a fight.

"Your looks deceive. You know more about sheep than I ever will." The mongrel cocked his head. "You only have to tolerate me for a couple more days before Domingo returns. At least, I hope so."

The canine's brown tail brushed the breeze like a feathery flag as he roused a wooly mass from the shade of a stone enclosure and herded the recalcitrant animals baaing and maaing toward an inviting meadow.

Kate took her cue and nodded a quick good-bye. "Madame Ibarra— *à bientôt*."

"No, wait." The wizened peasant woman hurried to the house, so Kate followed. She smoothed the hand-hewn arch with her fingers. In bygone days, someone took great care fitting pieces of carefully curved wood to aged stones.

Madame Ibarra thrust a burlap bag into her hands. "You must have food for the day, and drink." Then she reached up to make the sign of the cross over Kate. "Domingo declares even our corner of Lot unsafe now. May Gabirel guard you."

"Gabirel?"

"Our Champion, the heavenly angel who watches over us."

"Ah, so you named your youngest for him. And Domingo means ruler?"

"*Oui*, for he entered this world on a Sabbath."

Simple, undeniable logic stoked her obsidian eyes. Aunt Alvina used to regard Kate the same way, with motherly concern and pride. Near the ridge above the family dwelling, Kate looked back and the Ibarra family matriarch gave a nod.

The flock's dense scent led into an elongated valley bursting with early summer growth. Poplar saplings and chestnuts poked fresh buds skyward. In the still-dewy grass, some pink Lady Orchids Domingo had shown Kate a few days ago still held some color.

The war threatened even this isolated area. Rather than herding their sheep, countless young Basques like Domingo risked everything leading downed pilots over the Pyrenees or fulfilled other dangerous assignments for *La Résistance française*.

At word that the Gestapo had compromised her Clermont-Ferrand circuit, he might have left Kate to fend for herself, yet kept his word to guide her to the Department of Dordogne. Whether she ever reached that destination remained to be seen, but after meeting his mother, she'd gained an inkling of how much he sacrificed to help Monsieur le Blanc, the mysterious *Résistance* worker they stumbled over on the trail.

Just before *Monsieur* left this world, he'd revealed his identity as her father's brother. The experience still held Kate in wonder. Finally, she had what she'd always hungered for ... family. After his humble burial, their temporary host revealed the depth of his devotion to la *Résistance*.

But Monsieur le Blanc bequeathed her far more than a locket with her father's baby picture—he left his recollections of her father, *Le Renard Intrepid*. And while Monsieur died, Domingo waited in the shadows, keeping watch.

Halfway up the slope, prickles traced Kate's spine. A wary turn, and she burst into a relieved laugh. Some knobby-kneed baby goats with upturned ears the length of their heads trailed her.

"Hello little ones. Does this mean you've bonded with me so quickly? I have only visited your pen a few times." She smoothed their long cream-colored hair and pink ears. "Come along, then."

"Maa, maaaa."

One kid struck an appealing pose with a weed stem hanging from its mouth. Another baby rubbed its muzzle into the ground, adding a gritty layer of soil to its charcoal nose.

Remembering Domingo's quiet vigilance after Monsieur's death brought Kate inner warmth, not unlike this sunny spring weather. While remaining close at hand, Domingo allowed her time and space, and because he asked nothing of her, she told him everything.

Still shocked at her rashness, Kate's inner chidings had ceased, for the most part. If her outpouring had been in error, so be it. But in her heart of hearts, a calming voice told her Domingo's loyalty ran deeper than the *Ségala's* farthest reaches.

Wildflowers brushed her every step. Addie could identify most of them, no doubt, but Kate's lack of names did nothing to decrease her appreciation of the colors dancing in the grass.

Shiny charcoal hooves barely touching the earth, the kids danced along with her at a distance from the sheep. After the long winter's stark dun and white landscape, seeing so many emerald shades almost hurt Kate's eyes. At the top of the incline, she paused.

"Minus these rolling hills, I might be back in Iowa on Addie's farm." The locations she had called home since she came to France came to mind—such good memories of Le Chambon sur Lignon, much higher in the Haute Loire, and the countryside around Clermont-Ferrand. But now, this high country between the Viaur and Aveyron Rivers grounded her afresh.

She reached down to scratch a kidlet's head. "Right up there, see? That's where Domingo went." Rugged crags rose like sentries and Kate shivered in spite of her confidence in Domingo. In those *Ségala* wilds, thousands of *Résistance* partisans awaited instructions and British ammunition drops, but en route, the Gestapo lurked at every turn.

Simmering ferocity against the Third Reich burgeoned all over France, but so far, London limited the actions the Resistance could take against the enemy. Only covert sabotage was allowed—no direct contact with the Nazis.

Kate sensed limits, too, even though Domingo had found her a transmitter. Today, the Ibarra's neighbor Edorta called his brother Gabirel to work, so the sheep tending fell to her. Besides, Domingo warned her never to transmit with only his mother at home.

In this land of wildly divergent contours, the *Ségala* carried a particular mystique. When they first arrived in this department called Lot, Domingo had pointed out a peculiar crag.

"To the left of my baby finger, like a steeple—see there? From our property, you can see that peak. Northwest lies the *Résistance* encampment, so highly guarded that no one can approach undetected."

"Except you?"

He shrugged. "Whoever knows the passwords."

Now, Kate wished she'd asked more about his missions. Most partisans kept to their own territory, but Domingo seemed to range far afield.

The goats meandered up the hillside, their hooves leaving small pointed indentations in sod still moist from the spring melt. Westward, a smoke curl rose from another farmstead. Pungent lavender bundles from last year's harvest wafted their intoxication from a nearby drying shed.

Terraced up the valley's side, scraggly grapevine rows promised fruit in late summer, even with no one to tend them. But by then, who knew where she would be? Like Domingo, Kate had traveled farther than she ever dreamed. What might come next?

Southward, two sturdy sycamore rows guarded the dirt road. Their whitish outer bark layered over a deeper taupe foundation matched a stone outbuilding in a nearby pasture.

The flock spattered the hillside like light mortar smudges on a verdant tablecloth. Iowa had its beauty, but this serene landscape defied Kate to search out appropriate words. She dropped to the earth and pulled out her notebook. Lately, she'd journaled as if writing to Addie—oh, that she could!

"You would love southern France, with its endless variety of flowers, in shades that stir the heart. I hope you're gardening in spite of

London's recalcitrant clay soil. But most of all, I wish you happiness."

For the millionth time since December, Kate pondered the irony of Addie, an Iowa farm wife, taking her place in Mr. Tenney's London government office and living in his mother's upstairs rooms. Kate recalled her own days in those very rooms, after her husband's fatal crash.

She'd lost everything: Alexandre, then the baby, born too soon. Bereft of all that gave her meaning, she'd sought ways to contribute to the war effort. But who would ever have imagined she would join the Secret Operations Executive and become part of the British war machine?

The Baker Street office, her mentor Miss G, Ringway Airport where she learned to parachute, and Tatton Park where she practiced jumping, seemed otherworldly from the vantage point of these soft hills. London had become Addie's world now, and her husband Harold would soon storm France's northern shores.

Reminding herself to shred her outpouring into the pigs' swill back at the homestead, Kate set the notebook aside and pulled an ancient volume from her backpack. Though its French forms challenged her, the Midi-Pyrenees folklore piqued her curiosity.

Midway into the afternoon, the sheep startled when a solitary peasant crossed the hill. His dark brown velvet pants, green wool vest and espadrilles came straight out of her book. Probably a *Résistance* liaison, perhaps with clandestine papers tucked in his shoes. Captured by the Gestapo or the *Milice*, those hated French collaborators, he would swallow that evidence.

Kate's training taught her that the *Résistance* had yet to reach many obscure Basque areas. Many believed the Parisian government still owned this struggle with the Nazis. And unlike inhabitants farther north and east, most of the locals had yet to view a German officer or patrol pass through their area.

Le Chien circled the herd, but Kate could not forget the wiry stranger who might have lived a century earlier. Except for his clipped mustache, he resembled Maurice, her former circuit's organizer.

With SS Waffen tank units advancing northward to face the Allies and the Gestapo on every hand, this fellow crossing their land enjoyed about as much defense as the kids romping at the flock's edge. Like him, so many innocents stood to suffer all over the world.

Reports of horrendous Nazi *ratissages*—raids meant to strike terror in the populace—filtered in from Russia. Belgium, Poland, Greece, North Africa and Holland. Italy, now in the fourth battle for Monte Cassino, recorded its own agonies.

Day by day, this war's tentacles stretched. Now, unthinkable cruelty verged as close as Figeac, a little to the north. Kate and Domingo witnessed the aftermath after the Germans hauled young men off to detainment camps. Doors torn from hinges, fruit cellars ransacked, window glass shattered, stores plundered, woebegone children, and women weeping.

The oppressors took whatever they pleased, but especially sought young males to work in their war industries. At least their closest neighbor Edorta snatched Domingo's brother Gabirel from school and absconded to the *Ségala* highlands.

But Madame Ibarra could not manage without her youngest son, so Domingo had gone to fetch him from the high country before he returned to his own missions. But what could Domingo do if Nazi tanks suddenly descended on this peaceful place? What miracle could save these hard-working folk?

The answer rang as clear as today's crystal-blue sky—*L'Invasion*, or *Jour-J*, as the French called it. Liberty from the collaborating Vichy Regime rested on the promised Allied Invasion, so Kate merged her prayers with tens of thousands more rising from the heart of France.

TWO

Instead of periwinkle lavender buds poised to turn color by early July, fallow fields languished on every side. The slight wayfarer who joined Domingo a kilometer back rubbed a handful of last year's harvest in his palm.

"Field hospitals use this oil to treat burns. But it's bound to run out, with so few workers left to tend the fields."

This partisan's hunger for talk ran against the grain—the land itself proved comrade enough for Domingo. Always something new to notice, and every trip increased his speculations about the war. This fellow might provide more mental fodder, but Domingo remained silent.

His comrade chatted on until a signpost came into view. "Oh—I turn west here. Salut, *mon ami. Bonne chance—a liberté!*"

Awakened by spring, the countryside embraced Domingo's relieved sigh. Good fortune to you, and to liberty ... he definitely echoed the sentiments, but far better to forge his way to the *Résistance* encampment alone. He brushed at burrs sticking to his pants and sleeves.

How many times had he freed a sheep from such a hindrance? If only ridding this land of the *Bosche* oppressors were so simple. He paused to drink at a rivulet, and half an hour later, dusk faded into darkness. Farther, a dank sweet lavender scent lured Domingo to a shed used for drying. The herbal, hay-like essence calmed his senses as he sank to the floor against a wooden support for a nap.

But in a dream, one of the long line of British pilots he'd led over the Spanish border suddenly hovered inches away. In a scratchy voice, he murmured, "If it weren't for the longbow, I'd have been born speaking French like you."

Domingo remained quiet, so he continued, "I mean the Hundred Years War, you know."

Yes, I know, but who cares if you think me unschooled? Why explain that Euskara, not French, has always been my native tongue? French or not, you need me now, for we have a border to reach.

Just then, both of them froze at the sound of boot steps. Domingo shook himself awake, the pilot's statement still ringing in his ears. It ignited a perennial question.

Why had he been born into Basque heritage? That line of thinking brought Katarin to mind—she'd come so far from her American origins to aid the cause.

But that pilot also reminded him of a failure he'd rather forget— leaving behind one of the men entrusted to his guidance across the Spanish border. He'd shut out many details, but that energetic American who foolishly broke his ankle when he left the path still had a hold on Domingo.

He'd never imagined moving on without a pilot, but that time, he'd had little choice. Gestapo agents nearly closed in, and a British pilot suggested hiding the American under a stinking animal carcass near the river. "You can come back for him later, when it's safe—otherwise, we'll all die."

With the enemy on their tails, and the injured pilot urging them all to leave him, Domingo had finally agreed. But when he returned after guiding the others across the border, the American had vanished. Did the Gestapo find him and kill him or ship him off to prison in Germany? Had he gone off in this wilderness alone after they left and been attacked by an animal?

Dried lavender straw scaled from his clothes as he gnawed a hunk of *Maman's* bread. If not for the war, he'd be breathing in the richness of fertile soil with the sheep at pasture all day and anticipating a meal of hearty porridge tonight. Instead, he slept wherever he could and wrestled with these unknowns, both past and future.

In the cool misty dawn, he resumed his trek. Barring Gestapo interference, he'd arrive at the camp soon. But that pilot's eyes taunted him again. How could Domingo ever forgive himself for forsaking that man?

~

A day later, another night mission arose. Domingo had begun to expect these sudden assignments, but this one sent him across the border of Lot and plunged him into a fiery task.

"Hurry!"

He obeyed the order from his group's leader and set a wire sizzling toward explosives stuffed into an unused coal shaft, hustled away from the site and sprinted up a prickly incline. *Smash*! A groan as someone smacked into a tree told him others were following him toward his cycle's hiding place. He plunged through a ravine of scraggly chestnut starts, dousing his soles in a narrow creek.

"Dom..."

Must people chatter, even now? Gestapo would soon swarm this whole place like flies on manure. Nearing a rocky indentation opposite the inferno, Domingo collapsed. Another man followed him, and a third tripped over that one.

Figuring they had run about halfway between Decazeville and Montredon, Domingo crawled through lush growth at the mouth of a cave. Inside, a solid limestone wall supported his weight as he struggled for breath. The two other partisans crawled in, and one began speaking as soon as he gained enough breath.

"Where did you learn to run in the dark, man?"

Domingo gave himself to breathing.

"Who taught you to move like that?"

"Playing ... *pelota*."

Silence reigned, but not for long.

"Hopefully no miners lose their lives in this raid, especially after being employed this winter." The heavier of the two men studied Domingo. "I have some chicory in my pack. Do we dare make a fire?"

"I doubt they'll search this far away before dawn."

Soon, the scent of thick root coffee spread its fervor, and Domingo relaxed for the first time in hours. He welcomed the quiet of these hills, but as he often found, others needed to talk. At least by now, these two surmised he had no such inclination and addressed each other.

"You go toward Correze?"

"Unless I receive other instructions. My directions change like the wind."

"I travel to another munitions attack tonight."

His pack bunched under his head, Domingo feigned sleep. Outside the cave, wind whooshed in the pines while the men passed a cup back and forth.

"When Louis the Eighth gave Duke Decazes this land, he had no idea the Duke would one day hinder free France."

"At least he and Cabrol opened their minds to the English way and mixed ore with coal to cast iron. They birthed our industrial revolution."

"And we just destroyed their tunnels."

"Decazeville has other claims to fame. You know Timbaud himself lived here as a child?"

"Jean-Claude, our hero?"

"*Oui.* No light matter, joining the *Résistance* in two great wars. Did you hear that he sang the Marseillaise before the firing squad?"

"Indeed, and he paid with his life."

"But he still killed one German commander—long live Timbaud's memory." Someone spit into the fire.

"And good riddance, Feldkommandant Hotz."

Timbaud had grown legendary, yet *Résistance* tales reached Domingo only second-hand. He'd never heard the name of the commander Timbaud killed until tonight. Guiding downed British pilots over the Pyrenees dominated his past two years, but lately, the pilots often joined the *Maquisards* in this wilderness instead of returning to England. That was good, because his sabotage assignments increased by the week. Surely that meant the Allied invasion would inevitably come, and that could only bring about the end of this war.

After the two talkative strangers snored, Domingo pilfered a draught of tepid coffee and cautiously edged his way down the incline. Criminals and thugs ranged these hills. For all he knew, those fellows back in the cave only posed as saboteurs in order to turn him in to the Gestapo at first light.

~

A lazy sun saw Le Chien circle, prod, and nip, a vigilant warden to sheep intent only on filling their stomachs. The dog nudged Kate's elbow, alerting her to return home for the night.

She rubbed her scarred heels, almost healed after the hard trek just a few weeks ago. As she followed Domingo in his unabated passion to reach his home, her shoes had proven inadequate on the rough trails. When he noticed her blisters, he applied cool moss to her blisters and handed her an extra pair of espadrilles.

Today, gratitude flooded her once again as she slipped her feet into their comfort. Considering the gentleness of Domingo's touch and his willingness to meet her needs even though he longed to hurry home, she whispered a prayer for his safe return.

After the sheep crowded into their pen and the kids nuzzled their mother, Le Chien's eyes, one scarred across the pupil, caught Kate's attention. Some would call the dog ugly, but there was something appealing in the angle of his head

"When Domingo comes, I'll tell him a shepherd's life seems easy, since you do all the work."

Le Chien perked his ears at his master's name, gave her a reproachful look, and sauntered to the sheepfold gate. Kate sank to the low stone wall that seemed to grow out of the earth.

I am the door of the sheep. Through me they go in and out and find pasture. The verse brought her confirmation Sunday to mind, long ago and across the Atlantic in little Halberton, Iowa.

With Le Chien blocking the gateway, no one could hurt these sheep, and they couldn't leave the enclosure either. Kate whispered into a slight breeze, "Gives new meaning to the saying, *Over my dead body.*"

The heavy iron pump handle protested when she filled a stone trough and two pails to take into the house. Inside, Madame Ibarra sliced potatoes into a pot, with steam rising around her like hazy river vapor.

"*Madame,* I wore Domingo's scent this morning as you suggested, but the herd knows the difference. They're still bleating their protest." Kate glanced down at her borrowed men's trousers and shirt. If the Gestapo came, she certainly looked her part.

A small stoneware crock above the stove held her new identity card. Once again, she'd transformed into a milkmaid, as when she first arrived in France, but now as *Emazteona Giselle Ibarra,* twenty-four, born in the Department of Lot. The age tweaked her sense of humor—she must've matured quickly, since she'd turned twenty-one just a month ago.

Wrinkles littered Madame Ibarra's forehead. She took her time answering. "They're just being stubborn. Keep them in the nearest pasture tomorrow, and they will respond to you. Always remember, we drive cattle, but sheep must be led."

She slanted her knobby finger toward the window. "Gabirel should be home soon from Edorta's."

"Is Edorta the one who protected him? The man in Figeac said ..."

"Ah, *oui.* We call him brother, more bound to us than by blood, closer than family. He took Gabirel from school before the soldiers came. He did the right thing, but now..." She slipped into silence.

Kate eyed the wood supply. Probably Gabirel kept the box filled, but she could help. Three loads later, seeing the fruits of her labor satisfied her. She turned to the barn to do evening chores and found comfort on the ancient wobbly stool beside a nanny goat.

"Come on, nanny. Give us some milk."

The door squeaked, and as Madame Ibarra entered, Kate squirted herself in the face. She licked her lips—um, sweeter than cows' milk. Domingo's mother chuckled low in her throat, but her eyes communicated good will.

"Tonight, Domingo travels safely. I feel it." She pulled up a milking stool and milked the cow and another goat before Kate finished.

Did Domingo's mother refer to the same unique sense that often bolstered her? Sometimes when she thought of Addie, it seemed Addie might be thinking of her, too. Or did the matron of this household refer to some deeper wisdom?

The simple spurt, spurt of creamy white milk echoed against the pail as daylight eased into the evening. As Kate finished with the goat, a motor grumbled out on the road. On tiptoe before a high window, she spied a lorry painted the brown-gray of *feldgrau* uniforms.

Her pulse tumbled over itself when the motor stilled. Like a phantom in the dim light, a German officer emerged from a truck and strode toward the barn. Kate hissed, "Enemy soldiers," and raced back to her stool.

Madame Ibarra sat immobile, showing no other sign she heard. The brightness in her eyes momentarily calmed Kate, who buried her face in the animal's side. Outside, boots cracked against dry stones and harsh male tones rose and fell.

The barn door creaked, turning Kate's stomach. Heavy steps neared. Then cool leather-gloved fingers grasped the back of her hair.

"Tell me your name, light-haired one."

For a moment, Kate's mind went blank. Then she remembered. "Emazteona Giselle." A second soldier stationed himself a few yards away, but not far enough to mask his smell, the odor of stale wine overlaid with sweat.

"*Qui est la mere de la maison, eh?* Show me your *cartes d'identité.*" The first soldier barked his question and finally let go of Kate's hair, but his rifle butt brushed her nose. With a gentle swish, Domingo's mother rose from her stool and gestured for the Germans to follow. The upward tilt of her chin revealed dignity—indeed, she presided as the mother of the house.

The second Nazi ordered, "You—stay where you are." He followed his comrade, but stationed himself at the barn door. When Kate risked a glance at his back, his broad shoulders and wide stance in tall leather boots made her gulp—the picture of power.

A surreal sensation flooded her—she shared a barn with an SS officer. Could this really be? Yes, Madame Ibarra had just led enemy soldiers down the alley between stalls. Like a true heroine, with no training or previous experience, she acted with composure.

The radio! It was hidden just a few feet above this stall in the granary. If the Germans searched the premises, what could she and Domingo's mother do?

She should take some action, at least pray, but no words came. Images of Domingo's fragile mother reaching into the stone crock filled her thoughts. But a German fiend shadowed Madame Ibarra. Everything depended on those identity cards passing inspection.

And then the guard swayed back down the aisle. He slouched

against a divider a few yards away, eyeing Kate through half-closed eyes.

An eon passed. Empty teats slumped between Kate's fingers, but she pretended to continue. Ice ran along the course of her spine when the guard moved closer, but at the same time, Mrs. Ibarra led the other German through the door. The guard returned to the divider as coarse black homespun—Mrs. Ibarra's sleeve—brushed Kate's arm.

The first soldier gestured her away with his hand and pierced Kate with his stare. "You have lived here since birth?"

Kate froze—she couldn't have answered for her life.

"Don't tell me you can't speak French, girl."

"She has always been slow." Madame Ibarra's tone remained steady even as her cool, chafed fingers settled on Kate's wrist.

"Ach! Then what good is she? We should deport her like *les Juifs*."

"She cares for the sheep, makes goat's cheese, plants our potato field, and cultivates the lavender. I could not live without her, for my husband and son died in the Revolution."

The officer puffed his chest. "We have camps for such vermin." He spat into the straw. "So, you manage this place yourself?"

"With our close neighbor's help."

"Where is he now?"

"Working, I think." Madame Ibarra's French garbled into the Occidental tongue for a time before she summarized, "Perhaps in a work camp for Monsieur Petain."

"Don't fool with me, old woman. This area is a *Résistance* hotbed, but you say you're a Petainist?"

Time stopped. Nicotine stains marred the officer's raised hand. An animal brushed against a gate somewhere, and Kate ached for breath. Why did Madame Ibarra not answer?

Just when the tension seemed unbearable, the officer chortled. "You're certain this neighbor of yours does not meet British airplanes and carry explosives up the mountain to the fighters in the night?"

Madame Ibarra made a scoffing sound and took her own stool. Finally, the officer dropped their identity cards on a divider and turned toward Kate. "Tell me the meaning of your name, girl."

Perspiration broke on her forehead and fever flamed in her cheeks.

She glanced toward Domingo's mother. "*Maman?* My name? I think it means *good wife*."

A raucous guffaw echoed. "A mockery—some wife you would make." He struck a match on his boot and acrid smoke rimmed the lantern light as he bent over Domingo's mother.

"*Achtung, alte parasiten.*"

Kate shuddered at the meaning of his injunction—*Warning, old parasite*. His steps echoed down the alleyway. But instead of following him, the guard neared Kate again.

He leaned toward her with a faint smile, so close his green-gray eyes shown like a cat's. Then silently, he raised his hand and lifted a stray strand of her hair.

Eyes squeezed shut, Kate bowed her head. Slowly, as if to show her he could do whatever he wished, he slipped the hair behind her ear. Shivers coursed her neck and shoulders, and she felt sure he noticed her tremble.

An eternity later, he backed away. The barn door slammed, causing the goats to skitter. Then the lorry door banged shut amidst unintelligible German phrases. The driver gunned the motor, sending acrid fumes clear back into their stall. Only after the lorry turned onto the road and gained speed, did Kate hurry to Madame Ibarra.

"Oh, Madame, you are a true mother of *la Résistance*."

They clung to each other in the barn's relative safety long after the vehicle roared off toward Figeac. Shadows slanted darker around them, and Madame Ibarra's shoulders stooped a little more.

To change the atmosphere, Kate thought of an unnecessary question she could ask, for Domingo had already instructed her. "Madame, please show me how to feed each animal."

His mother took a mighty breath, cleared her lungs, and moved from stanchion to stanchion. "A scoop of corn in this trough, two scoops of oat groats here, and a pail of ground corn in the pigs' swill."

"Oh, thank you. I'll come in as soon as I finish."

Mrs. Ibarra ran her contorted fingers over the cow's backbone before leaving. Kate lingered beside the goat pen, observing her tortured gait. Her arthritis surely must be painful, yet Domingo said Gabirel was only fourteen. How old had she been when she'd given birth? She must have been in her late forties when he was born.

The urgent, innocent bleats of bright-eyed baby goats reminded Kate of her most recent loss. Last summer … her miscarriage seemed ten years ago, but anguish erupted as fresh as the raw milk in these pails. Tears burned the backs of her eyes as she knelt to tousle the kids' ears. Nothing to do but wait for the swell of grief to pass.

"Rest well here with your mother, little ones. I'll see you in the morning."

Ten minutes later, oat porridge in thick yellow cream swam in Kate's pottery bowl. Domingo's mother pushed the honey pot closer, its thick, translucent liquid still bearing the meadow's scent.

"You gather this from the hills?"

"Toward our far boundary, near Edorta's land."

After a second bowlful, Kate slid her chair back. "Oh, that tasted so good, Madame."

Domingo's mother said nothing. Mentioning the enemy visit could do no good, so Kate stacked the dishes and poured boiling reservoir water into the dishpan. But Madame Ibarra nudged her aside with a brief message.

"My work."

Kate donned her coat and circled the stone pen where *le Chien* kept faithful watch. She whistled her best imitation of Domingo's call and squatted beside him.

"If Russians can train dogs to perform dangerous missions, surely you can learn to accept me. Gabirel will soon be home, so I can begin my work. And then …"

She leaned back against the wall into the stuffy scent of warm wool and hot breath rising from the sheep.

Then what?

Domingo's priest would help her find safe transmitting locations, but after London issued the order for partisans to join the fight, wouldn't staying in touch with her circuit prove impossible? Always before when plans went awry, someone had sent a clarifying message, yet now …

Having to leave Le Chambon-sur-Lignon for Clermont Ferrand had taught her to manage uncertainty. After that, when her mind leaped into the future, she forced her thoughts back to the present. That was the secret, but having specific assignments certainly helped.

Distant sycamores stood like watchmen on either side of the road Domingo would follow. Compared to guiding downed pilots, negotiating this limestone plateau must seem as easy to him as feeding the pigs.

As if to remind her of their presence, a sow grunted, and several others squealed as afternoon gave way to sunset. Kate walked until flaming orange and russet outlined the *Ségala*, and halfway to the crag Domingo once pointed out to her, headlights glittered. A prayer sprang to her lips.

"If that's the *Milice* or the Gestapo, befuddle them. And please keep the tanks away from here." Then the soldiers' visit replayed.

"Oh Lord, thanks for keeping Mrs. Ibarra and me safe." Kate's mind skipped to Addie's pasture in Iowa, replete with smelly cow manure, and she recalled an agent describe learning to plant mines in cow pies. When a tank crossed over them, they went off--

Résistance crews from here to Toulouse surely did that very thing.

But tonight's visit still made Kate quake, and the idea of the Waffen SS carrying out reprisals on these peasants for aiding the *Résistance* sent a chill down her spine. As though stiff-arming a thought could prevent its implementation, she willed it away.

THREE

Late afternoon, and Gabirel should be home from Edorta's by now. "Bring him soon, and keep Domingo safe, too."

During her first isolated months in France, Kate pleaded the same for Addie, Charles, and his mother when reports of Germany's new Vergeltungswaffen rocket strikes on London filtered in. Such random news found her in conversations overheard on the street, or through glimpses of forbidden newspapers. She prayed even for Addie's controlling husband Harold, who prepared to cross the Channel with his unit.

But what of her own service to the Allies? Domingo had brought her radio from the Gaboudet organizer, but she chafed when Gabirel left for Edorta's this morning. Especially after that visit from the soldiers, she must not transmit without him here. Besides, she had no messages at this point.

The urge to stamp her feet possessed her, rousing a memory. When she was young, this attitude always produced a smile from Aunt Alvira. "Now Kate. Have patience."

The last silver-pink reflection of day faded into twilight. One more turn around the barn and a sweep of the yard for anything unnatural drew Kate near the back door. One more look for safekeeping.

"Maybe this is what it's like for people with a home. They feel responsible for everything."

Home—what did that mean, anyway? She barely remembered her first home. Her mother's face remained with her, probably because Aunt Alvina displayed her graduation photograph on the mantel. As for Kate's father, she recalled nothing.

Aunt Alvina had filled her childhood emptiness, but now she was gone, too. If only ... "Oh, what was my hurry to leave that dear woman and the home she made for me?"

Kate rubbed her shoes on the iron boot scraper. Maybe home was an elusive phantom. You enjoyed it until restlessness overtook you or disaster reared its head, and then you started over in someplace new.

Darkness dipped a final covering over sunset's last shaky fragment, and the sheep shuffled within their fold. For Domingo, such sounds signified the place where he belonged. What would it be like to belong here, to belong somewhere in this world? Wistfulness accompanied Kate into the house, where she barred the door.

Domingo's mother bent to her knitting. Kate fed the fire and asked questions, though Madame Ibarra's heavy accent rendered understanding her answers difficult.

Her people originated just over that ridge. She jerked a needle in the appropriate direction. "Providence gave us three boys and a daughter. I prayed for more, but four it was ... the will of the Almighty. Now, the eldest has already gone to be with his Maker—my dear Ander."

"Where does your daughter live?"

"She married an honest man from across the river and is now with child." Madame Ibarra pointed her needle south.

"Oh, that Ander," she mused, reverting back to her firstborn. "A fine lad, so like Domingo. I had a bad feeling when he went to fight in Spain, a divine warning. Domingo's father died there, too." Her mouth tightened. "And now... Godspeed my other sons' return."

A few minutes later, her head dropped forward, forcing black chin hairs into her shawl. Tenderness overwhelmed Kate and she determined to do her best for her.

The fire's crackle witnessed her silent vow as she peered through the curtains into the yard. Oddly, she felt closer to England here than in Clermont-Ferrand, high in the Haute Loire.

Very soon the Invasion would begin, maybe even tomorrow—how she itched to listen to the BBC! The long-awaited Allied advance would mean more bloodshed, but at least some of it would be Nazi.

Finally, Domingo's mother stirred. "What can be keeping my Gabirel?"

Had that lorry of *feldgraus* waylaid Gabirel en route? Madame Ibarra carried the lantern to the back room, so Kate banked the fire and layered thick quilts near the hearth. Her mission had changed again, from courier to guardian of a peasant woman.

Guardian ... what a joke, considering the courage Madame Ibarra displayed with those Germans. For tonight all was well, but what if real trouble arose? Kate's contemplations joined the fire's artwork on the wall, like the wispy cloud forms she watched this afternoon.

Some time later, tapping wakened her. A young man built low to the ground, with thick legs and torso, stood outside. When Kate opened the door, Gabirel slipped in like a shadow and hurried up to the loft without looking Kate's way.

His companion pushed his Breton beret back, uttering a mongrel mix of French and Occidental. Kate gathered he was asking for supplies. "... food for the partisans, en route from Gaboudet. Picked up bicycles at the Ratier factory in Figeac."

What should she send? Then she realized he also hungered to unburden his heart. Over a glass of buttermilk, he leaned into the doorjamb, a deep weariness reflected in his eyes.

"Today, the SS herded our men into a field. They discovered our hidden *Juifs* and made them carry rocks back and forth until they fell exhausted. Then they beat them and demanded they carry some more. When they finally loaded the Chosen into lorries, they let us go."

"Did Gabirel witness this?"

"No, we picked him up at Edorta's." He shifted his weight, drawing Kate's attention to his footwear, worn espadrilles dusted in powdery white and bearing the smell of flour.

"So far, I have been a *sedentaire,* helping the cause from my home, but today changed everything. I looked into my wife's eyes—we had heard how the Germans hate *les Juifs*—now we saw that hate for ourselves.

"She will manage our business while I cook for the fighters. When the time comes, I will fight, too. They say the planes from London drop Sten guns by the carton each night. Whatever the leaders ask, I will do."

He handed Kate a folded paper, then nodded toward the lorry. Before she could respond, Madame Ibarra bobbed through the main room.

"Gabirel has come home. He's upstairs already."

Mrs. Ibarra gave a quick nod before conversing with the visitor. Kate recognized only *cochon*—swine, and Gabirel's name.

The partisan tipped his beret and signaled to two others who had waited outside in the truck. They leaped out and commandeered a pig amid squeals wild enough to waken the Gestapo kilometers away in Figeac. With the hapless animal secured on the lorry bed, the old vehicle rattled to life. Blacked out taillights gave the faintest flicker before inky darkness consumed the exhaust.

Madame Ibarra touched Kate's shoulder. "Domingo may eat some of that *cochon*."

"You maintain hope, Madame."

Domingo's mother stared out into the night, and her voice emanated from a deep place. "War makes one hopeful."

"What do you mean?"

"In such times, hope becomes all you have." Before she retired, her eyes acknowledged her understanding. Gabirel had worked with the *Résistance* tonight.

In moonlight, Kate unfolded the note—logistics for a landing field. She must call Gabirel to stand watch.

She climbed the loft ladder and shook him. "Sorry to wake you. Will you keep watch while I transmit?"

The smell of evening dew still on his clothes, he leaped from his pallet. Thankfully, her radio responded, so she listened for word from London. Nothing. She sent the messages, and when she descended, bleary-eyed Gabirel made for his bed.

Morning brought no sign of Domingo, but helping with the sheep kept Kate busy. They completed late afternoon chores under a smoky gray and purple sky—the better to hide the partisans. When Gabirel arrived home from Edorta's, Kate breathed deeper.

"I'm going out to check for messages now."

Up in the granary, she detected a distant whine, the sound of planes circling, a sure sign of the Invasion. She checked the BBC, but no messages came through. If only she had more notifications to relay to London, but she must be satisfied for now.

Gabirel left when she descended the ladder. At dawn, he reappeared and slept for a while before pasturing the sheep.

While Kate hung clothes on the line in the afternoon, Gabirel came running from the pasture. "I must go."

He fled, so Kate hurried to the sheep. Domingo would be upset about Gabirel's activities, but what could she do? Some time later, a peasant wearing a simple homespun vest, tattered trousers and espadrilles approached, gesturing Kate to follow him with the sheep.

At his unspoken command, *Le Chien* nipped at the sheep's heels and drove them onward. Over a ridge, he collected the flock like a great wooly blanket. A birdsong cacophony blended with rustling leaves as a timid breeze lulled Kate's trepidation.

The stranger's actions indicated some sort of danger, but what? Visions of Domingo's fragile mother visited by those soldiers again haunted her, but the idyllic scene stilled her wild pulse and bade her speak aloud.

"This could be a sunny day in the English countryside, straight out of *The Wind in the Willows*."

Purple and lavender violets, a white daisy-like flower, wild periwinkle iris and some yellow buttons sprinkled the expanse. Addie would surely uproot some to nurture in Mrs. Tenney's clay-soiled London courtyard.

If Kate let her imagination go, she could visualize Waffen SS troops closing in, so she focused on her instructor's advice. "Lead your thoughts—don't let them lead you." Precisely why she'd brought a book along to read while the sheep grazed.

If this vagabond life taught her nothing else, she'd become less prone to cling to fear. Maybe that stranger warned her because this was the day for of requisitions. He had disappeared now, but Domingo had explained how Vichy constantly claimed food from the inhabitants here.

"Every week, we must tote our share of meat, milk, and produce to the roadside. But often, local *Maquisards* lock up the lorry driver, pick up the Figeac grain merchant's employee and deliver the supplies to *la Résistance.* After they free the Vichy driver, the merchant reports a burglary."

That day, he'd stood arms-akimbo, eyes sparkling, black waves swarming the tops of his ears. "We fight back however we can."

Kate gave herself to her book until the same peasant approached from the opposite direction. *Le Chien* read his signals, and Kate shadowed the flock west for a quarter-mile. The sight of Domingo's home warmed her, and she recalled Mrs. Ibarra's comment yesterday.

"You are like one of us already."

One of us. With her husband Alexandre, their baby, and Aunt Alvira, gone from this world, could Kate claim oneness with anyone on earth? Addie, yes—always. Northern France and the English Channel separated them, but they'd been apart before, and each time, their friendship grew.

With the sheep secure, she entered the barn. Inundated by the dusty grain scent under the barn's massive rafters, a wordless sensation enveloped Kate, like Aunt Alvina's country church liturgy so long ago. Even with her incriminating radio and the Gestapo hovering so near, a sense of safety caressed her.

Then, like a surreptitious wind, Domingo stood before her. Kate caught her breath—how had she not heard him enter?

He put his finger to his lips. "Shhh—do not let *Maman* and Gabirel know. I brought you some messages—highly important, the organizer said." He pulled at his top lip with his teeth.

"You must move the radio tomorrow. I will return." He slipped toward the back of the barn. Beyond him, through the window, a mere filament of light still brightened the horizon.

~

Clack, clack, clackety-clack. Pause. Kate's fingers made far too much noise on the radio keys. Gauzy pale blue dragonfly wings shimmered in feeble torchlight How would such a creature make its way from the creek up into this granary?

"As unpredictably as me tapping out signals from this granary," Kate muttered to herself.

The local organizer had sent highly sensitive information to her with a wayfarer, so once again, lives depended on Kate's transmissions. Below, a cow mooed, and some small nocturnal animal sprinted across the yard.

When she contacted headquarters during her wilderness trek with Domingo, an experienced operator oversaw her. But here on the farm, Kate transmitted on her own. Gradually, the details returned.

Messages at least two hundred words long, including a number corresponding to each letter of five words from your chosen poem.

Her instructor called Kate's chosen poem odd, but it worked. *By the shores of Gitche Gumee, By the Big-Sea-Shining-Water …*

After long minutes, confirmation arrived, so she relaxed. At ten o'clock, she tuned into the personal BBC messages, and after a few tries, the word ABERNATHY emerged in an illogical sentence.

The code's unintelligible phrases contained a message designed to throw off Nazi decoders. If they picked up her signal and succeeded in interpreting it, disaster might follow. The other danger, that her consistent *clackety-clacks* would alert the Gestapo if they drove by, worried Kate just as much.

At least if they cut the electricity to isolate and identify her signal, the battery would still prevail. Still, detection vans or agents with electronically sensitive apparatus might be canvassing the area between the Dordogne and Lot rivers tonight. Why did the enemy have to be so scientific?

When she switched off the machine, footsteps sounded on the ladder. Kate froze, but soon, Gabirel's black curls showed over the opening in the granary floor.

"Your machine wakes the night."

"Sorry. Stopping every twenty minutes slows me down."

"Why do you do that?"

"To break the air waves, in case the Germans detect my frequency."

"You think the Allies really prepare for *l'Invasion*?" Gabirel launched his question with an arched brow and the changing voice of adolescence.

His words bubbled freely, unlike Domingo. "Today is June third, right? Nearly a month ago, didn't the BBC broadcast all the right messages to signify the day?"

Gabirel flicked his hair back. "But no one came."

"The mission halted only because of bad weather, since pilots require clearance. Perhaps a storm blew up after the broadcast that night, but with so many drops all around us, we can be sure this time."

"At the encampment, I saw stacks of guns and grenades in crates. Domingo carries one, doesn't he?" His tone wobbled on the last phrase, finishing the question in a soprano.

"Many do. Did you ask him?"

Gabirel rolled his eyes. "And they carry pills that kill you, so you don't give away secrets under torture?"

The lipstick Kate's mentor gave her, with one of those tiny pills hidden at the end, lay in Kate's pack. No use denying facts.

"Only for impossible situations."

"Domingo has one?"

"I don't know, Gabirel."

"Perhaps the British and Americans, like General Petain, make big promises, but fail to deliver."

Compassion filled Kate. During the past four years, he endured one after another of Vichy's broken promises.

"Did partisans talk this way at the encampment?"

"No, but sometimes, I wonder if this war will ever end."

She touched his fingertips. "Of course you do. Domingo still believes."

Gabirel blinked "Yes, but tomorrow you both leave." He scooted down the ladder and murmured to the animals as Kate willed herself to focus on her final transmission.

Toulouse cells cite Waffen SS units heading north from refitting stations. Harassment increases at petroleum plants, coalmines, and railroad bridges. As a result, the Gestapo presses harder on rural departments.

Parachute welcoming committees required on Lot plateaus … high alert from now until Jour-J … le Débarquement at hand …

These reports all confirmed *l'Invasion*.

Understanding Gabirel's impatience, Kate sat back and rubbed her temples. After all, hadn't she eloped with Alexandre in youthful emotion? She clicked off the radio and lifted the gunnysack Domingo'd hung over the granary's high window. Cool evening air drifted from the darkness covering the countryside, but a full moon lent enough light for the parachute drops to proceed.

She let the gunnysack down, and the fragrance of sweet clover hay, heady straw, and ever-present manure carried her back to Addie's farm, but Gabirel's mood still settled over her. Surely, the Allies would come—unthinkable that General Eisenhower and Winston Churchill made all their preparations in vain.

Perhaps the magic words would float to her via the BBC during the next few hours. Kate flipped the switch to listen again.

FOUR

The darkness of the road to Montredon closed on Domingo like a dark tunnel as he navigated the five kilometers on his cycle, its headlamp turned off. Once, the lights of an oncoming vehicle loomed too late to kill his motor. Abreast of the shiny vehicle, he held his breath—most likely they were Gestapo investigating the conflagration caused by this night's work.

He shrank back from the vehicle's rush. Its shimmer took him back to the night of his beloved Sancha's death, but Domingo refused the familiar call—no good came from dwelling on what might have been. His next thought denied that truth, as that American pilot reappeared in his consciousness—impossible to shrug off those eyes, since Domingo bore responsibility for abandoning him.

His next thought, of Katarin staying with *Maman*, sent fiery emotion through him. No, he mustn't contemplate the American agent. Not now.

Thankfully, the vehicle maintained its speed, whipping his shirt-sleeves in its wake. Since he'd lit another fuse just several hours previously, a suffocating sensation gripped his throat. If someone stopped him, the smell of sulfur would testify to his participation.

Crossing the Lot River Bridge eased his breathing. He threw cold water on his face and neck before gunning the cycle toward Figeac. At long last, the glow from Decazeville faded. Figeac slept, except for two men standing in the street, staring east—friend or foe, who could tell? Domingo idled downhill, and two streets past a tall steeple, turned toward home.

The very word enticed him. Home. Months had passed on the trail until circumstances forced him to bring Kate to this isolated corner of Lot a few days ago. After the circuit supplied her radio, he relayed daily messages from the *Résistance* leader north of Prendeignes, and took whatever nighttime assignments headquarters supplied.

This time, they included a motorcycle, though he'd almost killed himself on the back trails earlier. Recalling that out-of-control slide constricted his throat, but this machine certainly cut down his travel time. Maybe he could stay home awhile, to lighten *Maman's* load.

Though she hid her worries, he must attempt to take his father's place. Perhaps now, with another woman, she would let down her guard. In spite of language obstacles, maybe Kate could comfort her more than he.

Around the final curve, Domingo turned off the motor and secured the cycle under a vine thatch. Good—no light from the granary. But halfway down the path, the transmitter's incongruous clamor met his ears.

His chest tightened. He must find a new place for Kate's transmissions tomorrow ... today. But where? He strode toward the barn, aware of something troubling him even more—how had he come to feel so responsible for her?

He pondered the first query and shelved the second at the sight of Gabirel standing watch outside the door. Heat burned the backs of Domingo's eyes as he touched his brother's thin shoulder.

"Thank you for watching. I'll do morning chores—sleep." Gabirel withdrew to the house in the ebbing night.

Past doleful barn animals asleep on the hoof and spent kidlets sprawled beside their mama, Domingo reached the granary stairs. Usually, clarity reached him in this haven, but the transmitter intervened. Still, his answer came to him as he climbed.

Only *Père Gaspard* could secure a safe transmission location, just as he had provided the agent a new Basque identity.

Mottled hair streamed from the knot at the back of the agent's neck. She must not have heard him steal up the ladder. The shock in her eyes when he appeared so suddenly the other night troubled him—mustn't repeat that error. He didn't want to startle her.

When he rattled the ladder, she focused beyond him, as if waking from sleep. No wonder. It was nearly four o'clock, and she'd started working before he left. But then, a relieved smile broke out and tawny waves brushed the hollows of her cheeks. Domingo glanced away.

"Your mission went well?"

He let his eyes answer for him. "And yours?"

She pointed to an envelope.

"A message for me to deliver?"

"I'm sorry. You need sleep." Her voice brushed his soul—such a gentle sound.

"We both do, but for the cause ..."

"Let me do the milking." Her black-brown eyes glinted up at him. On that December night when he carried her to safety after she injured her ankle in her parachute drop, her eyes had conjured Sancha's, but now distinct golden flecks marked the difference.

"Yes, and when I return, we visit *Père Gaspard*."

"I was about to click the switch." She did so and without thinking, Domingo patted her shoulder, then drew back. The night he left to search for Gabirel, he erred by standing too close to her. Maybe thinking of her as Agent Merce instead of Katarin would help.

Pre-dawn stillness accompanied them to the house, where Domingo submerged his canteen in the water pail, grabbed fresh bread, and wolfed some cheese. He whispered a final instruction to Kate.

"I'll ride the cycle, so I should be back soon. Rest until you hear the cows call you."

He pulled the door shut and retrieved the cycle. The sooner he delivered the messages, the sooner he could return, to *Maman*, to a few hours of sleep, and to Gabirel. But an insistent realization nagged at him. He would also return to this Amerikan agent.

He must cover the distance before daybreak, when the *Milice* brandished their fancy cars and pistols. A hidden turn-off gave way to high rocky country, and every kilometer increased Domingo's sense of safety.

Soon, his headlight grazed jagged woods concealing the entrance of the *Ségala* encampment. A guard took the cycle. He would find the machine full of fuel when he exited.

Free-French agents and Francs-Tireurs-et-Partisans members, or FANA, claimed the camp now, qualifying it for extra supply drops, though London questioned other organizations operating under the FTP's Communist arm.

The partisans borrowed the term *Maquis* from the Greek island of Corsica, where it meant *the brush*. And they stole other words, techniques, and ammunition from every quarter.

Jacques accepted the messages and waved Domingo inside. "Perhaps this intelligence comes from the National Council of *Résistance.* Tonight, the number of our local parachute welcoming committees exceeded last night's. When dawn breaks with no reports of deaths, I'm always relieved."

"Anything for me to take back?"

Jacques shook his head and sniffed. "You smell of sulfur and smoke. Except for that, I'd have guessed you had been sleeping after a day of tending your sheep."

"As I would, given half a chance."

Someone moved behind Jacques and he called, "Kerriac— more messages."

A slight man emerged from the shadows. His immediate eye contact and ready smile gave him away—Amerikan—perhaps a new OSS agent.

"Hang around a minute, in case a question arises."

Domingo shrugged. "I know nothing of the content, and today the agent moves to another location."

"You'll still bring us word?"

"Perhaps she must move too far away. The SS has reached the *Causse de Limogne.*"

"Brutes." Jacques cursed and offered a cigarette, but Domingo declined. "Still, we take heart. Last night, our men pilfered enough Hun dynamite from across the Auverne to decommission a hundred train engines. They repair pylons too quickly, so we blow the engines and transformers now, since one small charge disables them."

"You expect *l'Invasion* very soon?"

The squat leader ran his hand over heavy beard growth, and with two dirty fingers, pushed between his eyebrows as if fighting a headache. "One sure sign, *mon ami*—drops from a USAAF Flying Fortress last night."

"A B-17? Here?"

"Never doubt the importance of our efforts." Steel-gray eyes settled on Domingo. "Travel safely, and here's to liberty."

A team entered the encampment with rifles slung from their shoulders. Farther on, two tall Caucasians wearing khaki military-style jodhpurs chatted. Russians? Yes, their accents gave them away. Aitaita warned against such—*Bolsheviks, Communistas*—out *to change our way of life.*

But General de Gaulle's *Forces Français es de l'Interieur*—the FFI—all stood united to free France. Everyone answered to General Koenig, de Gaulle's chosen British commander. Some may have sworn allegiance to separate political organizations in the early days, but they'd now joined forces to dispel the Reich. From his grave, Aitaita might disapprove, but not if he were here.

One man in this gathering was a Spaniard. Another's espadrilles gave him away as a Lot peasant. He stirred a huge porridge pot—perhaps a cousin's cousin.

A guard guided Domingo's cycle to him, and he kicked it to life. As the camp faded in the distance, one goal enveloped him—that he, Domingo Ibarra, citizen of Lot, France, perform his duty for the liberation. Hopefully, unlike Poland, this country would emerge free.

He touched the brake where he failed to slow the last time. But seeing a large branch torn from its trunk, he idled the motor. This obstacle could hinder the *Milice*. French police loyal to Vichy irritated him almost more than the Gestapo.

He tore off his jacket and shinnied up, littering the earth with bark, and smashed the branch down. Soon Domingo had created the perfect roadblock, another hassle for the *Milice* and five extra treasured minutes for the *Maquisards*. Small things like this could tip the scales.

Toward St. Perdoux, early morning cooking smells emanated from vine-covered stone houses, and a peasant led his sheep across the road. Then a gendarme stepped from behind a thick stone fence. Dressed to the hilt, his revolver bulged from its holster, and a scabbard tapped his thigh.

"Destination?"

"Home from helping my grandfather."

"With a cycle?"

"His neighbor found a canister with this inside. He says we take what we get, payment for the trouble this war brings upon us."

The gendarme twitched his turned-up mustache. "Papers?" Domingo handed them over. "Ibarra. That name sounds too familiar. Come."

Domingo weighed his options. He could race off, but then would need a new card. He leaned the cycle on the wall and entered the building, greeted by a Petain bust.

Le Marechal Philippe Petain,

chef de l'etat français,

vainquer de Verdun

Under his kepi with its silly pillbox circle, arm outstretched, Petain portrayed a kindly older friend, but the message inscribed below soured Domingo's stomach.

"Français! Vous n'etes ni vendus ni trahis ni abandonnes.

Venez a moi avec confiance."

"French! You are not sold nor betrayed nor abandoned. Come to me with confidence." Who still believed this rubbish?

"You honor *le Marechal?*"

The lie came easily. "My grandfather keeps a bust on his hearth."

"False information, I suspect. Go, but watch yourself."

Along the way, a farmer strapped his iron plow to two oxen. The peaceful sight gripped Domingo. Could that *Gendarme* not discern how Petain had hurt these peasants? What motivated his loyalty to Vichy? His paycheck, or did he honestly believe Hitler's puppet government worthy of his service?

When the River *Célé* glistened in the distance, Domingo slowed the cycle. Soon, rocky cliffs gave way to murky water sprigged with late spring insects and humidity. He walked the bike through a frog chorus, the muddy river bottom defying him to breathe.

Suddenly, sun flamed through the chestnuts, and he reconsidered his route. He could take the easy road, but this back way saved time. A few extra minutes meant a little more sleep, a precious commodity.

An early fisherman nodded, so Domingo wished him well. How

often had *Maman* filleted and fried Papa's early morning catch?

But where was that rocky turn-off? Domingo sniffed the fertile, weedy earth until a break in some low bushes led him to yesterday's tire tread.

The long, quiet trail cooled his emotions, down through an area bedded with crushed rocks, then into a meadow and the sycamore-lined road winding past his generational homestead. Like this wide path, his life had become light and shadow, morning and evening and night.

Beyond the river, Ibarra land called his name ... ah, to stay here forever. But his conscience remonstrated. Katarin had no home, no family. She discovered her uncle only when he was dying. Long before this war, life left her with the same theft, betrayal, and abandonment Petain promised to stop.

FIVE

After appearing past the curve in the road ahead, the bicycle stopped, sending an explosion of dust up around the rider's black skirts. Kate watched the woman unwind her long legs from the chassis and remove her thick goggles and beret. No, not a woman. A man.

Intense violet eyes scanned her and Domingo. Set in a broad face tanned by sun and wind, they contained the hint of a dare. Burnt-red hair curled over the lanky fellow's temples and ears—the farthest thing from Kate's image of a priest. But when he straightened his robe, thought lines encircled his bushy eyebrows.

"Domingo, I have missed you." They embraced like father and son.

"*Père*—how ..."

"You live. Thanks be to God." The priest's rangy form almost disappeared in Domingo's arms, but he reached a hand toward Kate.

Domingo flashed a glance her way. "Agent Merce, meet Père Gaspard, who taught me most of what I know."

Strong hands enveloped Kate's, and Père Gaspard's voice shifted low. "You borrowed your name from Our Lady of Mercy *Espagnol*, who appeared with refugee children under her robes?"

"*Oui.*"

"But you look like a Kathryn to me."

At Kate's inquisitive look, Domingo held up his palms. "He has a seeing gift." He tapped the priest's arm. "How could you know?"

"It's the fire in her eyes—Kathryn means pure. *Mademoiselle*, I trust you like our lovely Department of Lot, the soul of France. Except, of course, for this miserable war."

"Your hills and valleys go easier on my shoes than *Le Massif Central.*"

"You've trekked up there?" Not waiting for a response, he sought Domingo. "What brings you home? I heard our partisans blew the Decazeville *collierie* last night."

Domingo merely cocked his head, so Père continued. "You know already, I see. Word has it the mine will be unusable for months. Since we shackled their electrical works in March, the Germans have assigned twenty-five hundred men to restore it—the Bosche don't like idle people. But you two must have passed through there when you came down from the mountains, n'est-ce pas?"

"We kept out of the way." Domingo glanced at Kate. "Rough climbing, but worth the safety. They must have rewired the *collierie* about that time."

"Yes, and all for naught." Père's wide grin overtook his entire countenance. "Since our humble *Maquis* has disabled France's largest opencast mine." Quickly, he turned serious again. "But this success will bring fury down on our local prefects."

"And the SS Waffen units?"

"With the entire winter for repairs and new recruits from Alsace to fill their quotas, they stand ready." A visible shiver crossed *Père's* shoulders. "But back to the mine. Losing it makes the local units look bad. Besides, the next level of command seems inefficient in carrying out Hitler's orders. It also hints at problems with the big bosses, Laval and Darnard."

He twisted toward Kate. "Perhaps you heard that last year, the Waffen-SS took Darnard, our own countryman, into its legions when he organized the *Milice française?*"

He squeezed his eyes shut for a moment, and Kate recalled what she'd learned about Darnard.

"Sickening—a Frenchman as *Sturmbannfuhrer* over the *Milice*— who'd ever have imagined such a thing would come to pass? At first, Darnard organized only five thousand, but now the *gendarmes* multiply seven times over, and practice even greater harshness. As if our enemies were not enough, we suffer this from our own."

Domingo's nod must have encouraged him to continue.

"They've already deported six hundred Figeac men to Montauban for German labor camps. Not one teacher remains at the College, no pupils over sixteen, nor an artist or skilled tradesman." Père rubbed the stubble dappling his chin.

"Never underestimate the Gestapo, the *Milice*, or Das Reich. Brutality marks the SS commander and his underlings. Every *ratissage* they carry out has clear calculations behind it—German storm troops leave nothing to chance."

Père Gaspard untied a packet from his bicycle basket and sighed. "I wouldn't doubt they soon give up on Vichy altogether. Then the last vestige of law will be gone from our departments, and the Germans will do what they please with our women and mortar our villages."

A flock of pigeons dived overhead, but the men paid no notice. "Your gifts are many, *Père* but I hope you aren't prophesying..."

Père moved to a low wall and gestured for Domingo and Kate to sit. "The *Milice* already penetrate far into the countryside. Abbeys and *maquisard* strongholds have become the only place of refuge. So many have already fled to them, they barely maintain supplies." He snorted. "And now, renegades like you blow mines and cut the German supply lines left and right."

Domingo showed his dimples. "You taught me how to follow orders."

"Indeed, and halting Das Reich is a worthy goal. We locals will pay in reprisals, but of all the groups this war has created, the *Milice* rank lowest. Already, the *Maquisards* have made examples of several collaborators."

"So I heard. Shot and roped up in public squares."

"These displays delight the locals, but every time the people celebrate, the Nazis plan reprisals. We must fortify ourselves for whatever comes."

A ground squirrel chattered high in an oak tree across the road, reminding Kate that nature continued as always. Domingo's dusty espadrilles, wide-necked shirt, and beret complemented *Père* Gaspard's black robe, embedded with dirt and bits of straw. Of course—they'd both been out on missions—who had time to consider cleanliness these days?

"Where do you strike tonight?"

"The railroad bridge west of le Bourg."

"You do God's work. How may I help?"

"Our agent must send messages to London."

Père Gaspard led them down a narrow walking path. "And move every three days, no less." He gestured toward a cottage. "Come in for some hot chicory. Together, we will ponder."

He ushered them over the threshold. "And your mother, Domingo? Is she well?"

"With Gabirel back home, yes. But we already received one visit from the Reich."

"Ah, indeed—they have penetrated that far into the countryside." *Père* Gaspard rummaged at the stove while they discussed local peasants, so Kate let her mind wander to the hand-plastered archway, the closed-up stuffiness permeating the cottage, and numerous deep scrapes on the heavy wooden door, as if an ill-behaved cat or dog once reigned here.

Soon, sweet-smelling chicory coffee filled brown pottery mugs, and heavy steam offered a foretaste of the almost chocolaty taste to follow. Thicker than American coffee and much stronger than London's watered-down version, the brew bore a bitter taste at first, but Kate had grown fond of this bracing drink.

Père joined them at the table. "At fourteen, your Gabirel has become a man. War has scant respect for youth." His frown spread. "The Gestapo has proliferated like rabbits since April. You know about the diversion our partisans created last month when they occupied *Cajarc*?"

Domingo raised one eyebrow ever so slightly, and *Père* accepted the gesture as a yes or no, Kate couldn't tell which.

"Their audacity took the pressure off the Communist Resisters farther north in *Correze*. The Gestapo has been onto them for some time. But our occupation of *Cajarc* gave those *Correzian* fellows a mild reprieve—the River Lot never saw such a feat."

He addressed Kate. "Can you believe our people rang up the Germans to inform them terrorists had overtaken the area?"

"Rang them up?"

"We'd hooked into their telephone transmission line months ago, so why not go ahead and ring them up? When we did, the Germans amassed *Miliciens* and *Gendarmes* for battle along the river. Our *Maquis* suffered few losses and convinced the Germans of their skill and determination. Of course, the corroborators looked like fools."

His sigh mingled with a feeble half-smile. "In Cajarc's town square, our *Maquis* also executed three *Milice* collaborator police convicted of denouncing resistors."

Domingo's jaw tightened and *Père* patted his elbow. "Some *Milice* do harbor patriotic motives, but things have been so confused since Petain stepped up. People who lauded him in the Great War couldn't comprehend that he would eventually succumb to the *Fuhrer's* bidding."

His sigh contained a tremble. "Discerning a Vichy collaborator from a citizen stalwart for liberty has become impossible. Did you hear that someone denounced me?"

"Who?"

"A regular at Mass. I'd blessed him just that Sunday, and would have guessed he supported us." Père turned to Kate. "You see, my so-called 'seeing' ability works only sporadically. Would that God bestowed more consistent gifts, eh?

"At any rate, *Cajarc* proved we could join several groups under one command. Before that, the Communists under the FTP refused to fight with a Fee Fee *Résistance* group. Of course, the FTP battles against Fascism, in order to set up a Communist France, and boasts hundreds of monthly kills.

"Whether by sabotage or knife blades, all come together with the de Gaullists now." He met Kate's eyes. "If you wanted excitement, you chose the right place at the perfect time."

He wound the wires of his spectacles over his ears and unfolded a map. Domingo helped him spread the crackly paper like a delicate lace cloth.

"I know of no collaborators in our area, though one peasant who fought under Petain still believes the general secretly communicates with De Gaulle. I hoped he might retain London connections, too, but when he sentenced one of our leaders to two years internment, I gave that up.

"Now, back to our challenge. "Do you prefer a chateau or a pigsty?"

Domingo answered for Kate. "Whatever is safe. These messages must get through."

Père's sloped forefinger traveled the map. "We have transmitters here and here. The higher the better." He pushed his glasses up his thin nose. "Perhaps we begin here, a fair climb, but difficult for the Gestapo to reach."

"The vineyards?"

"Surely the Gestapo has far more productive places to search."

"You will take her?" At *Père's* assent, Domingo flushed. "*Merci.*"

The same sudden flagrant heat swept Kate. After all they'd experienced, she might never see Domingo again.

"Very soon *l'invasion* begins. I have it on high authority." Index finger pointed upward, Père attempted to lighten the moment as Domingo donned his beret.

"Where do you want the transmitter?"

"Inside the door, for now. A lorry should arrive shortly with spring greens and potatoes for the camp." Kate trailed them toward the motorbike, where a strapped container held her heavy transmitter.

"We'll disguise this with vegetables or Jean-Claude's supply of baked goods. Perhaps a gendarme will accompany us, although that most often happens in daytime."

"You trust them?"

Kate strained to understand the Basque Domingo slipped into, but Père Gaspard studied her before responding in perfect French.

"Only locals who protect me on deliveries to my poorest parishioners. The truth has become a mixed parcel."

Kate followed his gaze to new growth brightening the countryside. To the east, an almost cloudless expanse of blue sky met hilly terrain.

"Thank the Lord, the seasons remain. Winter gave way to spring, and the Allies mount their attack. As for the gendarmes, if the Gestapo happens by while we are *en route* ..." His eyes held an extra twinkle.

"Seeing my protectors, they'll think all is well and leave me alone to continue my good works. Perhaps even those nasty *Gendarmes* will have a good deed on their side when it comes to dividing the sheep from the goats."

Père Gaspard hefted one side of the transmitter. "Save your strength for tonight, Domingo. You'll probably run for miles."

An itchy sensation enveloped Kate's throat. Blowing a bridge tonight, and tomorrow night, demolishing something else?

"You have a strong arm for the ascent?"

"You think of me as an old, weak man, but ..." Père flexed his biceps.

"Never. After all, you taught me how to score at *pelota*."

They lowered the transmitter and Domingo grabbed his beret. Kate swallowed a cry that poised on her tongue as he gave her a slight bow.

"*Va avec Dieu.*" Go with God—exactly what he said on her first night in France.

Kate's throat constricted, and she could barely croak, "*Merci, et vous aussi.*"

His glinting onyx eyes held hers for a moment. He touched her sleeve and a thousand sparks enveloped her arm. Then he hurried to the cycle, and the motor roared into action in an acrid haze.

Père Gaspard made the sign of the cross over his diminishing figure. "A good man, if one ever lived. Godspeed." He sighed and faced Kate. "We must pack supplies for your stay."

After the cycle's buzz faded to a faint drone, she followed him into the rectory, breathing in the enclosed scent of stored linens, binned potatoes, and shelves of books.

"Be sure to take plenty of potatoes, carrots, and any fruit still worth eating. Between winter and summer's abundance, we must scavenge."

Addie would play around with that word, but Kate knew their scavenging held no candle to how Domingo would survive these next days ... weeks. Who knew how long?

She filled her pack with necessities, all the while lifting him heavenward in silent prayer. Despite him leaving, excitement flooded her. Maybe she was, after all, born for this work, as Monsieur Le Blanc prophesied when they first met in London.

Père rummaged in a closet and thrust out a folded linen cloth. "I keep some sisters' garb handy for such times. What do your papers say?"

"Milkmaid, the Ibarra's dim-witted daughter." She wondered he had forgotten, having so recently reinvented her identity card.

"Ah, yes. We'd better fix that. I shall make you a teacher, with more travel allowances. If necessary, you can throw on this garb. Hum ... the Gestapo deported your family, *maquisards* overtook your school, and your priest sent you on this retreat."

He held up a length of coarse cloth and squinted at her. "Too big, but the less of your form those beasts view, the better. I'll see to your *carte d'identite* right away and we'll be off."

He handed her a large backpack, and his use of the word *we* staved off the pang edging Kate's breastbone. Barely used to her present identification, she sloughed off her attachment to Emazteona Giselle Ibarra, a plodding young woman with an idyllic Basque home and three brothers. Posing as an orphan after losing her family offer less challenge—not far from the truth.

Kate rehearsed her new family history as she packed the heavy linen robes, a massive cross necklace to complete her outfit, and plain black shoes. She hoped she wouldn't need them.

Somewhere, a bird tweeted. Kathryn felt sure she heard that sweet sound, and strained her ears. But a *swish-swish* of someone's skirt blocked out all else. She pressed her head and back against crisp sheets and accustomed herself to the smells around her.

The bird call faded. Nothing here of nature—wherever *here* was—but rather, invasive scents, ones that seemed pleasant at first. She'd wakened in a place where every sniff told her that each aroma covered something else, something you didn't want to smell. Oh, to be out in her back yard, where azaleas had started blooming, and the lilacs imbued every breath.

That *swish-swish* irritated her, though she realized it must be women's hosiery declaring to the world that their owners were walking down a hallway. A hallway? Yes, that must be it, although Kathryn couldn't open her eyes to look.

Why couldn't she open them? Nothing wrong with her hearing, and though a quick brush of her face with her fingers revealed bandages to high heaven, her nose still worked. That was something, at least. She concentrated—yes, she'd fallen, a ridiculous topple over that railing high above the pews at Good Shepherd.

Then Doc came, and a man wearing brown tweed and bearing that strong whiff of robust Gauloise tobacco. She'd never liked it back in France, but today—at least she thought it was today—it had an intoxicating effect. Even now, just remembering it swept her back again, against her will. No, she must stay here and wake up. She must see who walked up and down the hallway outside this room, and figure out how to get out of here.

But the swishing came closer, a cool hand held her wrist, and a man said, "Keep her sedated—the surgeon is on his way from Portland right now."

SIX

To the east, smoke plumes still rose from what remained of the blown *collierie*. His ears still ringing with last night's detonation, Domingo gunned the engine. He'd meant to ask Gabirel if he'd heard the blast, but something else happened just then—he couldn't even recall what it was. Things were like that with Gabirel lately. If you missed your chance, he might close his heart to you and the opportunity might be gone forever.

Maman's chin had trembled and Gabirel had blinked hard when he and Kate left. During his frequent disappearances, *Maman's* frame had shrunken more than ever. He hesitated to embrace her lest he break a bone, and yet, a fresh awareness made him want to hold her close.

Maman stroked Kate's hand. "You must visit us again in a better season." The emotion in her voice surprised Domingo. Standing there, he decided to think of this agent as *Katarin*.

This agent's glinting eyes gave him pause. "Madame Ibarra, you have taught me so much. I hope to return to visit you some day." Then she held out her hand to Gabirel. "And thank you so much for keeping watch. You made my work easier."

Gabirel gave her an awkward look, but stared at the ground when Domingo approached with his usual, "Take care of things here."

Domingo saluted him and gave his mother another gentle embrace before he whisked Katarin toward the cycle. "Have you ridden one of these before?"

"No, but I'll adjust." That was her way with whatever needed to be done. Her father went by *Le Renard Intrepid,* and undoubtedly

Monsieur le Blanc had earned a nickname, as well. Katarin could be *le caméléon*, with her ability to reinvent herself at a moment's notice.

Domingo's mind leaped to the moment they said good-bye. Had he allowed his emotions to show? He flicked back his hair. If only he could do the same with his increasing thoughts of this American girl.

Speeding toward his next mission, he took comfort in the Gestapo swarming Decazeville tonight. That meant they would pay less attention to this area of Lot.

Somehow, he'd become an explosives expert—ah well, he could follow instructions. *Leave the motorbike in Figeac, behind the city hall.*

Follow the rails toward Espedaillac. Reconnoiter before dark at an abandoned farmhouse three kilometers east.

Outside Figeac, he cut the motor and made for the city hall by a little-used back route. With the cycle hidden, he slipped into a tree-covered ravine that circled the buildings, for the Gestapo kept watch on the railroad depot. An afternoon breeze blew, reminding Domingo how his muscles ached from riding. The twenty-kilometer hike to Espedaillac seemed short, compared to the distance he'd covered with Katarin.

And she'd kept up with him without complaint, even with blistered heels. That knowledge fluttered as close to his heartbeat, along with the look in her eyes when he'd left her.

Pushing his way through a narrow foliage-covered path parallel to the railroad, he made good time. The sun sank lower, so he stopped to fill his canteen beside a frothing spring bubbling from a gash in a rock. At the Espedaillac signpost, he veered westward until a stone house, with windows like hollow eyes, emerged from among the trees. Finding a sheltered spot, Domingo leaned against a broom tree and gnawed bread and cheese.

A peasant near *Almont-les Junies* had supplied the same food when he and Katarin had followed the *Rousseau de Limo*. In his haste to get home, he'd barely noticed her until she bathed her sore feet in an icy rivulet.

He recalled one other time, before France's surrender to Germany in November, '41, when he'd traveled the same road. Probably he'd run an errand for Père before leading pilots over the Spanish border.

Even before the Nazi occupation cast its shadow over France, Père Gaspard sometimes asked Domingo to perform tasks a distance from Lot. That time, during the *Junhalmontois* harvest celebration, he'd feasted on *estofinado* and garlic potatoes. Even now, the spicy taste of potatoes cooked with fish, herbs, and *crème fraîche* would cause his stomach to rumble.

Finally, as dusk ushered in evening, something moved in the meadow, and a human being prowled below him like a lynx.

Wait for four low whistles, bowed out like a dove's call.

When another partisan found the first one, Domingo crept beyond the broom tree and advanced behind a thicket, thankful he'd avoided this foraging existence for the war's first years. Leaving the sheep in Gabirel's care had occurred gradually, for a day or two at a time, then a few more.

And then Katarin fell from the sky. Somehow he sensed this parachutist was a woman. He tamped down his concern for her dangerous mission—the worst Gestapo stories involved radio operators.

Only natural to think of her, especially now that I know her past, and that came about because ...

As he awaited another sign, the events that reunited them unfolded in his mind. Returning from a trip across the Spanish border, Domingo and his comrade Petra were diverted to attend a supply drop on a plateau west of Albi.

There, Katarin waited with messages for the pilot. He and Petra accepted separate missions after the drop, Domingo's to deliver her to a train station. Of course, he had no idea she was the one he'd met back in December.

But that night, they witnessed the railroad bridge near Albi blown to bits, and she recognized him. Her whisper still sent a shiver over his shoulders. "You met my drop. You nursed my sprained ankle and carried me all the way to that haystack."

Later, word came of her circuit's blown cover. It was impossible to leave her alone in the wilds with the Gestapo on the hunt, so they trekked on. Then, scrabbling up a mountain trail in a murky pre-dawn, they found a wounded agent, Monsieur le Blanc, sprawled in the path.

Who but the Almighty could have arranged for Katarin to hear his deathbed confession that he was her uncle? Without question, Père Gaspard would pronounce this a divine appointment.

While he turned over the last morsel of cheese in his hands, Domingo turned that experience over in his mind like a many-faceted jewel. Père might tell such a story during Mass to relate how the Almighty reunited people and fulfilled their deepest desires.

Monsieur's deathbed scene, like the moving pictures Domingo first experienced during his teacher training, defied logic. Yet he himself watched Katarin's transformation as she witnessed Monsieur's last feeble breath. Perspiration grazed Domingo's hairline at the memory of comforting her with *Maman's* sorrow song.

He'd never held anyone but Sancha so close, and could still feel Katarin quake in his arms. If not for those intense hours, he wouldn't be thinking of her so much. Surely he wouldn't.

Trill … trill … trill … trill … Domingo jolted upright. Two more fellows from opposite directions joined the first ones, so he shinnied down the hill. A gruff-faced partisan nodded toward a steep incline.

"From up there, the bridge rises only a kilometer away. Follow me." The earth shook as a train crossed the bridge, and from higher ground, the leader pointed out the wooden trestle. "The next train is due around three in the morning with tanks and munitions for Normandy."

After wending their way through a scree of oak and blackberry bramble, a dilapidated cottage came into view, crowded by the growth of young saplings. A sulfur smell permeated the building where a younger man waited, so obviously weary that he seemed old. Plastic cylinders and other apparatus covered a rickety table, so everyone gathered around.

"Welcome. Observe our blasting caps, Bickford lighters, detonators, and TNT." He rotated a safety fuse. "Familiarize yourself with the Bickford. At this end sits a glass ampoule of gunpowder." He ran his finger along the edge. "A spring-loaded striker. And here…" He unrolled a small paper with numerical columns.

"Note the delay times for various temperatures. We set the charges at ten p.m., up on that ridge, estimating eleven degrees Centigrade.

"See the color-code? Check the inspection hole like this, then the condition of the ampoule end before crimping a blasting cap to the fuse. Next, insert the well of a TNT block like this, crush the ampoule and recheck the striker. Then and only then, remove the safety tab and run."

He studied each man. "We have a two-hour climb. We leave in half an hour."

Everyone scattered. Domingo walked a short distance, surrounded by rough, rocky beauty. Deep undulations peppered the landscape like human fingers, with caves where the Jews found refuge. Père Gaspard told of priests who led them to abbeys, so they could navigate the mountains to Spain, or in some cases, where they still awaited the war's end.

A footfall sounded, and the leader touched his shoulder. "I remember you. From Figeac? You have experienced demolition?"

"Last night."

"Ah. Decazeville. Then you'll light the charge at the north end."

Dark eyes flashed before Domingo's inner vision. Once, those dark eyes belonged to Sancha, his betrothed. But the Gestapo murdered her more than a year ago, along with innocent children. The hills where she died, close to the refuge city of *Le Chambon-sur-Lignon*, seemed a world away.

But these eyes before him now flashed gold flecks—Katarin's eyes. He liked the feel of her name on his tongue, like flowing water.

How strange for Père Gaspard to have guessed her name. Stranger still that she stirred emotions Domingo had secreted away after Sancha's death. He shook them away once again and considered his rag-tag partners.

Perhaps one wrenched the neck of a German guard last night or drowned a collaborator, in spite of London's rules—until the *l'invasion* occurs, avoid direct contact with the enemy.

Tonight, he would take life, for these trains bound for Normandy carried guards. He must believe Père Gaspard—war turned things around. As if to prove that concept, two partisans discussed a Dutch inventor who moved to Amerika long before the Great War.

"His bombsight is so accurate it can drop a bomb in a pickle barrel, taking into account the wind, human error, and other interferences. The inventor knew war's waste of precious life, and hoped an accurate bombsight would prevent thousands of deaths."

A meadow bird launched its last evening call, and the story quieted Domingo. This bridge blowing would in the end save many Allied soldiers, and hopefully shorten the war.

The leader gathered the group. "Tomorrow night, we expect a shipment of Nobel's # 8 waterproof *plastiques*. They're pliable, easy to work into any crack or hole, but I'm glad for what we have. The *plastiques'* stinky fumes cause headaches."

Another partisan, older than the rest, joined them. "Who lights the fuses?"

"We work in three teams, one at either trestle end, one in the center. The best runner goes with me." The men pushed forward a lean young fellow wearing espadrilles from Dordogne.

"One man guards, while the other lights the explosives. At the north, *La Foudre* over there will do the lighting." He flicked his thumb toward Domingo.

So this was how a man acquired a nickname. Suddenly, someone called him Lightning—*La Foudre*. Gabirel, even more of a natural at tracking than Domingo, would smile at this some day.

"Keep low to the ground. Our pay is nothing, but at least it's equal, the Communist ideal." The leader snorted. "Disperse in separate directions when we're finished, unless one of you travels toward Figeac."

"I'll find you, *La Foudre*." He handed the first explosives box to Domingo. "No stumbling."

The gritty wooden carton scraped Domingo's fingers. At the top, some of them set to work with the explosives, but the leader sent Domingo and one other member sidewinding below the trestle.

"Check for anything amiss. Meet us here in twenty minutes."

Domingo let the other man lead. They halted once, their backs to the trestle posts.

"Not a German for kilometers."

"I hope."

"You from around here?"

"No, from Lot. You?"

"Toulouse. Student turned woodcutter." Domingo might have asked how he ended up here, but kept silent. The young man's smile showed in the growing moonlight, and a story brewed in his eyes.

"My uncle, a priest, saved my neck when I turned *refractaire* because of the German deportations. My parents told me to hide in the hills until the gendarmes made their quota, so I made my way to my uncle when our band began to starve.

"He decked me in an extra robe and took me with him on his rounds. When the Gestapo stalked us, he intoned prayers, so they didn't even ask for our identity cards."

"Sounds like a priest I know."

"Père Gaspard, from Terrou originally. You know him?"

"My parish priest. So now you blow bridges?"

"That's the only way I know to get back to law school, if any law remains when all this is over. And you blow bridges as well, I see."

"*Mais oui.* What else is there to do?"

SEVEN

Slowing the lorry for a gaggle of geese, *Père* turned studious. "The main road and Parisian rail-links still connect us with the far southwest. Our peasants took in refugees who swarmed here in '40 as Vichy demanded young men for German work camps. They now work for *La Résistance.*

Exactly as Kate's instructors described the growth of the Resistance effort, and this morning's breeze reminded her of their predictions concerning the weather, too. Beautiful, like spring in Iowa.

"The plateau's forests couldn't be better suited to hiding defectors. The *Ségala's* chestnut groves, trout streams, and small villages provide food, and the heights offer a wide view, plus natural niches to store supplies."

"The gendarmes avoid those areas?"

"Yes." He gestured to the road, where a clutch of innocent goslings followed their mother. "To be honest, sometimes I feel sympathy for them. On the one hand, as French police, they must earn their pay to feed their families, though the Nazis force superhuman tasks on them.

"How could Vichy possibly agree to produce a million workers for the Fuhrer? Surely they know the *Massif Central*, the Pyrenees, and the *Ségala* hide every man of age who ventures here, and the *Maquis* eagerly accepts every new registration in an effort to win back their own pilfered land."

When the last goose straggled across, he bumped the lorry down a hill and over a rickety bridge. "There, you see the homeland of our *Maquis.*" Père pointed high on the eastern side where sheep speckled sparse vegetation.

Kate's shoulder rammed into her door when they hit a bump. "How do these people make a living? They must be very poor."

"One might say so, but the *Maquis* find them rich in support and friendship." He gunned the engine around an uphill corner. "Many camps stay on the move, except for the group we supply today. But you understand that well?"

"Oh yes. Since I parachuted in, I've lived in—let me see—three villages, and slept in far more beds."

"Many have helped you along the way?"

"Oh, yes. In *le-Chambon-sur-Lignon*, at the Presbytery, then in *Clermont-Ferrand* and to the south, when Domingo led me away from Albi and we discovered the Gestapo had infiltrated my circuit." Her gut clenched at the memory.

"Ah, *Le Chambon*? I understand that city shelters many."

"*Oui.* Banished Jews, defectors, and so many children separated from their families."

"France desperately needs such safe havens. What did you learn there?"

"The pastor's wife welcomed me so heartily, I felt at home right away. She had room in her heart for everyone. And the children—I've never witnessed such innocent, beautiful faces and smiles. *Le Chambon* showed me a bold kind of love—and honesty. The citizens band together to protect all those little ones, and do their work in the open."

"They don't lie to the authorities?" The priest raised a bushy eyebrow.

"I don't think so. Of course, they hide the children if there's danger. That's a level of trust I'll probably never reach." Probably? More like definitely. She changed the subject. "Have you visited many *Résistance* camps?"

"Several closer to the southern border, near Aveyron, with their fair share of shadowy participants, to be sure. But Jean-Jacques Chapou relegates those types to the fringes. Even so, I fear all control will soon cease. Anyone who can manage a weapon..." Père swerved to avoid a rabbit.

"If I had the desire to escape the priesthood for a life of crime, it would be easy. But the bulk of partisans became *refractaires* for conscience's sake rather than support the Nazi war machine in factories here or in the motherland."

"You mean when Vichy issued the *Service du Travail Obligitoire* edict?"

"*Oui.* The STO instigated an impossible choice: obey Petain's new ruling, enforced by Laval, who also signed away French Jews to deportation and death, or obey the call to freedom for France. You can imagine how our ranks swelled."

He goosed the engine around a sharp curve and sent Kate crashing forward.

"Sorry—I never learned the finer points of handling this machine." Père scrunched his forehead in contrition, but returned to his topic. "How could my countrymen in good conscience support Hitler? At that time, I visited a *curé* near Cahors, where our own *Maquis* originated.

"He supported those unorganized young defectors even then. When Chapou doubled the group to eight, living like Saint John the Baptist, eating off the land, the *curé* continued his work. Later, the STO brought in far more fighters. We had had enough of Pierre Laval's so-called *Relève.* Do you know about that?"

"The exchange of French workers for prisoners of war from the 1940 invasion?"

"Your training serves you well. Before that, the *Maquis* struggled, and many came to me for counsel. Under the circumstances, becoming a *refractaire* seemed the most moral choice."

"You guided them into the *Résistance?*"

"For better or for worse. You understand that many guides pay with their lives. *La Résistance* highly values Domingo's abilities, but if anything were to happen to him, it would kill his mother. And I would bear responsibility."

"But having him work in Germany would have devastated her, too."

"True. In that so-called *Relève* exchange, no prisoners returned until August, and then the Bosche released a mere nine hundred. City folk fell for the enemy's lies because they formed soup lines. *Feed me and I'll obey you.*"

"Obeying the STO order would have meant aiding the enemy?"

"Indeed, even though we had no idea if 'work' meant actual labor or detainment. If Domingo had gone, he would have deserted on his first leave, like many others. Later, regulations tightened again, doubling the gendarmes' work.

"They already searched for *refractaires* who refused to fill their prefects' new quotas, but last summer they had to search for deserters, besides. In September, Vichy demanded that women work as well, promising they would stay in France. But in October, one local *gendarme* confided in me his new orders.

"Suddenly, Laval offered amnesty to *refractaires* in exchange for working here. That unfairness enraged families whose sons had complied with the original STO."

"So, Vichy cannot win?"

"Exactly. Imagine a parent whose son went to work in a German factory, now watching other young men and women laboring here with no punishment. People wrote to Petain *en masse*, and Vichy failed to raise the Nazi quota."

Père Gaspard swerved again, this time for what Kate thought might be a mink. He wiped his forehead. "In the midst of vast human carnage, our hearts still reach out to a hapless animal, don't they?"

"So you sympathize with the *gendarmes*?"

"The Reich makes a hard taskmaster, and Laval signed unrealistic quotas. Surely General Petain couldn't have believed our young men would volunteer. Their fathers fought against Germany in the Great War—why should their sons slave for the Nazis?"

The red in his cheeks heightened with each argument. He released the clutch and braked before a hapless young marmot squatting in the middle of the road. Père yelled out the window, but the dazzled creature hopped only a few feet away.

"Danger stares him in the face, but he fiddles around, like our people. Some felt they owed Petain allegiance, but last December, the Germans killed two *gendarmes* and badly injured two others. Why obey a government that hires you one minute but shoots you the next?

"Discovering the right thing to do has become a tightrope walk. Every day the rope tightens, and with each decision, the *cravasse* below deepens."

"But you keep on."

"What else can we do? Our fate lies with Churchill and the Allies. The Free French say one thing, Vichy another. The Gestapo threatens at every turn, and now, Das Reich encroaches—tank units crossing our beautiful countryside. Ach!"

He slapped the steering wheel. "I fear for my people, once safe and secure in the heart of France."

Quiet enveloped the cab, and Kate's thoughts wandered to Madame Ibarra and Gabirel. If the Gestapo came, what would they say about her absence?

Her mind returned to Domingo, then to the other trainees in her SOE group, Charles and his mother, and then Addie—dear Addie in London, working as a secretary. Maybe she'd even have a chance to write, always her desire. Père's foot on the brake brought Kate back to the present.

"See that stone house back in the trees? This kindly old couple provides much for our cause." He wrestled the lorry to a shaking halt behind a tree in full bud. The canvas flap hit the top of the lorry and in a few moments, Albert grinned from outside Père's filmy window.

"You're doing all right back there?"

"No worse than other times."

"Give the man and woman who live here as much as we can afford." Père ruffled his hair and Albert hopped toward the back again.

"Once loyal to Petain, loyalists never would have dreamed of deceiving the government, but now their four sons have dispersed with the *Maquis*. Four of them, mind you! The Fuhrer must scratch his head concerning the French—how can a country that surrendered so quickly a few years ago produce such opposition now?"

A slender peasant emerged from his barn, pitchfork in hand and pipe between his lips. The lorry shuddered when Père turned off the motor.

"This clutch always slips." He sent Kate an appealing look.

"As they say, beggars can't be choosers."

Albert offered the parishioner an armload of food, and Père tumbled out, hands extended. "All is well with you? Is Madame inside?"

As if waiting for the call, a woman bent nearly double limped forward. Père Gaspard rushed to take her hand, and Kate waited a distance away. "Madame Merlat. You fare well?"

She clasped his hand. "Well enough. And you?"

"SS Waffen units are advancing from the south across Lot. I can't imagine them meandering onto this *route blanche*, but we've angered them greatly. Do all in your power to stay out of their way."

The farmer raised his pitchfork like a weapon. "Of course. And who knows? Maybe they may get in *our* way."

"All goes well for your daughters?"

"Ah, yes, and five grandchildren, one more as of yesterday."

"Oh my—we'll have to baptize that little one soon." Père glanced toward the house as though reluctant to leave.

"God's blessing upon you and your family." They stood still for the sign of the cross, like humble confirmation students receiving a final blessing. Then Kate followed Père to the cab and he started the engine.

When they heard the canvas flap drop, he let out the clutch and proclaimed, "Onward." Kate clutched the dashboard with a last look at the man and his wife, a French caricature of Grant Wood's *American Gothic*. At the Chicago Institute of Art, the painting had sold for three hundred dollars—another piece of the trivia that constantly circled through her mind.

"Madame Merlat must be in pain." That delicate woman's condition wasn't trivial.

"Rheumatism. The two of them started school together, they once told me. So they're the same age, but women weather worse than men in these times."

"Like Madame Ibarra. That Gestapo visit took years off my life, too."

A slow-moving herd of cows challenged them next, blocking the road, and Kate's cultural training identified their breed—Limousin cattle. *Tolerate vast temperature extremes. Thick winter coat varies from deep yellow to reddish-brown, sheds at first warm weather. Distinguishing pale rings surround eyes. Bulls reared for beef.*

Though the description seemed insignificant, she memorized what she was told, for a milkmaid ought to recognize common local breeds. But now, she'd become a teacher. Only hours ago, Père presented her with a new identity card.

"Mademoiselle, consider yourself a member of the novitiate at St. Joanne de Castonelle." His smile revealed rows of sturdy teeth. "One never knows who one might become, eh? Careful—let the ink set a while longer."

One never knows could be her motto. The cows' owner lagged behind, confident they would wait for him. His black beret shaded his forehead like an awning and his gray and white moustache twitched when he came abreast of the lorry.

"My cows are holding you hostage?"

Père smiled. "In a manner of speaking."

"What news have you?"

"Hard times ahead, Monsieur Chapou."

"Though I can claim no ancestral link to our leader, still, I am proud to bear this name. Our son met him in Labastide. Long may Chapou live—*Vive la liberation!*"

"Amen to that. But the Liberation fighters may go hungry if we fail to deliver their potatoes."

The peasant nudged an animal with his stick. "Move ahead, there, off the road." His wards obeyed him, sending tufts of coarse hair floating onto the path and leaving behind other smelly deposits

"*Merci*, Monsieur."

The man lifted his hat and kept on his way. Above the racket of starting the engine, Père leaned toward Kate.

"He's told me that story more times than I can count. Meeting Chapou obviously impressed his son. I don't know if he realizes how Chapou surprised us in February when he professed allegiance to the Communists."

"Yet he still leads the *Résistance* here?"

"*Oui.* I believe his main reason was practical, for the Communist FTP provides arms."

Père turned silent and a pungent odor rose from the road—the lorry must have smashed a large cow pie. The image the smell produced brought Addie's farm to mind. Ah, but Addie had tried hard during those years with Harold—always did the best she could to mollify his consistent anger.

Then, incredibly, Harold found a way into the armed forces, and

Addie came to London.... *and I left her there.* Kate winced at the memory. Why did every decision have to be so complex?

After three more stops, Père wrangled his long legs from the lorry. "The camp lies up there." He gestured toward a steep incline. "Someone will soon arrive to carry up the supplies. Stretch your legs, but keep the lorry in sight."

Along a path spattered with chamomile and chickweed, Kate relaxed in the luxury of walking. Ducks quacked in the distance, and the serene scene before her belied the war's rising intensity.

She and Addie had once formed bouquets with these small white pairs of chickweed flowers—ten petals each, like conjoined hearts. Addie's hens loved the plentiful chickweed behind her chicken coop. Kate grinned, remembering her fond name for the hens.

"The girls love spring, because then they can ravage the chickweed patch. They peck until nothing's left, but every rain brings it back."

So much had changed since that week Kate spent on the farm two years ago. Addie had grown strong enough to stand up to Harold, or maybe he became more honest—blatant would be the correct term. At least now, as a soldier, he could spend his rage on the Nazis instead of Addie. Maybe this old world still boasted some justice.

What was it about women like Addie, hardworking, meek, and faithful? They held the world together, but suffered so much in the process. Surely, her mother couldn't have been like that. Being married to *Le Renard Intrepid* might not have been easy, but would her mother coalesce to his wishes like Addie did with Harold for so long? Kate groaned—why waste time asking such questions, when she knew they were unanswerable?

Domingo said *morille* mushrooms flourished here, so she searched in the shadows, but she saw no sign. Then she found a place to relieve herself and started back, looking over her shoulder, to the safety of the truck—the last thing Père needed was her capture, along with the messages for London sewn into her pant legs.

Before she arrived, he'd completed the transaction. A couple of ragtag men wheeled loaded wooden carts up an impossible path—all she would see of *La Résistance* today.

En route again, Père turned to Kate. "Mission accomplished, and may the same prove true for your transmissions. Now, we proceed to your new location."

He lowered his voice. "By the way, I told those fellows a nun rode with me, so they fled."

"You're better at lying than you are at driving." As if to prove her point, the lorry narrowly missed sideswiping a massive tree.

"I hope you will suffer no dislocations, child."

Where three paths converged, he veered left. "I also hope you will not take my deceits as foolhardy."

"Remember, I'm not who I appear, either, and you have provided my latest deception. At least you are who you say you are."

His belly laugh buoyed Kate. "You mustn't be too sure."

If not for the glint in his eyes, she might have doubted his priestly call. Domingo knew what he was doing, turning her over to this jovial fellow who charmed his way through this twisted world. Addie's Harold would fault Père's practical theology, but then, he would find fault with the Lord Himself.

But would he risk his life to save a Jewish child or an agent from another country? She couldn't imagine that. No, Harold would make a perfect gendarme, loyal to Vichy, following the letter of the law.

Père yanked the lorry into one more turn. "A final stop. I almost forgot."

He and Albert dragged a burlap sack of potatoes and carrots still musty with the smell of earth to a small cottage. Kate straggled along toward a slender middle-aged woman who emerged and craned her neck up at Père.

"Madame Beaulieu, I hope you are well."

When she nodded, he continued. "And your family also?" The priest's voice held comfort. "Your husband and sons are safe?"

She held up her palms. "God willing."

Père raised his hand over her. "May the Almighty protect your household."

The woman bowed and sank back into the shadows. Every farmstead had a story to tell because of the war—oh, for the time to entertain each one.

As they traversed the sharp curves of the road, a mix of trepidation and excitement battled within Kate. At the top of one hill, Père shifted into neutral and rolled to an idle.

Albert appeared outside his window. "We're finished?"

"Thank you for your help, son. Please go straight home, and tell your father I'll have the lorry back early in the morning."

The lad trotted off into an oak forest, where the growing afternoon shadows swallowed him.

"He'll walk all the way back to the village?"

"Only a few kilometers from here, though it must seem to you we've traveled far afield. We only wound around to the other side of the valley. Albert knows the route. Our next stop will be your temporary home."

He hurtled around yet another curve, slowed, turned into a gated pasture, and gave Kate a nod. She clambered out and worked loose the rusty chain. With some pushing and screeching, the ancient wooden contraption swung wide. After the lorry passed, she re-latched the chain and a short distance farther, they parked in a dense stand of poplar and pine.

Père hurried to the back and hoisted the transmitter. "Follow me." He shook his head when she lifted her hand to help him.

"At least let me take your bag." He eyed her askance and lumbered on.

Soon they angled deeper into the forest, and evening coolness closed in with a clean pine scent. The last rays of sunshine cast feeble light, and it took careful attention to mark each step.

After making their way around a curve, Père cocked his head. "There, ahead. Do you see it?"

At last, Kate's eyes adjusted to the dimness. A building stood about ten yards away, partially obscured by undergrowth.

"The door should be unlocked, if you could ..."

She strode ahead, fumbling for her torchlight, whose feeble rays revealed a table, two chairs, a fireplace, and wood stove with logs stacked nearby. The smoothness of the metal torch gave a measure of comfort, and her pack held three more torchlights if this one failed.

"Bless whoever filled the wood box before they left. We'll get a fire going once I haul this thing upstairs."

In a back passage, Père caught his breath. "See? I'm stronger than

I look." His smile widened, and despite his robe, he conquered the deep rungs of a homemade ladder, ascending to a loft.

By the time he backed down, Kate had lighted the lantern and fired up the stove.

"An amazing feat, climbing that ladder, especially with your garment, sir."

"At times, my *soutane* seems a bother, but more often than not, it proves a blessing. Let's have supper. You need strength for your work."

He pulled parcels from his stained canvas bag. The tightness between Kate's shoulders relaxed at the thought of having company for a while.

"So, Mademoiselle, I sleep here, by the fire."

"You'll stay tonight?"

"Is it not customary for someone to keep watch while another transmits?"

An inadvertent sigh escaped Kate's lips. "Use the bed—my transmission list is long."

"The better for me to prepare my sermon." Père held up a paper packet and raised his eyebrows. "I pilfered some real coffee from the parish. Looking forward to this in the morning will help us, like prayer."

His face stayed as serious as it was long. Finally, he cracked a smile. "All things work together..."

"... for good. I know that verse. It comforted me when my husband died, and again when I lost our baby."

"You lost a child? May I ask how long ago?"

"A little over a year."

"And your husband ... to the war?"

"RAF—his plane crashed on a mission."

"I see." He paused, eyebrows furrowed. "Je suis désolé. This senselessness makes it difficult to see the good, or shall I say impossible? The concept must contain a time lapse, don't you think? How did you decide to enter your present work?"

"It's a strange story. A Frenchman recognized me on a London street when I was walking home from work one day. He recalled my mother's face from the Great War and encouraged me to volunteer."

"That sounds peculiar enough to be holy. Your mother—she was American?"

"Yes, she worked at the front as a Bell Telephone girl and married a Frenchman. They moved back to the States after the war, and..."

"You must tell me more about that." He filled the coffee pot. "Look here, the last person to use this place even left us a pail of water. Stacked wood, a full pail, and we have real coffee. Small things make all the difference.

"But I'd like something big, too, like having Domingo stop in, unharmed, or a sudden armistice, or..." Père's ample eyebrows did a polka. "My desires rarely seem to find full satisfaction."

"You wouldn't have to stay tonight. You could go home and sleep in your own bed."

Père's shrug replayed on the whitewashed wall. "With detection vans on the prowl, you need a watchman. I hate to picture you locked away in some prisoner of war camp."

"You think the Gestapo would find this desolate outpost?"

"Never underrate their tenacity—or God's. My double motto."

"Would you mind if I take the lantern up, so my torch lasts longer?"

"By all means." He rummaged in the cupboard and pulled out another lantern. "I happen to have connections for lamp oil, but don't ask me if my network merits the bishop's blessing."

"Well, it has mine. Does that count?"

"Indeed."

Climbing the ladder, Kate felt secure with those brilliant blue eyes watching her. She peered down before entering the loft and her new friend lifted his hand.

"Do call me if I can help in any way."

EIGHT

The French loft faded from view, and confusing thoughts and images took the place of the transmitter. Aware of low conversations, Kathryn tried to open her eyes. Where was she?

"Nurse, give her another dose. The pain's going to be intense when she wakes up." A needle jabbed Kathryn's arm and she eased back into that other world.

But that other world had changed from France to London, where a smartly dressed woman proclaimed her a courier. "And you rated high in radio operating, as well."

Clackety-clack-clack. Suddenly Kathryn found her fingers hitting the keys, but the racket faded, and she slept again.

Next, a man with curly red hair trekked with her across a high plateau. "We'll get through this somehow, but our homeland will never be the same."

His rare blue eyes and gangly figure stood out against a late afternoon horizon, and a rocky limestone path threatened to trip them. But where were they headed? Glimpses of summertime in terrain awash with green and gold and smelling of ... what was that luscious scent that reminded her of Iowa in late May?

Her comrade signaled a stop, and off the trail, the answer came, for purple, white and yellow irises ranged through the grass. Their intoxicating perfume vied with a nearby stand of pine, and above jagged rock cliffs soared a kite—or was that a buzzard? Were they in Central France, and those cliffs Le Massif Central?

Then, as if a curtain opened on another stage, the scene shifted again—a small study lined with dark wood bookshelves. Voracious,

Kathryn read about the efforts of French churches on behalf of the Jews and details about authorities tearing children away from their parents.

Another man set simple food before her, and told her someone would arrive under cover of darkness to bring her a bicycle for her trip. Then, as if traveling between worlds, she found herself whisked into a kitchen where a woman kneaded bread.

"Etes vous américaine?" Panic struck—had she not disguised herself well enough?

Next, Kathryn climbed the stairs of an old building with a small child sitting on her shoulders, and in a large room lined with beds, she tucked the little girl in. Then she went outdoors and hid in some bushes to eavesdrop on two men conversing about a new agent's arrival.

All these figments seemed real, and the spoken French beckoned her deeper into that world. But why did these incidents contain no logical thread? How had they gotten out of order?

When a dark eyed young man approached, she felt certain she knew him. He placed his hand on her wrist, and in his calm gaze, her puzzlement lessened. Behind him, a white-haired woman cooked porridge at an iron stove, and outside the window, a dog collected some sheep in a stone pen.

Suddenly, analyzing everything became unnecessary. Without making sense of the flood of scenes, Kathryn knew all would be well. Freedom and serenity engulfed her as the young man uttered one simple phrase.

Va avec Dieu—go with God. She took her first long, deep breath since she entered this place. Her shoulders eased into the mattress. The ether smell drifting around her subsided, the doctor and nurses crowding her room receded, and natural sleep overtook her at last.

~

The narrow loft left little room for her head, but Kate held her lantern high as she stepped onto a sturdy plank floor. Someone already covered the lone window. She pulled extra stitches from her hemline to remove papers with parachute drop coordinates, checked the battery, and sat down.

Soon, mathematical directives and variables engaged her so fully, she lost track of time. The ladder creaked, a mellow coffee aroma ascended, and her watchman's busy red hair greeted her from the top of the ladder.

"My mother always hoarded the best for another day, so we'd have something to look forward to. She'd say, 'Now, Henri, Jean-Luc, Marietta, and Noelle, save your holiday treats for the coming days. Don't you remember how gloomy January can be?"

He flicked the side of his mug with his fingernail. "I once claimed her motto, but now, tend to think just the opposite. Enjoy what lies before you—you need it now as much as you will in the morning. Take whatever good this moment brings—see it as your gift."

Kate reached for the cup. Père read her gratitude and held up his palm. "In all honesty, I needed this, too, to construct my Ascension Day sermon. How's your work going?"

"If I can only finish this last message before my listening time from ten until one, I'll be satisfied."

"I want you to know, I'm using you in my Sunday sermon, unless I notice any Gestapo types infiltrating our service." Père leaned on the top rung and sipped from his cup.

"Me? How?"

"The disciples had trouble accepting that their leader must leave. He explained everything, but that changed little. Yet after he passed into the cloud to heaven, they experienced great joy." Deep thought lines crisscrossed his forehead. "You know the story?"

"Aunt Alvina saw to my education at her country Lutheran Church."

"Ah, good. It occurs to me that the Ascension has to do with communication. In the Incarnation, our Lord revealed God's incredible love, and His leave-taking did the same."

"How is that?"

"Once He ascended, the Holy Spirit came. His followers preferred to look into his eyes to read his meaning—how could anything surpass that close relationship? But after He'd gone, and the Spirit entered their very souls, they finally understood. What once seemed better to them had actually been second best, for now he would remain with them forever."

"But the crucifixion already showed God's love. Why did he have to prove it again?"

"My answer verges on heresy, I suppose. Although our Creator God made us in his image, we can be stupid, like sheep. To be shown something as life-changing as His love, one lesson will hardly suffice."

"Sounds like realism to me. But what does my transmitting have to do with that?"

"Oh, I'll think of something." Père's mischievous grin made Kate giggle. "On with your work then, you courageous girl."

Courageous. She rubbed her eyes in the scintillating coffee steam, considering her mother at the front lines, and her father, the Intrepid Fox, performing spying feats. Now, twenty-some years later, here she was in France. But courageous? She wasn't so sure about that.

The coffee worked magic, and while her machine rested, Kate stretched her muscles. Only then did she wonder how Père Gaspard managed to navigate the ladder with two full cups. It wasn't enough to tote hers up to her—he must have wanted to share the joy.

Nothing pertinent came from the BBC tonight, so after her monitoring time, Kate switched off the machine, crawled down the ladder, and fell onto the bunk. Père still read beside the fire and pattered over with a blanket.

"Good work. Now, sleep as though you were born for it." His hand swished the sign of the cross over her and she heard him blow out the lantern.

It seemed as though only minutes had passed when a shaft of light struck her closed eyelids. Kat stirred, incredulous that morning had arrived already. Someone moved near the stove, in sync with the coffee pot's burble, burble, burble. What was that other aroma— something with eggs?

A quick trip outdoors for a whiff of the new day invigorated Kate. The tall pines seemed friendly, but soon she would be alone.

Père had worked a miracle. Kate gaped at the full plate he set before her. "Crepes? How did you manage?"

"Four eggs and a cup of milk don't come along often these days. I took it as God's smile upon your work."

"Someone has been here already?"

"No, I paid someone a visit." He puckered his brow. "Would you like to hear my Ascension Day connection?" He grinned as she dived into her food.

"Just as German spies convey important news to the Fatherland, so our Creator longs to hear from us. London devises machines to transmit messages, too, but I'll use the Reich as an example, in case of unwanted Gestapo visitors this week." He steepled his long fingers.

"Long ago, our Heavenly Father created a communication system far better even that German enigma machine. He imprints His messages on our innermost being. Then because of the Ascension, His Spirit translates them." His nose wrinkled like a curious chipmunk's. "What do you think?"

"Bravo, but I'd like more wisdom to understand those heavenly messages."

"My sentiments, also."

"How do you think infiltrators would respond to your sermon?"

"Not at all, at least outwardly. But secretly, who can tell? The messenger never knows the fruit of his message."

He reached for some papers from the shelf behind him. "Speaking of which, about twenty minutes ago a courier brought these messages for you to send. I must be going, but my prayers remain with you. Stay close, although the day bodes well for a lovely walk."

He gestured for her to follow him to the back passageway. "See how this latch pushes the ladder into the wall, so you can hide it from above? This simple action could save your life."

He donned his beret. "You'll stay indoors after dark? No telling who or what might happen by."

She touched his sleeve. "*Merci encore.* Now, you entrust me to Him who keeps Israel, who neither slumbers nor sleeps."

He blinked. "I needed that benediction. Today I must visit an Abbey, for..." He inspected behind him. "*Pour les innocents,* God's Chosen. Be assured that you help them too, with every tap of your keys." He opened the door and hurried toward the lorry.

Kate worked until pounding developed in her left temple and radiated behind her ear. She descended for leftover coffee and opened the door a crack, then a little more. Spring greens against dark furry pines called her to explore.

But she stalled, kicking at a pebble. "No. No. You will stay right here, Agent Merce. If Miss G dropped in from London, she'd say, 'Breathe in slowly, now out again. Do some calisthenics, and then back to your work.'"

Later, when day waned, Kate circled the house three times while a dove murmured to its mate. That low, intimate sound produced Alexandre's profile in the trees, but all she could do was lift her eyes.

"Help me carry out my mission, just as he did."

Hours later, she'd deciphered five complicated messages, but the latest one loomed even more difficult. She startled at a knock downstairs, descended the ladder without a sound, and stood listening for the password.

"ABERNATHY."

She breathed again and opened the door to a man she had never seen before. "You have messages?"

"Yes, come in."

His intelligent eyes urged her to honesty. "Can you wait? I'm doing battle with two more."

"I've transmitted some in the past. Maybe I can help."

"Oh, I hope so. Follow me."

He bent over her notes. "There must be a way. Let me think."

Grateful, Kate stretched her back and legs. Even if he found no breakthrough, sharing this perplexity released her tension. Then she remembered Eugene. What if this man, too, had turned traitor? As he scanned and calculated, analyzed and plotted, she swallowed her fears.

"See here ... if A equals quadrant and G equals four, and this configuration stands for airfield, then don't you think ..."

She studied his figures. "That makes sense. So the drop will come in the north quadrant, tonight. You must have trained at Baker Street?"

"British Security Coordination recruited me and sent me back here for counter-intelligence work. But with so many drops, we ran short on couriers today. I must say, in some ways, working out these codes comes easier than foraging in the hills. Do you mind if I try the other one?"

Without waiting for a reply, he went to work, and Kate copied down the first. Half an hour later, mission accomplished, he started down the ladder.

"I'm happy to carry news of landing spots. This month alone, we've received over one hundred containers. Finally, we have enough weapons for the fight. Already, we've derailed five engines south of here and blown bridges on the Toulouse-Capdenac line and from Capdenac to Decazeville."

Kate followed him down. "Do be careful."

"You remind me of my daughter, only I hope she does less dangerous work. I last saw her on the first of May, when we occupied *Gramat*."

"Your home?"

"It used to be. After that day, people either loved or hated the *Résistance*. Early in the morning we occupied the city hall and post office. We requisitioned food, and citizens brought plenty. Then some of our partisans marched straight into homes and demanded weapons. In one afternoon we amassed many, and pilfered all the *gendarmerie's* guns, too.

"Our leader stationed men in the square with weapons drawn, but the *gendarmes* willingly handed over their knives and guns. Many of them have been stealing ration cards for us for a long time."

"And you saw your daughter that day?"

"Yes, a special moment, since I've been back and forth since '36 when I fought against Franco. My father taught us that each man deserves his chance rather than being bound up in a bundle of sticks, fascist style." His dark eyes flashed, and he swept back his fair hair with a jerk of his neck.

"I followed my older brother off to fight and we came back refugees. When he went to work at a northern cheese factory, I stayed in *Montauban*, met my wife and eventually brought her to *Gramat*. When our government capitulated to Germany without even putting up a fight, you can imagine our discouragement.

"Not long after that, a British organizer needed experienced fighters with language ability to train British intelligence. We had two little ones, but my wife encouraged me to go. I worked in Scotland and Canada, and by the time they sent me here, all kinds of intelligence had surfaced.

"I warned my wife about the *Maquisards'* parade to the war memorial. Clearly, the Germans would react, so she promised to take our children north to my brother while the trains were still running. His boss offered her a job. He welcomes all, and there is food."

"I hope she went."

He let out a long breath. "I'm certain she did." His face clouded. "And on May 11, the Bosche rounded up all the men of Gramat in a field. Our town sheltered Jews, and the beasts found out."

"Did your family hide any?"

"My cousin worked for the mayor, and learned how to forge identities. She kept stores of *Résistance* supplies in a village shed, a bad example for my wife." His crooked smile belied his concern. "I'll be proud, whatever she does."

"Do you have enough food in camp?"

"A priest up in the mountains claims a special calling. He hunts game to roast, even poaches from others' traps. We forage, too, and haven't starved yet."

He swung out with a final warning. "Stay close. The Gestapo lurks everywhere."

~

At about eleven that night, Paul Verlaine's poem came through on the radio. The verse froze Kate to her chair:

Les sanglots longs
Des violons
De'lautomne
Blessent mon Coeur
D'une langueur
Monotone.

The last six words confirmed her hopes that the Invasion would begin within twenty-four hours. She continued to tune in, and the announcer threw *Abernathy* into the personal messages. At this signal for the local circuit to forge ahead, Kate's fingers turned white gripping the table.

If only she could whisper the news in Gabirel's ear, to still his doubts forever. Restless, she climbed up and down the ladder a few times, then boiled coffee and peered outside. Images of Allied planes and troops storming the northern beaches passed before her.

Her radio, an irrepressible magnet, drew her again. Every second, every sound, took on enhanced meaning.

NINE

The explosion, followed by a strange prolonged crackling, made its own unique, tinny music. Acts of destruction had never delighted Domingo, but this train transported troops to kill the Allies. Each sharp crackle marked the demise of a wooden bridge support. Every bridge destroyed halted the German advance, if only temporarily.

During the first blast, he shared the shudder with a laurel tree. Fawns would die tonight, along with birds and lambs just beginning their lives in this valley. But such was war's way—innocents suffered.

The fierce rumblings faded, and two massive smoke pillars melded into one ominous cloud, forming an avalanche that filled the valley. Domingo pulled on his pack, and a faint rustle met his ears—probably the leader of this mission, who indicated they would travel together to Figeac.

"If we handed out Legion badges for valor, you would receive one." The demolition leader's voice pierced the cool night air. "Ready? Once we get to Figeac, I have directions. Lead on."

"No one else comes with us?"

The leader shook his head, so Domingo plunged headlong down the path, down, down, down. Night breezes zinged his ears. Relentless through bracken and bushes, he set his sights on Figeac. Some time later, at the outskirts of a town, they paused for cheese and bread, so his comrade turned to him and spoke.

"For this night, call me Giriotte."

Giriotte—a stone beehive hut built to protect peasants from storms out in the wilds. A likely nickname, like many partisans were given.

"And you, what shall I call you?"

Glancing at Giriotte's ruddy complexion and greasy hair, Domingo considered. "How about *Cazelle*?"

"Ah, another name for the same shelter. However, I have already heard others call you *La Foudre*. Now I understand why, for you run as fast as lightning." Giriotte picked at his boot lacing. "I prefer not to mention my real name, with Gestapo and Das Reich encroaching."

Domingo swallowed what he wanted to ask—*then why must you talk so much?*

"But the blood of the ancient *Cadourques* flows through my veins. Those warriors acted the hero even though they knew the enemy would cut off their hands." He leaned against a tree. "Now, two dozen people have been shot to death in Saint-Céré, and the Bosche even deport our women."

A wave of sickness pummeled Domingo. *Please keep Maman from such a thing.*

"Montpezat-de-Quercy has been looted, along with many other villages. Whoever imagined Orniac ransacked, women shot in Cardaillac and Lauze, and others yet unknown?"

The buzz of insects in the brush called to Domingo. He and this Giriotte rested between two feats of destruction, but birds still warbled from their perches, and a couple of wrens, orange-brown in the sun, swept over the area. Were they upset or simply playing with each other, like two airplanes doing acrobatics?

He might have instructed Giriotte to jabber less. But the fate of those women he had mentioned—plain, rural women—festered in Domingo's heart.

Katarin gave up her name for the cause. The thought rose unbidden, just as this agent had come into his life. For all Domingo knew, Père Gaspard had imposed yet another identity on her by now. She might have stayed in her homeland, where his Basque leader sought refuge, yet she risked her life here.

Her country had become one of few safe spots left in this world, but unlike many of his schoolmates, Domingo harbored no desire to go there. Intense desire to regain his homeland quickened his pace, and Père's sentiments from the pulpit a few months earlier swept over him. "We are *les inconnus*, the unknown. But our heavenly

Father sees us, and our faith summons us to treacherous involvement.

"We must save *les Juifs* and restore the liberty of France. I follow the bishop's orders, and so, my children, must you, each in your own way. We may not see or touch *les innocents*, but no effort we expend on their behalf goes unnoticed."

On the Sunday all the parishes had read the bishop's letter, Père praised the brave woman who rode a bicycle for two days straight to deliver the sealed encyclical in time for all rural priests to read at Sunday mass.

"This, my friends, equals an encyclical from Pope Pius himself, who shows restraint after the terrible aftermath of his public stand in the Netherlands. Perhaps you recall those dark days."

After the service, Domingo questioned Père, and his answer came fiery-eyed. "In '40, Pope Pius sent expressions of sympathy to the Dutch Queen, the King of Belgium, and the Grand Duchess of Luxembourg when the Nazis invaded. Accordingly, the Dutch bishops sent an anti-Nazi letter to every Dutch Catholic parish. In no other country did the bishops protest so strongly."

Père's gaze swept the backs of his little flock taking their separate ways home. "Mussolini charged that Pius made himself enemies with Italy's ally, but Pius said he would rather be deported to a concentration camp than deny his conscience. The result of the Dutch bishops' protests still haunts him to this day—ninety-two Jews killed. With every new outcry for a public papal statement, he recalls that proclamation's disastrous effect."

"These days, a particular choice may appear the moral one, but the next minute, proves the opposite. The Pope's example leads us to stand against the forces of evil regardless of our personal safety or reputation.

"Do you recall when the Germans overtook Rome, they hauled away only one thousand Jews? A small fraction of all who lived there, and the Nazis knew it. But what could they do? Even now, behind the scenes, parishes, scholars, and no doubt the Vatican itself, shelter hundreds, perhaps thousands of God's Chosen. One day, the truth will come to light. When we alter above water, we submerge."

Pere's words on that day still echoed in Domingo's ears. And now, this agent from America had joined the fight. He guarded her given name more closely than his own.

A gritty, low shout brought him back to the present. The schoolteacher-turned-*Résistance* leader brandished his fist in the air, very much like Père did that long-ago Sunday.

"Those collaborators, as evil as Hitler himself, shall not prevail. Surely you have heard what happened in the small village of Fraysinnet-le-Gelat just two weeks ago on the route from Fumel to Gourdon?"

Domingo well remembered, but felt no need to speak of it.

"The SS rounded up and killed all young males from one-child families, so their family lines would die with them. But every cruel strike fuels our fury."

Domingo stayed silent until finally, Giriotte's tales ended. "You live nearby?"

"Not far." Surely he observed their differences in dialect and espadrilles—why spell them out? During teacher training, Domingo's professors called these distinctions divisive, like using his native tongue.

He completed his teacher training to make *Maman* proud, but then wayward pilots needed help. How could he teach and watch over her, Gabirel, and the sheep while traipsing that route at a moment's notice? When this was all over, Giriotte might return to teaching, but Domingo had no wish to do so.

Something rustled in the brush and he held up his hand. A beret appeared, and Domingo stole along the ravine to get a better look … a partisan whose pinched face declared his hunger. They shared bread, and like a snake charmer, Giriotte's singsong tone brought forth the fellow's history.

"Our southern band has lived in *giriottes* and *bergeries* since '41. Now we unite south of Figeac with Limoges, Tarn, Lozere, and Ardeche.

For once, Domingo cleared his throat "Remember those near Carcasonne, where the Cathars fought against the Albegensian crusades? They attained the name '*les purs*', but lately it's used for the *Maquis* in general. Can we claim to be the pure ones? And how did you happen to come north?"

"We heard that London dropped Maxime at Carennac with his WT operator in January, and you have a Colonel once associated with the *Résistance* Central Council. Then we heard you received Maxime's arms instructor for arms training."

"All true. He turned us into a fighting force." Giriotte turned to Domingo. "But you were not there?"

"No." No need to explain his wild trek with Katarin.

"On May eleventh, during the SS occupation, the *Milice* arrested our leader in Figeac. You know this, right?"

The stranger shook his head. "No. Tell me."

"They deported him, some say to the Carlsbad camp in Germany. Can you believe that underground word travels so far?" Giriotte rubbed his ear. "His instruction gave us confidence, but his arrest put steel into our souls. At Figeac, they paid us back for destroying their Ratier works in January."

"You helped in that raid?"

Domingo wanted to clap his hand over Giriotte's mouth. "We stopped the Luftwaffe's production of variable pitch propellers. They still haven't been able to resume. Maybe they never will." A proud smile softened Giriotte's weary features.

"Tomorrow we meet a descendant of the Camisards with the *Résistance Fer* and trained by the British in sabotage. He fights with the FTP, and with his railroad knowledge, we'll destroy a large center tomorrow night." Giriotte ran his sleeve over his mouth and stood.

"Whether I fight beside a Communist or a man drunk with the idea of liberty, from Poland, Belgium, or Spain, or with a German Jew who escaped before the Reich took over, what does it matter? To *l'invasion!*"

Traces of dawn showed along the horizon, and the stranger saluted them. "I must hurry. *Bon courage.*" He ducked back down the ravine, and soon his beret bobbed out of sight.

Giriotte nodded once and took the lead at a maniacal pace, heading downslope in the opposite direction. His rhythm enervated Domingo, and for once, he followed another's lead without chafing.

~

In late afternoon a lithe young man in a dapper Parisian hat, incongruous knee-length socks, short pants, and espadrilles handed Kate more messages. She lost no time climbing the ladder, with the courier's exclamation ringing in her ears.

"*En effet, l'Invasion est venu!*" His eyes darted, matching his news of the Invasion beginning.

Hours later, at a muffled tap, Kate descended.

Another tap-tap-tap. She obscured the ladder and faced the door quavering. Why hadn't she thought to look out the upstairs window? Moonlight might have given her a clue who waited out there. She put her ear to the door and stilled her pounding pulse.

A coarse whisper loosed her tension. "Ascension Day." She breathed again—Père Gaspard. They'd never agreed on a password, but this worked perfectly. Like a refreshing mountain breeze after a long, hot climb, Père beamed down at her with his soutane wafting a mysterious chocolate scent.

"You've come back."

"I missed the warmth of the fireplace. All is well?" He wiggled his eyebrows and pulled something from his robe.

"Your soutane proves a blessing again?"

"This garb hides a multitude of sins. False identities and baptismal records, grenades, your American pencil explosives..." He stepped back to study her. "Your eyes widen, Madame. Did you think these hands dealt only in bread and wine?"

"No, but I never imagined a grenade in those folds."

"Some call it a cassock—same root as the great Russian warrior Cossacks. My vows promised a stimulating life, but tonight I bring only bread and cheese, with more coffee."

Kate sniffed a couple of times.

"Ah, yes. And a bit of chocolate from ... an undisclosed origin."

"I have nothing to offer in the way of sustenance, but I do bear news from London."

"Have you heard then? Is tomorrow the day?"

"Unless my mind fails me, indeed it is."

He crossed himself. "*Merci, mon Dieu.* At last."

He set the supplies on the table. "The planes in the skies alerted me, but I knew I mustn't jump to conclusions. We must celebrate, but first, let me take in this glorious news."

He waved her to a seat. "I supped with a family just down the road, and news of *l'Invasion* filled the room. The Allies hold us spellbound with expectation." He looked thoughtful for a moment. "Did you ever picture yourself aiding a secret army, traipsing the Massif Central, handling life and death transmissions, and making an enormous difference in a vast war?"

"Never. My husband yes, but not me. Yet I always hungered to make a difference. At the news of Alexandre's first crash, I admit that I left for London ready for adventure. So many men had joined up, but women were just beginning to see the opportunities."

Père Gaspard's quiet acceptance instigated questions about Kate's father. Would le *Renard Intrepid* listen to her like Père? Would he allow her to ask her questions? The old rafters creaked, jiggling the windows.

"Must be windy out. Did Albert make it home all right?"

"He spotted Gestapo, but took shelter in to a farmhouse, the one where I received this bread and cheese a while ago. Jean-Claude spent a sleepless night worrying, but joy came this morning when Albert appeared, hale and hearty. Hungry?"

Her eyes must have spoken for her, so Père set out the food.

"Albert often accompanies me on produce runs, since his father owns the market. If anyone stops us, his regular deliveries fit our mission perfectly."

"Do they check your papers often?"

"Plenty. But so far, all is well."

"Albert doesn't attend school?"

"The local schedule instructor doubles as a *Résistance* leader. Even our children pay a price, it seems. How is your work going?"

"Better, like playing the piano after a long absence. The responses, bode well."

"For a week last winter, someone transmitted from the rectory attic." Père shrugged. "Things have probably become more complicated since then, but let me know if I can help. I've arranged for transport in the morning, and also brought a small diversion."

He pulled a hinged board from under his soutane. "Perhaps we might have time to play checkers?"

"You're full of surprises."

"What better way to assuage my wayward contemplations?"

A brilliant defeat later, Kate acknowledged she'd pitted herself against a checkers master. But she learned a new move and several of her questions about Domingo found answers, because Père described Sancha's mission.

"She went to Haute Loire, to help the children—only because they needed workers, or she never would have gone."

"To Le Chambon-sur-Lignon?"

"Yes. She was so young, so much of life before her, but the Gestapo ended it all, and murdered the children, too. They earned their retribution." In silent agreement that the rest of the tale belonged to Domingo, Kate only nodded. But then Père described the deaths of Domingo's father and brother in the Spanish Revolution.

"No wonder he raced so fast from the heights, and paled at Gabirel's absence."

"I call all my young parishioners 'son,' but Domingo has always been special. Obedient but thoughtful, he read his lessons long before I assigned them, and entertained questions of integrity."

Père emphasized his last word. "The Almighty can see us through the worst, you know—as long as we hold to an honest course." He thought for a while. "I have shared too much, perhaps. But Domingo's experience taught me about the place of violence in love, as at the crucifixion."

The gale rattled the windows again. "You know about the Basque president, Aguila, now in your country?"

"A little." The chicory's invigorating aroma filled the room. Sip by sip, the long night ahead seemed less daunting.

"My Euskara helps me, as does the Spanish tongue, with so many Spaniards descending on us. The government calls the *Langue d' Occident* outdated, but Domingo's family keeps it alive. When a language dies, what hope remains for its people?"

"Many of our Indian tribes have died out, like their languages."

"What about the Cajuns?"

"In Louisiana?"

"Yes, I met an agent from there who filters information on the Reich's plans. Is his language valued in the United States?"

"I doubt it, if we treat Cajuns anything like the Indians. How did he come here?"

"Army intelligence channels." Père pulled a book from his pack. "Time for you to work, and for me to study."

TEN

In early morning light, Giriotte inspected a blistered toe. "These boots should serve me better. Do your feet give you trouble?"

"Am I studying sores on my toes?" Domingo chuckled under his breath.

"I may have to go back to the old ways." Giriotte grimaced. "Leather boots seemed to have more to offer, at first glance, anyway." He dipped his feet in a cold stream. "After Papa visited Paris, my parents decided to modernize us."

"If you want good espadrilles, you must attach yourself to a village, you know."

"Would yours adopt me?" Domingo left the question hanging as Giriotte scraped his heel on a rock. "When did you join the fight?"

The horrific beginning of his personal commitment rushed before Domingo's mind. That awful day when he and Philippe discovered innocent children's bodies hidden in thick brush, along with Sancha's. The reality still stung—murdered by vile oppressors, thrown away like rubbish.

Even now, the memory of the coppery smell of blood assailed him, but he shook it away.

"For me, it wasn't a matter of joining. Has anyone ever told you that you talk too much?"

"Once or twice." Giriotte dressed his feet and sighed. "But I am who I am, just like you. You were born to range this land like an antelope. Fortunately for me, they're picking us up in Saint-Céré. Another thirty miles beyond that would only energize you, but might render me an amputee."

He would make a good *comedien* in a traveling troupe, Domingo reasoned. But then Giriotte brought up a detested subject.

"Have you ever seen the interment camp at Vernet?"

"Once, I neared the camp at Gurs. That was enough for the rest of my life." Bile climbed up Domingo's throat. Even though he and Petra, his comrade at the time, had viewed the camp from afar, the stench stayed with him. What was it about odors that forever labeled a place or experience?

"How many pilots have you taken across the Pyrenees?"

Domingo shrugged, but Giriotte wanted to know more. "Were you with those hundred Jewish children from Chateau de La Hille, near Foix? What a story—from Germany to Belgium, and when the Nazis took Belgium, they fled to some chateau barns near Seyre, in Haute-Garonne.

"The Swiss took them to *Les Succors Swiss aux Enfants*. A Red Cross nurse arranged passage for twenty over the mountains, but her superior besought the Vichy Chief of Police when French Police hauled forty more to Vernet, built for Spanish war criminals."

Domingo conjured up perilous routes through raging snow and ice storms. Adults created enough trials, but such a trek with children ... unthinkable. He crossed himself. *Bless those who guided them.*

"And the Chief of Police agreed to let those forty go. Only a few days later, the Germans deported all the rest to death camps."

A deep curve in the trail led to a slight incline, and Domingo ventured, "Isn't this our pick-up point?"

"Yes, thank heavens." Giriotte dropped beside a nearby stream to soak his feet again. A baby bird, fluffy down still visible under sprouting feathers, hopped near the water, the image of vulnerability. From a branch, its mother lifted an urgent call.

"So you guided pilots, but not through that territory?"

"You speak of Ariege. Many travel that route, through Agen, Toulouse, and on to St. Girons in Ariege. We moved farther north, on ancient family paths."

"Those in the south headed to Tabescan. And your destination?"

The faint hum of an engine caught Domingo's ear, so he lowered his voice. "Near San Sebastian. Shhh."

Giriotte gathered his socks and boots. Domingo rose as a vehicle approached. Two minutes later, they boarded a lorry that sloped port side and reeked of something rotten. Twenty-some kilometers ahead, the road descended sharply. For the fourth time, Giriotte rammed into Domingo.

"Sorry. Nothing to hang onto in here."

Domingo held his peace. He might fly into someone next.

Two strangers rode in front with the driver, and six others lined the back. A scruffier lot Domingo had never seen—hopefully none was the munitions expert.

But Père Gaspard's perspective instructed him. "We are *Les inconnus*—we appear powerless, but every secret act matters to the whole."

In rising dust, Domingo pulled his kerchief over his nose and closed his eyes. *Les inconnus*—the unknown. Père's label brought Katarin to mind once again. Where was she? Was she safe? There was no way to know, but at least he could check on his family.

The lorry finally jolted to a stop. The team unwound cramped legs and waited at the precipice of a drastic incline. A man from the front handed a wooden crate out and returned for more, and a new leader spoke.

"You all have blown things before. No operation should ever fail, but this one *must not*."

The leader swept his beret toward the last partisan to leave the lorry. He fell asleep minutes after the vehicle took off, workman's cap flopped on the floor, jaw slack. Now, he appeared alert and in control, as his next instructions showed.

"Tonight we will call our expert, Paul. But afterward, we never saw each other or heard that name, you understand?"

Around the circle, faces hollowed by deprivation and lack of sleep nodded. Behind them, prolific wild vines sprouted along myrtle trees, and spindly poplar and sycamore saplings. In full leaf, they would provide full cover from the enemy.

Domingo breathed deep of fresh air. A sense of purpose staved off his anxiety about *Maman* and Gabirel. Tonight's action would bring SS reprisals, all too often against innocent civilians, as in

Saint-Céré, where the Gestapo interrogated even the Sisters, and killed twenty-four citizens.

A quiver traced his shoulders at the thought of the enemy in that beautiful medieval city, performing their vile deeds in sight of the towers of Saint-Laurent and the River Bave. No respect for even the Sisters there—Domingo felt his back stiffen at the unthinkable idea. When an important pelota game approached, he experienced the same determination—his team must win. But this was far more important than any game.

The little muscle in Paul's cheek jerked as he gestured with his hand. "We follow that ridge to the city's edge, and commence at eleven o'clock, when the shift changes. Twenty minutes later, *Résistance Fer* members will muffle all protests within the ranks. These iron workers have committed themselves at great risk."

After a voluminous breath, Paul's visage enlivened. "But they understand the threat. Tens of thousands of troops are on their way here. Seven Panzergrenadier units, 20,000 Das Reich troops, two hundred tanks and armored vehicles."

Electricity ignited the circle. Partisans set their shoulders.

"We will sting General Lammerding, a conscienceless brute, like a hoard of wasps." He squatted, and everyone else followed suit.

"At the ridge top, you'll see the rail yard." Paul unfolded a dilapidated paper square and pointed with his dirty finger. "We'll set charges here, here, and here on the west side. Opposite the station, here, here, and here."

His finger smudged a circle. "After eleven, insiders will station themselves in the central switch house, and we'll hit all six centers. No train will enter or leave here for at least two months."

He surveyed each man and stopped at Domingo. "Follow me."

What did Paul see? On the other hand, what difference did it make? The others fell in line behind Domingo, and half an hour later, Paul gathered them behind some bushes.

"Now we check the sites, prepare the *plastiques*, and set the charges. When the whistle blows, we move into position."

He instructed Giriotte, "Take three men. Check the northern tracks."

Giriotte's eyes glittered like fireflies as he skittered off. Paul motioned for Domingo and two others. "We'll investigate the station house."

He eyed Domingo. "You are the one they call *la foudre*?"

Domingo almost laughed out loud. His fame had spread.

~

Roses in December ... how did the rest of that poem go? Something about memories, but lying here on her raised hospital bed, Kathryn could only recall those three words. Still, they reminded her of something good, something pleasant, so she clung to them.

In December, good things happened for her. Yes, that was when she found passage to London ... Red Cross—those words had a special meaning that escaped her right now, too. Leaving from Canada, she'd typed all the way across the Atlantic.

She'd wanted to find somebody over there. Someone important, but who? She opened her eyes when a female voice commanded her to help out a little. *Help out with what?*

"We're turning you over so you don't get bed sores, ma'am. If you can hear me, throw your left arm over your chest. Do you think you can?"

Left arm ... chest. Kathryn attempted to connect words with meaning, but that other world pulled her back. Oh, that lovely chest of drawers in her room at that lady's house. A very proper lady, connected to her employer. What was his name?

Mr. ... Mr. ... Tenney! Yes, and his mother. They'd been so kind while she searched for ... someone. At hospital after hospital, people commiserated with her, studied their patient lists, but shook their heads.

"I know how hard this must be, and I'll call you if anything changes. We get new transports nearly every day, you know."

One day, Mrs. Tenney took her to her dentist friend. "You've nursed that sore tooth for weeks. We've tried oil of cloves, strong tea, and who knows what all. It's no use, the pain won't dissolve on its own."

The dentist drove hot air into her tooth with a metal tip before he filled it, and she cried actual tears. Embarrassing, considering all the pain wounded soldiers faced.

The dentist tried to salve her pride. "Ah, I'm so sorry. Sometimes these bloody cavities have to get worse before they can get better, and tears aren't all bad. I learned that at Dunkirk—gave me a metal plate in my head, and a jolly good dose of perspective as well."

Then she noticed the scar along his temple. *Get better.* The other day, Darlene told her to do just that. "Oh Kathryn, everyone misses you so much. If it weren't such a drive to Boise, Gabby would be here. Dear little Mara said she's praying for you. Oh, and her pony has learned to work a cow."

"It does me a world of good to see you, Dar, even though I know it's a sacrifice." But Kathryn's words hunkered down in her throat like recalcitrant germs.

"Just you keep in mind that I've gotten to see my new little grandson more often. Staying overnight makes the trip a lot easier, and I'm sure you'll be better soon."

The surgeon said the same thing when he checked her. "We had to wire your jaw. This will take some time, but it'll get better. For now, you'll be on a liquid diet, and by the way, I have every assurance you can hear me, so we're going to continue to talk to you."

Better ... better ... *Better is a dinner of herbs where there is love, than a fattened ox with ...*

But she'd been thinking about December, the month she floated through the air and landed in that beautiful place. Like a giant bird, with something heavy strapped on her back. Stars and moon as witnesses. Pulled some strings, important to do it at just the right time.

Memories ... roses in December, and the mellow sweetness of lavender stored over the winter. Oh, for that heady scent again, or a steaming bowl of porridge with wild honey.

But where had she been? In a simple kitchen, a diminutive woman stirred a big pot over an old iron stove. She turned, her black eyes sparkling. In a barn, they milked some goats, but then soldiers came ...

Utter terror returned, but Kathryn realized she'd called out only when a nurse came to her side. She rubbed her cool hand over Kathyrn's arm.

"Something troubling you, hon?"

Troubling me ... yes, those soldiers. Yet that spry little lady maintained control. She must've been as frightened as I was...

Then she was back in London, with Mr. Tenney telling the staff a worker from the office had been killed in a bombing raid the night before. The worker had been a warden, like his mother. That night, Kathryn donned a metal helmet and served as a fire warden with Mrs. Tenney. They might have been killed, too.

She learned how to snuff out incendiaries, how to find hiding spots. In that other beautiful countryside, the little woman made do each day in her stone cottage. Worried about her sons—yes, what were their names? So concerned that her youngest would join some fighters...

The dream—or whatever it was—transported her to her first day of school in Aunt Alvina's town. In the school cloakroom, the warmest brown eyes and a shy smile won her heart, and when a boy started to taunt her, Addie stuck her finger in his face and yelled, "Johnnie Jorgenson, you stop it right now, or I'll tell her why you had to go home from school last..."

The boy's face flamed and he fled. Better yet, Addie whispered, "Don't ever let him bother you again—he had an accident and had to go back home to change his pants." That Saturday, Aunt Alvina said she could invite Addie over to play, and they skated on the river together.

Better a dinner of herbs where there is love ...

But she returned to that small woman's house, and someone knocked at the door. Another one, out in the woods, with pine trees all around. Frightened, she climbed down a ladder, and someone handed her papers. Messages for someone—so important they arrive tonight ...

Clackety-clackety-clack-clack-clack.

What was that racket? Always in the background, making her mind whirl. Doors shutting and opening. Climbing secret stairs, pulling up ladders, hurrying out back doors and ducking through alleys. Granite stairs then, and a hidden closet opening up into more rooms.

Nothing like roses, these memories taunted Kathryn with scanty details and constantly skipped around in time. So many different places... Who had she searched for? These memories made her jaws ache, even though she still hadn't uttered a word.

ELEVEN

Moving off like an animal in the wild, Domingo tore off through a wild berry patch. Thorns ripped his hands, and he flattened when a German guard issued a sharp command. His partner breathed far too loudly.

Boots again clacked on stone, so Domingo crawled to a break in the bushes and stared into the rail yard. Not a soul. He pulled out Aitaita's gold watch: 10:30.

Half leaping, half-crawling, he made room for his comrade. Tension flowed between them, and soon, his partner pointed left down the tracks. The light from their cigarettes clearly marked three Bosche guards as they smoked, chuckled and intermittently broke out in loud guffaws. Their guns dangled from their shoulders.

Domingo gulped cool night air and stepped across one set of tracks, then the second, his flexible espadrilles making no sound. The outer wall lay in dark shadows. For that, he breathed *merci*, and continued in a crouching run.

Around the corner, a signal post rose between the two sets of tracks. Loud laughter wafted from the guards as he darted back to the berry patch with his partner close behind.

The distance between this and the next detonation location allowed five minutes to set each charge, unless *plastiques* took longer. Well, they would soon find out.

Most of the group, hunched down like jackals, waited for them. Domingo's chest leaped at every chestnut that crunched under a boot, but the German guards still talked and chortled, unaware of anything amiss.

In the warmth of close bodies, Paul's eyes flamed against the night sky, his gestures mimicking an orchestra director.

"You two take out the guards on each side. I'll set the charges nearest the station house, with *La Foudre*."

"Girotte, you and your partner kill the other three, and the rest of you, keep watch with the guards' guns."

A twig fell from the nearest tree and someone startled, but then the group quieted, a silent intensity connecting each man. Like a panther, every nerve taut, they awaited their prey.

Stay low, watch, light your charge, flee with hell at your heels.

Engine brakes squealed, train cars clanged together and tore apart with nerve-jangling wrenches as workmen unhooked heavy iron latches. Shouts rang across the rails. Axle grease and coal dust wrapped the yard like a shroud.

After picking and shoveling all day, the workmen's soft conversations carried on the slight breeze. *Help them hear the alert and stay clear.* Domingo had no wish for innocents to die.

The smell of Nobel's number 808 explosives, oddly akin to almonds, but stronger, hovered. Then, like a shrill night bird's call, only much louder, the yard whistle shrieked. The killers loped along the path between brush and tracks.

Domingo shadowed Paul, stooping and twisting, all the while balancing his delicate box like an egg basket. Once, a sharp cry was stifled abruptly, followed by a heavy thud. One Kraut would never again see his fatherland.

They enacted a swift-paced scene, Paul in the hero's role. At one point, Domingo glimpsed the partisans-turned-patrollers, now toting heavy German Karabiner 98k's. All moved according to plan. He might be watching a movie.

Paul slipped ahead of him as if he had blown this very station ten times before. Domingo handed him tools. One by one, Paul used and exchanged them.

Aluminum-colored wire, tape, tweezers, pliers—ordinary useful items one might employ to fix things, hold pipes together, or even pull a child's painful loose tooth. But tonight, they became lethal instruments.

Wire ends scattered at their feet—such a slight noise—but the gentle twang echoed in the stillness. Paul's fingers twisted, his elbows jutted. At last, his shoulders relaxed. Sweat doused his forehead as he motioned for Domingo to light the farthest charge.

The charge barely ignited before Domingo slid to the next. Snort of sulfur-blue ... splash of light ... sizzle. A flaming trail darted along the fuse, but Domingo rejected his childhood fascination with fire.

Run—jump those bushes. Torpedo as far and as fast ...

Paul crashed into him and they tumbled along a ravine. Moments later, a blast rent the night with a stunning display. The force almost covered the screams coming from the yard. Then another blast, and silence. Finally a third, and two more on the other side.

Domingo held his breath. *One more. Come on Giriotte.*

Low to the ground, Paul held his temples. A groan, prayer-like, escaped Domingo's lips as two more men slid against him.

Paul braced his fist in the air. *Pow! Ker-slam!* The final detonation shook the earth with a magnificent fireworks display.

Paul exhaled. "We did it."

Père Gaspard seemed very near, with Good Friday words followed by the annual crack of a book he slammed shut behind the altar. Every Holy Week, this ritual in the darkened sanctuary signified Roman soldiers sealing the tomb. Then Père's "It is finished!" rang out. Domingo felt the same rejoicing this night. It was done.

By the time they reached the incline's crest, the rail yard swam in flames and fumes. Smoke spiraled above the tallest pines. They watched, entranced, as three more of their team crawled over the ridge.

But not Giriotte. Where was he?

Paul stared into the conflagration. "Five more minutes before this place crawls with Huns."

Time stalled. *Hurry, Giriotte. I won't mind you this time. You can bump into me on harsh turns—come on, come on!*

But when Paul gave the signal, Giriotte still had not arrived. *Help him, Lord.* All the way to the lorry, Domingo pled. *Please, in this last few seconds ...*

The engine sputtered to life. Explosions rose from the valley like the maelstrom he and Katarin observed that night over Albi.

"That's the munitions arsenal blowing."

Someone produced a flask, and Paul commented. "Ironic—we call them Bosche after their scientist who figured out how to convert Haber's atmospheric nitrogen into ammonia on an industrial scale ... for explosives."

Another partisan chuckled, and Paul continued. "They both got a Nobel prize for their work, and what do we get?"

"Sweet success!" The flask circled again, but Domingo had no heart for this empty victory. Dust and sulfur ringed his tongue, and he could think only of Giriotte. An urge to plunge into the darkness and launch a search nearly overwhelmed him.

At the same time, calm logic reigned. If they turned back, even more men would perish. The night offered no figure loping toward the lorry, wild flailing arms against the orange and yellow background.

"Above all else, maintain hope." Domingo closed his eyes against his knees. "Remember, we are *les inconnus*." Père's words helped him as dirty sweat rolled down his face.

He drank from a canteen his neighbor offered and passed it along. When he wiped his face, Giriotte's eyes rose before him. Who could ever fathom the price he may have paid for that rail yard?

Unknown—but known to God. Père shared one of his family stories, using his uncle as an example. "He was gassed in the Great War, and my grandfather found him in a field hospital. Grandfather watched over him until he died."

Starlight reached down through the cracks, and Domingo let his mind wander back to that other war. So many men fit the meaning of *les inconnus*—buried far from home and remembered only by their loved ones. The lorry faltered, and Domingo shook himself back to the present.

Perhaps Giriotte had gotten away. Maybe the inferno disoriented him, and he'd run in the wrong direction, but still away from the rail yard. One day, they might meet again on some back woods path, and Giriotte could exult in telling him all the details.

One by one, the other partisans dozed. Good, they needed the rest before their next missions. Domingo leaned his head against the rough lorry wall, but sleep remained a stranger.

~

Into the darkness before dawn, Kate continued transmitting. Once, she glanced out the window and recalled what Père said earlier. Domingo's home meant everything to him, like that Cajun who left America. Did people with a home live without the restlessness that never left her?

Finally, she packed up the set, wishing she could haul it down the stairs for Père. During the weeks since her mission to Albi, she'd longed for another courier assignment. When Eugene blew her circuit's cover, another of her temporary homes had passed into the realm of mystery. Left without even a mailbox for messages, she felt at loose ends.

Then Domingo became her guide and they discovered Monsieur le Blanc. Something had happened inside her as she waited with the injured Monsieur alone on that rugged wilderness trail, vulnerable to the Gestapo. She found his briefcase, learned his identity, and pondered the flawless timing involved in this unlikely reunion.

Then Domingo brought partisans to transport Monsieur to the *Résistance* farm. Amid animals and manure, Monsieur's dying became a sacred time, for he gave proof that he was her father's brother.

She and Addie used to giggle over Aunt Alvina's matronly brassiere with its severe stays, but the contraption provided a perfect metaphor for what happened inside her when she heard his revelation. Monsieur's dying message reinforced Kate like that brassiere reinforced her aunt's figure.

Finally, so many of her questions found answers. At last, her meager fragments of information about her father came together.

What were the chances of meeting a relative would bless her with clear recollections of her father and mother? Much like her first rendezvous with Monsieur in London, the scene defied understanding, yet Domingo had witnessed it, too.

From now on, she could cast aside anxiety about her next move. If the Almighty could bring her uncle to her on a trail at the edge of the wild Massif Central, was anything impossible?

Beside a dwindling fire, like a long smudge on the floor, Père

Gaspard slept. Kate sank onto the bunk and tried to clear her mind of SS troop movements, bridges blown, rail yards destroyed, and supplies needed. But lists of coordinates ticked before her like a hundred clocks. Which mission had included Domingo?

Impossible to know, and she must sleep. She buried her face in her pillow.

The aroma of boiling coffee woke her in full daylight. She wiped sleep from her eyes—a new day, and tonight would bring another location, along with more meaningful work. The thought spurred her out of bed to splash her face with hot water burbling on the woodstove.

The door creaked, and silence bade Kate to look up. One glance told her something terrible had happened. Père's drawn countenance paled against his black hood. Even his wild hair seemed limp and its roguish red diminished.

But he made an attempt at cheer. "I trust you had a good sleep?"

"What is it?"

"The SS has gone into a fervor, burning villages, looting everything in sight. They've even ransacked peasants' farms. From the smoke..."

Kate's heart leapt into her throat. "Domingo's mother?" Père Gaspard whitened even more at the echo of gunshots in the distance.

"I'll fetch that transmitter and we'll be off. The lorry will meet us at ten o'clock. Perhaps the driver will have some idea ..."

He mounted the ladder and straggled down under the radio's weight. She handed him coffee, and they drank in quietness. Then he lifted the radio again, and at the meeting point, settled his burden on the earth. He sank on a fallen log, twisted like a pretzel.

A squirrel clattered down a pine, scattering bark every which way, and Kate hurried to see what chased it. Good pretense for a walk, after being inside so long. In the heavy pines, she mouthed fervent prayers before turning back.

Père Gaspard's rested his head on his arms. A while later, he paced between two massive pines and a chestnut, still silent.

On one pass, Kate dared a question. "How do you keep from hating the SS?"

"Who says I don't hate them?"

Digesting his answer led to a question that haunted her since the war began. Alexandre gave his life for freedom—she accepted that long ago. He knew he risked death, like Charles Tenney and so many others.

But why didn't an all-powerful Being intervene for all these innocent lives? For those children murdered with Sancha, and the helpless elderly, like Madame Ibarra?

Something stirred in the bushes across the road and alerted Père. Then, like a lamb's mewling, a far-off noise drifted from somewhere.

Ramrod straight, he strained until the noisy lorry appeared over the last bump, a veritable khaki warrior. Its dented front fender trembled when the driver braked. He leaped out and broke into the Langue d' Oc. Kate caught only some village names, the SS, Gestapo, and *gendarmes*.

He apologized for keeping them waiting. Then, palms uplifted, he croaked, "Where can we go now?"

Père looked years older today than yesterday. "Henri, you know these parts. Where would a transmitter be safe? The communication with London must continue tonight."

Henri, a long-nosed fellow with scabby ears from sun and wind, cranked his enormous hands to his hips. His elbows stuck out like bony chicken wings—yes, like those raw bones Kate and Addie once split while butchering a dozen roasting hens.

When Henri silently rubbed his forehead, Père's face distorted in thought, and Kate's heart fell. Surely, there must be a place—there simply had to be.

TWELVE

A peculiar acrid odor woke Domingo. He stuck his head out the back of the lorry to get his bearings. They'd veered off the mountain road onto a gravelly *route blanche*, but murky haze obscured his view.

Then a slim moon slid from under a cloud and revealed a familiar outline. Ah, they traveled close to Saint-Céré, parallel to the river. He grasped the vertical edge of the lorry and sniffed. The heavy odor of smoke—much too powerful.

A heavy sensation under his breastbone foretold trouble. *You have a strong spirit, but you will rule that spirit, my son.* Intensity laced Aitaita's words on that long-ago day of their hunting excursion.

"What does it mean to rule my spirit?"

"Life itself will teach you at every crossroads."

Now, that prophecy mocked Domingo. Surely he reigned as lord over nothing. Even the snores of the weary partisans around him seemed to scoff at him.

Five minutes later, the lorry pulled to a stop. The driver scuttled toward the back, but not before Domingo hurled himself out.

"Your ride ends here, gentlemen. *Bonne chance.*"

As if to ridicule the meaning of *good luck to you,* a dark figure sashayed out of nowhere, gun in hand. "You must be the demolition team?"

The fellow inched closer. "Good work. But around Figeac, Frontenac and Terrou, the Second SS and the 189th Division have gone mad. *Completement fou,* I tell you."

Domingo's heartbeat scathed his ears. *Completely crazy...* Terrou, Père Gaspard's village, and Figeac—he must get to *Maman* and

Gabirel. Panic washed his throat, and he longed to rip more information from the messenger's throat.

"Everyone who can has fled to the mountains." The messenger wiped his brow. "And now the tanks have begun hitting the countryside. Be sure to break up when you travel—you'll be too obvious."

Another concern rose like fire in Domingo. Had they pinpointed Katarin's latest transmitting station? What if they had taken her prisoner? The thought stole his breath away.

"The Allied landing has begun. Tens of thousands swarm the Normandy beaches, and our people are determined to dismantle every railroad in the whole of Lot by tonight." The messenger's tone strengthened.

"General de Gaulle says our nation lost her heart when she surrendered to the Reich. Well, we may have faltered when the SS marched into Paris, but now we will prove that France retains her soul. Come with me, if you will."

Unable to stand still another second, Domingo tore off southeast like a wildcat. Trees and vines swallowed him, but he pushed on toward his valley.

~

"Come on, Sister." Père bent for the transmitter. "We must be on our way." They scrambled inside the lorry, where he turned quiet.

Henri jammed down on the accelerator, backed halfway down the hill and waited for Père. But advice took a long time coming. "Straight. Go straight until we figure this out."

A sharp corner took Kate by surprise, throwing her into Père's shoulder, but he paid no attention. Before them, a dirt road spread, seemingly endless. The driver downshifted with a loud *grind*.

"We ought to head for the Ségala, but I hope you understand I cannot leave my parishioners. I must discover what has happened to my family, too. Do you understand?"

Kate nodded. Half a minute later, Henri asked, "Can she transmit from a burned-out village?"

Père hunched his shoulders. "If we only knew which one to choose. How many times can the SS destroy the same place?"

Henri spat out the window. "Once they've looted and killed as many as possible, why should they return?"

"*Oui* ... that gives me an idea in keeping with our sister's disguise."

Did he mean the time had come to enter the cloistered life? Despite such grim circumstances, a slight grin edged Père's lips.

"To the dismay of my spiritual superiors during my training my dramatic talents have always lent toward creating diversions. And at present, they might come in handy."

He drummed his fingers on the dashboard, and Kate held her hand to her stomach. Too much strong coffee, no food, and wild, bumpy curves.

"First, we'll see how Figeac fares."

"From what I hear, the hospital and doctors at Cahors and Saint-Céré provide medical aid, so you can go directly to them."

"Yes, indeed." Père folded his hands and lapsed into his own world.

Kilometer by kilometer, they covered about a third of the way from Halberton, Iowa to Cedar Rapids, where the Collins Radio Company manufactured transmitters for the military. Strange how she still judged distances by comparison to points back home. Perhaps Collins even supplied radios for the SOE. Kate reminded herself to turn hers upside down sometime to check.

Père's eyes shifted under his veined lids. How did one pray at a time like this? Kate could only plead—*send help for Père's family and his parishioners. Give the Allies success. Deliver Madame Ibarra and Gabirel, and keep Domingo safe. Do not tarry, oh God.*

From all outward signs, Père might be asleep. His pasty color added to his vulnerable look, but thoughts, ideas, and prayers somehow meshed when he shut out the world. Kate knew this because when he roused, fresh insights poured forth.

Her mind clung to that old word, *tarry*, implying purposefulness, or the choice to be late. And she mustn't be late tonight—the messages Père brought this morning contained German troop movements and logistics for several parachute drops. Her fingers itched for the keys.

Henri struck a pothole and set the brake so suddenly, Kate's head hit the roof. Before she realized anyone stood outside the lorry, Père Gaspard launched into a conversation with a scruffy man, three-fourths of it lost to her in the local brogue. The wayfarer's face crumpled when the priest added something about Terrou, waving his hand like a traffic flag the whole time, with Gallic expressiveness.

Craning his neck to see past her, Henri gaped at Père, whose fingers quivered against the door handle. Finally, Père responded, his voice terse and hoarse. "Keep moving. That's all we can do."

Fear billowed in the small cab like the dense, milky aroma of a steaming pot of porridge. Kate pondered whether the millions of requests going up to heaven right now overwhelmed the Almighty. Why did He seem so slow to respond? Why did He allow people to suffer so?

At every turn where freshly leafed out foliage allowed a view, smoldering fires marked the horizon. Many local people aided the *Maquis*, but some did nothing to harass the Germans. Why should reprisals fall on them as well as the guilty?

The answer rose like Kate's sigh—of course, Das Reich had no list of names to consult before they mortared an area. Aunt Alvina's pastor back in Iowa suffered, too, because of his German heritage. People like Harold judged him a spy without even meeting him or considering his kind heart.

Sunshine for good and evil, reprisals for both innocent and guilty. Had the Gestapo come down on the churches and organizations sheltering Jewish children in Le Chambon sur Lignon by now? Was little Linden, the fragile Jewish waif who delighted to ride Kate's shoulders, still safe? Had her brother ever returned, or would she never see even one of her family again?

In retrospect, that precious child had eased some of Kate's pain at losing her baby. Right now, she could almost feel the orphan's warmth.

"Divine provision," Père would say, "just like your rendezvous with Monsieur le Blanc." But at this moment, he withdrew.

Navigating a severe slope, Henri's elbow narrowly missed Kate's jaw. A man of fifty, perhaps, with an arched nose, deep forehead, long neck, hairy nostrils and ears, Henri's beret swayed mere inches above his nose.

Sweet-sour wine scented his breath, something Kate became used to in Clermont-Ferrand, when she often visited the square where lots of people drank wine. She leaned her head against a metal pipe extending horizontally above the tattered leather seat and let her thoughts rove.

Did Addie still enjoy her work for Mr. Tenney? Had she overcome her fear that Harold might discover her whereabouts and shadow her to London? If Kate could transport herself anywhere in this chaotic world, it would be to Mrs. Tenney's for just one evening with Addie.

The next moment, Kate almost landed in Père's lap. His eyes shuttered open and he patted her shoulder as she rearranged herself. The driver blurted something and Père issued a comment.

"*Ca va.*" He referred to Henri's wild driving, and he would say the same about everything else, too. It would all work out.

The sun warmed the cab, and understanding stole in—God joined with them right here in this smelly old lorry. Even when her world turned topsy-turvy, Kate had always hoped for this to be true. But something about this situation tipped the scales toward belief. Truth settled down in her soul.

As if to juxtapose with her insight, smoke funneled behind a church spire. What did it mean? Perhaps the Gestapo had already entered the village set a fire—but how could He be present in such an act of destruction?

THIRTEEN

"Truffles. Je cherche les truffles." The startled peasant dropped his basket, of rich, soil-crusted mushrooms. Under his wool beret, his chin revealed a quiver. Even the crushed brown velvet of his trousers trembled.

This simple man with his pig, snout to the earth, was simply minding his business. But Domingo, keeping a straight line toward home, had collided with him headlong.

"*Pardonez moi*, I was in such a hurry ..."

The peasant's dark eyes traveled skyward what is he looking at in the sky. Then his slight shoulders relaxed. He retrieved his basket and re-settled his hat.

"Has Das Reich come to your land?"

"Das Reich?"

"The SS—tanks. Have you seen them?"

"No, but I heard them rumble two valleys away." The man launched a forefinger southeast. "The earth shook as it did in my youth, when the mine at Courrières blew up in the Pas-de-Calais. I felt the earth move."

So many kilometers away? Surely, he imagined that.

But the peasant continued. "Gasses in the mine caught the work-ers' lamp flames. My brother Louis survived by eating the victims' lunches, and someone slaughtered one of the horses. They held on for twenty days. When Louis walked down our path alive, *Maman* shrieked with relief ..."

He wiped a stray tear from his cheek. "Yesterday the earth shook again. Even Jean-Paul felt it." The peasant gestured toward his pig.

"This morning, I met some people from Terrou on their way to higher ground."

"And?"

The man flopped his arms at his sides. "Most of the men had already fled, except old useless dogs like me. Women and children ran up there."

He jutted his chin toward a high point. "The feeble ones, they stuffed into carts, like loads of potatoes and onions."

Domingo shuddered. *Maman* would never survive such treatment.

"But you stayed to gather truffles?"

"What better occupation?" The peasant's cracked lips spread over irregular brown stained teeth. "My wife prepares a *fête du cochon*."

Then his mind slipped into the past. "After the rumbling, I hurried north to search for Louis. *Maman* cooked a feast when we returned home. Only a few survived—over a thousand died. *Maman* declared that Louis had been visited by grace."

Friends gathered for pork and mushrooms in a humble home—a pleasant memory, but so incongruous with present reality. Had this peasant taken leave of his senses?

"If soldiers come, we have little to offer, only truffles. They may eat our *cochon* and our truffles, but will leave us alone."

Domingo shook out his legs, for pausing had become harder than running. "You have seen no soldiers yet?"

As if responding to a different inquiry, the old man replied, "I am Martirena Sheriden by name. My grandsons follow the wind, as I once did, to Spain. Now, I cannot leave my wife alone."

One tooth caught on his lower lip. "The soldiers stay far from Sheriden land—perhaps they fear me." His wild grin startled Domingo. "Your father fought in Spain, too, I venture, but we have become useless."

Papa's countenance rose before Domingo's mind. If he lived today, would he be leading a *Maquisard* band?

The peasant's mind seemed to clear as Domingo swigged some water. "The enemy raided Terrou twice before, but this time, they burned the whole village. They have issued a new order now, for those who do not cooperate."

He spat into the grass. "Why waste their time on us? We know nothing. We only pray for *l'Invasion* to come soon."

"It has, my friend, this very day."

"Indeed?"

"*Oui.* Protect your wife, and blessed be your hunting."

Domingo took off again, his thoughts racing faster than his feet. The old fellow had a point. Why not hunt truffles? Do what your hands find to do.

Once again, dark eyes swam before his vision. *Maman's*, Gabirel's, and now, an Amerikan girl's—so many pairs of dark eyes.

Then Père Gaspard's blue gaze danced with the brown. With this fresh havoc raining down, how would he ever find a safe place for Katarin? Domingo had no idea, but Père's word provided assurance.

The swish of grass between Domingo's legs whirred like the rustle the threshers made when they sifted chaff from grain on great canvasses held high. The process had mesmerized him as a child, longing for the day he would be old enough, strong enough, to help.

But there would be no harvest this year. June had come, but field after field lay empty. Would a normal harvest ever return? Would the seasons one day pass without bringing more tragedy? Domingo wavered on a ridge, but the weight in his chest allowed him only a second of contemplation before he plunged forward again, splitting through the underbrush and winding around hedgerows designed to stop powerful beasts.

Closer to his valley, dread pressed in on him. It still seemed unlikely that that old fellow searching for mushrooms had felt the earth rumble so far away from where his brother worked. But his premonition had tuned his heart to the predicament Louis faced. Could this sense of foreboding that shadowed Domingo be the same type of intuition?

Twice, he stopped to listen for familiar sounds in this wood far too quiet for an early June day. No one called to teams forcing plows through stubborn soil, or whistled walking home from market. Such an odd, uneasy silence.

Martirena Sheriden, that *wayfarer* had called himself ... Surely, Aitaita would know him. But so many new names swam through

Domingo's consciousness, so many faces, pilots, agents, and an ever-growing parade of partisans.

Their fates, especially *Giriotte's*, haunted him. He conjured up all sorts of scenarios—*Giriotte*, broken and bloody, rolling into the brush, where a sympathetic railroad man found him, carried him home and nursed him. Or he stumbled on an injured worker and refused to leave him behind.

Was he to know *Giriotte* no more, like Philippe, with whom he avenged Sancha's death? Would he never again see Petra, who had trekked so far over the Pyrenees with him, with an extra pair of espadrilles—*alpargatas*, he called them—slung around his neck?

Could individuals be replaced like a worn-out pair of *alpargatas*? It seemed for every new partisan he met, he left two others behind.

Wild geese fledglings taking their first flights ought to surround him right now, but even winged creatures forsook the stale, low-hanging smoke clouds. Domingo passed a farmyard where not even a sleepy, long-tongued dog lazed in the sun.

Since when had his pack hung so heavy? The cords of his neck hurt. His arms ached. With dust in his mouth and his teeth on edge, he reached the final descent to Ibarra land. There, below the stone fence's outline, Aitaita's aged weathervane caught a glint of sun from the milk house slates.

But the sheep pen lay empty. Domingo coursed the ditch, then the road ... Faster, up and over the ancient stones and down into the lane.

Filmy grey shrouded the farmyard. His heart faltered at the eerie sight.

Unnatural, unpalatable, this lack of sound. He longed for Giriotte's noisy camaraderie, for Père Gaspard's hand on his shoulder. And yes, for the sight of Katarin wearing his smelly old chore clothes and attempting to reason with unreasonable sheep.

He tried the barn first, whistling the secret tune Gabirel would respond to in an instant. A shiny kitten meowed and took a step toward him. He shinnied up the ladder and unlatched the granary door. Surely they hid here, where a few days ago, Katarin had sneezed when he first carried up her transmitter and arranged the wire antennae over the rafters.

But only the usual oat groats and dented, yellow corn waited inside.

Down the rungs and around the pigpen, he discovered no sign of life. What did pigs matter, anyway? He and Gabirel and *Maman* would find food to eat next winter somehow. But a deep swell of pure terror threatened to erupt inside him.

Là-bas—another idea occurred. *Over there*, possibly, in the underground storage compartment ... he would find them hunched together in that earthen space. The short door squawked open, but no eyes shone out from the darkness, only the dank, heavy odor of wintered potatoes, turnips, carrots, and damp soil. Domingo's breathing, loud in his ears, taunted him.

Outside the house, his lungs burned. *Maman, Gabirel ... where have you gone?* The others, Papa, Aitaita, and Ander, had left for that other world, but *Maman* always remained, like the lintel, the hearth, and these solid stones. She simply had to be here somewhere.

A pot lay tipped onto the table, but *Maman's* scent—the unique mixture of yeast, raw buttermilk, lye soap, and a thin thread of lavender, lingered. Domingo held out his hand in this room where she spent most of her days.

His glance fell on the heavy old sideboard, painted white but chipped here and there. *Maman* had shrunk even more since he'd left last winter, so now she could barely reach its top shelf. He yanked the massive protrusion out from the wall. No one knew about the receded stairway except their family, not even their closest neighbor.

Faint hope wavered within Domingo. The tall old chest fought him every inch of the way, and dust swirls rose like ashes in a wind. A dried-up mouse lay behind it, a furry skeleton amid windswept papers and fallen coins. Domingo pulled the door clasp and climbed the shortened stairs to the triangular space that had fascinated him as a child, when they stored fruit and hams here.

Angular light rays from the opening behind him accentuated the stillness. Thick, merciless stillness. It was empty. Dust flecks sparkled in the dull air.

Maman. The word became a pant. *The old ones in carts like bags of potatoes or onions ...*

The oxcart. Had he seen it outside? Yes, the reliable contrivance sat in its usual place. Domingo stared as if its ancient wood could whisper a secret.

The garden dugout—maybe Gabirel took *Maman* there. The refuge lay close by, filled with rakes, hoes, pincers and tongs, a small spade. But only a rat family nested in a far corner, their beady eyes glinting.

The other small shed, under the ash tree, where they cooled the butter and milk in summer? The dark space, built a few steps into the hill, exuded the heavy intoxication of cream waiting to be churned, day-old milk, and a granite pan of lush butter. The ladle sprawled like a body on the shelf.

Domingo lifted the pan's coarse towel covering, stuck his finger in and peeled off a mass of golden foam. But the spread, so sweet and hearty on *Maman's* fresh-baked bread, left a solitary, slippery taste in his mouth. He shut the door and dropped his face into his hands.

"*Maman*, where are you? *Mon Dieu*, help me now, if ever." His voice resonated like a stranger's.

One place remained, the miniature fortress far back in the woods, across the creek, where he and Ander played as boys. Their closest neighbor had guided Katarin there with the sheep during an alert while she stayed here with *Maman*.

But first, the house beckoned to him again. Seeing an apple in a basket on the table, his stomach raged, and Domingo realized he last ate this morning. He gouged the peel with his teeth, aware of its tough, saggy texture after a winter in storage.

His eyes lit on the shelf and his throat filled. He stuck his fingers into *Maman's* crockery, pulled out mere dust, and tore out toward the back pasture consumed by an even greater hunger.

The way wound in and out of pastures, and he stopped once to test the sheep droppings—yesterday's. So, this pasture emptied then. How much warning had Gabirel been given? He visualized his brother guiding *Maman*, urging her to come quickly. He studied the ground for clues.

Domingo stepped down the bank to the creek, skipping through the meter-wide water to the slippery bank on the other side. Gabirel would have to carry her here. The image roiled in his mind like the burning of Terrou—impossible. How could *Maman* in her brown woolen skirt and shawl, her fringed scarf tied under her chin, allow her youngest son to port her like a baby?

Grass waved above Domingo's ankles and pawed his calf muscles—far past time to turn the sheep in here. *Far past time* ... the words beat a rhythm with his heartbeat near a cave-like indentation beyond a rock wall. Another creek flowed here, dividing Ibarra land from Edorta's.

Grass gave way to bare soil, a few weedy patches and tufts of bitter vegetation even the sheep refused. Then the land sloped toward the rocks. If the space lay empty ... A battle wrangled in Domingo's chest, but he directed his feet forward.

The rough rock wall scraped his hand as he leaned into its dampness. A few steps beyond, he paused to acclimate his eyes.

"*Maman* ... Gabirel?"

His echo mocked him. His inward parts felt like stone. His fingers traced what he knew, but could not see. Lichen, thick and soft on the boulder's underbelly. Aitaita said in the old days, long before kings divided these Basque lands into Spain and France, worse came to worse in the fight for freedom, and the men boiled this growth for soup, or ate it raw.

Its earthy scent soothed Domingo like a sign from heaven. Even here, away from the light of day, life persisted. But where had his people gone?

He shook his head to clear his mind. So many daily joys and sorrows could not dissipate into thin air. Then he realized the worst horror of all, beyond the SS troops or Gestapo, torture, and even deportation or death.

To lose his family—to have *Maman* and Gabirel gone forever ... With no family on this earth, Katarin bore this depth of pain already. She had lost everyone.

Domingo staggered outside. No gentle murmur of sheep gnawing grass. Nothing to do but walk on past the creek, up the next rise onto Edorta's land.

Time held itself distant, creating the sensation of being suspended in air. Somehow, this rich valley had suddenly gone vapid. He checked the barn, called names, while squelching a rising tide of panic that threatened to engulf him.

All is never lost—keep your senses. Aitaita taught him so, and Père Gaspard.

The wide front door of Edorta's cottage hung haphazardly on wrenched hinges. Violence had occurred here, for Edorta, above all men in the valley, cared for his buildings and his animals. The buildings still stood, but where were his sheep?

The overturned cupboard spilled flour and salt, skillets and pots, towels and matches. A single, stained apron littered the floor. Domingo's stomach retaliated at the oval shape of the stains, dark red-black, and he fled behind the house. There, a shovel sprawled against the well. Fragile early vegetable plantings had been trampled into a wet green mass.

Onions—such a mix of bitter and sweet ... Boot prints marked the bare pigpen and the barn floor, and Edorta's milk cow and pig had vanished.

Domingo's voice sounded hollow in his own ears. "Have you taken everything?"

His screech echoed back on the breeze. He re-entered the house, scrunching pottery shards under his feet. A single quarter of cheese hid under an overturned pot and a heel of dry bread lurked in the corner. Spying them, Domingo heard his stomach complain.

At the same time, the passion sprouting within him would not be tamed. His stomach, he could feed, but only a cleansing from outside, an *epuration sauvage*, a wild purification, would suffice for the agony in his throat.

He ran the full way home and grabbed whatever food he could scrounge. Stopped at the threshold. Touched his heart and placed his hand over the family insignia.

In doing so, another puce-colored stain caught his eye. He scraped it with his fingernail, held the copper scent to his nostrils.

Oh God of my fathers, God of my dear Maman.

His finger traced the cross Aitaita's father engraved to mark their family, to protect them. Domingo searched the distance in vain—if only Père Gaspard would saunter down the road, with his unflappable trust that all would be well.

A sudden recollection from last July inundated Domingo, when

Père hurried down this road with news from Rome. His Vatican contacts sent dire word—Pope Pius prayed near bodies blown from crypts in the Church of San Lorenzo.

His parents and brother were buried there, and he had his driver take him there, to commiserate with the grieving. Fifteen hundred citizens had died in the allied raid intended to stall Nazi operations in Rome.

"Thousands more are wounded, Domingo." Père's somber tone communicated the incident's gravity. "If Rome suffers so, who can be safe? We must adopt constant watchfulness."

His prophecy rode at the base of Domingo's throat when Nazi paratroopers stormed into Rome on September eighth, surrounded the Vatican, and drew a white line on the ground. Swiss guards on one side and Nazis on the other. The Vatican itself had been placed under siege—when had evil ever been so rash? The faithful must rise to the cause.

Recalling these ominous events sent sudden fresh energy through Domingo. He had risen to the cause, blowing bridges and wiring trucks to detonate on major roads, taking his turn at cranking the generator handle for American agents up in the camp to transmit their Morse code, setting explosives between railroad ties to burst when German supply trains crushed them with their front wheels, ambushing a German truck loaded with ten tons of cheese.

All this he had accomplished, and more. But with the Allied advance across the Channel, London now required further action of the Resistance. the order had come down to engage the enemy face-to-face, in hand-to-hand fighting if need be.

Fiery purpose coursed Domingo's spine. Indeed, he would live up to his name, *la foudre*, fueled by this searing pain of loss, and by furious love of country, of home, of all that was holy. On his honor, he would fight to the death.

Domingo turned a wide circle around the farmstead. So many suffering, so many already lost ... the fields themselves barren and ghostly. The question that had taunted him rose again—was the fight worth all this? And then Katarin's face rose before his eyes. She, too, had devoted her all to this cause.

With one last wistful look at the place of his birth, he loped toward the steepest incline he could find.

FOURTEEN

"I'll inquire here." Père left Kate standing outside the St-Cere Abbey, with her head still reeling from the effects of the lorry ride. Even if only for a short time, having solid earth under her feet felt wonderful.

Under a lingering fog, the murky Dordogne flowed by, and all around the Abbey's three-story stone buildings the town nestled, with the Abbey as its pole star. A solitary clip-clop sounded through the ghostly haze, but otherwise, this strangely quiet June day seemed surreal.

Finally, Père exited the Abbey and rounded the truck to speak with Henri. Then he beckoned to Kate to climb in. Henri goosed the engine and they headed east instead of north, until another wide river came into sight. Her qualms increased. Why would they cross the Lot River now?

"Trust." Her answer sounded internally, as real as if Père had spoken the word.

After some distance, the old vehicle lurched across a bridge onto a cobblestone street and turned into a massive church complex. High towers and buttressed stonewalls surrounded cloistered walkways worthy of inspiring *A Mighty Fortress is our God.*

For the entire drive, Père's closed eyes had warded off her questions. Kate relegated them to a crowded mental shelf established long ago, when her mother failed to return after their last good-bye and the image of her father's face faded from memory.

After a shuddering stop, she followed Père under a carved arch, tamping down her curiosity again, and focusing instead on the tune of Aunt Alvira's favorite hymn. *A mighty fortress is our God. A bulwark never failing. Our Helper, He, amid the flood of mortal ills prevailing.*

Such a strange mix, she and Père Gaspard, Catholic and Lutheran--but these days, those distinctions became irrelevant. When Martin Luther penned those words over four hundred years ago, he fought against heresies—today, everyone united to subdue evil incarnate.

A massive wooden door swung open, and with the firm swish of heavy starched linen, a strong-boned woman peered out. Her eyes glinted hazel and gold.

"Mother Hélène." Père extended his hand. "How does today find you?"

Tall and statuesque, the matron angled her head. "We have lost no one from this life. But then, I've sent nearly everyone away."

"I've brought an agent who must make radio transmissions tonight. The SS has rendered the St-Cere Abbey far too vulnerable."

Deep lines crossed the aged nun's sturdy forehead and bloody stains marked her white habit's sleeves and skirt, but Mother Hélène stood aside to wave them in. Afternoon sun blazed through high stained-glass windows. Mother Hélène craned her neck toward one of three spires towering above, and her sigh drifted like the light rays.

"Who would have thought we would become such a haven for the clandestine?" Behind her, a series of walls jutted into each other like a child's make-believe block village. Despite the airy sunshine outside, a closed-in sense pervaded the halls, cool and damp.

"We had a little warning before the tanks came, so I sent most of the children and several sisters to fortifications beyond Decazeville. Our faithful informants report they found safety."

For a moment, her gaze held Kate's. "Welcome. You may call me Mother Hélène."

She held up her palm. "With so many victims brought in, blood is everywhere, or I would offer you my hand. Days like this should occur only once in a lifetime, but I must admit, they do show us how much we can accomplish."

"We know what you mean." Père scrambled out the door and returned with Kate's bag and Henri toting the transmitter.

Heavy iron keys clattered, and Mother Hélène inserted one into a lock. She folded a long forefinger indicating they should follow, and opened a second set of doors.

Père motioned for Henri to go ahead, and Kate brought up the rear. Their guide's voice echoed over the solid granite staircase. "The wounded rest in the main hall. Some need you, Père."

Under a long set of arched columns, she delivered a report of S.S. movements. "Ladirot, Gorses, Saint-Medard-Nicourby, Labathude, Mollieres, Saint Maurice-en-Query ... some lie in utter ruins ..."

The list went on, with the degree of damage to each village. The names ran together in Kate's mind as they passed along a foyer-like space with high windows. Mother Hélène turned through a narrow hallway into a dormitory bedroom.

Père Gaspard held out his arms to Henri for the radio box, his skin ashen. "Merci, Henri. I know you have other loads to deliver."

Mother Hélène pointed past Henri's nose. "This way, Monsieur. These stairs take you directly to the courtyard. God go with you."

He disappeared as she headed toward a vast oak wardrobe opposite a series of narrow iron beds. The wardrobe's clasp gave way to a hidden doorway, and with a bit of finagling, Mother Hélène pushed her ample frame through the cramped space.

Père Gaspard's breath came hard, and Kate had the feeling someone chased them.

In the next room, Mother Hélène tugged on a pull rope that released a set of wooden ceiling stairs. They climbed to a spacious hallway with doors on either side. At the third door down, their leader vanished into a walk-in closet and pushed aside some robes.

Like a sheep, Kate followed Père up five steps, careful of his swaying robe. Mother Hélène allowed them to pass, and gestured toward a long wide library table with a chair underneath.

"Will this do?" The room's only window looked out on a vine-covered brick wall. Unvarnished floorboards made Kate feel at home.

Père lowered the radio and stared out at sky and rooftops. "I wonder how many have found refuge here throughout the ages?"

"Hundreds. We've kept the children safe for more than two years, but in recent weeks, I thought mountain hide-outs even more desirable."

"No one can detect light from outside?"

"Only from above, and to do that, they must rappel down a high wall. But just in case, we'll cover the window. Can you believe we're discussing such things? But we're in good company—I hear the brothers at Assisi take even greater risks."

Père gave no response, but touched Kate's elbow. "This will suit your purposes?"

"It's perfect. We'll figure out a way to string the antenna."

"Good."

He turned to go, but Mother Hélène faced Kate. "You transmit mostly at night?"

"Yes, after the BBC broadcast."

"Downstairs, we have a smaller set, but when you finish listening, you must turn the dial from that frequency. People have been punished for tuning their radios to the BBC."

Back through the maze of doorways, rooms, and hallways, Kate memorized the route. Near the row of beds, Mother Hélène announced, "You'll sleep here."

Then she listed more atrocities. Père's replies revealed how closely he knew the population. And the enemy—nothing seemed to surprise him.

"You think the beasts have headed on to Normandy now?"

"If they've caught a whiff of *L'Invasion,* surely. But the commander seems not to mind lingering here in Lot, for our *maquisards* have thwarted him at every turn. He lumps us all together as one disobedient child, and shot some partisans and innocent citizens outright.

"No one has explored farther than the closest village. On the outlying farms, injured people may still wait for aid." Mother Hélène's wide gesture spread the deep arm of her robe. "You will visit our wounded now?"

"Um. Then, I must go to Terrou. On the way, I'll visit every homestead possible."

"Through that door. I'll be in soon." Mother Hélène turned to address Kate. "Please follow me."

A wide parlor opened before them, centered by a wooden table, a settee and an armchair. Mother Hélène reached into the table's single drawer for a miniature radio.

"I've never seen one that small."

"Once, another agent brought a large transmitter like yours. But she said this crystal one made listening easier, though it doesn't transmit.

"When she left in such a flurry, we acquired our own 'ears.' You'll spend enough hours up in that stuffy room. You may as well listen here, but first, come along."

She brushed under an archway to the kitchen, with a square black and white tile floor. Who would guess men bled in the sanctuary nearby? "Help yourself to whatever you need." Mother Hélène left, and Kate leaned her head against a cool cupboard door.

Things had greatly worsened for the people of Lot. Last night when she dared a peek at the sky, flashes from north to south marked hundreds of parachute drops, but otherwise the countryside was dark—these peasants had learned not to build bonfires when they awaited a drop. The sheer number of drops would have been a clear sign of *l'Invasion*, had Kate not already deciphered London's message.

The ordered progression of succinct checkered tiles quieted her restless thoughts. She carried a glass of water to the foyer and tuned the tiny radio, hunting for the BBC. A voice from London cackled random information, and somewhere in that mumbo-jumbo might be a message for her circuit.

The courier who helped her decode yesterday said someone would come tonight for further messages, but how would they know her whereabouts? The answer had to be Père, who functioned like an electric company's central control.

In any case, worrying wouldn't help—she must focus on transcribing everything correctly, as yesterday's courier emphasized. "We mustn't lose even one drop. If S.S. troops bivouac anywhere near the flash of our welcome committee's lights, they'll kill the committee and use the ammunition against us."

With so much static, Kate could barely make out the first four notes of Beethoven's Fifth Symphony introducing *les messages personnels*. The opening notes corresponded to Morse Code for V ... for victory.

"Give me clear reception." If angels could bring bread and water to Elijah in the desert, surely they could tangle the enemy jamming devices creating this static.

The room's wall hangings intrigued Kate as she listened. Plaques, painted flowers, and hand-stitched Bible verses hung interspersed on the walls. Over the decades, many sisters must have gathered here in the evenings.

Now, these cloistered women chaperoned little Jewish children over the hills of this hostile world, a daunting task in pants, much less robes.

"The cellar door is open," drifted over the airwaves—the clear cue for her new circuit's message. A few minutes passed. "The sun shines on the Acropolis today." And a little later, "The woman clenches a broken spigot."

Sure enough, the two remaining messages followed. A thrill ran through Kate from head to toe—Operation Overload had indeed begun.

At about the same time, Mother Hélène answered a knock and called, "Someone seeks you, my dear."

The same man who helped her yesterday stood there. But Père hadn't even left yet—how had this partisan found her? His greeting gave Kate no clue.

"Enough planes have passed overhead, this must indeed be *Jour-J?*"

"The BBC just verified the message. I haven't written it down, but you won't forget, will you?"

"Hardly." His deep-set eyes gleamed as he handed her a packet tied in white string.

"Urgent messages for London. I'll return later tonight." Before she could ask him anything, he fled.

Kate turned right into Mother Hélène, who grabbed her shoulders. "*Jour-J* has arrived, no?"

"*Absolutement.* I must send these messages."

"The number of detection vans has increased. Keep your transmissions to nine minutes each."

By the time Kate reached her Type 3 MKII transmitter, marked C on the side, G on the top, she was panting. "All right, MK two, there's hard work ahead." Her fingers jitterbugged from latches to dials and her mind raced with the news—British and American soldiers had indeed landed on French soil this morning.

Hours later, Père Gaspard rounded the corner and set down a cup of chicory. One look told Kate that fear no longer clung to him. He whispered, "I must go again but will return for you."

"How did you find your fam..."

He put a smudged forefinger to his lips, raising the scents of the forest, cheese, and ink. "Now to your work."

Later, someone brought a plate of steaming vegetables. As Kate gobbled the food, planes whizzed above amid distant explosions, like symphonic tympani drums. For an instant, it seemed Alexandre hovered near.

Once, during a short walk to the window to lift the heavy quilt nailed there, she spoke to him. Outside, starlight caught on the Abbey's metal-capped corners and chimneys.

"Alexandre, you'd be out there tonight dropping bombs on hydro-electric plants, factories, and train tunnels if you could. But maybe one of my messages will save a pilot's life."

Addie's face went through her mind. "Oh Addie, I'd give anything to have you here with me."

Perhaps Harold already wrangled with the enemy on Normandy's northern beaches—hopefully, Addie knew that and no longer concerned herself with him showing up in London.

Several reports came through of Rommel with the seventh German army on the coast. Such a war-hardened commander's presence created an ominous picture of lovely French countryside ravished by bombs and tanks--but in the end, the Allies had defeated his troops in North Africa.

Returning to her radio, Kate set her mind to complete her work in this sitting. No use contemplating what was happening hours north of here, except to plead for mercy for the invasion. But since this war had to be, she wouldn't mind if every Allied soldier brandished Harold's pent-up rage.

FIFTEEN

Sunlight glinted through thick sycamore and chestnut foliage, as Domingo listened to a leader at the camp. The slight commander addressed an unkempt crowd perched on tree stumps and logs. *Maman* would call them ruffians, but now, her very life depended on them.

"Headquarters has sent us new codes—*vert* for railroad sabotage, *bleu* for electrical facilities, *marron* for engaging enemy forces to reduce their power at Normandy, and *violet* for cutting underground cables.

"Some of you may have already taken part in raids, but now, we fall under the Allied Forces direct command. The BBC confirms *L'Invasion*, and today our northern contingent makes over 500 railroad cuts, severing all telephone communications in Normandy. Gas and oil will be unavailable to the Huns—we'll delay or stop their advance however we can."

Nearby, workers stirred three huge pots hung over open fires. Ragged clothes waved haphazardly on a line stretched between saplings. Brush piles and hand-dug trenches ranged over the hill.

"We continue to receive Operation Jedburgh supply drops in the German rear areas. The Special Air Service brigade operates behind the lines too, so we've tacked posters of their uniforms around camp. Be aware of their locations to avoid confusion. If anyone here has questions, see me afterwards."

Groups of three or four gathered toward the front. Domingo's doubts might have propelled him forward, but a loyalty deeper than patriotism harangued him. How could he leave without knowing Gabirel and *Maman's* fate?

All things are possible. Père Gaspard proclaimed that even mustard seed-sized faith could accomplish amazing feats. Still, Domingo felt certain *Maman* could never survive such a journey.

He'd searched at every farmstead along the way. Older peasants unable to fight shook their heads when they heard about *Maman.* "Such terrible times—if we see her, we will take her in."

In half-deserted Figeac, Domingo checked the school, the grand hall, the church and city hall. What could he do now but join the fight? He lifted his face to the sun. "Show me."

The simple utterance shifted his burden. Then he waited, a beggar desperate for bread. At some point, a shadow fell over him, and he opened his eyes to a familiar face.

"Domingo." Wide coals for eyes, tipped black beret, dirty canvas pack slouched over one shoulder, and worn espadrilles defined Petra.

Petra. Over a year ago en route to the Spanish border, Petra's presence had been like an older brother's. His powerful handshake jolted Domingo.

"What have you been doing, playing *pelota?*" Petra's quick smile showed a broken bottom tooth. He leaned against a tree and waited.

"When you left with your load, I headed east with that agent who climbed up to the landing field, and we watched the Albi railroad burn."

"Ah, yes, now I remember. A woman. How did the trip go?"

"Word came that someone betrayed her Clermont-Ferrand circuit, and an organizer said the Dordogne workers needed help. But on the way, we met a wounded agent." Domingo shook his head. "The agent nursed him, and strange as it sounds, before he died, he confessed he was her father's brother."

Petra scratched his head. "She seemed American to me."

"Yes, but her mother married a Frenchman."

"The agent met this man here?"

"*Non,* in London. He led her into secret work. Now she operates a radio, and my priest is helping her."

"Any more trips to the border?"

"Only one." Domingo winced at the memory. "If you had been there, we would have found more success."

"Tell me."

In spite of himself, Domingo opened his heart, the words flowing like a torrent. "A British agent and two American pilots ... one American insisted on talking, no matter how I warned him. Close to the border, he fell and broke his leg, and before I knew it, the Gestapo was upon us.

"We carried him, but they gained speed—we could see their lights closer and closer. Then a stench rose, and we stumbled on a deer carcass. The American had the idea of hiding his comrade under it."

"So you did?" Petra tilted his head.

"Yes, and I promised to return for the wounded man on my way home. But..."

"He was dead?"

"Gone. Dragged away. Not a day goes by that I fail to see his eyes peering out from under that mangy pelt."

"What else could you have done?" Petra rubbed his forehead.

"You would have thought of some way to save him."

"My friend, you know nothing of my own failures." They sat in silence for a time, and then Petra inquired, "Your family?"

Domingo's throat tightened. "Gone—our home ransacked."

"The S.S.?"

He nodded, staring at the dirt at his feet.

"Ah."

"And you delivered those radios?"

"*Oui*, and plenty more. They call the *Ségala* the land of a hundred valleys. Well, I am the deliverer of a thousand canisters. My feet threaten to separate from my body." Petra stared beyond the fresh trench below them. "Das Reich razed our homestead, but my people escaped. I keep on, especially with the Allies here. This is our hope, *non*? You sense the certainty, don't you?"

A petulant crow jawed at a yammering squirrel in a nearby tree. The squirrel flitted down a branch and leaped to more hospitable territory. Domingo stretched his neck and shoulders, but Petra made no move to stand.

"Your young brother and your mother are missing?"

Domingo's voice caught in his throat. "No sign of them anywhere. Perhaps they were hauled to Montauban."

Petra's rough hand on Domingo's shoulder eased the catch in his breath.

Petra read his mind. "Perhaps the railroad suffered irreparable damage before they arrived in Montauban."

"But then *Maman* would be in a camp like Gur ..." The very thought soured Domingo's stomach.

Petra swung his beret between his fingers. "My Aitaita said this world's darkness sometimes defies the truth, but we continue to move forward—this is our faith."

"Faith can shrivel."

Petra emitted a groan-chuckle. "Or it seems so because the odds increase. Come with me to blow bridges or whatever they tell us to do. I entrust my life to you, and you to me. We will stay together, and who knows? Perhaps we will come upon your family."

~

Petra hunched along a mountain stream, gagging for breath. He collapsed on the earth and Domingo's heart raced. They'd covered so many rocky inclines already. Most men Petra's age would have succumbed to the heat and exhaustion long ago.

Domingo peered over Petra's shoulder, as if checking on a sleeping child.

Petra's eyelids fluttered. "What?"

"You're all right?"

"Umm."

Domingo filled his canteen and held it to Petra's lips.

"Give me a few minutes. Then we go again."

Step by step, Domingo walked out a cramp in his calf. Petra drank more, crawled to the stream and dunked his head. Then he turned back, shaking his torso like a dog.

"Might as well keep moving."

"When they called us *liaisons*, they might have said runners." Petra chuckled. "If only we could send our feet off on these assignments and meet up with them later."

He hoisted his pack and they prepared to move out. But suddenly all bird chatter ceased.

Snap, scuffle, tramp ... they both froze. Boots, not espadrilles. Four or five men, not just one or two. Petra bade Domingo follow him under a higher rock overhang and they strained to see.

The travelers arrived at the spot Petra and Domingo had just vacated, and a coarse voice echoed, *"Jemand var her."*

"Vielliecht ein reh."

A third guffawed, *"Vielliecht eine Frau fur uns."*

"Ruhig. Die lage ist ernst."

An animal, probably a deer, thrashed near the *Feldgraus*.

A soldier's comment floated loud and clear. *"Siehen sie? Es war ein Reh."*

"Yah, yah."

When their voices faded, Petra turned to Domingo. "Did you understand?"

"Something about a woman."

"They knew something was just here. One said maybe a deer, the other, maybe a woman for us. The leader warned them to be quiet. If not for that deer, they might have searched up here."

Petra's eyes glittered like gold nuggets. "We could sneak up and kill them. We have every advantage."

His finger caressed his revolver while he stooped to check the knife tied at his ankle. But he hadn't accompanied Domingo last summer on the search for Sancha. The Gestapo's carelessness with the bodies kindled such fury that Domingo and Philippe sought out the killers and slashed them to death.

An eye for an eye ... Did Philippe ever recall that night? Mindless slaughter, fierce, all-consuming rage...vengeance.

Domingo had no desire to kill in cold blood again. Burning the Gestapo's clothes and burying the corpses had brought no satisfaction. He saw Philippe, once again transferring Sancha into his arms. Now, he stared at his forearms, where her body lay during that impossible trek back to her valley. After he delivered her to her family, a great heaviness, emptier and stronger than any before or since, claimed him.

Then Père Gaspard came and wept with him. Without

condemnation, he somehow understood and embraced Domingo's fury. When he finally spoke words of eternal mercy, Domingo became a small boy again, guilty but accepted, full of shame, yet loved.

Now, he touched Sancha's orange scarf inside his jacket and waited for Petra to make a decision. Petra pursed his lips, closed his eyes... but in the end, they allowed the Germans to go their way.

They delivered their messages, and someone asked them to help partisans cut railroad ties and telephone lines in a town to the southwest. After a night of racing against time to complete the work, Domingo and Petra dropped onto beds of straw in someone's barn for a few hours and wakened to run again.

The days flowed together, with repeated news of *Jour-J*. The invasion had truly begun, and with it, opportunities abounded to contribute to the cause.

Today must be June eighth, Domingo thought—no, the ninth or tenth. Petra managed to keep better track of time. He determined to ask at their next halt, but in one instant, the whole world changed.

One moment, thrushes sang and baby rabbits scurried across the path. Blue sky gave no hint of parachute drops the night before or local peasants gathered with their carts to deliver the London supplies to the fighters.

The next, a distant thrum caught his ear—an engine, but what sort? Something made of wood shattered, and then no more than twenty meters away, a full-grown hornbeam tree split into three pieces before his eyes. Petra's face twisted as he waved Domingo to a shallow limestone cave.

A massive metal apparition nosed through heavy brush, sending a shudder under their feet. Thick slatted rubber sheets around revolving spigots moved the monster forward.

A tank, a German tank, here in this peaceful countryside. Wonder and terror flattened Domingo's arms against the side of the cave.

Oh mon Dieu, non. Not on the Causse de Gramat, so near the farm of Gabaudet.

Petra wasted no time jerking Domingo up a raw stone cliff. "See that jeep—an officer, look at his lapel." In the incessant roar, Petra's hiss barely reached Domingo.

"Beside him sits a *gendarme*—a collaborator, as my name is Petra Couderq." A half-sob issued from his throat. "Oh no, *mon ami*, they're steering straight for the farm we just left."

Half a kilometer away, two hundred new recruits prepared for the night. Domingo and Petra had just met them, young men who heard about *l'Invasion*, ready to contribute to the fight.

Concern and rage forced uncontrollable energy through Domingo. "We must warn them."

Petra slammed him back against the rock. "Not enough time—you know it as well as I."

His eyes swam with tears. Domingo turned away, his head throbbing. But then a rush of heat swamped his chest and his collar became a noose. They ought to have killed those *feldgraus* the other day, but he'd failed Petra, failed the cause.

"No. We can try." Ignoring the shadow over Petra's face, Domingo raced away from the tanks, circling toward the farm's far reaches and the flood of volunteers.

The two of them might still be there right now, in the path of those tanks. Surely, God sent them ahead for a purpose. Domingo's espadrilles carried him faster, faster, his weariness vanished in the urgency of his need.

When Domingo and Petra left, those young recruits had been preparing straw for beds and helping with evening chores. An air of gaiety prevailed, for word reached them that every Lot railroad line had been cut, and the Allies brandished their way into the Normandy countryside. Relieved grins and jokes filled the air.

Domingo panted as he flew over rocks and brush. No guard had been posted at the farm. Those good-natured *garcons*, some no older than Gabirel, would startle at the terrible rumbling and run for shelter, but where could they hide?

Though another deep inner voice told him Petra was right, Domingo could only run. Foolhardy—who could outrun SS tanks? This dim awareness accompanied his blind rashness, and another understanding, too.

Petra followed him. Petra, with his solid head to think things through and act with prudence, would not let him go alone. Yes, he heard the footfalls behind him, but he dared not turn his head, no, not for a second.

Now he spotted the barn roof. Then he heard a wall crash and saw men flee the courtyard only to be shot down. Young fellows rocketed into the air from the force of the tanks. Terrified barn animals shrieked and screamed, audible even above the roaring engines.

Petra pulled Domingo back. "Come. For now, we can only watch."

An advancing tank crushed someone like an insect. Another. Severed human legs flew upward like whirring matchsticks. A wild, incessant vibration sucked everything under the behemoth's treads.

Smoke erupted as the hated Bosche fired the farm buildings. A young recruit scampered across the scrub at Domingo's feet, stared up wild-eyed, and scrabbled on.

Swastika armbands and rifles flashed as the soldiers pursued the partisans. Some partisans fell, others they rounded up in lines. Germans hoisted the captured partisans onto the tank fronts and tied them with wire. Domingo went for his gun.

"No. They outnumber us by far. Someone must help the wounded and carry word of this."

Carry word. The bitter realization showered Domingo with shame—that seemed to be all he was fit for, carrying word. He crouched low as an inhuman shriek lanced the early evening air. He sped to the brush to forfeit whatever remained in his stomach. When he duck-walked back, Petra laid a hand on his forearm.

"Those men on the tank fronts serve as hostages. All along the way, the *Maquis* will be poised to attack the tanks, but think of their terrible choice. How can they, with our own men strapped on them?"

Clearly, this SS unit aimed to destroy everything in its path— peasants' farms, *Maquisard* holdouts, helpless villages. They would head toward the town of *Loubressac*, north between *les Quatre Routes* and Saint-Céré, where he and Petra had helped cut the rails.

Traveling between Argentat and Noailles, these dull green killers would finally reach Tulle. Their obvious route swam before Domingo. This impossible reality raked his throat hoarse, but even now, Petra thought one step further.

"They will attack Tulle, the crossroads between Limoges and

Clermont-Ferrand, where partisans proclaimed liberation on *Jour-J.* The Bosche seek revenge. In the morning, I think they will re-take the city."

Domingo sank to the earth. "What can we do?"

Petra rubbed his chin stubble. "We could run all night. But we have seen how futile that is, *oui?*"

Heat enveloped Domingo's face—yes, utterly futile.

"Let's go down when they leave, provide first aid, and perhaps..." Petra's eyes took on a faraway look. "Perhaps we can find a cycle or a lorry still in working order."

"We should have killed those men the other day."

Petra grimaced. "Who knows whether killing them would have made any difference?"

The tanks finally rumbled north, and the peasant's family rose, one from the well, one from a manure pile, one from a shed's burning rubble. A woman wept over a little girl's shattered body.

A man stood shell-shocked, blood steaming from his arm, but anything they might use as dressings had been razed. Domingo tore off his jacket, ripped his shirt into strips, and bandaged the wound.

At one point, as he held another man's head and tended his dying rasp, from the corner of his eye, he noticed Petra slip off. Domingo closed the eyes of another youth and tucked another's gun into his own boot.

He knelt beside another victim, not much more than a boy, and looked up into the eyes of a woman swaddling a younger child in her arms. The child's leg dripped blood.

Then Domingo remembered Sancha's scarf. Feeling like an automaton, he pulled out the orange mass and stretched the flowing silk lengthwise.

"Here, let me bind up her leg." He knelt, and the mother did her best to help. Then he spied another child with a mangled forearm and bent to help. Earth and blood and sweat mingled with crushed garden onions. Their paper-thin skins littered the yard with shiny translucence and clung to the boy's bare feet.

Domingo's shirtsleeve made a hasty bandage around the little fellow's neck, and the lad quieted when he plastered cool mud over the wounded arm. He carried the child across the gutted farmyard toward another woman.

Far too many lives sacrificed—in a daze of horror, Domingo turned a slow circle.

Then someone clasped Domingo's shoulder. Amid this hopeless scene, Petra's low, controlled voice sustained him.

"I've found an old lorry. There are plenty here to bury the dead."

Domingo reached for a knife lying nearby, though Petra could see he already had knives and guns aplenty. But it seemed to Domingo he could not amass enough weapons.

Petra faced him. Forced him to meet his eyes. "Come, then."

SIXTEEN

A thin moon cast enough light to remind Domingo of a distant goodness. Otherwise, he and Petra moved through an endless, starless bowl of shadows and intrigue. At every sudden sound that penetrated over the racket of the lorry engine, Domingo's head swiveled like an owl's.

Intent on one goal, Petra urged the rattletrap to the high road. "The tanks will avoid the Causses—these limestone ridges would slow them down too much."

The wide elevated path, largely untraveled, had its faults, especially where heavy spring rains rearranged the already bumpy surface into gullies and drop-offs. The inky night lent its dire message: in such a time, your loved ones could disappear like sighs on the wind.

Yet Petra's confidence thrived here—his assurance throbbed between them on the stained seat. How, in this peculiar mix of petrol fumes, limestone dust, and urgency, could such a thing be true? It was as if Petra possessed special powers that kept him focused in the middle of fury.

Domingo willed his spirit to embrace Petra's ability to trust, like Père Gaspard's faith. One could borrow another's assurance, he'd learned, until your own had time to revive.

Though the engine had taken precious minutes to roll over, they burbled along now with the wind whizzing by and the road taunting, "Conquer me." Potholes defied them to maintain a steady course, but Petra charged ahead.

Once, he reached over and jabbed Domingo's shoulder, as if to say, 'Stay with me.' Another time they jolted off the road onto a

wagon path so rutted it seemed impassable. But Petra kept on, ever
northward toward Tulle. Domingo braced his feet against the floor,
wishing he could do the same against the fresh recollections diving
at him like phantoms in this strange, insufferable night.

Human eyes crazed with terror, human limbs hanging at odd
angles—the raw scenes hovered close, though Domingo attempted
to fill his mind with the future. How many kilometers did they still
have to travel to Tulle? What would they do there?

But only past and present existed, with Petra here beside him in
this musty cab. Peeling leather seats emanated grease, sweat and
manure, farm air, full of richness and promise, humble odors. Feeling
split leather beneath his palm soothed him, somehow.

Though Petra gunned the engine as fast as he could, Domingo
had the sense that they sat still. And as long as they remained in
this small space, together, en route to somewhere, he could maintain
this mock serenity.

But Tulle. The city would be sleeping. Should they canvass the
streets like madmen, then, banging on doors, shouting the alarm? Yes,
Domingo's heart said. But surely Petra had his own ideas, better by far.

Finally, the arthritic lorry reeled to a shaky halt at the edge of a
village—or some sort of habitation. Domingo yanked his numb legs
upward. No spire marked the town. Maybe this was an encampment,
then. Perhaps they'd come to the camp where the Gaboudet organizer
had sent them with their messages before the tanks arrived. He'd
forgotten about that.

Petra left his door hanging open and approached a faint light as
if he knew his destination well. Always purposeful, that Petra.

Domingo got out to stretch. No use attempting to shake off the
grisly sights of Gaubodet that clung to him. He had learned his
lessons well—only time could cause such images to fade.

The cool night air invigorated him and intensified his determination. When he returned to the lorry, Petra held out bread
and cheese.

"Eat."

An hour earlier, Domingo couldn't have managed, but a sudden
ravenous streak bade him attack the hard crust. He snorted. Some

foudre he had proven, resisting conflict and then running madly to no avail. He averted his eyes.

Petra leaned against a tree, watching. He refrained from asking, "Are you all right?" But Domingo read his thoughts: *Will you control your impulses from now on? Will you act the soldier and fight with a will?*

"They told me the road out of *Argentat* runs through a break in the ridges. Who knows if the Germans will choose that way, but if so, we'll hear them and abandon the lorry. If we make for the ridges, we can wait for them to pass." Petra scratched behind his ear. "But we'll do our best to beat them there."

A partisan brought a petrol can. "Use what you need." He flicked on his torchlight while Petra removed the metal cap and poured. The sickeningly sweet chemical odor filled Domingo's nose and tainted his tongue.

When he finished, Petra handed the partisan the can. "*Merci.* You will be repaid some day."

The man's chortle stopped short. "Here's the favor I ask—shoot that collaborator if you see those tanks. Shoot him dead for me." He stood back. "I hear something." He turned southwest. "Is that what they sound like?"

Domingo closed his eyes. Far away, a low, distant growl wafted through the darkness. As it died away, Petra confirmed the man's suspicions.

"You say the officers and that collaborator rode in an open jeep? Surely other collaborators wait for them along the way. Perhaps we'll give them a midnight startle."

"With my blessing. That is, if you have long-range weapons. Otherwise, what good will it do for you to draw your last breath under a tank track?"

The partisan's thinking lines deepened, and the small muscle above his jaw worked as Petra sought more information. "How far away is Tulle, and what can we expect to find there?"

"Several hours by foot. We heard that when the FTP took the city, the German garrison fortified themselves in the normal school for girls. The *Maquis* attacked and liberated some of our men.

"One report said thirty former *Maquis* prisoners identified nine members of the Sicherheitsdienst, Gestapo members known to have committed atrocities. Before the *Maquis* burned the school, they took those men to the graveyard and shot them.

"Control of the train station passed back and forth, with some innocent watchmen murdered by the Germans. When the Bosche attempted to leave, the partisans used the confusion to attack with automatic weapons and take prisoners.

"Sixty or seventy surrendered, and the *Maquis* circled the weapons factory and the Souilhac school to the south. They created a public show, like the one at *Cajarc*. One thing is sure. These tanks will bring terror down on the city." He hesitated and angled his head. "You're certain they're going that direction?

"Yes, from *Gabaudet*."

The partisan worked his jaw back and forth. "I want to sneak up and untie those poor men, even if they're dead. They deserve an honorable burial."

"If you ask my opinion, daylight becomes our comrade in this instance. The tanks bulldoze everything in their paths, and morning may help us think more clearly."

The man hurried back to headquarters and Petra leaped into the cab. "With luck, we'll arrive soon enough to warn them."

The lorry lurched forward again, and more than an hour passed before the motor sputtered. Then the vehicle gave a disheartened cough and died completely, Petra steering it off the road with a sour look.

"We're better off on foot, eh? I've known hatred to fuel a run as powerfully as love."

He might be describing the night of Sancha's murder, such a combination of hatred and love. Domingo held his peace and padded after him into the blackness. At the first inkling of light in the eastern sky, they sped even faster. When dawn half-lit the horizon, Petra halted, panting.

"A few minutes." He drank and ran his sleeve over his mouth. They separated to relieve themselves, and Domingo refilled the bladder at a stream. He peered west, but saw nothing of the tanks. Better yet, he heard nothing.

Petra spoke first. "They must have gone around, along the Correze River." His eyes flashed. "We might beat them there yet."

"Always, you think we'll make it, and I doubt that we will."

"Yet you keep moving ahead. That's what counts—it's all we can do."

Morning broke with light infiltrating thick foliage. They ran on in silence, as if racing with the end of the world. The plateau's peacefulness beckoned to Domingo, but how could he shed last night's memories so quickly?

Unbidden, the words Père Gaspard intoned after Sancha died came to him. "Some things we must accept, though the evil appalls us. Only thus do we prevent them from reigning over us forever." But how to accept the utter devastation at Gaubodet?

Farther down the trail, Petra collapsed. "Forgive me … I must rest."

Domingo's legs also begged for respite, but after long years of traipsing these hills and valleys, Petra knew his limits. These men Domingo accompanied over the past months had all vanished, but he must not let that happen with Petra.

The glance Domingo stole at Petra crumpled at the foot of a tree revealed his age—glints of silver in his hair and such immense shadows under his eyes. How was it they could spend so much time together, yet not really see each other?

This time, fate had reunited them, so they must stay together. After a few minutes, Petra stirred, drank water, and seemed to take strength from the rising late morning temperature. They fell into rhythm again, and ran until midday became midafternoon.

At last, steeples slit the blue northern sky. They hurried even faster, but about a kilometer away, Petra held up his hand, and Domingo squatted with him to listen. Nothing. Then, at Tulle's outskirts, a distant thrum they knew all too well singed his ears.

After an uphill sprint, they reached a church and found an unlocked door. Domingo thrust aside the heavy wood like paper, flew to the belfry and pulled on the rope. Clanging filled the air. A priest exited into the courtyard, staring up, looking confused.

Through an arch, Domingo watched Petra grab the man's shoulders. Without hearing, he knew what Petra said. "Tanks, German tanks, they're out for the kill…"

The priest cocked his head before hurrying toward the rectory. Across the street, a citizen came out his front door, scratching his beard. Petra shouted the news and the man spun into action.

Petra raced down the street while Domingo still swayed on the rope, watching the scene unfold. Finally, he let go and stood staring at the homes surrounding the church. Evening descended, and lights gradually graced their windows as that distant thrum increased to a muffled roar.

People called to each other and closed their doors against the sound. And then, in the cool shadow of the belfry walls, Domingo viewed the second SS Division, Das Reich, storm in from the west toward the city's heart.

He imagined *maquisards* scuttling away like ants in the face of this obviously superior force. What an understatement. He could almost hear the clatter of boots and the *shluss* of worn espadrilles on cobblestone in the center of town.

No doubt, Petra continued to issue his warnings. "Run far! There's no cowardice in surviving to seek your revenge."

Darkness encroached. Against cool stone, Domingo eventually dozed until footsteps alerted him. Delicate candlelight created ghost-like shadows on the belfry stairs, so he flattened against the wall, but a steady voice wafted up.

"Son, I have brought you something to eat."

The priest, older than Père Gaspard, stood shorter and more rotund. Yet his eyes communicated exactly what Domingo knew his own priest's would—selflessness and concern.

"You must be hungry." He slid forward a bowl of potage.

"*Merci, merci.*" Domingo downed the soup as he would a cup of coffee.

The priest rubbed his temples. "You traveled far to warn us?"

"Far enough. What's going on down there?"

"The tanks sleep, but some officers have retaken the normal school. Lights still burn inside, with much murmuring, and sometimes they rise to a shout. Morning will tell the tale."

"Stay away. I have seen them at work— they're remorseless."

The priest held his forehead. "So it is. All that bloodshed on

Jour-J has come to this. The excitement of conquering a few of our oppressors entered into us all. Like Chapou, many considered that local victory a permanent liberation, and believed it stood for France's overall freedom. Now once again, only two days later, we cower."

Domingo tried to orient himself to days and hours, but it seemed as though a month had passed since Gabaudet. Those scenes spurred him to make a suggestion. "Maybe your church can serve as a hospital."

The priest leaned in close. "You have seen much. Do you wish to speak of it?"

Domingo shut his eyes. No, maybe never. His wordless response must have communicated as much, because the priest changed the topic.

"A hospital—you are right. We'll need bandages. I'll see to it." He reached into his bulging pocket and handed Domingo a hunk of bread. "I almost forgot. Will you come down and spend the night in the rectory?"

"No, I'll stay here. Which direction is the school?"

The priest pointed. "Sunrise will show you."

"You will not go down to the square, then?"

"I will follow my heart, my son." His quiet shuffle down the stairs faded into silence.

Sleep seemed impossible, yet sometime in the night, Domingo dozed off. He had no sense of the time when Petra entered the belfry and roused him from restless sleep.

"They brought more than tanks and armored cars—artillery pieces, too. They've cordoned off the streets."

"How many men?"

"More than enough."

"Did you locate any partisans?"

"No, but I sent a message with a local boy." Petra dropped on the stone floor. For a fleeting moment, the moonlight revealed doubt in his expression. "So little we can do." The whites of his eyes rolled upward. "If we could only transform this bell into a cannon."

"We could build a catapult and launch it into a tank..."

Petra managed a lop-sided grin. "With twenty more bells, that might work."

"Remember, you said we do what we can. Rest. I'll get your supper. The priest will be up, anyway."

And he was, presiding over a growing pile of fabric strips in the rectory kitchen. While he scurried for food, the wooden table intrigued Domingo. Scarred by knives, burns and scuffs, the homely piece carried him away from Tulle, the capital of Correze, to his own small Department of Lot.

Always, his family's table centered their lives. Around that wooden circle, they gathered their wits as well as their bodies. There, they thought things through. The last evening everyone had sat in the kitchen together, sunset flaring through the window.

Maman stood quietly behind his father, who explained why he must leave. "They need us, and I must heed the call."

The pain in her eyes told Domingo she knew something already, maybe about Ander. But even Aitaita would tell him nothing, and when he accompanied *Papa* part of the way to Spain, Domingo assumed Aitaita would bring Ander home. Then Papa, too, would return.

For months, that hope braced him, until Aitaita returned, bringing dreadful word. Neither Papa nor Ander would ever come home again.

The aroma of hot soup and the priest's voice returned Domingo to the present. "Here, my son. May your comrade be in health."

Be in health. Feeling as brittle as this old table, Domingo wanted to hide in some secret room, never to be found. He longed to sleep forever, to hear nothing, ever again, about war. Yet the look in this humble brother's eyes urged him to persevere.

"Godspeed, my son."

Petra roused at the smell of hot soup, and his expression softened. "Many have eaten their last meal tonight. I fear what tomorrow will bring." He chewed without hurrying. "But all for liberty, *oui?* As Charles de Gaulle proclaimed, 'Pour les fils de France ...'"

Domingo took up the message that had once energized him. "Yes, 'for the sons of France. Wherever they may be, howsoever they may be ... they must fight the enemy by all means at their disposal.'"

Petra gnawed a crust. "I fear that means will prove far too weak for the sons of France in Tulle. Yet they have no recourse."

Leaning on the cold stone wall eased a steady pain in Domingo's neck. "What would you be doing, Petra, if not for the war?"

"Ah ... what use to talk about it?"

"I don't know—I just realized I've never asked you your occupation."

"You've never asked me much of anything, my friend. Why do you now?"

"Maybe for that reason—because I never did. Because this all can end so quickly."

"Yes. Well, I will let you guess."

"You worked in your father's business."

"Um ... what sort of business was that?"

"Something with your hands. Maybe stonecutting."

Petra's half-grin revealed nothing. At least the guessing game quieted Domingo's racing thoughts.

~

Darkness eased, then settled again. The swish of skirts and nylon hosiery grated on Kathryn's nerves. Why wouldn't they let her sleep? Someone prodded under her ribs until she wanted to scream. But before she could muster the energy, she drifted into that other world.

Once, she woke to see wires extending from her mouth and someone working at them with a pliers-like tool. She tried to touch her lips, but something—or someone—held her hand down. Twisting to free herself, she looked directly into a woman's eyes. The stark white cap pinned in her dark hair never moved, and her taut lips announced that she was in charge.

"Now, ma'am, calm down. You're in good hands. They brought you in last night. Kept you in surgery for quite a while—the surgeon said he'd never seen anything quite like your injury. From what I hear, you're mighty lucky to be alive after the fall you took."

Lucky ... fall ... what was she talking about? Kathryn wanted to ask, but she couldn't make her jaws move. Something fastened them together. Her chest tightened, and perspiration rolled down her temple. Thankfully, the nurse wiped it away with a moist cloth, but the next moment, she jabbed a needle into Kathryn's arm.

Coolness swabbed the spot, and the scent of alcohol drifted up.

Then the room's white walls swirled around her, and whatever the nurse said faded away. Kathryn had no choice but to close her eyes.

SEVENTEEN

At dawn, shots rang out. Petra stared down from the belfry and waved Domingo over. "See there, straight over from the highest roof? That's the school courtyard, with houses surrounding it."

"You went down there last night?"

"Close enough to see their positions. Tanks sit there, there, and there, to make a show of force." Petra's index finger stabbed the directions.

"Pssst ... pssst. Men, are you still here?" An aged voice wafted up the stone steps.

Petra grabbed his pack and Domingo followed him down the stairway.

"I'm going down there, my sons." The priest met them with seeming serenity. Thank you for warning us."

"But the Nazis have lost all respect, even for..."

"For men of the cloth? Well, then, I become one with my people, as I have always wished to do. The enemy disrespects them, too, but *notre Dieu* cherishes us all."

He turned to go. Petra strapped his pack over his shoulders in wordless agreement. His glance told Domingo they would accompany their determined host, at least for a distance.

With each step, daylight grew. Doors opened along cobbled streets, dispersing the scents of home—fires burning, coffee and porridge boiling. People moved from their front stoops as their priest passed. Some came forward to touch his hand. Several older men joined him, canes or walking sticks in hand.

Near the town's center, the priest turned to Domingo and Petra. "Go into this restaurant and give Monsieur Faisant my blessing. Tell him you have need of his upstairs room, and mark well what happens here. Then you must continue to warn others."

The proprietor saw them coming and swung his door wide. He gawked at the priest and shook his head. "Surely you will not go down there, father? They're arresting all men between sixteen and sixty."

"Then we shall see if they count me a man—actually, I am well past sixty, so they daren't take me in." He gave a slight smile and kept walking.

Petra broke the silence. "Perhaps he believes his *soutane* will protect him."

"*Oui,* and so it may. Come in, come in. I am Monsieur Faisant. You two should be in the Ségala. Our men fought a successful offensive here, but evacuated last night. Our two sons fled, as well."

Something in Petra's face gave Monsieur Faisant pause. "Have you not heard about those SS officers in Frayssinet-le-Gélat? They killed at least ten citizens, even a woman." He shook his head. "And now this—the Second Panzer division right here on the streets of Tulle."

Petra removed his beret. "Your upstairs room—may we use it?"

Up a narrow stairway that gave Domingo a suffocating sensation, the stout baker led them to a room where they hunched together at the window. A clear view of the town center showed the school's courtyard filled with uniformed Nazis. They marched up and down while others paraded the main street, their tall black leather boots clicking mercilessly on cobblestone.

One of the soldiers halted and another handed an officer a bullhorn. He raised it to his lips. "Citizens of Tulle, you have defied our Fuhrer. You have decried Das Reich and your city will pay, life for life. You have declared yourselves liberated, so we shall see. The day begins."

Several soldiers banged on the door of a home, crashed through and brought out a man. A woman followed behind.

"See how you will pay."

Another woman ran from the house, screaming. "No, no. André, no!"

But the soldiers passed the man like a clothespin, along to others who bound his hands and feet, rushed him inside past the screaming woman, and a few seconds later, carried him out onto the balcony. Then they pulled back his shock of hair and throttled his neck.

In a blur of black and brown and *feldgrau*, the soldiers tied the neck rope to the iron balcony posts, thrust the man's legs over the railing and gave him a push. Below, the woman shrieked and flailed against her captor.

The victim gave a few errant kicks before he dangled from the grillwork like a ham hung for winter. The soldiers in the street grinned up at him. Officers barked more orders and groups of three soldiers each spread like gnats to other houses, where the first scene replayed over and over until citizens hung one by one from balconies or lampposts.

When a few onlookers attempted to intervene, the soldiers roped their necks, too. Now and then a slap resounded. A guffaw rent the early morning mist. The whole time, women of the city sobbed and wailed.

At some point, the restaurant owner, ashen-faced, sagged against the wall. "I counted thirty hanging from the lampposts." He cried out louder when the soldiers throttled a tall, slender fellow.

"*Mon ami*, Monsieur la James. How can this be? My dear friend, ah *Mon Dieu!*" He bent over in anguish. "This cannot be, it simply cannot be."

Then Petra pointed out soldiers nearing the priest. They grabbed his helpless gaggle of men, and someone pulled the priest into the shadows. Within minutes, those who had joined him hung from balconies or lampposts.

The numbers, shouted by a German officer, transfixed Domingo. Thirty-seven men killed. Forty-four. Fifty-nine. Sixty-five. Eighty.

Eighty-three. Eighty-seven. Petra bunched his shoulder against Domingo's. Eighty-nine. Ninety-two. Triumph tinged the officer's bellowed announcements.

Ninety-seven. Ninety-nine.

The commander, a miniature puppet from their viewpoint, turned his men on anyone standing nearby. Chaos ensued. Shots echoed from the courtyard, blood flowed over stone, and Domingo counted at least twenty more slain.

Somehow, Petra maintained command of his tongue. "Surely they have finished. Let's move."

Domingo followed him down the stuffy stairway, his legs like wooden sticks. Sickness rode his throat. Surely, he would soon waken from this terrible nightmare.

Petra stopped to speak with someone in the street, and Domingo's mouth went dry as a new idea struck him. Perhaps the same vicious commander that bloodied Tulle's streets had ordered Gabirel and *Maman* taken away. A day ago, his mind held room only for them, but then all those killed at Gabaudet crowded in.

Now, these unfortunate ninety-nine swung in his consciousness, too. Though he knew that the commander could not be in two places at one time, all German officers ranged through his mind as one—the epitome of evil.

What would Père Gaspard say to the slaughter he had just observed? A sudden longing to pour his heart out to him overwhelmed Domingo as he followed Petra by a back way to the edge of Tulle.

They would run until Petra could run no more, of that Domingo felt certain. And so they did. The aching in his muscles soothed his guilt at being gone from home when the soldiers came, and for allowing those Huns to live a few days ago. Compared to his shame, the fire in his muscles amounted to a good pain.

If only he and Petra could keep on running forever. He wished he could vanish into an isolated chasm of the Causse de Gramat. Yet he wanted to fight. He'd determined to do so before, but now, he must.

When Petra finally dropped beside a flowing stream, Domingo panted beside him. A short while later, he detected someone crawling their way, and touched Petra's shoulder. The bushes parted, revealing a shivering young fellow with elbows torn from his jacket. He stared at them in singular terror.

Petra took a step toward him and motioned for Domingo to give him water. Finally, the stranger stopped trembling. Then the grim details from Tulle flowed from his mouth. Finally he ended his tale. "I watched them kill ten of us for every Nazi."

"*Oui*. We saw them too. Come with us."

Petra led the lad, who looked far too much like Gabirel, to wash in a nearby creek. Then they raced away again with him between them on the path. A new comrade—someone who shared the bloody visions that visited Domingo.

Once again, the eyes of that pilot he'd deserted under the carcass confronted him. But this time, they seemed a bit further away. Perhaps time would render them less disturbing, less searing—like Sancha's.

In the *schluss...schluss* of the young man's espadrilles, the future unfolded in Domingo's mind. He and Petra would take him to headquarters to witness to what he had seen. They would do the same, and then they would fight together until this wickedness ceased.

~

Insistent banging woke Kate from heavy sleep. Pale light streaked the edge of the window hangings. The unmistakable scrape of boots on stone reverberated up staircases and through hallways to her sheltered room. Then a man's voice echoed, loud and unrelenting.

"Oh dear God, help us." She clung to her blanket. If she could hear their boots, they must be...

But then Mother Hélène's voice rang out. "*Messieurs*, I have now shown you all that is possible. You have seen our wounded, thanks to your own attack. I have allowed you into our sacred worship space. But you will *not* defile my sisters by entering our private areas."

Authority filled her declaration, but trembling still swept Kate. Gestapo inside the Mother House ... today she must move again, no putting it off. She steadied herself and pulled on her underclothes, splashed her face and slipped on the habit Père supplied. After transmitting the last two nights, her color probably matched the habit's faded straw hue.

By all means, she must listen for incoming reports this afternoon, for by now, the London transmitting team would have passed on the list of needs she'd sent last night. At Harrington, the S2 would have forwarded the information to the Operations room. There, an officer had already marked tonight's targets on a large situation map, added the circuit agent's name, selected take off times and issued flight organizers radar clearance.

How could she get the new coordinates to a courier before tonight?

If she failed, precious supplies might fall into Nazi hands. Worse, for any parachutists, rifle fire instead of loyal French peasants would greet them, and they would perish instead of aiding the *Résistance*.

A man's voice broke into her thoughts. "What about this whole southern wing? Surely, you have room for a transmitter there."

"*Monsieur*, I assure you, we have plenty of room for many transmitters. However, do you suppose we would risk the lives of those wounded in your malicious raids? Would women devoted to saving life barter precious human beings for the sake of a few radio transmissions? I wonder if you are thinking clearly today."

"Harrumph ... we'll see when I report your insolence to Monsieur Laval. Sister or no, lying to the Gestapo cannot escape notice. We will find you out, and believe me, once a betrayer reaches Lyon, Herr Barbie will enjoy torturing them until they blurt the truth."

Two sets of boots resounded on the granite stairs, their steps fading away, so Kate lifted off the itchy habit and found a window with a view of the front parkway. An immaculate black sedan waited outside the Abbey doors. Within minutes, two German officers exited the building. Even through closed windows, she could hear the strike of their spit-shined boots on stone.

Near the door, Mother Hélène's profile showed, keys in hand. She appeared placid as she watched the men depart, but surely she trembled?

As quickly as she could, Kate retraced the maze that first led her to this safe haven and met Mother Helene on the stairs.

"You derailed them."

"For the time being. But that threat about Klaus Barbie unnerved me. He has no conscience at all." Mother Hélène took Kate's hand with icy fingers. "Why focus on him, though? To be a woman of integrity means being the same on the inside as we are outwardly, but this war teaches me I have a distance to go."

"To live honestly these days, one must lie."

"Indeed. Loyalty demands a high price." Mother Hélène locked the inner door and turned down the hallway toward her office.

"I must go very soon."

"*Oui,* but I do not know where to send you, and you will not leave without a destination. Let us pray Père returns to us." Mother Hélène's green eyes sparkled against her ashen skin. "You do know they call him the phantom of the *Résistance*?"

"No, but I can see why."

"Yes, only the Almighty can keep track of his movements." She turned her doorknob. "Our bandage supply has nearly run out..."

"Ah. I roll them like a professional."

By the time the bells tolled two, the air grew oppressive. Kate wiped her forehead after passing the morning cutting cloth and rolling it into strips. At one point, Sister Margareta, one of the few remaining sisters on the premises, invited Kate to accompany her on her rounds.

"Every day I check the eternal flame." She opened a small muted room with an altar at one end. "See there, above the altar? If I allow that candle to go out, God's presence will dwell here no longer."

Kate bit her tongue. As if she sensed her questions, Sister Margareta turned.

"This box contains the host, our Lord's body. It is most holy."

An image of the battered, bloody bodies languishing in the Abbey sanctuary flashed before Kate. Then she thought of Monsieur le Blanc's worn-out flesh and his final exhalation.

She wanted to ask, "But isn't Jesus with the wounded, too? And surely He was with Mother Hélène when she forestalled the Gestapo this morning?"

No, this was a time to consider a different way of looking at things. She stilled her inquisitive nature and once again, Addie's husband came to mind. He would have a heyday here. Even with his slim knowledge of Catholicism, he often ridiculed the institution.

"Keep away from those Catholics. They worship a statue, you know."

But perhaps her father had been born into a Catholic family— she'd had no time to ask Monsieur le Blanc. Sister Margareta smoothed the linen cloth around the host, kissed the latch, backed away and bowed three times.

In the hallway, Kate whispered, "Do you only come here to check the light?"

"And for adoration. I sit before the host and ponder what our Lord has done for me."

Near Mother Hélène's office, a sign of God's presence arrived in human form, as comforting for Kate as the eternal light. Père Gaspard's resonant voice drifted down the hall.

A great sigh overwhelmed Kate and she flung her arms around him. "How did you find Terrou?"

His smile quivered at the corners, so Mother Hélène took over. "What about the chateau? The owners have given over most of it to the *Résistance*, but...?"

"The Gestapo watches it too closely." Père twisted toward Kate. "Isn't your listening time almost here?"

"I was so worried about my next move, I almost forgot, and today listening is more important than ever."

In the next room, she slipped out the miniature radio set. Amazing—in the midst of such suffering, Père still remembered her listening time. In the background he and Mother Hélène continued their search for her next location.

When Kathryn completed her work, Mother Hélène gave her a serene smile. "We've come up with the right spot for you."

"Although getting you there may take some doing." Père Gaspard rubbed his chin. "But then, you've become used to wild rides, *oui*?"

"The lorry again?"

"That and some other contrivances. We have a distance of only, umm ... I think about twenty-five kilometers to go, though the trip may resemble ten times that. But the effort will be worthwhile, for the Abbey of St Pierre at Beaulieu-sur-Dordogne will provide superlative protection. I doubt even Hitler himself would trespass on an Abbey so rich in relics."

"What do you mean?"

Mother explained. "The Abbey owns a medieval golden Virgin and child. And two arm reliquaries, if legend serves us well."

"Reliquaries?"

"The arms of kings or other important people. German blood may have flowed through those monarchs, so even the Nazis would hesitate to disturb their forebears' eternal rest. I know Mother Juliette there, who has worked with the Correze partisans from the beginning—probably has her own code name by now.

"I know no one else as formidable as Mother Juliette. If anyone could convince a storm trooper the Abbey boasts a German king's arm, she could."

Père added, "Unfortunately the time has come for you to don your sister's garb."

Kate obeyed, and when she returned, Mother Hélène raised her eyebrows. "I'll have someone fetch your radio."

"Thank you. Do you have a map? I'd like to know the route, in case we get separated."

Mother Hélène reached into a desk drawer. "Here—before the war, I gave this to our novices. Even cloistered folk ought to know their environs."

Kate spread the map on the desk and viewed the Departments of Lot and Correze, the western section of Aveyron, and the easternmost slice of Dordogne. She pinpointed the spot near Capdenac where she and Domingo crossed en route to his home.

Père Gaspard joined her. "The initial influx of tanks and troops has filtered north." His finger traced a route through Souillac, Gignac, and Brive-la-Gaillarde into the center of Correze.

"I have heard reports of their doings in Tulle." He locked eyes with Mother Hélène. "Mercifully, they moved north, but new units may still arrive. You did the right thing, Mother, to send the little ones away."

"Both conscience and fear counseled me. My mentors taught that faith and fear cannot co-exist, but I have to disagree." She went out, and Père bent over the map.

"We'll follow the rail lines, shorn of their power, up through the center of Lot." He traced his forefinger over a plateau from north to south. "They say the Causse de Gramat has some sort of road paralleling the railway. From there, we can view the whole area.

"Sorry I can't offer you a tour of the Alzou and Ouysse Valleys, with their quaint medieval structures, nor the cliff village of Rocamadour, a unique pilgrimage site for centuries."

"Let's make a date after the war." Kate's comment eased the severe lines between his eyes.

"I'll go out and get the radio settled."

Kate tucked the map into her habit's hidden pocket as Mother Hélène returned with a pair of espadrilles. "I doubt your shoes will last the climb."

"Why, thank you—such a thoughtful gift."

Mother Hélène also held out the tiny transmitter. "You have more use for this than we do."

"You would send this with me?"

"Of course. It was never ours to begin with."

"Mother Hélène, do you know anything about Terrou?"

"Père Gaspard found his village as reported—razed, burned out."

"Did he find his family?"

"No trace of them, but that could mean anything." Mother Hélène pressed her lips together. "In some ways, it would be easier to know, but with everyone scattered..." She patted Kate's shoulder. "Perhaps on your journey you will act as his confessor."

"Me?"

"You two have a bond. In these times, we must all uphold one another."

Domingo's face flitted through Kate's mind. Mother Hélène described exactly what he did for her when Monsieur le Blanc died.

"Crossing the Causse after tending the dying and grieving here will seem light work to Père. Let's pack some supplies for your journey."

When they returned with provisions, Père Gaspard had lugged the radio into a hollowed-out hiding place beneath the seat of a cart attached by wooden joints to a bicycle. At first glance, the apparatus looked flimsy, a creation only the foolhardy would trust.

Père caught Kate's eyes. "Behold, a unique form of transportation designed just for us." His arm circled the contraption as if he presented her with a royal coach.

"Some of our more mechanical *Maquisards* developed this contrivance. It requires no fuel, is faster than walking, totes heavy loads, and rouses less suspicion because it makes far less noise than a motorized vehicle." His underlying paleness belied the cheery look he gave her. "In appearance, it may leave something to be desired, but that's true of me, as well."

He jumped onto the seat. "You see, I pedal here and you ride beside me. If worse comes to worst, you can lunge for safety while my priesthood protects me."

From behind them, a deep chuckle erupted. "Well, Père, I've seen a lot in my lifetime, but this might qualify as the most bizarre." Mother Hélène tapped Kate's elbow and then embraced her.

Sudden emotion engulfed Kate. "I don't know how to thank you for your kindness." She handed Mother Hélène an envelope. "Please give this to the courier who came yesterday, and tell him I'll transmit my new location to London as soon as I can."

"I shall not forget you, child. And be assured, you may count on our prayers."

EIGHTEEN

The burly commander's collar dripped with sweat in the afternoon sun. Domingo touched his own, just as wet, and listened to the man's every word.

"Now that London has given us free rein, we can break into our ammunition stores. We have enough to arm at least five thousand men, with close to that number of partisans waiting in the forest.

"A Belo-Russian squad that found its way here tells of strapping explosives to dogs trained to run under tanks, but the Soviet diesel fuel confused the dogs. We have a better idea."

Domingo noticed men in the crowd stiffen. Surely this commander must know these partisans tended sheep and loved their dogs. But he continued.

"The Russian army fit forty thousand dogs with a ten to twelve kilo mine each and removed the safety pin just before deployment. On the eastern front, the Germans were desperate, too, and shot them without hesitation. That at least helps us understand why the Nazis kill every dog they see here."

"But you say you have better ideas?" Petra's calm question staved off Domingo's disgust.

"With bazookas and leisure to hit the weak place in the back of each tank without hundreds of infantry on hand, it would be easy. But armed troops accompany the tanks, so we must kill the guards, send a man underneath the tank to place the mine, pull the pin, and flee to safety. A complicated procedure best accomplished by night." He scanned the group of men before him. "Obviously, this task requires a wiry frame, a fast runner, a cool head, and strokes of good fortune." He looked Petra and Domingo over. "Does either of you qualify?"

"We've seen those iron beasts in motion—that qualifies us."

"I see, but I hate to lose good men." The leader rubbed his dense beard. "Tanks do have one disadvantage. They can't make it through deep water, and to reach Normandy, these units must cross both the Dordogne and the Vezere Rivers, and if we hit the bridges first, we stop more tanks than if we physically disabled each one.

"The enemy has already brought tanks forward to guard those bridges. Still, with twenty thousand Panzer troops approaching from Toulouse, armed with the newest Mark IV Panther—the Reich's largest single armored unit—we aim to stretch their four-day trip into fourteen."

Petra ground his teeth. "Or forever."

"Our forces have scattered, yet we must kill twenty guards while others place the mines. Are you ready?"

"*Oui.*" Domingo and Petra spoke as one.

"You can swim?"

At their nods, he gestured them closer and lowered his voice.

"You'll be heading toward a bridge over the Dordogne. North of there, the citizens welcomed forty thousand Alsatians in '39, so they'll be mighty glad to see you. We assemble in a few hours, over there. Get some rest."

In the luxury of having alert sentinels posted around them, Domingo and Petra made themselves comfortable under a tree and lost no time falling asleep.

The next thing Domingo knew, Petra's gruff shake woke him. "Don't want to miss the excitement, do we?"

For the first time in days, his eyes showed more white than red. Domingo scraped together his pack and followed toward a troop assembling around the man who spoke with them earlier.

"Men, when our armies surrendered to the foe, one leader, General De Gaulle, refused. From London almost four full years ago, on June twentieth, he called on us to regroup, reminding us that we could not capitulate.

"We took heart that day, but now, the enemy encroaches even more, so we move through the Causse de Gramat toward the black Perigord. Through those shadowy forests, the enemy will soon approach the River Vezere. Another unit travels farther west, south of Bergerac." He paused for a breath.

"We know this land. Perhaps you recall the old Perigord saying, *'Stone for nasty people, your heart for your friends, iron for your enemies; if you are these three, you are a Perigordin.'*

"We count on the people's magnanimity, as did the large influx of Alsatian refugees. Those who speak Occitan ..." The leader bobbed his chin at Domingo and Petra. "... may have to translate. But once the peasants understand our purpose, no one will argue."

Domingo lost patience with his verbosity, though he wasn't the first local leader bent on glory. As the day's heat mounted, an itch started between Domingo's shoulder blades. *No need for a history lesson every time his mouth opens.*

"We follow the Dordogne two kilometers until it juts into a finger. The bridge ... how many of you know it already?"

Several hands shot up. "Good. At last report, the next wave of tanks approached Fraysinet-le-Gelat, so we shall stop them here." He pointed a ragged fingernail at the spot on a frayed map.

"We cross the river in Lot, pass over into Dordogne, and surprise the guards from the north. Thanks to the latest drop, several bazookas accompany us—here's to success."

For a moment, a familiar face visited Domingo—Katarin's dark eyes, the smoothness of her skin... No time now for that, or to ponder *Maman* and Gabirel.

"Decide who will silence the guards and who will swim underwater to place the charges. The killings must be swift and soundless. We have the moon on our side, and remember, destroying even one end of the bridge will stop the panzers."

Petra muttered under his breath, "Crossing a wide plateau in daylight, eh? Our angels will have to do double duty."

They followed a rocky path meandering through limestone outcroppings. Here and there, a pasture full of black-eyed sheep grazed between fields that ought to be producing grain by now.

Around Saint-Céré, with the Bave glinting in the sun, and then on past Rocamadour, with houses straggled almost straight up the incline. An ancient stone church lazed placidly in the morning light as it had for centuries, its turrets and steeple roofs rusty red.

Its careful stonework created a mottled mosaic of gold and dun, tan and brown. Patches of moss on the shaded north side made designs like those on the sheep pen back home, and beyond the church, the blue Alzou River crossed a green valley.

Aitaita spoke of the miracles that had occurred in this place—King Henry Plantagenet and Saint Louis IX's healings. He'd climbed the two hundred steps on his knees, and believed Zacchaeus, whom the locals knew as Saint Amadour, was buried here after witnessing the deaths of Saint Peter and Saint Paul in Rome.

Of all places to build a chapel, why pick cliff walls four hundred feet high? But after this one, Amadour's followers built six more, one housing the mysterious Black Madonna. Clearly, they had no Nazis to consider in those days. But surely the Reich would not destroy these ancient buildings.

When they paused for water, Petra asked, "Do you believe the tales of those who came here for healing? Will you bring your grandchildren here one day, as our Aitaitas did with us?"

"Ask me when the war is over."

Near Geoffre de Padirac, the entrances to vast caves and grottos took Domingo back to his own visits with Aitaita, who retold legends evoking the devil. "Yes, the evil one kicked his heel into the earth here. That kick supposedly created a massive hole, into which the devil challenged Saint Martin to jump, in order to save the souls of the peasants from hell. Saint Martin and his mule jumped into the hole to defeat the devil, who then vanished in the chasms below."

Years ago, Aitaita showed Domingo the hoof print where Saint Martin's mule landed, and told him that flames occasionally erupted from the chasm. These natural phenomena explained the legend.

Around this natural wonder lay houses made of stones fitted closely together. Men like Saint Amadour used what they found at hand—these stones—to express their faith and protect their families.

Soon Domingo and the men with him would destroy a bridge built by human hands, but he could think no further than that. Would he survive this war to father children or enjoy grandchildren? He shrugged, knowing Petra understood.

At dusk, they entered Souillac. Beyond the houses, they slipped past the ancient Abbatiale-Sainte-Marie to barter for boats to cross the Dordogne. Domingo stuck his oar into the water and Petra gave a low whistle.

"The water runs so quiet here. Maybe the war has stopped."

"Then you and I merely imagined those tanks, *mon ami?*"

"*Oui,* the fruit of our grand imaginations."

In darkness, they hauled the boats ashore, their hulls crunching against the pebbles of the bank. Then, like ghosts slipping from shadow to shadow, the men scaled the riverside and found a path paralleling the Dordogne. At every curve and ravine, Domingo listened, hoping to hear crickets chirping and small animals in the woods instead of tanks humming.

They faced an enemy in impenetrable armor. Fresh from their winter refitting near Toulouse, these vehicles never grew weary. But Domingo reminded himself of the M16's, pistols, and most importantly, bazookas.

"Aim those big B's at the back of the tank, its only weak point. The turret can still turn and blast you, so aim, fire, and run. The three best shots here, find high ground to provide sniper cover."

Orders filtered through his mind in no particular sequence. In the glow of twilight, the team serpentined their way along the bank toward their prey. Just before dawn, word reached Petra and Domingo. "We're within three kilometers of the bridge." Four of the men in their group hurried forward to assess the situation up ahead.

In a few minutes, more orders came. "Those carrying explosives, gather here."

Petra led the way, and Domingo shifted his pack to the earth for a little rest before the onslaught.

~

Was it twilight or just before dawn? So many words—messages from somewhere—swirled in Kathryn's head. She'd just stopped working— but what had she been doing, anyway? Voices carried as she descended a long stairway. As if the speakers became excited and then remembered to hush their tones, words undulated in and out.

She shouldn't be listening, that much she knew. But after a night of hearing other voices ... why on earth was she isolated so far away from everyone in this enormous building? After long hours, her shoulders ached, and she paused to rub the back of her neck.

"Kidnap the Pope? Well, I would put nothing past Hitler. Where did you hear ... couriers straight from the Vatican ... take courage from our brother in Assisi ... have no doubt he'll continue hiding the Chosen ... pockets of courage spring up in this desolation ... keep hearing of feats I would never have dreamed..."

Following the stairs led her to a long foyer ending in a room with a black and white floor. That smell—not coffee, but something close. A rich dark aroma wakened Kathryn's senses, and still the chatting flowed. Where were those talkers?

"I look back at my big hopes ... Sometimes I wonder what tangible good our exertions have accomplished, Père?"

"...cannot see the end yet ... still make a difference ...Remember, after Peter fished all night in vain, the Master came and swamped the boat with fish ... never understood Peter's reaction until now—he ought to have been overjoyed. But it wasn't about fish at all. No, at some point, finally, we see the poverty of our anxious efforts and cry, "I'm too sinful—get away from me!"

Such a peculiar conversation, but intriguing.

"... but our Lord remains ... knows our dire need, our fumbling, and still blesses our actions ... partly the war, partly our aging—the more we see of Him, the more we can face who we truly are, shadows and all."

"Ah, yes. Create in me a clean heart..."

Footsteps began out in the foyer and grew closer. "Another day has come, the sun has risen once again ... let us see what great deeds He can accomplish through us, Père."

Shadows, robes, and human scents developed into the warmth of people present in the room. "Ah, and here's our girl, Père. How did your night go?"

Père ...father. The gush of spoken French enticed Kathryn. If only she could open her eyes, she might remember who stood over her back then. But that place whooshed away when a cool hand touched hers.

"How was her night?"

"Far less restless—she slept much better. The pain meds seem to be working."

"Good. Cut them in half and we'll see how she manages today. Maybe we ought to bring in a radio and turn on some music to stimulate her. We can't let her sleep forever."

NINETEEN

Sudden shuffling and muffled voices emanated from the dark foliage along the trailhead. Petra touched Domingo's elbow. The volunteers who went to scope out the area around the bridge could not have returned so soon. A few moments later, unfamiliar men conversed with Domingo and Petra's leader.

"It's a heist. The biggest on the continent, possibly the largest ever, and right under Nazi noses. We've got part of the take, and have run as far as we can. Would you exchange your two best runners for us?"

"You're being chased?"

"At first we were, but our other comrades detoured our pursuers."

"A heist ... then you must be *Résistance Fer?*"

A muffled guffaw. "Those Bosche ought to know better than to trust railroad men."

Petra stirred. "Domingo, did you hear that?"

Domingo shifted his beret to peer at the strangers, whose shoulders sagged under weighty packs positioned on their backs.

"Railroad workers combined with the regular circuit to accomplish this one. We've stolen enough gold to..."

"Shhh." His partner chimed in. "This delivery has to be made in St. Julien de Lampon, about ten more kilometers, but with the weight, we've run ourselves out. The pick-up agent will wait until six o'clock tonight. Could you spare your two best runners? Whatever your mission, we'll rest a bit and join you."

"Any experience blowing bridges or disabling tanks?"

"Yes, as long as you have bazookas."

The leader advanced toward Domingo and Petra. "You two normally work as couriers, correct?"

Petra nodded.

"You have rested, *oui?*"

"*Oui.*"

"Your mission has changed. We need you to make St. Julien de Lampon by nightfall." He scratched his ear. "With an extra heavy load."

Petra turned to Domingo, who nodded despite his qualms. Now they would be delivering stolen goods?

But Petra already stretched his legs. "We'll do it."

"All right. Work out the rest with these fellows."

One stranger wanted to give details, like Giriotte, who lived on story. But his comrade stopped him short.

"Eduardo, there's no time." He dropped his pack and circled his shoulder muscles.

"Stay close to the river. Under no circumstances, surrender the delivery to the Germans. Drown the packs rather than hand them over. And you," he pointed to Petra. "Better take this pack, it's one bar lighter."

"So, we have no room to fail." Petra's eyes shone as he shouldered the pack the partisan indicated.

"Fail? *Ah non, monsieur,* you must not fail."

Petra grunted. "In St. Julien, what then?"

"In the afternoon, a woman will park a lorry behind the *bibliotheque* and carry in a stack of books. At closing time, six o'clock, you are to lift the lorry's back canvas and hand over the packs to someone inside."

"Simple, eh?" Petra saluted and turned toward Domingo. "Ready?"

Domingo adjusted his strap, but there would be no comfort on this journey. He wiggled his shoulders to adjust to the weight. "Ready."

Two minutes later, they left the bridge-blowing crew, and in spite of his freight, Domingo's feet felt light. He lifted his face to a southern breeze, grateful for this random turn of events. Once again, he and Petra ran, unimpeded and alone, surrounded by the lush Dordogne River Valley. They'd shared this silent intensity before, in the Pyrenees— one with the land, one with the mission.

Did Katarin sense this when he led her from the Massif Central encampment to Lot after Monsieur le Blanc died? Had his urgency to get home overtaken her, too? At the time, he never even wondered.

The soft drum of Petra's espadrilles guided him forward. To their right, the Dordogne swelled as it ran its banks, mist rising into thick midmorning air, and Domingo's thoughts reverted to Katarin again—but for the war, he never would have met so many foreigners in his lifetime.

Above, stippled light filtered through countless layers of leaves, and on either side of the path, small animals rustled through the brush as though this war were a fantasy. Domingo turned a singular truth over and over in his mind—Katarin possessed no people, no home on this earth.

~

Another ramshackle lorry, as dilapidated as the first, ploughed through a mass of branches nearly obscuring the entire road. The engine groaned and fierce vibrations shook the stuffy cab where Kate sat, clenching the door handle. The peculiar bicycle mechanism housed in the back of the vehicle seemed far more desirable.

The Spanish driver was in no mood to talk, just like Père, who closed his eyes. After a particularly violent lurch, she turned toward the inscrutable fellow who forced the steering wheel to cooperate.

"Where were you born?"

Either he didn't understand or didn't want to. But she persisted with her broken Spanish.

A distinctive black eyebrow moved up a bit. "Beyond Foix."

So he came from the Ariege, closer to Spain than to Lot, farther into the Pyrenees.

"How did you come here?"

"To fight." His tone included a silent reprimand.

Counting herself lucky to receive an answer, she gave up trying to make conversation. A minute later, the lorry heaved over an unruly bump and more than the normal amount of dust sprayed in.

Père Gaspard coughed, but kept his eyes shut. He was garnering strength—she almost felt the process.

With a series of rattles, the vehicle swerved to avoid a big rock and bounced Kate to the ceiling. Whump! Soon after, the driver downshifted and coasted to a halt.

"The rest of your journey begins here." He opened his door and climbed down. By the time Kate and Père Gaspard reached the back, he had already maneuvered their cart onto the path and turned the bicycle over to the priest.

"I go now." His salute produced a matching one from Père.

"*Merci.*" Père Gaspard dusted off his robe as the Spaniard maneuvered the lorry—turning it around on this path would have challenged the best of drivers, but somehow, after a few jolting reverses, the vehicle gained the road and disappeared in a cloud of petrol fumes.

"Quite the ride, eh? Still, I would rather do all that climbing in the lorry than afoot." His voice regained its usual tenor. "Now our real challenge begins."

Kate mounted her bicycle as he manhandled the cart, his hair orange as a jack-o-lantern against the pure blue sky. "Lovely day for a ride. Shall we?"

Thanks to Mother Hélène's map, she figured out their location and approximately where they headed, more than she could say of the other trips she had taken during the past six months. Besides, she knew her companion and trusted him, unlike the many guides who delivered her from point to point before. What more could she ask?

It took a while to coordinate their pedaling. Getting used to the cart's wide sway took longer, but once she did, the views captured Kate's attention.

"We're slicing the Department in two, like the big yellow grapefruits my brothers and I used to receive around Christmas time. Did such delights make their way to Iowa?"

"Sometimes Aunt Alvina included an orange and an apple in my Christmas stocking, because she remembered receiving them as a child. But after the holidays, she always produced a full box of red Delicious apples from the fruit cellar, which we stretched as long as we could.

"My best friend Addie, from a poorer home, eyed them with

longing when she visited. But grapefruit ... no, I think my first taste came much later."

"Your Aunt liked Addie? Did she share your hoard with her?"

"Oh, yes. In fact, Addie probably saved her, in a manner of speaking. She lived alone before I came. Having Addie over to visit gave her some time to herself.

"Nothing of ours was off limits for Addie. I think when she first came to play with me, she must have felt we lived in a palace. Nothing like the chateaus here, of course. We lived in a three-story square wooden house with an open oak staircase, though, and I had my own room."

"And the first time you went to her house?"

Far below, meadows alternated with fallow fields and forested spaces. Kate feasted her eyes on flocks of sheep shorn of their winter wool, their eyes masked by dark circles.

"We played there only a few times, mostly in winter, to build snow forts. Addie's father ... well, he wasn't the most welcoming person. But after my parents died, my nurse transported me by train across the country. I knew no one, not even my aunt, but on the very first day of school, Addie won my heart. I must have seemed like an abandoned bird, so she took me in. Having a new friend meant so much to me.

"Would you describe her house for me? I doubt I'll ever get to your country." For some reason, Père kept her talking, and Addie made a delightful topic.

"They lived in a little wooden shack teetering on its foundations. Americans call men like her father good-for-nothing. He drank away their living. Addie recently discovered he gambled, too. She never forgot her mother's despair at him losing their sole milk cow, but as a child, she didn't understand.

"When her neighbor Jane helped Addie can corn for winter, she described her father betting his paychecks on the old-time Chicago races. A puzzle piece from Addie's childhood slipped into place. Hearing how Jane's father bet their entire farm one night and lost his bet, Addie realized that must have been how her father lost their cow."

"Things come into focus as we grow strong enough to accept them. Do you believe her father gambled away the cow?"

"Yes, but you're right. Addie couldn't have embraced the truth earlier. She always stood up for her father."

"Ah ... little girls defend their Papas at all cost. Such a need in their hearts for a man they can respect."

"And that's why I felt such a loss before Monsieur told me..."

"When you first told me about your uncle, what was his name? Monsieur..."

"Le Blanc."

"Ah, yes. Your story took me right into that situation. Finding him changed your life greatly."

"Or him finding me."

"Better yet, God directing your paths to cross. At that point, you must have become ready able to process what Monsieur shared."

"Yet the encounter still carries an unreal feeling."

"Sometimes that which is most real seems less so. We get so used to judging reality by physical means, we often fail to recognize eternal certainties."

"I still don't understand why he had to die before I could get to know him better. He could have shown me my father's birthplace after the war."

"But perhaps one day you will still visit there."

"How would I locate it?"

"Did you ever think you would discover all you now know about your father, or meet his brother?"

Clattering over an unruly patch, Kate reduced her pedaling to compensate for the cart's jerking. Far to the west, dark forests covered the land. To the northeast, rocky terrain melded into wooded heights. The sun rose to its zenith, but the air remained comfortable.

"So, did you ever think you would come face-to-face your uncle?"

"No—his identity shocked me."

"But earlier, he found you on a London street?"

"True."

"And then your paths crossed again in a most unlikely circumstance, is that true?"

"*Oui.*"

"You have experienced the mystery of God satisfying your deepest desires. So I must ask you again: why should finding your father's childhood home seem impossible?"

Père had a point. She could never have arranged her first meetings with Monsieur le Blanc in London, nor again on the train to Albi. That time, she hadn't even recognized him, and the odds of him lying on the path when she and Domingo fled the *Milice* and Gestapo were astronomical. Domingo might have chosen another way, and so might Monsieur.

Addie's Harold would call each case *God's will.* But questions still troubled Kate. Surely her longing to see her father's birth site and the church where he married her mother amounted to selfish desires compared with people's real needs.

The war had made everyone needy—many for everyday sustenance. Perhaps she ought to be satisfied with what she knew, already far more than she ever expected.

She considered asking Père's opinion, but realized that in all their wanderings, she had asked him nothing of his childhood. Maybe it was time.

On a relatively smooth area, she began. "Tell me more about your family. How many children were there?"

"Twelve. Nine boys, three girls."

Kate whistled. "You were the oldest?"

"Not at all. The seventh."

"How did you decide to become a priest?"

"My mother always proclaimed my temperament perfect for this vocation. I accepted her wisdom, as did two of my older brothers. We considered such a calling an honor—something above the ordinary."

"Do you still?"

"Not a fair question during war." He raised his heavy eyebrows and grinned. "From time to time, I do."

"Three of you became priests?"

"Yes, and two sisters entered the convent. My mother once worried that she would never enjoy a grandchild, but our one sister has given her eight. Of course, with six of us marrying, she ended up with plenty—more than thirty at last count."

"Do you ever see your brothers and sisters who serve in the church?"

"No. One has died, and the order called two of them to work in Italy."

"In Rome?"

"Um ... yes, one lives in Rome."

"Who of your family remains at home?" This last question slipped out without considering Père's recent news. His face blanched, and he focused on his pedaling. So did Kate, but not without berating herself—how could she have forgotten? After a long upward stretch, his labored breathing concerned her.

"Shall we switch places for a while? I've biked often since I came here, and ..."

He sent her the next thing to a scowl. "First Domingo, now you. Always thinking me old and decrepit. Thank you, but no."

They lapsed into silence. For some reason, Mother Hélène's comments about Klaus Barbie ran through Kate's mind. In a world of harsh oppressors, he still managed to make a name for himself— sometime, she'd ask Père if he knew anything about him.

They traveled several kilometers with only a few small animals racing across the trail, mouths full of grass or weeds. Sporadic bird-songs wafted, and once, the undeniable odor of skunk. Otherwise, the Causse received its afternoon rays in mellow quiet.

Then, an unnatural sound resonated in the air. The second time she heard it, Kate touched Père's sleeve. With a great deal of wobbling and jiggling, he brought the ungainly cart to a halt.

"Good, it's time for a water break."

But she put her finger to her lips. Distant yet distinct, the sound continued, like a transmitter's clack, but more regular. From east or west?

Just when she decided west, Père pointed northeast, where rugged landscape created a gorgeous backdrop. A narrow, winding road divided the terrain below them, but otherwise, trees in full leaf surrounded meadows spread like dark green carpets.

At any other time, such beauty would have relaxed her, but the clacking made Kate calculate the potential for Nazi soldiers to turn up, as they had in the Ibarra's barn. The memory evoked sadness, but also pride in Mrs. Ibarra's calm behavior.

"It's a printing press, a proof printing press." Père Gaspard turned with a grin. "I'd bet my *soutane* on it."

"You must be really sure."

"Word has it an FTP Lieutenant established a press northeast of Terrou, closer to Latronquiere. I wager that's what we hear, and prophesy we'll come across vestiges of its production soon enough."

Kate returned his self-satisfied smirk. "Who am I to argue with a prophet?"

TWENTY

How many weeks had she wasted laid up in this hospital? With an attentive nurse at her elbow, Kathryn swished down the antiseptic corridor in the fuzzy carpet slippers Gabby had brought yesterday. Her daughter had made the drive alone, with Mara and her older children in school. The surprise on Gabby's face when Kathryn had walked in the room had been plenty to handle.

"You don't like my new look?"

"Oh Mom—you must be in a lot of pain."

"Not really, at least not compared to earlier." Gingerly, Kathryn ran her fingertips along the indentations where the doctor removed the wires a few days ago. "These scars define my jaw, don't you think?"

Gabby bit her lip and dropped her head, but not fast enough to hide her tears. "Come here and give me a hug."

After their embrace, Gabby pulled up a chair. "The first time I saw you, I was afraid to touch you. The third time we drove over, I began to believe you might make it. But you seem all right now—I mean ..."

"Oh, I'm still me, don't you worry, honey. Still a stickler for ... I can't believe I've missed planting my garden this year."

"Oh, we took care of that—even added a new kind of squash. Mara's a pro at weeding, and little Henri pulls out as many carrots as weeds."

"I'm missing them something awful. I wish..."

"You're healing—concentrate on that. It's all you can do right now, and the nurse says you'll be able to come home soon."

"She does? Did she define *soon*?"

"No, but she also told me the doctors say it's a miracle you survived that fall. Should've broken your neck, not to mention your back. I have to ask, but I wonder about it all the time. Do you remember what happened?"

Kathryn shook her head. "Not much. Well, sometimes I think I do, but then ..."

Gabby's tone turned even more serious. "Darlene swears she saw a stranger in the church. A man. Did you see him?"

"Yes, but only after I fell. I remember his clothing and his smell. That's about all."

"Did he come close to you?"

"Yes, but I can't remember what he said."

"He actually spoke to you?"

"I'm pretty sure he did, after I fell. But I was in such a state. Doc Randall had told me not to move a muscle, and I didn't want to upset Darlene more than she already was."

"For a long time, she couldn't talk about it without crying."

"The best of friends—she's definitely a true heart."

A nurse brought lunch. "Look at this, dearie. You've finally graduated to toast with your broth. I bet you'll never drink from a straw again once you leave here."

Abby helped cut the toast into small pieces that Kathryn dipped before she ate. Still, chewing challenged her.

"Seems so strange for you to fall like that, Mom. You've always been so agile, and heights have never bothered you."

"I know—that troubles me, too. From now on, I might have to ask you to help me wash the high windows."

"Yeah." Gabby dabbed crumbs from her chin. "But by the time Dad and Ander come home, you'll be all..." She searched for suitable words, so Kathryn finished for her.

"Beautiful again."

After Gabby left, Kathryn carefully walked into the bathroom and stood before the mirror. All in all, the surgeon did pretty well sewing up her face. Sure, a few scars zigzagged here and there, but considering she'd come through the war with nary a mark to show for it, how could she complain? A dizzy spell threatened her, so she struggled back to bed. At least now, sleep came when she wanted it to.

~

Petra halted ahead of Domingo on the path and cocked his head to listen.

"They said to stick to the river, but we're not about to run into that rifle fire up ahead. What if we angle toward that steeple barely showing through the trees? There's bound to be a road leading from that village to Saint Julien."

"I believe that's Saint-Mondane, and you're right. There has to be a back way."

Panting over his open canteen, Petra slanted his head. "Those shots ... perhaps someone alerted the Gestapo about us, but two other wanderers crossed their path. Would you call that fortune or misfortune?"

"You wish someone else to die in our place?"

"Not really. We have earned a long rest, carting this heavy burden so far." Petra's face cracked into a smile, and Domingo's tension released a bit.

"No rest for us. We still have an hour, maybe two, ahead." He tamped down his anxious thoughts. Of course they would get the gold there in time.

But an agitating niggle taunted his nerves, like a fish working at tempting bait. Ever since he'd led Katarin to Albi, his missions kept changing in the middle.

That night when he and Petra first left Gabaudet, the same thing happened, so he ought not be surprised at the sudden appearance of the gold and its exhausted carriers, just when he had begun to look forward to shouldering a bazooka or taking down the guards.

Petra wiped his mouth, shoved his canteen into his jacket, and shot off toward the steeple. Domingo pulled his mind back from their original bridge-blowing mission to the task at hand.

Before he and Petra left, he'd handed half of his weapons to the strangers. Now, he felt almost naked with only one knife rubbing against his ankle. A wry thought made him grin as he raced up an incline along a gurgling stream. From there, they wound around a twisted cliff side above the Dordogne.

What if Père Gaspard prayed he would be spared more killing before the war ended? Quite likely, since he'd entered into Domingo's misery so fully after Sancha's death. He wouldn't be surprised if Père's prayers had a hand in diverting his missions, but he would never know for sure.

In spite of his soaked shirt, a shiver traced Domingo's spine. Sometimes the ancient faith of his fathers seemed just that, ancient. Their trust in the Almighty had flowered in different times, long ago and far away. And yet, they'd faced calamities and dire adversity.

But they remained steadfast in the Basque ways, especially their faith. What would life mean without that steady foundation? A vast emptiness enveloped Domingo at the thought.

Lately, something else troubled him. Last night, a wayfarer spread word of partisans torturing some captured Nazis. The victims weren't even fighting men, but office workers who had never laid a hand on a French citizen.

He'd heard of the Gestapo pulling out fingers and toenails, burning agents with smoking cigarettes, and the like. But this ... Even as he loped behind Petra, he tried in vain to blot out the reported scene, yet couldn't stop imagining being stripped naked, digging his own grave, and being thrown into it before succumbing to a gunshot.

Père must be aware of these actions, yet he continued to do everything in his power for *la Résistance*. Did Katarin know about such things? She entered his mind naturally, not that she ever left for long. *Kathryn Isaacs.* Her name held a musical lilt, foreign and invigorating. The Basque version rang stronger to him—Katarin— but also softer to the ear.

The thought of her ought to keep him positive, for the presence of agents from England here in this isolated territory, and now so many Americans, too, signified hope. But for Domingo, that hope warred with fear for her safety. At Gestapo headquarters in Lyon, he'd heard, that mad butcher, Klaus Barbie, tortured women and men alike.

What if the vans detected Katarin's transmissions and she were captured? Unbearable helplessness washed over Domingo at the idea, for what could he do to rescue her? About as much as he could to find and help his own family.

A projecting tree root returned him to the moment. He stumbled forward and barely caught himself before crashing into Petra. The packet of gold, besides being heavy, prevented any air from reaching his back, and the straps rubbed through his shirt.

Petra made a sharp right turn down a path skirting Saint-Mondane. Normal middle-of-the-day noises carried from the village, and cooking smells stirred rumblings in Domingo's stomach. They had last eaten early this morning, when one of their team fried a vast amount of fish he caught during the night.

"By natural means?" The fisherman kept silent at Petra's question. Obviously, he'd employed a grenade, Domingo and Petra agreed. So unfair to the fish, but coupled with hard bread, they tasted wonderful.

Now, hunger roared through him like fire, but there would be no stopping, not until they made their delivery. Domingo rehearsed the instructions. *Find the library. Go around the back and wait for a lorry with a female driver.*

Katarin—there she was again—dealt with similar instructions all the time. That day when she received a message lacking the exact word proving the sender's authenticity, she figured it out right away. Had that man been Gestapo? What if she had fallen for his ruse?

He felt privileged that she'd told him about her wild past two years. From Amerika to London, losing her pilot husband, becoming an agent, training, dropping into France in December, climbing to Le Chambon-sur-Lignon, transferring to Clermont-Ferrand, and then to the parachute drop where they met again.

The list stretched on, and she endured all these changes in a strange country. How could he complain about his own reversals?

Determined to rein in his wayward thoughts, Domingo shifted his pack and scurried after Petra. An hour later, with another steeple in sight, his shoulders cried for relief, and his stomach ground inside him. Petra stopped at the village outskirts, where a plaque proclaimed they'd reached their destination at last.

"The library should be at the center of town, don't you think?"

A nod was all Domingo could manage. He wiped away sweat that threatened his eyes.

"Do you want to stay here with the gold or check on the lorry?"

"Stay. Bring food."

Petra's wide grin showed a gap where he lost a tooth since he and Domingo last traveled together. "I'll see what I can do."

They paced from the path a good distance, found a rock that stuck out like a nose, and stashed their packs under it. Domingo sank beside them to keep watch.

Petra shook his shoulders loose. "Do I look like a hapless traveler passing through town for not much reason at all?"

"I would say so, except for your drenched back."

Someone raised a second-floor window in the nearest house, so they ducked farther back into the foliage. Maybe they were being watched.

"Get going. I'm ready to pounce on any food that comes near, rats included."

"Don't speak too quickly. They say they grow larger than cats in Marseilles."

Petra left, and Domingo positioned himself on the earth, using the packs to rub his sore shoulders. His gut caroused again, so he took out his canteen, but seconds later, a violent cramp in his leg muscle jolted him upright.

About the same time, a lorry turned down the road. He squinted as the driver maneuvered a curve. A woman, he was almost sure, though a beret hid her hair. In a village this small, he would wager that lorry was the gold's destination. He pressed his palm against the painful area in his calf.

Up to this point, he had no desire to see the treasure he and Petra carried, but now, with an afternoon breeze stirring the treetops and time to pass, the urge struck him. What did gold bars look like, anyway?

He shook out his calf and paced until the discomfort subsided. Then he eased onto the pine needle carpet again. As he leaned into the tree and found the leather latches on his pack, a criminal sensation enveloped him.

But why shouldn't he at least view the contents? He glanced around, but saw nothing and heard only birdsong and animal chatter.

A lazy June afternoon with no one in sight, yet Gestapo agents might emerge at any minute. If they did, what recourse would he have?

His knife still awaited use. And he forgot to leave something else with his bridge-blowing friends—the grenades. They rubbed against his ribs from the inside pocket of his vest. More perspiration broke out on his forehead. Without even realizing it, he'd trekked all this way with explosives a centimeter from his heart.

That discovery settled his quandary—if caught, he'd blow the Gestapo up, and himself, too, rather than be taken alive. He touched his pack. How many lives would this cache save?

Again, the urge to see the gold overwhelmed him. He lifted a latch, checked his environs again, and lifted the other. Only a slim, shiny surface showed, but his fingers told him more. Smooth and cool. Heavy, he already knew. But how heavy? He picked up the top bar and guessed—about twelve kilos, maybe a bit more.

Compared to the hay bales he hefted since his youth, or a swine fattened for market, or a pregnant ewe that slipped into a crevice, each bar weighed nothing. But all totaled, how many pigs or ewes or bales had he carried along the Dordogne in these three gold bars?

The bushes moved, and he slapped the latches shut. Instinct sent his fingers to his inner jacket pocket. *Grasp the grenade, position your fingers to pull…*

But Petra's grimy hand, crawling with a forest of black hair, passed through the branches like a white flag.

"The lorry just parked."

"Brown, with an olive canvas?"

"You saw it go by?"

"Just after you left. How far away is the library?"

"Not so far."

"But we eat first?"

Petra tossed him a crusty loaf of bread and set another packet on the ground. Then he pulled a long smoked sausage from his knapsack. Another, and several more.

"Only the best for my partner."

"Where did you…?"

"Let's say I requisitioned this well-deserved meal in the name of the French Forces of the Interior, compliments of a local villager. You know what they call it now? The Fee Fee."

Domingo bit into a sausage. "Whatever they call us is all right with me. He gave it to you without argument?"

Petra sat down cross-legged. "Try to imagine this scene: the local barber out in the street, shaving the heads of collaborator women while other men hit them. In that sea of flesh and hair and blood, all eyes naturally turned from me to the main attraction. Maybe some of those women really have slept with the enemy, but I wonder.

"Anyway, no one even noticed my requisition." He shook his head and sat down. "'La coiffure de '44', they call it." He stuffed half of a sausage into his mouth, ending the conversation.

Thinking of those women, Domingo's wild appetite waned. He'd heard partisans call such women *collabos horizontals*, for giving comfort to the enemy. The idea disgusted him, but so did visualizing them dragged naked into public squares and shaved.

What if his sister used her own body to bargain for *Maman* and Gabirel's lives? People might misunderstand her action, but what justice would lie in condemning her? *Find the mercy in every situation* ... straight from Père's mouth. The trouble was, no one took time for mercy these days.

"Petra, did your Aitaita tell you the devil lives in those deep caverns we passed yesterday?"

"Of course. They formed when he dug his heel in and tempted Saint Martin near Padirac."

"Do you think it is so?"

Petra wiped grease from his mouth. "No, that's only a legend, a child's tale. I'd say the devil dwells up here among us. He came with the Huns when they invaded. He lives in grenades and cannons and tanks."

~

Behind a mass of clouds arranged across the sky like clumps of clotted cream, the sun stayed hidden. At fresh bad news from a stranger, Père Gaspard's shoulders shrank even more. Next to him, the traveler pursed his lips at Kate's question: "What do you mean, the Gestapo took them away?"

She grabbed Père's sleeve to pull him closer, as if closeness might protect them from the details. The bedraggled fellow had overtaken them a few kilometers from their destination. Now, he worked his upper lip with his teeth. A young man, but his thinness and pallor gave the aura of one far older.

"I do not wish to dishearten you, yet I'm sure I met the people you describe, an old woman and her son. The boy was a few years younger than me, Ibarra by name. Yes, I saw them near Figeac, in the countryside. We stood in line at the back of a lorry."

Père Gaspard's voice turned sharp. "How do you know that name Ibarra?"

The young man looked off into the brush. "The soldiers recorded all of our names, sir. I heard them, one by one. The boy was Gabirel, the woman ... forgive me, I cannot remember."

"Did this happen before our *Maquisards* cut the railroad line to Montauban?" Père Gaspard strained forward, even more agitated than when he'd returned from Terrou. Watching him, the base of Kate's stomach formed a hard knot.

"Before. I swear it. In Figeac, everyone but me boarded the train, two carloads full, bound for Montauban."

"And those from Terrou?"

"I know nothing of them. I am sorry. I only passed through the countryside at the wrong time. Otherwise, I would never have entered that line myself. One minute, I sneaked through a barn south of Figeac, where a mama goat bleated for her kids, and the next minute, a German soldier blocked my way."

Père jerked his head at Kate's sharp intake of breath. South of Figeac—did he mean the baby goats that romped in the meadow with her a few weeks ago?

"You say you escaped at the Figeac station?"

"*Oui.* A woman holding a baby started screaming. She fell to the earth and others surrounded her. I was last in line, so when the officers ran to her, I saw an opportunity to slip away. At least they never discovered my mission."

"And you carry word northward for whom?"

"For the camp near Argentat. Would that I had not heard you ask about that name, Ibarra, for now evil tidings have found you."

Père Gaspard clasped the young man's shoulder. "The fault lies not with you, son."

"A coincidence. A bad coincidence."

The priest's eyes sparked. Kate knew what he was thinking—no coincidences exist.

"We have longed for word of the Ibarras, and you were sent to tell us. Even though the news causes pain, we thank you."

He reached into his pack and handed over some bread. "Be on your way again, and may God speed your feet to Argentat. Remember, the messenger sometimes suffers for the message he bears."

The courier bowed and took off as though a hoard of devils chased him. Kate and Père watched his feet puff dust from the roadbed until his form faded.

Then the life left Père Gaspard's face. "*Mon Dieu.* How can this be, Madame Ibarra thrown into a lorry and taken to Montauban?" He hung his head. "How can this be? They have taken her and Gabirel to Germany."

Deportation. Related words swamped Kate. *Interrogation. Torture. Death camps.* But nothing could be worse than Domingo's mother being treated this way. Simply being uprooted would destroy her. Departing her valley, this land of her birth, and in the back of a lorry, handled like an object of disgust. Worse, she surely observed the look in her youngest son's eyes as he stood by, helpless.

A wave of that helplessness enveloped Kate, but she brought herself back to Père Gaspard, still literally shrinking before her eyes. She had no language for what she witnessed as the news settled in. For a moment, a great darkness threatened her mind, but then she remembered something Mother Hélène said just before they parted.

You may serve as Père Gaspard's confessor … Hot tears scathed the backs of Kate's eyelids. Some confessor she would make. If Père uttered one more word, she would collapse, too.

The sun's rays peeked out from behind the clouds, but gloom hovered around them like dense fog. Had this terrible report reached

Domingo yet? Wherever he traveled, Kate sent him strength. Even as she did, she imagined him following a rail line all the way to Germany after the war.

If he thought he could somehow find his family, nothing would stop him. As she considered his mind working, a longing as sharp and defined as the gorges in the Causse de Gramat enveloped her.

With all her heart, she wanted to be there when he found out, to hold and comfort him as he had comforted her at Monsieur le Blanc's passing. The intense physical desire she'd experienced the night Domingo left burgeoned into something broader and stronger. She desired not only to share his loss. She wanted to be part of his life, broken or whole.

TWENTY-ONE

Petra raised the canvas, hoisted his bag into the lorry with a grunt and stepped aside. Domingo unleashed his straps and just like that, transferred his ponderous burden to the custody of some unknown person inside the lorry. The dim interior shaded the recipient's features, so he and Petra would never know who'd received the heist.

Arms light with the sudden weight reduction, Domingo pondered. Would it feel like this if he could let go of all his burdens? Maybe sincere prayer did that for Père Gaspard.

But he had no time to consider the question, for Petra already slunk out of sight into the cover of a low-hanging grove. Half an hour later, they paused on a trail leading northeast along the Dordogne. Domingo assumed they would head back to the Lot encampment, but Petra, as always, thought faster, deeper.

On a curve in the path, he halted to point out a crossroads visible below their position, where the trail widened into a road. "See how those two trails meet ours down there?"

Domingo craned his neck. Petra stood as still as a gnarled gneiss outcropping, waiting. Domingo did the same, but his instincts told him little, only the approximate direction to their original encampment, as well as the certain knowledge that the river would keep turning on itself, back and forth, making thumbs and fingers all the way to Souillac, as rivers often did.

But Petra saw more, or heard more. How to describe the unique skill this man possessed for searching things out and making sense of them? Over countless trails and missions, its reality became clear.

Petra could make decisions in a flash, but only because of what he ascertained before the fact.

While Domingo merely reacted to scanty details, something more refined took place between his comrade's heart and mind. With his head twisted toward Domingo, Petra's hand dropped from his pack strap. He held his tongue a minute longer, and then instead of sharing his thoughts, asked a question.

"What do you think? Should we turn south here, toward the encampment, or continue a little farther along the river?"

He deserved more than a shrug, so Domingo conjured a question. "What do you sense about this place?"

"The breeze tells me that stretch ahead swims with activity. Most likely the local partisans have set up ambushes for any Wehrmacht units passing this way. Who knows? Maybe they need our services here to fell foot soldiers more than back in the Ségala."

"Maybe." Domingo had no doubt they would find out.

But Petra waited longer, so Domingo added more. "Perhaps we could go a distance along the river. There's bound to be another road heading south not much farther along." After all their travels together, he could have voiced Petra's reply.

"A good idea. As strangers here, how can we know without checking? You have spoken well."

Domingo jogged along behind his leader, for Petra had become exactly that. Such a guide orchestrated options and set up alternatives. In this way, he made his followers feel they chose the way themselves.

After another kilometer, Petra paused again, and Domingo drew up beside him. Petra barely whispered. "Hear them?"

Domingo concentrated and finally heard—or sensed—the shuffle of feet against rocky path. He no longer analyzed how Petra heard the sound or felt the vibration when they were still moving down the trail.

But his gift amounted to more than physical senses. He possessed a knowing beyond Domingo's comprehension—God's gift. He might have coveted Petra's ability, but only gave thanks to be reunited with this man endowed with such invaluable intuition.

While they waited, the murmur strengthened until Domingo

realized more than one or two men approached. Petra squatted and shifted downward, ear to the earth. Then he held up four fingers.

Domingo would have bet a bar of gold they would soon see four men hiking along the trail, and they did. The group's forward man pulled back when he saw them, but Petra held out his hand in a peaceful palms-up.

The strangers smelled of musty sod and mulch, river water and perspiration. One of them smoked a handmade cigarette, a jaunty railroader's cap tipped over his forehead.

The leader took the initiative. "You need an assignment?"

Yes, they awaited another mission. Why not here? Why not now?

"*Oui.*" In Petra's simple reply, a surge of power engulfed Domingo in spite of the ache in his muscles, the heat, his tiredness, and his anxiety about *Maman*, Gabirel, and Père Gaspard's people. It even surpassed his newfound realizations concerning Kate, and he knew he could perform whatever these partisans required of him.

"We keep watch between here and Souillac, and onward to Bretenoux. There are only two big bridges here, but we have orders to kill any *feldgraus* that approach."

"You have seen many?"

"One or two have found their graves in the ravines." The man jerked his head toward the waterway on the other side of the path. "We must not let them get through, but we need more men. Many of our best have gone north to join the ambushes all the way across Correze. Our weakest place, the other side of Souillac, cries for more watchers."

With a look, Petra sought and received Domingo's silent assent. "We'll be your watchers. Tell us exactly where to go."

~

Little by little, Kathryn sensed the rhythm of her normal stride return. Back and forth to the far end of the hallway, four times a day, walking all by herself. Back in her room, she collapsed in her chair and stared out the window at a concrete parking lot.

On the way to her room, she always paused at the nurses' station, where the calendar contained so many scrawls and notes that, without her glasses, Kathryn couldn't make out the date. Surely she'd known that fact earlier in the day, but now, it escaped her.

"Why did I leave my glasses back in my room?" Her question reached no one, so she kept moving toward her destination.

Back in her hospital room, a pleasant surprise waited. "I've been watching you walk—almost normal, dearie."

From her chair next to the door, Kate still panted, but Darlene's contagious cheer called up a smile.

"So, how's our church cleaning lady doing today? Your color looks a lot better. Here, I brought you something to read." The newspaper headline immediately piqued Kathryn's interest, as well as answering her question about the date.

ANNUAL RODEO JUST ONE MONTH AWAY

"Why, I've slept away half the summer!"

"Honestly, hon, I wondered if you'd ever wake up. But here you are, rarin' to go." If Darlene could be accused of anything, it would be eternal optimism. "And I'll tell you one thing, I'll be glad to hand the cleaning job back over to you. People have no idea how many volunteer hours you spend over there. We had an ice cream social last Sunday, and you wouldn't believe..."

Oh yes, the annual social—so she'd missed that. First time in years her famous chocolate cake had been absent from the dessert pickings.

A man in a white doctor's coat crossed the threshold. "Mrs. Ibarra? We have a test to run on you. You've done so well here that you're being considered as a member of a medical experiment on recovery from head injuries."

"What...? I don't want to..."

"Come with me, ma'am. Others will benefit greatly from your cooperation. It won't take long at all." He placed his hand on Kathryn's wrist, but Darlene spoke up.

"Didn't you hear her say no?" Her spunk touched a deep chord in Kathryn, who took it from there.

"No one's spoken to me about any experimental group. Did my doctor send you?"

"Why, yes. He said you'd be glad to take part."

Darlene raised her right eyebrow and squinted, so Kathryn knew she wasn't the only one with doubts.

"Well, I'll think on it, but you'd better bring me something in writing first. I like to know what I'm getting into."

He backed away, and as he did, Kathryn noticed his shoes. Somehow, they looked familiar. A shadow passed over her spirit as Darlene started to chat again.

"The things these hospitals do these days ... why, I heard the Mayo Clinic in Minnesota runs groups like that all the time. Ralph's cousin's mother went to one last winter. Guess they studied how people sleep or something." She chuckled. "That'd be a good one for you, eh?"

"Not funny, Dar." Kathryn bit her lip. Something about that stranger ruffled her nerves. Then, as Darlene turned to cheery news about local goings on and Mara getting ready for the rodeo, a puzzle piece clicked into place.

Those shoes went with a pair of brown tweed pants—the pants that stranger wore the day she'd fallen in the church. A shiver ran across her shoulders.

"Are you cold? I can shut the window ..."

Kathryn held up her hand. "No, it's just—did that guy look familiar to you, Darlene?"

"I don't think so. Have you seen him before?"

"Maybe." Darlene chatted on, but Kathryn's thoughts swirled.

She'd been too busy relearning everyday tasks to give much thought to her fall. Besides, the memory of her infamous accident haunted her.

How could she possibly have been so clumsy? In a way, she dreaded going back home, and out in public. Surely people in the community had been wondering the same thing.

"So, I told Mara that maybe ... maaaaybe Grandma would be able to watch her perform. Have they said anything about you coming home yet?"

"Hum? Sorry, what did you say?"

"Nothing important. I only asked about you coming home, the subject you've been talking about ever since you woke up."

"Oh, yes. Maybe in a week or so, they say. Will you be able to come and get me, Darlene? Gabby would, she said, but she's already missed so many days of work, I hate to ask her."

"You bet, my friend. Everyone's dying to see you again."

Sudden embarrassment caught Kathryn in a vicegrip. "I... I can't believe I've created so much trouble for everybody. You've already done so much for me--for my family."

"As you would have for me if the tables had been turned. Why, when I think how you helped me out that time Antonio broke his leg...what would we have done without you?"

"Antonio broke his leg?"

"Of course he did. Take a minute to think, and it'll come back to you. Picture me fifteen years younger, with three little ones, and a very icy winter..."

"Oh, yes, now I remember. He slipped unloading wood, and Gabby happened by to play with...what was that little girl's name?"

"Come on, now. Our children practically grew up in your house, Kathryn. What was her name?"

"Let...Lettie?"

"Of course! And I was busy inside—what was I doing?"

"You were...someone had the flu, and the doctor came..."

Darlene ran over and gave Kathryn a hug. "See? Everything you've ever known is all still in that noggin of yours—we just need to coax it out. Now, who had the flu? Who were we worried about?"

"Antonio's...his mother?"

"Absolutely. Yup, we just need to coax all of those memories out of your head, and I'm just the person to do it."

"You remind me of somebody, Kathryn."

"Someone you knew a long time ago, way back when you were little girls?"

"That's right."

"Somebody you write to every week—somebody over in England?"

"Yes."

"But she grew up in Iowa with you, right?"

"Yes—oh, how could I ever forget her name?"

"I'll give you a clue. Her name starts with an *A. A d...*"

"Oh, for heaven's sake. Addie. Kathryn dropped her head. Darlene,

I don't understand my brain. The things I know best seem the hardest."

"Well, it's going to take an awful lot of patience."

"Which I have in spades, my friend."

TWENTY-TWO

Two shabby maquisards jumped out of a lorry that screeched up to one of the portals. Not ten feet away from Père and Kate, they flipped up the canvas. Moans came from inside as the men reached in for wooden gurney poles. Blood oozed onto stained canvas as a wounded man cried out and rolled to the side, his trousers splotched dark red from knee to hip.

"Hurry. This other one has already lost consciousness." The gruff order from inside the lorry sped the stretcher-bearers through a heavy side door that opened from the inside as if by magic.

"So, Saint Pierre's has transformed into a hospital, too, a refuge. They can scarcely look up, but help awaits them here." He turned to Kate. "Just as our help awaits in the triumph of the Cross."

The men returned for the victim inside the lorry, and Père Gaspard took a step away. "Wait here. I'll be back soon."

The chiseled artwork far above Kate, still intact after all these centuries, held her attention. What led the designer to choose the second coming rather than the last judgment? And why had the judgment been the common choice back then?

The more she craned her neck, the more she saw hope in the midst of earth's trials, and strength in seeming defeat. She hadn't given much thought to the second coming, but Père certainly had. She'd have to quiz him some more.

Words Kate had heard in tiny Emmanuel, Aunt Alvina's country church, wafted through her mind—*Wonderful Counselor, Mighty God, Everlasting Father, Prince of Peace.*

Maybe this wonderful counselor with His arms outstretched

in stone, had soothed the pain she'd caused Aunt Alvina. Surely her aunt had turned to Him for comfort. And what if right now, Aunt Alvina watched her from eternity with compassion instead of condemnation?

So focused on her training and secretly nursing her own losses, Kate had missed the annual proclamation of Christ's names last Christmas. She regretted that now. *Prince of Peace*—that sounded so ironic in these present circumstances. *Mighty God*—some would find the concept laughable now, too, for where was divine protection for all the innocent people of the world when they needed it?

Yet the suffering captured in the tymphanum juxtaposed other-worldly power with life's most impossible situation—death. If death claimed even God's Son, what hope remained? But the crucifixion signified a great, eternal power beyond any present distress.

And Père believed that humans could claim that strength. Claim forgiveness. Kate hugged herself. She needed it—that was certain. But how could she forgive herself? That would mean putting the past to rest, but the memories resurfaced to taunt her just when she most needed to sleep.

By the time Père hurried out with a brown-robed brother, hope harnessed Kate's imagination. In spite of her rashness and selfish actions, maybe Aunt Alvina *could* forgive her. Maybe she did long ago, and immersed in heaven's mercy, cheered her on now without holding a grudge.

And when the time came for Domingo to hear the frightful news about Gabirel and his mother, perhaps this same mercy would somehow surround him. He mentioned his grandfather's presence being so real to him, even though years had passed since his death. Maybe now, *Maman* also hovered near him in his distress.

So much we cannot know—so much mystery unleashed by the war. Kate studied the lorry, another vehicle seemingly unfit for the road, yet usable. She longed to be useful to Domingo, too, if only to shoulder a portion of his grief. Even thinking of that produced a torrent of heaviness that tightened her throat.

Père unlatched the cart's compartment and someone else hefted and unloaded her transmitter. She followed them along the side of the church and through a different door, away from the one used by the stretcher-bearers.

Then Père fell back with her. "They offer us temporary shelter here, but we must climb to the camp tomorrow. You see, this place welcomes both *Résistance* and Nazi wounded. You can be sure of secure transmitting only until morning."

"With Germans in the church?"

"Stranger things have happened—safety right under their noses. From what I can see, only the severely injured end up here. Even if they had the strength to find you out, they would have no way to contact their units."

As usual, Père was right. Besides, what choice did she have but to trust? He'd never led her into danger yet. A fresh quietness filled Kate as she followed a robed man through a maze down some steep stairs and into a locked basement.

All of a sudden, arrangements for a single night sufficed. She settled into a dank, cramped space far from where Père tended to the wounded. Far from the Nazis.

~

Those silly shoes nagged at Kathryn, along with the tweed. The fabric had a few yellow specks mottled into brown, black, and white, not something you'd normally see around here. It was almost as if someone dressed for thirty years ago magically found his way into her world.

She slipped her dress over her head, anticipating Darlene's arrival. In a couple of hours, she'd finally get home. Nothing ever sounded so wonderful. Small joys enticed her—she visualized walking through the simple bungalow, touching her countertop, the cherry wood doorframes, her yellow gingham curtains.

The newspaper Darlene brought her last week lay folded open to Mara's name in the rodeo listings. Barrel racing, at her age? Well, Mara certainly lacked nothing in the risk-taking department. Hadn't she balanced on the garage roof last fall? Part monkey, everyone said. Just like Gabby.

And just like you, Agent Merce. Remember parachuting out of that

Lysander? You embraced the flowing air, the night sky, and yes—the danger.

Kathryn shook away the memory. Some things you did just once, not even understanding your choice. If you survived, you blocked the memory of those decisions out of your mind. If you could, that is. She picked up the newspaper—such a joy to be able to read without dizziness overwhelming her. The rodeo was still three weeks away—she couldn't wait to cheer for Mara and capture the experience with her camera.

One of her regular nurses came in. "You're all checked out, Kathryn, so you can go to the exit down the hall to the left. That's probably closer to Darlene's car." She picked up the suitcase, set it down again, and enfolded Kathryn in an unexpected solid hug.

"You even know her name."

"Of course I do. She must've visited you fifteen times—such a loyal friend. I'm going to miss you, Kathryn—wish you lived closer to Boise so we could have lunch together once in a while. I'm so proud of how hard you've worked to get better. You had quite the challenge, but your perseverance has paid off. You're almost like new."

"Well, you did a lot of work, too, Sarah."

Sarah waved her hand in the air. "It's my job—it's what I do."

"But you do it with style. Thanks for all the extra time you spent listening to my woes."

Sarah stripped the bed. "You could never whine, dearie. You're a trooper *par excellence.*" She carried out Kathryn's breakfast tray and paused at the threshold. "I do hope you'll stop in to say hello if you ever come down to Boise."

Through the window, Kathryn spied an unfamiliar car pulling up, and for some reason, her heart skipped a beat. "Come on, old girl, only a few minutes, and you'll be out of here."

Seemed like forever since she'd left home to clean the church that day in May. She picked up her suitcase and paused a moment to look back. Funny—even a hospital room could start to feel like home.

Halfway down the hall, a strong odor suddenly caught her attention, so she twisted to see behind her. A man maintained his distance, but she still identified his distinct tobacco smell. Tweed pants, hazel eyes—a slight fellow with weathered skin. She shrank back against the wall.

He caught up with her, planted his feet and squared his shoulders. "We need you, Agent Merce."

A shiver raged through Kathryn. She hadn't heard her code name for thirty years, and thought she never would again. The intruder studied her as though weighing his words.

"We believe we've found one of the henchman of the Butcher of Lyon, but we need a witness. Did you ever see him?"

A virulent mix of emotions inundated Kathryn. She grabbed the nearest windowsill for support. The man's hazel eyes never left her, and she felt sure he never deviated from his goal.

Her only hope was to close her eyes. For a moment, she considered lying, because the sensation at the pit of her stomach assured her that if she told the truth, her life would alter again. Hadn't she experienced enough of that already?

~

As Petra guzzled water from his canteen, Domingo leaned against a tree, sipping a little at a time. After felling two Germans who stumbled into their path, they rested a while, each in their own world. A wisp of humor came to Domingo—Père Gaspard must have faltered in his prayers.

Blue sky with a slight hot wind—this was the kind of day for weeding a field or coaxing sheep into the shade. Domingo attempted to suppress the vivid image of the enemy he'd just sent from this world. But Petra, always focused, already contemplated their next move.

"What do you think?"

"The weight of that gold we carried hurt my brain. I've forgotten how to think."

"Forgotten, eh? So, you no longer think about your family?"

Fire raged in Domingo's chest. He jerked his head away.

"Of course your answer is no. Your brother and your *Maman* weigh on my mind, too. Since we passed Souillac, we're nearer to the Correze camp. What if we seek information there? Perhaps word about Figeac has reached them."

"Word about one old woman and a boy unrelated to anyone in the camp?"

"With so many people on the move, peculiar things happen, Domingo. How will we know unless we ask?"

Domingo kicked at a stone. This time, Petra's instinct must have failed him. The news he craved about his family would come, perhaps, but in its time, and surely not so easily.

But Petra persevered. "Friend, listen to me. Finding your answers, in my opinion, has become as urgent as our assignment."

"But we cannot leave our post. We signed on to this task."

Petra's eyes glimmered. "One of us could leave. I don't recall swearing an oath that we would both stay here every minute. And with their final breaths, those soldiers we killed told me what I wanted to know."

"They did?" Domingo recalled one set of hazel eyes, one blue, young men caught unawares and fearing for their lives. What could Petra have learned from their chaotic garble?

"The taller one said to the other, 'Don't let them know we're trailing the rest of the unit.' It seems we caught the last two of the bunch, so I can handle things here until you return."

Domingo's sigh met an increasing wind. "*Merci*, brother. Your idea makes sense, but for now, I have given up on finding answers."

Petra's scowl made clear that giving up" had no place in his vocabulary. His eyes flashed. But for Domingo, letting go of his expectations seemed logical, even desirable, under the circumstances. A grander scheme calling for self-sacrifice played out around them, and that meant putting his search on hold—it also distracted him from his growing sense of helplessness.

Once again, Petra surprised him. "I understand. But when we met a few days ago, you prayed for guidance. I still do ... for our missions, and for information about your family. In finding our way through this puzzling time, we must act on our wits, and the idea of going to the camp has haunted me since yesterday."

A bird intent on its destination swooped low, and Domingo swallowed down his trepidation. From the riverbank, a frog croaked, probably aroused from slumber when they dragged the Germans into the brush. The distasteful recollection of the heavy *thunk* when his victim collapsed on the earth sent a shudder through Domingo. A well-muscled fellow, he might have put up quite a struggle, but with Petra's help, one swift blow behind his ear sufficed.

The deed complete, Petra instructed, "Go watch the path while I hide them." When Domingo returned, all sign of the bodies had vanished. They scraped twigs and branches over the area until only a placid country scene remained.

But now, a sinking sensation overcame Domingo. How could he doubt Petra's instincts, when over and over, he had proven his trustworthiness? He knew he should keep his thoughts to himself, yet his argument sat ready, as clear as the sky overhead.

Petra's insistence forced him to face a truth that he would rather not know. Not yet. He'd been considering how people vanished in this war, never to be seen or heard from again. In some ways, not knowing his family's fate might be easier.

But faithful Petra squatted there, waiting. His deep slow breathing told Domingo his patience would prevail. Why wait? He might as well let loose.

"Something tells me they are gone."

"Gone? What do you mean?"

Domingo squeezed his eyes shut. What *did* he mean?

He toyed with the word that drenched him with fear. *Mort.* Dead. The concept came to him so often in recent days, it had ceased to startle him. He turned its brevity over in his mind, like its meaning. Surely, *Maman* had perished by now.

Maybe Gabirel still survived in some German work camp, but Domingo could not imagine the same for her. True, Katarin praised *Maman's* courageous will in the face of that Gestapo visit, but what could she do now?

Gestapo swine in the Ibarra barn—a sick taste washed his throat as a gust assailed them. What had they come to? Yes, *Maman* rose to that challenge, but this ... being taken far from their home ... Though he struggled against it, an insistent inner nudge declared that her time on earth had ended.

Did Petra agree? He hadn't said, but only made clear his belief that knowing one way or the other would be better than this uncertainty.

Silence grew between him and Petra like a swarm of gnats. Petra worked his jaw and stared off into the woods. Sudden clouds gathered, accompanied by a sinister rumble in the heavens. They drew their tarps from their bags and Petra came so near Domingo smelled his trail scent and noted the intense light in his eyes.

"Will you stay here or go?" His set chin told Domingo all he needed to know. If he chose to stay, Petra would proceed to the Resistance camp himself and ask after *Maman* and Gabirel.

Arguing would do no good. Stay here or go to the *Résistance* Camp—his choice narrowed like the riverbed a few kilometers back. The billowing dark clouds provided an excuse, but what difference did bad weather make in the midst of tanks and murder and mayhem?

Petra, never fearful, relied on his innate sense that all would be well, even if one of them left. And though Domingo could not imagine it being true, his partner's intuition about finding some information at the camp must be very strong. How could he fight against that?

"I'll go. I like loping along the river."

Petra's shoulders dropped, and his easy humor returned. "Part wolf, eh?"

"No, haven't you heard? They call me *La Foudre.*" Domingo's chortle echoed hollow in his ears, but making a little joke eased his tension. "So you must be *Le Tonnere.*"

Lightning and thunder—as if to mock him, the summer wind turned cool, and a rainstorm slanted down from the southwest, followed by hail clattering like jackboots on cobblestone. Not the time Domingo would have chosen to huddle under a rubber tarp or begin a journey afoot. But as usual, this war offered little choice.

For a moment, he pictured Aitaita, Papa, and Ander, gone on to war long before him. They did what they felt they must. That image strengthened him to muster the heart for this solitary jaunt.

Cramping calf muscles compelled him to rise, and Petra clasped his hand in a steely grip. "We will meet again soon. If you don't return, I will follow you. *Venez avec Dieu.*"

A second later, a gale raged down around them, lashing rain interspersed with stinging needles of sleet. Petra's steady gaze ignited Domingo's confidence. Off into the tempest, and a few feet onto the trail, something about the miserable, freezing downpour exhilarated him. One more force of nature to confront, one more obstacle to overcome.

Icy rain slapped his face, but he merged with the storm and took on the wilderness.

TWENTY-THREE

"Thank heavens that storm settled the dust, but we'll have to watch for mudslides on sodden paths in the morning." A dole-faced partisan addressed Père Gaspard in an anteroom at Saint Pierre's.

"At least the weather will slow down the SS, too."

"Maybe a little, but unfortunately, most of them aren't traveling afoot. We'll have to wait for the wind to dry things out. Be ready to leave about two."

While Père made arrangements for their trek to the camp, Kate continued rolling bandages, an activity that transported her back to Mrs. Tenney's church in London, where she learned the finer points of this task. Mrs. T and her friends made a game of their rolling.

But on her check for messages, a shocking one came through. *Repatriate to London tonight.* She checked again. No, there was no mistaking these orders. Nothing to do but tell Père Gaspard.

Peeking into the makeshift hospital where he sat beside a wounded man, Kate waited to catch his attention. On a cot behind him, a soldier's black Waffen S.S. uniform stood out.

A peculiar mix of odors—blood, perspiration, strong wine, and chloroform—filled the room. Père stood up and passed to the next patient without looking her way. She might as well roll more bandages while she waited. But revulsion struggled with her sense of purpose—some of these rolls might be used for Nazis.

When Père Gaspard found her, he announced, "We're bound for the Promised Land. Are you ready?"

"We'll have to change our password."

"What was it before?"

"Don't you remember?"

His bloodshot eyes went blank. Kate rolled her hand upward and arched her neck until she surveyed the delicate embossed ceiling.

"Ah, yes. *Ascension.* Now what?"

"Canaan."

"Perfect—the promised land. We're promised land people. Like the musketeers of old, all for one, one for all."

Kate checked one more time for information from London. The dank, enclosed space reflected her mood. Go back to England? How could she? Not now, when she finally felt so purposeful. She gave herself a talking-to.

"You signed up for this, and orders are orders." She calculated the coordinates in the next message, perhaps not so far from here. Not impossible—of course, not impossible. Orders could never be impossible.

After tapping out a positive reply, Kate shut down the transmitter and allowed herself a shudder. *Promised land people* ... the term took on fresh meaning. But England surely seemed far from the promised land of her dreams.

She ran her fingers over her radio's smooth wood. Odd how one could become attached to a mechanism like this—this radio had brought her a sense of purposefulness. But once again, the time had come to thrust herself into the unknown.

Heavyhearted, she went to find Père again. "I have something to tell you. I've received orders to return to London."

"When?"

"Tonight." She showed him the directions. "Here's where they'll pick me up."

"Why, I never imagined ..." He studied the logistics. "You're certain?"

"It's not out of the ordinary—agents get called back all the time."

"Hmmm ... So now we must find a guide who can take you to this plateau in time for the flight. If only Domingo were here. Let me see what I can do."

He started off, but turned to ask a favor. "Check again, will you?"

If only ... no time to let her mind wander there. Hadn't Miss G reminded her during her training to replace *if only* with *next time*?

"The first wastes our time in the sea of regret. The second points us to second chances."

Thankful for the small crystal radio set from Mother Hélène, Kate set to work. No new messages.

The next time Père appeared, he brought her some coffee. "Your orders still stand?"

Sudden emotion inundated Kate, and what issued from her mouth was hardly intelligible. But her nod communicated.

"I've found someone, but it'll be a while before he arrives. I have a confession to make. When we left Lot, I could have sought one more location there—maybe I should have, so we might have stayed longer. But *attentisme* has always challenged me."

"What do you mean?"

"Waiting on events. I would far rather solve life's puzzles than wait and watch for something to happen. Waiting for word to come is even worse. In my heart, I know my family hid too well for even me to find them." He sipped his coffee and gave a great sigh.

"Though I believe God watches over them, I chafe at the waiting. There's far too little control in that. Action—even if it's the wrong action—appeals to me too much."

"I'm afraid we're too much alike, Père. My mentor warned me that times of waiting and resting would be worse for me than taking risks. At least when I do something, I feel my life has some meaning."

"Even if you don't particularly like the meaning?"

"You understand me, you really do."

Later, when her pile of bandages filled a heavy hall table, Père sought her again. "Your guide is ready."

"You'll take my radio somewhere safe?"

"Indeed." He drew a deep breath. "I'm going to miss you. I suppose you have no idea if they'll be sending you back?"

"No, but I hope so. If they don't, maybe I can..."

"Come back to *La France* when this is all over, to find your father's birthplace." Tears glinted in his eyes. "If you do, I hope you'll come and find me—do you hear?"

Père handed Kate a provision bag he'd somehow managed to put together, and when he hugged her, her eyes overflowed. But then he pressed her fingers with his. "You'll be all right. This means you've learned so much that those in charge seek your wisdom. Perhaps you'll be treated like royalty." He meant well, but the attempt at humor did nothing to temper Kate's sense of loss.

"Remember in whose name you came here—all will be well."

"But what if I never see you again?"

"All will be well. Rest in this thought."

"But..."

"Shhh, now. I know it in my soul—all *will* be well." He grasped her shoulders. "You've endured difficult changes before—true catastrophes. As He has in the past, so God will continue to be your strength. He knows how to guide you back to us if need be."

His gentleness and the depth of his tone calmed her. "*Oui ... absolument.*" But her heart broke when he dried her tears with his sleeve.

"There now. Off you go, then. Grace lights your path and my prayers travel with you."

The guide, a diminutive fellow with a twinkle in his eye, shouldered his pack. "*Venez avec moi—vite!*"

Come with me—fast. Was there any other way to travel these trails? His voice melded with an inner one that had strengthened Kate more than once.

Along a strenuous ascent, recollections paraded before her. During her childhood, on the Atlantic crossing, while she searched for Alexandre throughout London, when she met Charles and he offered her a job and a place to stay—the list of times she'd been cared for extended on and on.

Grace lights your path... Not once had guidance and protection failed her, although she'd entertained such doubts. Though she longed for a chance to say good-bye to Domingo, serenity filled her as she lifted him and his family to heaven.

Père's prophecy steadied her instinctive wild urge to bolt and run back to him. "All will be well." Strange how such a familiar phrase gained momentum as the words replayed in her mind.

All will be well. Yes, even the frantic fear that she'd never see Domingo again.

All *will* be well. The light in Père's eyes shone again as if he stood before her.

All will *be* well. Suddenly Kate was transported back to high school literature class, with Mrs. Morfordson proclaiming the intention of state of being verbs—"They reveal the very present truth about a situation, class. They show us the way things *are*."

All will be *well*. Step by step, the final portion of the statement resounded, a proclamation that this moment had become acceptable. She could manage whatever lay ahead. She would.

By the time her guide pointed into the distance and cited, "*Seulement trois kilometres, mademoiselle*," Kate's equilibrium returned—the three-kilometer walk would do her good. The dizzy, out-of-control feeling that overcame her when she first read the message from headquarters faded.

Back to London—her next mission, though so sudden and unexpected, beckoned her. What if, on the outside chance, this unexpected interlude meant she would somehow get to see Addie?

~

The C-47 touched down like a jewel riding the darkness to earth. This moonless night, when pilots ought not be flying at all, still saw a successful landing, with the pilot coasting down from about four hundred feet. Flying dark like this, he had to rely totally on his bombardier's navigational skills.

And so did Kate. She gave a sigh when the process worked. These hardy fellows flew ridiculously low over the radar-soaked French mainland. Then, with German flak surrounding the French side of the Channel, they'd quickly ascend to eight thousand feet when they took off again, to avoid the coastal guns.

At the thought of dropping down seven thousand feet again once Channel water appeared below, Kate's stomach churned. But before they continued on to England, the pilot said, they had some more cargo to pick up.

Cargo—that could mean just about anything, but considering the brutal battles underway in Normandy, Kate guessed they would carry wounded Allied soldiers back to London.

As they carried Alexandre from Norway after his first crash. Yes, someone had found him and taken him to a safe house until a guide could lead him to a rendezvous point and eventual transport to London.

Keep your mind on the facts ... she grasped for something to calm her mind. No use dwelling on her hurried leave-taking. Those glints in Père Gaspard's eyes nearly brought her to tears, but before her lay a tough climb, and they had to race.

Better concentrate on the amazing new airplane taking her back to England. From her transmissions, she knew the C-47's first flight had taken place just a few days ago. Americans were involved, and the latest report said no crashes yet—good news.

Once she climbed into her seat, the pilot wasted no time, and his conversation with his mate diverted her attention. Facts and figures—safe territory.

"RAF Witham expects three more new planes just like this one. These babies are a dream—don't you love having the aerodrome above you?"

"Yes, but the shorter tail cone excites me more. Someday, maybe we'll tow a glider across the Channel. Besides, who has time to look up?"

"Well, we'd definitely be in worse shape without Bomber Harris's night raids over Germany. At least he keeps a lot of Luftwaffe pilots busy there."

The engine noise increased after takeoff, so Kate heard only snatches between the pilot and the bombardier. "Hidden flak batteries ... wonder why they named this the Dakota ..."

The ride took Kate back to the Lancaster that brought her here last December. Seemed like far longer than that, but war played games with Father Time. Moments could take on the significance of entire days, and days could swell into months.

Speculating about the future did her no good—would she be sent back to France, or spend the rest of the war in England, perhaps training other agents? That seemed unlikely, since she still felt she had so much to learn. Would she...

No, no. That line of thinking would never do. She closed her eyes and let the roar convey her back to that other flight, far above the Auvergne.

On that gorgeous moonlit December night with stars spangling the sky, the pilot had alerted her when they came close, and her training had come to the fore. Strangely calm, she'd rehearsed her next steps.

Then the metal hatch had scraped open and wind whipped her face. Stars and moon teased her to gawk at their glory, but she'd somehow focused on her instructions.

Remember, the parachute does most of the work, but you can steer a bit by pulling on the canopy's risers and suspension lines.

The pilot called, "Ready?"

She replied in the affirmative, though her whole body trembled. He pushed her out, her static line tightened, and the pilot chute jerked free of her backpack. The inflation *whoosh* brought her breath back, cold and fresh.

Release the main canopy. Extended lines parted the binding at the shock of her weight and cast her to the heavens until the main chute billowed.

Eyes open, chin tucked, knees locked to the rear—so far, so good. Time suspended, melding her body with the night's indigo blanket and creating an odd sense of comfort. Adrift between two different worlds, the ache in Kate's chest from her miscarriage let go momentarily and she declared her new identity to the universe.

"Agent Merce descending."

Months earlier, SOE officers exchanged looks when she requested Code Name *Merci*.

"How about *Merce*? *Résistance* Spaniards and Basques celebrate her festival every year, and like her, you're on a mission to the oppressed."

Bend slightly forward from waist, elbows tight into sides, hands over reserve parachute ends, fingers spread.

With all four risers secured, the canopy came under control, and a vast starlit dome over misty valleys surrounding a plateau welcomed Kate to southern France. Her spine tingled as though she embraced a happy surprise.

Turn into the wind, let go the toggle ... balls of feet, calves, thighs, buttocks, and side of back must touch down in a continuous roll.

"Continuous roll—the story of my life ... if only I could float longer." But the earth loomed closer and closer. Next, silvery grass glistened with dew.

Bawhoosh! The impact burned her calf to the knee. Her chute puffed and fluttered, canopy release assemblies clicked and, jaws clenched against the pain, Kate still carried out her instructions.

Lift latches to free parachute from pack and roll over.

"Please send help." Back on earth again, staring up at the flawless heavens—but she already needed aid. Her nerves grated at this pathetic landing, despite her perfect training performances.

An approaching shadow started her heart knocking against her ribs. One seven-letter word invaded her senses—*Gestapo*. She tried to think what to do next as the shadow bent down. Then, warm breath grazed her ear with a man's whisper.

"Code Name Merce."

A different concern overwhelmed Kate as she realized the hopeless tangle around her ankle. Panic threatened at the sharp sting radiating her calf, but the stranger knew what to do. He loosed the cord and in one silent, efficient movement, balled it with the chute and buried them in the brush.

When he returned, she attempted to stand, but fell against him, so he palpated the throbbing spot and dressed the entire ankle with cool moss. His obsidian eyes under heavy dark brows calmed her as he retied the string and leaned low, waving her onto his back.

Heat flushed her face at causing him trouble, but the guide's unflappable demeanor quieted her. Without hesitation, he shouldered her one hundred and ten pounds, ten more in boots and clothing, plus her pack and the radio.

Rock-hard muscle stabilized her. To the east, snowy Massif Central peaks glinted. This plateau must lead to the Pyrénées foothills in the opposite direction. Even after smoky, chaotic London, Kate felt instantly at home. They might have crossed an Iowa pasture instead of south central France.

You'll drop in south of Vichy, Pétain's occupied capital. There, villages harbor Jews, downed allied pilots, and others of Gestapo interest. Remember, if you are found out, you understand only French.

Perspiration niggled the back of Kate's neck when she remembered another of her instructions. She'd failed to smudge her light hair with mud and change into her milkmaid's garb. But electricity still sizzled up her leg, and her landing trousers kept the blessed coolness in place.

Use your ingenuity. Keep a cool head when you make mistakes.

Ingenuity—she almost chuckled. "The most creative thing I can do is pray. May this man not suffer on my account." Her guide's wool jacket absorbed her prayer.

What seemed like hours passed as he pushed through thick brush, stark branches in winter dress, and prickly broom bushes that snagged at her trousers. Finally, another meadow shimmered before them like spun glass. The guide dropped her radio and pack with a solid *thunk* and eased Kate against something scratchy and dusty, but yielding.

She caught at the stuff with her fingers and sniffed a handful ... hay. The guide hissed a muffled password, rousing a faint response from the dusty mound, as though someone called up from a deep basement.

Satisfied, her guide hoisted her pack and radio into the haystack and with his hand on her forearm, directed her fingers to a warm, chapped hand inside the hay. A moment later, a French phrase dipped in his thick Basque accent brushed her ear.

"*Allez avec Dieu.*" Go with God. The simple phrase had soothed her like a benediction. Then, like a moon-shadow, her deliverer had disappeared.

But not from her heart. Would she ever see her indomitable Basque angel again?

Scrape ... bang. The sounds of men loading the cargo interrupted Kate's reverie.

Nothing to do but wait while they loaded the plane, since the pilot's final words to her echoed stern and clear. "Stay here."

Kate never knew what they loaded, and once they passed through the airspace over the coast and returned to normal flying height, she relaxed. In fact, the wild day's events took their toll, and she fell asleep until the pilot's announcement woke her.

"We made it again."

Just as she had in so many lorries with Père Gaspard, she bounced in the seat. They'd landed already?

A few faint lights revealed a runway. She shook herself awake—Wickham field.

The bombardier yelled, "Almost there."

Then a change in the pressure, a bump, and another. Kate's heartbeat throttled her chest. After a few more jolts, though, the pilot switched off the motor and opened his door.

Or someone opened it from outside. A gloved hand reached for hers, and Kate gulped the damp English air.

"Follow me, ma'am."

Within minutes, Miss G wrapped her arms around Kate. "Welcome home."

Surprised by her mentor's emotion and the strong smell of cigarettes blanketing her, Kate drew back. But Miss G seemed not to notice. "We'll get you installed for the night, and someone will come for you early in the morning to begin your debriefing. I hope you enjoy a good sleep."

A million questions floated through Kate's mind, but Miss G's calm posture quieted them. *A good sleep*—suddenly, weariness cloaked Kate, in spite of her nap, and it seemed all she could do to obey. Miss G opened a door inside a dormitory.

"Are you hungry?"

Kate shook her head.

"All right. Now, try to still your wild thoughts, since sleep is of the essence."

But such a gift was not to be. Thoughts of Père Gaspard haunted Kate. She slept, wakened, and dozed again. In a dreamy haze, she envisioned a courier fill the priest's pockets with more notes to transmit to headquarters.

Clackety-clack-clack. Her radio keys sounded like the noisy ducks Madame Ibarra fed each morning and evening.

Some noise startled Kate awake. Alone in a dismal little room, the sweep of a strobe light over the area befriended her. Would England ever be free from these endless beacons searching the night sky? Technically, London was the closest place to home she knew, but with the constant threat of rockets falling from the sky, it had little safety to offer.

When she woke from another miserable snatch of sleep, Kate shook herself and sat up. Better to sit in a chair until dawn than float between Southern France and here—wherever *here* was.

Someone brought her breakfast and directed her down the way to a second-story Baker Street room. There, an officer greeted her.

"Good to see you. I trust you slept well."

"Not exactly. I feel like I'm in the nether world."

"Mmm ... typical. In a way, you are. Pour yourself a cup of coffee and sit down."

Real coffee. A spotless cup. A plain old oak chair. Kate took in her simple surroundings, thankful for the hearty coffee. Mrs. T and all of London sacrificed for this brew.

"This morning, it's that other reality you just left that we'd like to explore. You've done well, even with your original assignment foiled, Agent."

"Thank you."

"So, tell us about your missions, starting with that original one."

"My...? You mean with Maurice and...?"

"Yes, that one."

"Maurice—is he alive?"

Facing Kate over a clean desktop, the officer shrugged. "I'm unable to give you that information."

"But, surely ... only if he's alive or not."

He angled his head. "Actually, I'm not able to tell you because we don't know yet. Maurice dropped out of contact weeks ago. We had a report of him being imprisoned in Lyon, but no confirmation."

Kate's heart plummeted—Gestapo headquarters. "Oh."

"Perhaps you can give us clues. That's one reason we called you back. When was the last time you saw him?"

"When he sent me to Albi."

"From Clermont-Ferrand?"

"Yes. He gave me such specific instructions. I had no idea the circuit was endangered."

"Mmm... He might not have known yet, either. What about Eugene?"

"I delivered a message to him a few days before that."

"And what's happened with him since?"

"I heard he was the one who outed the circuit, but I don't know if that's true." Kate searched the officer's eyes for hints, but he maintained a poker face except for one raised eyebrow.

"Well, then. Tell us what happened after Albi."

"We stumbled over Monsieur le Blanc. He was injured, and died a few days later. We left his papers with the *Résistance* leader, who said I'd be needed in Dordogne. But on the way there, the SS went wild, and..."

"Who is *we?*"

"My guide and I—a Basque. We passed through Figeac, where they wreaked destruction, too. When my guide's brother went missing, I transmitted from their granary until it became too risky. Then his priest..."

Kate ran out of breath, or thoughts. Suddenly, it seemed as if nothing she'd accomplished seemed worth reporting. A multitude of transmissions and many deliveries, but what did they all amount to?

Her debriefer looked up from taking notes. "Please continue."

"But looking back, it all seems so ... so random."

His grin preceded a chuckle. "Precisely. Call up your training, Agent Merce. Our work, you will recall, revolves around randomness."

TWENTY-FOUR

Through a small window, Kate stared at a London courtyard. The interview droned on, but her eyes felt far too heavy to stay awake. When the officer shoved back from his desk and left the room, she dropped her head on her arms. To be left alone, even for a short while, amounted to bliss.

But soon, the officer re-entered with a full coffee cup, and one for her. At the powerful scent, Kate lifted her head.

"This war will produce some inveterate caffeine addicts—myself, for one." He allowed her time to savor her first sip. "I have just a few more questions, Miss. Did you ever meet a fellow named Lanyard?"

"No."

"How about..." He consulted some notes. "Bernardo, or a woman named Bernadette, or Yvette?"

"I don't think so."

"Who else did you meet? Think back to your time in Le Chambon sur Lignon."

"The people at the Presbytery, the cook, the au pair girls, and of course, lots of children."

"A girl named Sancha?"

The name riveted Kate and enlivened Père Gaspard's description. To think, she and Sancha both visited Le Chambon. "No."

"You're certain?"

"I heard about the Gestapo ambushing a young woman by that name, along with some children, but I never met any of them."

"Mmm ... who told you about that incident?"

"Dom ... my guide's priest, Père Gaspard."

"You're altogether certain he's a priest?"

"If he's not, he certainly knows a lot about faith."

"You spoke with him often?"

"Oh yes, the last few weeks, he's been helping me find transmitting locations. And he's made me a new identity card—twice."

"Do you recall his code name?"

Kate shrugged. "I'm not sure he has one."

The officer's other question replayed in her consciousness—what if Père disguised himself as a priest? She almost giggled out loud. Maybe some day she'd return to France and discover him teaching religion or philosophy at some *Parisienne* institute. Or perhaps all his talk about the priesthood and his soutane disguised a devout day laborer with a penchant for philosophizing.

"This guide. Tell me more about him."

"He's a Basque shepherd." The officer's dark eyes merged with her memory of Domingo's, and Kate shivered.

"He hurt you?"

"Oh, no—he helped me out of trouble more than once. He met my drop and nursed my twisted ankle. He's ... before that, he led pilots over the Pyrenees and now he's carrying out *Résistance* sabotage. I mean, before the invasion."

"What type of sabotage?"

"Blowing bridges and railroad yards, cutting telephone wires— whatever he's assigned."

"And then?"

"I don't know. I haven't seen him since a few days before the invasion." The overcast morning beckoned Kate to glance outside, and the gloom cast a pall over her emotions. What if she never saw Domingo or Père again?

"Do you wish to speak with anyone while you're here in London?"

"Is that possible?"

"It depends. Is there someone?"

"Charles Tenney, sir."

"Mmm."

Kate wanted to ask if she'd be returning to France. In one respect, her real life waited for her back there, but she knew the officer would waive her question. At the same time, his inquiry created a chasm inside her—she hardly dared hope to see Addie.

After another fifteen minutes of questions, someone returned her to her room along with a meat pasty. She could have eaten three of them, but devoured this one and lay on her bed.

Her mind swarmed with the interview questions. Who was the last person she'd seen before she entered the airplane for her return trip across the Channel? The day before that, who had she spoken with, and the week before that? What news had filtered in of the invasion?

Where had she been on that exact day, and how had she heard the news? Had she ever been followed? Could she be certain? What about this Mother Hélène she'd mentioned—how much had they talked?

At least this plain room with its narrow bunk provided a reprieve. She slept until someone knocked.

"Kathryn Isaacs, are you in there?"

That voice—so familiar, yet ...

Kathryn, they told me to knock here. Are you in there?"

Her head swam. Was she dreaming? But the visitor seemed insistent, and the cotton coverlet under her hand felt real enough. She sat up.

"Hello in there? Kathryn Isaacs, are you there?"

She made her way across the room, and nearing the door, her heartbeat quickened.

"It's Charles Tenney, Kathryn. They've allowed me to..."

She unlocked the door and gasped. Could it truly be him? He peered down at her with a bemused smile.

"Why it *is* you, after all, dear girl."

Kate fell into his arms. "Mr. T—Charles. I can't believe you've come..."

Then behind Charles, she spied a wisp of rose-colored fabric—a woman's blouse, perhaps. Next, eyes as brown as Iowa farmland came into view. Kate went limp. If Charles hadn't been holding her up, she'd have...

Addie clasped her hand, then, and embraced her. The scent of wool and faint lavender returned her to England even more fully than the cool, damp air. Charles and Addie half-dragged her to a chair and finally, Kate's tongue was loosed.

"Addie, you've come. Oh, I can't begin to…"

"It's all right. I'm in shock, too. We're … Charles just heard you'd arrived, and…" She glanced at him as he took a seat at the desk.

"Beyond wonderful to see you well and whole, dear girl. London's been dismal with you away." His eyes glinted, and Addie reached for his hand. The movement caused a ring on her finger to flash.

That deep flush on Addie's cheeks, Charles's ruddy color … Kate looked from one to the other. What was it about them?

"You're—you two are…?"

Addie's glow answered for her, and Charles beamed.

"Where's…? What's happened to Harold?"

"Oh, my goodness, Kate. Of course, you wouldn't know—we've got so much catching up to do."

"Right." Charles looked at his watch. "I'll let Addie answer all your questions, Kathryn, for I must get back to the office. We've been told we have until eight p.m. with you, so…"

He looked into Addie's eyes. "I propose you and Kate spend a couple of hours together, and I'll pick you up at five fifteen. Mum doesn't know you're here yet, Kathryn. But she'd…"

"…never forgive us if we left her out of this." Addie's freckles almost popped from her smooth skin.

"Ahem …right. I'll ask Mr. Firth to fetch her and perhaps we can all eat dinner together. How does that sound?"

"Sound? It sounds like heaven…" Kate burst into tears. "They'll let you take me away from here?"

"You doubt my connections?" Charles grinned like a mischievous lad. "I didn't suffer through the last war for nothing. Well, then. You must stay on the premises until I return, but they said you're allowed to walk around the grounds."

Addie squeezed his hand. "We'll see you soon."

Charles gave a little bow, donned his hat, and walked out. Addie faced Kate. "You look … just like always, Kate, but I imagine you're reeling."

"You've found the perfect word, as usual. You haven't changed a bit, either, except you look radiant. You can't imagine how many times I've wished we could talk."

"Well, we have a couple of hours, although I'm sure you can only tell me so much. Does a walk sound good to you?"

"You're right about the *only so much*, but I have enough curiosity to kill twenty cats about what's happened here. Tell me everything."

Addie's hushed tone fit with the low mist hanging over the courtyard. "I should start with Harold. It's been ... I never would have believed things would turn out the way they have."

After hearing the details, Kate pulled Addie onto a bench. "All your struggles, all those years of waiting and hoping and working so hard. Still, hearing about Harold's death had to be hard."

"Yes. Letting all those fears go—I never lost the one that had him finding me and—I don't know what he would have done. Anyway, releasing all that anxiety took such a weight from me. Charles told me afterward that I held my head higher from then on."

Two half-grown bunnies raced across the courtyard, and one hesitated to observe the humans before pursuing his mate. He cocked his head as if he realized this rendezvous might be momentous.

"Hey, little fellow. Wish I had a breadcrumb for you, but I guess you're on rationing now, too. Speaking of that, you've lost weight, Kate."

"Probably. I haven't even thought about it. But you look healthy."

"Oh, I'm stronger than ever. Charles and I have become regulars at a government farm on the weekends. I had no idea he liked that kind of work—actually, I don't think he did, either, when we started. But he's become a champion at weeding."

"So, you became friends..."

"Yes. It came about so gradually, and then one night he asked me to dinner. I confess, I borrowed your skirt and sweater that first time we went to a restaurant together."

Kate waved her hand in the air. "Good. You know anything I have is yours. And your ring...?

"Charles's grandmother gave it to him before she died. It was her wedding ring." Addie fingered the small garnet.

"What does it mean for you and Charles?"

"We're engaged, Kate."

"Engaged! Oh, Addie. I couldn't be happier for you, and for Charles too. When will you get married?"

"We ... we haven't set a date yet, because he's called away so often. But neither of us can think of a good reason to wait. His mother doesn't know about this yet, so I only wear the ring away from home. I'm pretty sure she has an inkling, though. You know her—mother's intuition and all that."

"How is she, then?"

"As busy as ever. It's good you're sitting down, Kate. Here's another surprise. She's been spending a lot of time with Mr. Firth. They started working for the..." Addie gave a quick glance around the courtyard. "For the children—you know. And then she began helping out at the bookstore. But lately, I've been thinking their friendship has moved farther than just that project."

"Women's intuition?"

Addie giggled. "Yes, I guess so. Remember when you wrote me that we can trust our inner leanings and thoughts?"

"Sure do."

"Well, I'd say I've come a long, long way in that ability. But it's much easier to trust them when I'm focusing on someone else's life than on my own."

"If that isn't the truth! Let's walk some more. Being with you does me a world of good, and so does walking. Being cooped up in an airplane most of the night, and spending all day yesterday in a stuffy office made me antsy."

"Do you spend much time outdoors in France?"

"Quite a lot—seems like I'm always traveling between locations. Someday, you'll have to go there, Addie. Especially to the Department of Lot—so many scenes could be straight out of *The Wind and The Willows*. I thought of you especially when I was tending sheep there."

"Tending sheep?"

"Oh, there's no end of the occupations I've tried—but I'm not supposed to talk about that."

"I wish I could take you out to the gardens, but for today, this dismal courtyard will have to do. I'm glad to be in London, but the gray on gray does get to me sometimes."

"It couldn't be dismal with you here."

"I suppose you don't know ..."

"What will happen next? How long I'll be here, if I'll be sent back to France? If I'll ever see the people there again?"

"Yes—oh, I'd love to hear about the people."

Kate shook her head. "Sorry. And you're exactly right, I have no idea how those questions will be answered. But I have gotten a little better at handling my impatience with all the mystery." She waved her hands at the building behind them.

"Really? That's remarkable, Kate. You could never wait to read the end of a book—don't you remember how you always cheated?"

Kate squeezed her hand. "Oh, I remember. Mind you, I said I've gotten a *little* better."

~

Charles raised his glass. "Attention, everyone. Addie and I have called you here because of Kate's unexpected visit, but there's also another event this evening." He glanced at his watch. "In fifteen minutes, to be exact, a few blocks from here, so we'd better be going."

Amidst friendly chatter, Kate, Mrs. Tenney, and Mr. Firth followed Charles and Addie down the street.

"Oh, Mrs. Tenney—I can't describe how good it is to see you again. I thought you might faint when you first walked into the restaurant and saw me."

"At my age, it was quite a shock, but Mr. Firth sustained me." She turned accusing eyes on him. "Did you know?"

"Absolutely not, my dear. Charles knows me far too well. I'd have a dreadful time keeping such a secret from you, even during the drive over. I've become an old softie. Back in the last war, I felt I could jolly well handle anything."

"Oh my—that makes me think of our troops fighting in Normandy right now. They've made progress, but at such terrible cost, I..." Mrs. Tenney would have continued, but Mr. Firth interrupted her.

"But they've gained the beachheads now, my dear. Compared to what the Canadians suffered in the raid on Dieppe two years ago, success is ours. Let's not talk about the war tonight, righto? A small diversion will do us all good."

As the steeple of Mrs. Tenney's church came into view, Kate's eyes misted. "Oh, what a time we had there, rolling bandages. You and your friends taught me so many tricks, Mrs. T. I never would have thought to roll the fabric down my leg to tighten the ball."

"Nor would I. Those ladies know their business." She patted Kate's forearm. "Oh, I shall hold the memory of this evening tightly, dear. It's so wonderful to speak with you again."

At the church stairs, Charles turned like a father gathering his children. "The event we're attending will take place right here, and very soon. Follow me."

The quiet candlelit atmosphere swallowed Kate up. Serenity filled her, and an undeniable sense that she was loved. To be back here, even if the time was short, to share her heart with Addie—what an immense gift. She wiped away happy tears.

At the end of the old sanctuary's main aisle, Mrs. Tenney's vicar awaited them. Everyone proceeded toward him, and once there, Charles gave his mother a peck on the cheek.

"I think you might have given up on me ever marrying, Mum. But I have finally found my soul mate, and the hour has come."

Mrs. Tenney clutched her neck. "Now? Tonight?"

The vicar took over. "Ma'am, Charles declared his intentions weeks ago, and has been holding the license for the perfect time."

"Charles? You knew Kate was coming?"

Addie answered for him. "No, but we thought to be prepared, with Charles traveling to the coast so often. And then, just this morning, he received word about Kate being here. Isn't it wonderful?"

The vicar cleared his throat, blocking out Mrs. Tenney's reply. "At any rate, this seems a divinely appointed time to join this man and woman in holy matrimony."

Charles and Addie settled in front of him and Mr. Firth took his stand beside Charles. Then he pulled Mrs. Tenney in beside him.

"So if you would please adjust your thoughts to this momentous occasion, we shall begin the ceremony." The vicar surveyed the evening gathering. "Sometimes, I believe these cozy family weddings are the best."

Mr. Firth and Charles took off their hats, and Addie beckoned Kate closer. *Family weddings ...* Remorse stabbed Kate. Why, oh why had she eloped with Alexandre? Aunt Alvina would gladly have given them a beautiful wedding.

When she shook off the cloudy recollection, all the times she and Addie had dreamed of their weddings, the novels they'd read together, hoping for the heroine to marry the hero, flooded Kate. Scarlett O'Hara, Jane Austen's Elizabeth Bennet and Emma Woodhouse, plus so many more. And now, to be united with her dearest friend again, and even to witness her marry Charles ...

"Into this holy union Charles Tenney and Adelaide Bledsoe now come to be joined. If any of you can show just cause why they may not lawfully be married, speak now; or else forever hold your peace."

The sanctuary's shadowy interior, illuminated by a handful of candles due to the blackout, lent an air of intimacy, and tears burned Kate's eyes again. Good tears, cleansing tears, for this moment of starting over, of embracing the good that life had brought Addie and Charles.

"Addie, will you have this man to be your husband; to live together in the covenant of marriage? Will you love him, comfort him, honor and keep him, in sickness and in health; and, forsaking all others, be faithful to him as long as you both shall live?"

"I will."

Mrs. Tenney's sniff broke the stillness.

"Charles, will you have this woman to be your wife; to live together in the covenant of marriage? Will you love her, comfort her, honor and keep her, in sickness and in health; and, forsaking all others, be faithful to her as long as you both shall live?"

"I will."

"Will all of you witnessing these promises do all in your power to uphold these two persons in their marriage?

"We will."

A sob broke out, and Mr. Firth circled Mrs. Tenney's waist with his arm. She laid her head on his shoulder for a moment, and Kate gave thanks they had found each other, too.

At some point during the ceremony, Kate realized she was holding her breath. She straightened her shoulders. A new beginning—a lovely fresh start in the midst of all the hatred of war.

The flickering candles suggested Père Gaspard's blessing. *Grace lights your path...*

Mrs. Tenney wept into her hankie, and Mr. Firth leaned his head to hers. Alexandre's face flitted before Kate. Such a different beginning they'd shared, before a small-town judge in his cramped parlor. But then the memory of Domingo's eyes brought her back to the present. What was his fate?

"Witnesses, I need you over here." Kate signed her name at a small table with a lighted candle and a register. Afterward, Addie gripped her left hand.

"Oh, Kate, I know you'll soon be off for parts unknown again, and we might not know when you're leaving. But having you here means everything to me—what a special gift God has given us."

"I can't imagine a better one. I can't put into words how happy I am for you."

"Well, you introduced us, you know."

Mrs. Tenney and Mr. Firth exchanged pleasantries with the vicar, and Charles motioned for Addie to lead the way outside.

Saying good-bye to Mrs. Tenney and Mr. Firth incited another flood of tears, and when Charles and Addie let Kate out at Baker Street a few minutes before eight, they walked her to her door.

Addie's hug lasted forever, and Charles added, "Do ring me up at the office if there's another chance to see you, Kathryn."

"You can count on that." Such a blend of joy and pain—it was all Kate could do to go inside.

TWENTY-FIVE

"**Y**ou look much better this morning. Hopefully, today will bring you more clarity."

"Thank you for letting my friends visit last night."

"Highly irregular, but others here were of the opinion an outing would jolly well do you good." The Baker Street officer got down to business again. Soon, he realized that yesterday's visit with Addie and Charles had also produced clarity.

Picturing the newlyweds together this morning made Kate smile. Addie had offered few details about Harold's death and Kate didn't probe. Probably some military secret—the war overflowed with them. So many people walked around with riddles in their heads. Last night at the restaurant, she'd wondered how many other customers kept confidences that would be locked away in files for decades?

But one thing really mattered—the furrows in Addie's forehead had all but disappeared. Warmth welled up in Kate this morning, even though she faced another round of inquiries. As usual, life's unpleasant parts merged with the good to create a complicated pattern. This morning, some things Addie had said interspersed with the officer's questions.

"I planted a laburnum tree as a memorial to Harold—I've always loved their golden chains, and next spring, it might blossom. Nobody back home knows about him yet—Berthea still visualizes him flying over the French coast. Charles said his name will be included on the invasion casualty list."

"So Harold never got to fight, after all."

"That bothered me, too, but at least everyone in Halberton believes he did." Addie's voice wavered. "Mama used to say life's a mixed bag."

"I know what you mean. Tell me more about you and Charles, then—I'm not surprised. I still remember the look on his face when he first spied you at Liverpool Station. Love at first sight."

"I don't know about that, but he's been so kind to me, as patient as hens pecking for grain. I can't imagine anyone more conscientious and devoted to doing what's right."

The officer cleared his throat, jerking Kate back to his spare office. "I shall repeat my question."

Heat razed Kate's cheeks—she hadn't even heard him the first time.

"We've grave concern with the Gestapo. Klaus Barbie's viciousness creates a new standard. Even though you've not been in Lyon, have you heard or seen anything concerning him?"

"Why, yes. I saw him back in the winter, near Clermont-Ferrand."

The officer took his turn at being at a loss for words. Kate contained a chuckle at his bemused expression and continued.

"Maurice sent a partisan with me to deliver a message to Eugene, our radio operator. He had changed locations for safety reasons, so my guide led me some distance, and told me about his wife. She worked as a telephone operator for the Germans, and gave him tips for the *Résistance* straight from the Reich's phone lines.

"Along the way, we met a group in outdated uniforms. 'Naphtalines,' my guide whispered, 'Spanish holdovers from the war for liberation.' London will soon be dropping in Americans like flies, so these old fellows have headed up north to fight. When the Allies take to the hedgerows, they might be surprised who will support them.'

"About fifteen minutes later, gears ground somewhere close, so my guide did reconnaissance. His report sent shivers down my spine.

"'Gestapo. I wouldn't doubt it's Barbie himself, en route to Vichy from Lyon. I'd recognize him anywhere—I escaped from Holland, you know. In my book, he rivals the Devil in hell.'

"A few minutes later, he pointed out Eugene's latest hideout, a deserted barn. But before we went any farther, a black Citroen flashed into view and a man in a dark Fedora and trench coat stepped out. He turned a slow circle and a guard with a Schmeisser submachine gun followed."

"You could identify his weapon from a distance?"

"Our instructors taught us to shoot it during training. Of course, the blowback and lugging that extra nine pounds on one of our forced runs left me with a sore arm and shoulder."

"Aha...please continue."

"Before the guard entered the barn, he canvassed the area. He passed so near our hiding place, I thought he'd let loose with a volley any second. I won't forget his scarred face, either. But he finally strolled on and approached the barn.

"Barbie walked our way, so we backed deeper into the bushes. Finally, he stopped and unbuttoned his coat to relieve himself. Midday sun clearly outlined his face, and I vaguely recalled his photograph from our training, because he was so different from the typical blond S.S. officer."

"You're altogether certain this man was Klaus Barbie?"

"My guide had no doubts. By the time Barbie returned to the vehicle, the guard came from the barn and handed him an envelope. Barbie got in, but his squire sniffed the air and made one more pass in our direction before following him."

The officer blinked. "Amazing. You came that close to the villain who tortured and killed Jean Moulin—I must say I'm impressed."

Kate shrugged her shoulders. "All I did was hide in the bushes. After they drove away, my guide sat back and rubbed his forehead. 'We might have avenged the murder of Jean Moulin, who organized us as the Free French.' I knew he would never have tried, given our circumstances, but he certainly enjoyed mulling the possibility out loud."

"So you watched Barbie relieve himself, but what about Eugene? Did you deliver your message?"

"We attempted to. My guide checked the barn, but Eugene had disappeared. The message had to wait until later."

"You're sure Eugene wasn't there?"

"If my guide could be trusted—Maurice had chosen him. When we reported back to Maurice, he said there had to be some explanation."

"So you made the delivery the next day?"

"No, Maurice had something else for me to do by then. I left the message with him and assumed he found another way to reach Eugene."

"That guide—did you ever talk with him again?"

"No, I believe he went east to gather more information from his wife."

"Hmmm ... and he was absolutely certain about Eugene."

A full minute ticked by on the wall clock. When Kate fidgeted, the officer continued. "Do you feel the same way?"

"About Eugene not being there? Yes. Maurice trusted the guide, so I believed him. But I didn't go into the barn to search for myself."

"Why not?"

"We'd already wasted nearly a day, and the guide assured me ..."

The officer held out a photograph. "Is this the man who relieved himself?"

"Yes."

He shuffled through some papers for another photo. "And this fellow?"

"That's the man with the gun."

~

Poor Darlene. Kathryn hoped she would believe what her doctor agreed to say ... they'd discovered a nervous twitch in some facial muscle that would only worsen with time, so he recommended therapy in Denver. A regular transport was scheduled this morning, so although Kathryn said Darlene was already on her way to take her home, he'd insisted. Why wait a full week for the next transport?

Then Darlene would read the brief note she'd left.

I'm so sorry, Darlene. This just came up. Please tell Gabby I hope to be back for Mara's rodeo.

Barely giving her time to write the note, Kathryn's captor had hustled her past the parking lot to a tree-lined street and opened the back door of a maroon Chevy. A sinking sensation in Kathryn's stomach prevailed through the city's southern outskirts. This felt like a kidnapping.

Several times, she thought to leap out at a stoplight and disappear into a gaggle of shoppers, but a voice from long ago quelled the urge.

After all these years, she could almost hear Père Gaspard's voice.

"*Quel que soit le risque, nous allons, parce que nous croyons que la vérité reste importante.*" Amazing how his words still affected her—*No matter the risk, we go, because we believe the truth is still important.* Nothing else could have calmed Kathryn at this point—the mission she'd consented to seemed outlandish, no—impossible.

But Père would have undertaken it, she knew. And so would Domingo, for the sake of truth, or any number of her comrades during the war.

On the other hand, her simple rural life tempered by the seasons and serene country joys had grown so comfortable—living on the edge of such a small town assured that her first sight every morning would be rolling hills. How could she possibly be leaving, especially without explaining to her loved ones? But Gabby had no idea of her secret involvement in the war.

Père's words also brought Kathryn's parents to mind. Perhaps their final mission paralleled her present choice. After all their service during the Great war, maybe they loathed the idea of leaving home, too, but made their decision for the truth.

And then Monsieur le Blanc's death scene rolled through Kathryn's memory. Monsieur took such great risks later in life—he'd been even older than she was right now. Still, he made difficult decisions for freedom, for the cause. And they ultimately led to his death. What right did she have to make a selfish choice when injustice still prevailed?

Weary from her inward struggles, she closed her eyes as dry southern Idaho landscape passed by. The long drive into Wyoming made her doze after a while, until a sudden stop blasted her into disoriented alertness. What was she doing in the back seat of a car, clipping along through the countryside? Nothing looked familiar, and neither did her companions.

The rear-view mirror revealed the driver, a small-shouldered fellow with a Fedora, heavy eyebrows, and dark eyes. He held a smoking cigarette out the window, but a whiff carried back to Kathryn. *Gauloise.* Of course, what else?

Maybe it would be best to pretend she still slept. She slitted her eyes, but scanned the roadside for clues to their location. Her eyelids grew heavy again, and when she reawakened, they passed a sign.

Denver airport, twelve miles.

At a stop sign, the driver studied her in the mirror. "You're going back into your past, but trust me. It's for a good cause."

Trust me ... Exactly what Jesus had whispered last spring when she'd sailed over the church balcony and lay helpless on the sanctuary floor ... But this voice, the same one that spoke to her in the ambulance, carried her much further back. That slight French accent ...

"Just remember, I need to be back home in three weeks for my granddaughter. It means everything."

He angled his head so the top of his hat resembled the peaked ones of German Wehrmacht officers. His next glance sent a shudder through Kathryn.

"Yes, and you must remember, too. Your superiors instructed you to put the war behind you and never speak of it again. But now it's time to call up your memories. On our long journey, you'll have plenty of opportunity to recollect faces and events. And once you identify the man we seek, I promise to bring you straight home."

"Will I be back for my granddaughter's rodeo?"

"That depends how fast your memory works." He threw his cigarette into the wind, and she noticed the greying hair above his ears. "By the way, you can call me Benjamin."

~

A gust of untimely cool summer air widened Kate's pant legs and chilled her through. Underneath, she wore a dark yellow chore dress fit for a milkmaid. She grinned at the thought—she'd come full circle, back to her original identity.

But knowing how many kilometers she might be required to conquer before this night ended, the trousers made sense. On the ride across the Channel, she'd spoken with another agent being dropped farther south to prepare for the Allies in the south of France. Their conversation sent a shiver through her.

"Nowadays, they just gore out a big old bomber's ball turret for us to jump through. Not nearly as terrifying as landing in the wrong spot—I've heard too many pilots tell about their horrendous misses. Of course, when you're flying dark, anything can happen."

Kate cherished her orders back to France, which Miss G had delivered the evening after Addie's wedding. *Addie's wedding*—how could she have been there? Kate's heart still burst at the memory of standing in the sanctuary with those dear people. Such an unexpected sign of the grace Père Gaspard had mentioned so eloquently before she left him. If she could have chosen any event to witness, that marriage ceremony would have topped her list.

Miss G said that this time, they would drop Kate off on a makeshift airfield along with a mountain of ammunition for the partisans—no need to parachute in. Ambivalence accompanied that news. Parachuting again would be such a thrill, but with it would have come a trip to Ringway for refresher training.

That flight, again on a moonless night, seemed smoother and shorter than her first jaunt on the C-47. No stopping for cargo on this leg of the trip—she and the other man being flown to France had become part of the cargo.

She'd arrived at the airfield early and watched muscles bulge as the ground crew hefted military machinery and crates into the plane's belly. Chances were, the pilot would stop along the coast for wounded men on the return trip. What must it be like for him, back and forth across the Channel night after night, with little or no sleep?

Once the plane lifted off, Kate's thoughts drifted to the past few days. Questions ... so many questions. She almost felt sorry for the officer assigned to her. Her memory of Klaus Barbie took him off guard, but after that, his inquiries had come fast and furious.

Remembering the onslaught made her head swim, so she turned to the brightest spot of her time in London—Addie and Charles. Impossible not to smile at their tender vows. As Mrs. Tenney quipped, they deserved each other.

Charles gave Kate a wink when his Mum straightened Mr. Firth's tie—yes, another twosome in the offing. Addie shared Iowa news about some weddings, too, and of course, deaths. One of their classmates had lost his life in the battle for Saipan last month.

It was still hard to believe she'd been able to see Addie, even though the time had been short. Addie shared a brief snapshot of the near future with her, too. Charles had been called to the Isle of Man to train young Jewish men who'd matured since their emigration to Great Britain.

Now, they prepared to parachute behind enemy lines for the rest of the war. Addie might be able to go along to the island, to work in an orphanage. "Charles has warned me about a huge prison there, where the Ministry keeps criminals and other undesirables. Otherwise, he regales me with stories about his childhood rides on the island's small trains and playing along the coast."

It seemed so natural and right, the two of them making a difference in this way. Another positive about seeing Addie—Kate had finally been able to relax, and slept for hours and hours that night. The whole world looked brighter in the morning.

Then came another happy surprise—her orders back to France. The next part of her assignment shocked Kate. She felt certain her mouth had dropped when Miss G mentioned Père Gaspard.

"We've heard of this priest through another source, and it seems logical for you to connect with him again—why waste such a valuable contact? Didn't your Teddy Roosevelt say, 'Do the best you can with what you have where you are?'

"Mainly because things have gotten so tight with the Gestapo, your association with Père Gaspard may smooth your way. Based on what you've shared here, we're positioning you closer to Gestapo headquarters, even though you'll first need to find your priest friend.

"You've shown your pluck when cast into uncertainty, so we feel confident asking you to shoulder a certain amount again." The plane wavered against the wind, and an inky darkness rewarded Kate's attempt to see a star. Though Miss G's next question made sense, it troubled Kate.

"Do you think this priest might have connections in Lyon? With the Gestapo headquartered there, any contacts we have can make a big difference."

"He's never mentioned any."

"Well then, we'll move forward with our plan."

For a moment, the odds rattled Kate. How could she possibly

locate Père again? Who knew where he went after seeing her off? He might have changed his plan to climb to the encampment. But she could check with Mother Hélène, and in Domingo's village.

During the debriefing, she'd referred to Domingo only as a guide. True, but he meant so much more to her—every time she mentioned him to the officer, Domingo's dark eyes arose before her and her pulse quickened.

This time, the plane had settled onto a field in a gentle rain. A guide met her and breathed her code name, shouldered her radio, and moved on without a word.

Nimble like Domingo, he seemed barely to need water, stopping only once just before dawn. He left her for a few minutes, and Kate tried to orient herself as light streaked the horizon. Not far away, an iron plow poised mid-field, surrounded by drenched earth. The guide remarked about it when he returned.

"The SS probably turned the oxen into stew."

"Where are you taking me, and how much farther is it?"

The young partisan studied her. "I assumed you knew. We're headed toward Saint Pierre's, where your partner tends the wounded. On a normal day, we'd be there by midmorning, but with this rain, who knows?"

Another two hours found them drenched, but within range. When the rain stopped, the sun came out and turned the air sultry. Kate's pantlegs were more mud than not. Père Gaspard's soutane would gain ten pounds on this trek—she could almost hear his off-tune whistling.

We're promised land people. What exactly had he meant? Once, when she visited Harold's church with Addie, a hymn extolled the virtues of that land of milk and honey, fruits growing on trees that never withered, no more sickness, sorrow, or death. Above all, the Almighty reigned there. All the verses rhymed in a cheerful tune, as though the journey must be a joy.

Trudging ankle deep along what seemed a God-forsaken path, that rosy picture clashed with reality. It was hard to imagine this guide leading her straight to Père Gaspard—too easy. But Père would make a good *Canaan*—could a person be a promised land?

Slow progress gave her plenty of time to consider promised-land people. What were they like, anyway? Maybe Père meant good traveling companions, set on the goal, positive most of the time, and ready for whatever came along.

Suddenly, her guide halted with his hand upraised. "Wait." He checked ahead and gestured for her to follow.

What greeted Kate next shocked her almost as much as seeing Addie standing at her Baker Street door. Under a chestnut tree stood Père Gaspard. She closed her eyes and looked again. Unmistakable in his soutane, two-toned from the mud, he angled his head and waved before hurrying her way.

"So—you have returned, *mon amie américaine*, and in one piece."

TWENTY-SIX

In spite of thick foliage overhanging portions of the path, June sun beat down on Kate as she followed Père. En route to the *Ségala* camp high above Saint-Céré, the familiar swish of his soutane, even in this caking mud, created a comforting rhythm.

From the moment he met her and her guide on the path, the same love surrounded her that she sensed at Charles and Addie's wedding. How could she doubt that heaven watched out for her now? To witness their vows and be sent back here would have been enough. But Kate acknowledged her incessant need for proof, and proof traipsed the path a few feet ahead of her once again, in the form of this gangly priest.

Somehow, Père Gaspard had already been informed of her mission, so she hadn't even needed to explain. And he'd already been busy making plans.

"I'll travel with you as far as the encampment. There, we'll find a guide for the rest of your journey—I'll do anything I can to foil the Gestapo."

Kate almost felt guilty that everything seemed so simple, but what awaited her in Lyon would surely make up for this easy start. Word had it that interrogations there often led to death—she sent up a plea for Maurice.

"Take care, it's a little slippery after last night's storm." A few minutes later, Père half-turned his head. "I suspect my ancestors used this trail on their pilgrimages." At a level place in the trail, his incredibly blue eyes gleamed at her with purpose and mischief, like a cat's.

"Getting quiet around here, isn't it? With our fighters going north, I'm betting the Limousin will be liberated by summer's end. And then, freedom will move south to us." Père's fiery red curls slid into further disarray as he retrieved a soiled kerchief from his voluminous robe.

"You used to prophesy, but now you've stooped to betting?" Kate wiped off perspiration pooled at the nape of her neck and slapped at an insect.

"Why not? My guess is as good as anyone else's." Suddenly, Père stiffened. Their guide raised his hand at muted steps from the tangled brush.

Kate closed her eyes and waited until the *schluss ... schluss* of espadrilles decreased her tension. But these days, collaborator *miliciens* and even the Gestapo took to disguising themselves with Basque footwear.

With Père, she shrank deeper into the bushes and joined his silent prayer. *Please shield us.* But their requests produced the opposite results.

"Over there to the left ... that's the priest."

In seconds, several partisans surrounded them. One of them pulled Père aside and murmured to him in *Occitan.* Then he positioned himself before Kate, his dark eyes boring into hers. "You served with Maurice, *oui*?"

Père's protective stance demanded an explanation, and finally, the stranger glanced his way. "We have need of this fair-haired girl." He turned to Kate again. "Your ID, please." He squinted at her card and read aloud. "But you once were Ibarra..."

At the sound of Domingo's family name, Kate froze. Père murmured something, and whatever he said satisfied the stranger. "Père, you may come along if you like."

Without asking, Kate knew why they wanted her. The distasteful truth encroached like a nasty itch. She wanted to scratch this reality away, but knew better than to try. These partisans needed her to confirm a traitor's identity—who cared if she ever reached her proposed destination?

After she cooperated with these patriots, *la Résistance* would give the betrayer a double-barreled traitor's farewell. Ambivalence rode

Kate's midsection—she hadn't looked forward to going near the Gestapo headquarters, but of all her missions since she parachuted into France, this one might be even worse.

The leader studied her as if measuring her fortitude. "You must identify a turncoat for us." He spat and waited.

He took her silence for compliance and ushered her past his comrades. They backed to the side and she fell in behind this new leader.

Nothing had changed here since her stay in London—detours rose on every hand. Choices still faced her, but each one depended on others made by friend and foe alike, including heartless Waffen S.S. commanders.

Who could be trusted for a night's sleep or some food? Who collaborated with the Nazi-friendly Vichy government? Who remained loyal to *La France*? And who had betrayed the cause and must pay for that foolhardy choice? Nearly overcome with gratitude for Père's steady footfall on the path behind her, Kate kept up the pace. Maybe he could help Eugene face an ignominious death.

That's what Père was about, making a difference, and he did so in many ways. Since *l'Invasion*, Kate's travels with him fused nightmare with inspiration.

Because of his perspective, beauty had surprised her everywhere. In the rocky heights surrounding their paths, in his interactions with everyone from lorry drivers to Mother Hélène, Père radiated uncommon serenity, opening her eyes to the landscape. At the same time, he'd made her laugh, and even surprised her with that checkerboard—another kind of beauty.

The present view provided the perfect example. Limestone cliffs shouldered against an azure sky, wildflowers peppered meadows that invited Kate to lie down for an afternoon nap, and a sun-dappled stream flowed from the heights. Yet her destination held a new horror—she would be instrumental in Eugene's demise.

Again, she gave thanks for Père Gaspard. His acknowledgement of human weakness in general, as well as his own in particular, won her heart. And today, that frailty would be on display in Eugene. Yet come what may, Père still trusted in an ultimate, though seemingly distant goodness.

"Remember how this war turns things around—what seems so far away may really lie quite close at hand. Through all their trials, the apostles claimed *God with us*—indeed, even in martyrdom. And we follow their example."

A ground squirrel chattered up a tree. Even creatures sensed disturbance in the natural order of things. Midsummer ought to display fields planted, peasants at work, and carefully tended grapevines, but so many had fled the tanks, none remained to do the work.

Like the musky rise of late fog still lingering in river hollows, Père's convictions persisted in spite of everything. That steadiness calmed and sustained Kate, though any second, the Gestapo might rain down on them.

Closer to the camp, she recalled weeks-old news of a double agent called *la Corneille*. She'd entertained questions then, of course. Had she ever crossed paths with him—or her? Now, her questions multiplied.

Could Eugene be *la Corneille*? Kate recalled the shock of hearing that her network's wiry radio operator with his heavy shank of black hair had turned traitor. Could he also be the one who traveled all through the southern Departments, affecting many other networks as well?

To think he had betrayed Maurice, their organizer, and so many more, all the way back to London—such a thing seemed impossible. Every time she'd delivered a message, she'd come so close to touching his hand. She'd always considered herself a good judge of character, so how could she have failed to read the treachery in his eyes?

The partisans led them past a small hamlet set into the hillside and upward past a large two-story house. A central set of rooms rose above the second level, with a brown-roofed tower and two stories on the other side. Kate longed to stop and walk through the rooms. But chances were, the place had been absconded by the *Milice*.

A hundred feet higher, the leader grunted a password to a guard stationed in a low branch of a tree. Soon, the dreaded moment of truth would come—if only she could dissolve into the day's heat.

Something else troubled her. Someone had sent these men to find her, but whom? And the leader knew Domingo's family name—what could that mean?

He would never have told them—no, he would hold her secrets until his dying day. But even though her original agent name had been *Dumont,* these men had searched for her under her more recent identity. Of course, London had just sent her back with yet another persona.

In a sudden burst of sunshine through layered leaves, camp sounds reached their troupe. Dense foliage obscured the camp entrance, and farther into its depths, she imagined Domingo's ebony eyes glinting at her. She could almost hear his voice on this breezeless air.

If she saw him again ... *When* she saw him again, it would be enough to hear him breathe her name.

Another guard stopped their progress and brought Kate back to this day, this distasteful reality. Would she have to watch the *maquisards* torture Eugene or raze his body with bullets? The firing squad, swift and sure, had become their favored execution style.

High in a chestnut, a crow protested this invasion of its territory with its hoarse cries. The huge black noisemaker reminded her that in this world of subterfuge, some surely lost their faith. But Domingo ... somewhere, maybe not so far away, he carried out missions that would pulse terror through her veins. Ah, here she was, thinking of him again.

I lift him up, I lift him up ... please protect him and grant us victory.

In heavy foliage, the leader again paused to give a password. A man gave directions, and Kate finally spotted the guard. They must have entered the camp, at last.

Around a curve, a partisan addressed Père. "Do you wish to visit the refugees?"

"Not yet. I'll accompany this young lady for a while." He made Kate a promise with his eyes—he would not leave her.

The partisan nodded and headed past a canvas tent smelling of bread baking, obviously the kitchen. Kate and Père trailed him down a gully, across a meadow, and finally into an obscure shelter.

"We have the prisoner roped in here. If you stand where I tell you, you can see him without being seen." He led them ten paces before making a turn into a heavily shaded area. But as he predicted, a light shone farther on.

Perhaps six feet from an opening in a heavy curtain, they stopped. "Take a good, long look."

Eugene—clearly, Eugene.

"You recognize him?"

"May I see him from the front?"

The partisan flitted like an insect through the opening, and two guards turned the prisoner. Doubly sure, Kate let out a long breath. Père touched her elbow.

The partisan returned, expectancy written on his features. "Is this the one they call Eugene, who transmitted for Maurice's circuit?"

"Yes."

"You are certain?" This time, Père posed the question.

"No doubt at all. I saw Eugene many times."

Père's sigh engulfed Kate, but the partisan gestured her back the way they had come. "*Merci.* You serve *la France* well."

But Père advanced toward Eugene. The partisan led her away, and when they approached the kitchen, he gestured toward some fresh bread loaves. "Perhaps you need to eat?"

When shots rang out, he showed no emotion, but told Kate to wait here. A few minutes later, Père approached. A heavy knot sat in Kate's stomach, but the dullness in Père's eyes told her nothing.

"He refused to speak with me—hopefully he found some peace." He shook his head. "Ah, *mon amie,* the troubles of this war. I'm going to see how I can help the refugees—nearly a hundred on the other side of camp, they say. Headquarters sent some urgent messages, and that partisan will return shortly to take you to a radio. Do you think you can work?"

"Of course."

"Be kind to yourself." He hesitated. "So far, I have located no one here headed to Lyon. Everyone able to travel has left the camp in the other direction. This derails your assigned duty, but we'll have to wait."

"Randomness—I'm not surprised. Maybe the war will end before I can get there."

Père touched her shoulder. "Maybe indeed. But for now, we both have work to do. I will find you later."

A few minutes after he left, the partisan led Kate to a cave-like dugout. At the entrance, he handed her a lantern and some folded papers.

"You'll find another lantern inside. You're safe here."

Kate hung the lantern and in a nearby stream, washed off the worst of the mud. Then she sank into a squeaky chair set before a substantial wooden table. That same serenity she'd experienced at the Ibarra homestead descended. She pulled out the messages and gave herself to London headquarters and the BBC.

~

Hours must have passed. The two lanterns flickered, dispelling the darkness, but at the cavern's entrance, sunset reigned. In fresh evening air sweet with blossoms, Kate stretched her arms and cramped neck.

An image of her mother hunched over a Great War telephone switchboard tickled her thoughts.

"Mother..." The hallowed word drifted like cottonwood tufts or milkweed fluff. Oh, why hadn't she asked Monsieur le Blanc more about her before he died?

"I so wish we could talk, Mother, if only for five minutes. I'd like to know what your life was like at the Front, and how you decided to come to France. When did you first meet *Le Renard?* Did he notice you first? How did you know he cared for you, and how long did you wait to marry? Did he woo you with wildflowers, if any dared to flourish so near the battle?"

A chilly wind bade Kate pull her sweater closer. "How did you decide to move back to the States? Was it hard for my father to leave his country? Most of all, what call did you answer when you took that last flight?"

She walked a distance away. *Did you cry when you said good-bye to me that time? Did you have any premonition that you'd never see me again? And what caused your plane to go down?*

Back at the entrance, Madame Ibarra's face undulated like a feather on the wind. How was it for Domingo, now that he had lost her? To think, he might not even know yet.

Surely, everything would be different for him. His mother's voice and laughter, her gestures and the light in her eyes, her unique scent—hundreds of intimate memories must swirl inside him. After living together all these years, how could he possibly let her go?

Some time after Kate returned to her work, a whiff of hot chicory drifted in. Père Gaspard stood there holding a steaming cup. The brew, tangy yet sharp, beckoned her from her work for a few moments.

"How did you manage?"

"Always wondering about *how*, aren't you? Simply enjoy this, and hand over any messages you have ready. I'll find a courier." His eyes gleamed against the darkness. "Do you know what I've been considering?"

"How could I ever guess?"

"Something about Saint Pierre's tymphanum. I'll be back later to check on you."

A coarse wool blanket warmed Kate as she sank against the rock wall, its earthy scent enveloping her. Nothing like hot chicory and the chance to close her eyes, even for a short time before the BBC's personal messages.

In the distance, she could hear the refugees at their everyday tasks—cooking supper, talking over campfires, preparing children for bed. That rhythm of humanity created a sudden shaft of desire.

Then out of the night rose an impression from the past. She swam in that nebulous state between sleep and wakefulness as someone braced a hand near her and warm breath touched her ear.

"*Dormez bien, mon enfant.*" The same words she spoke over sweet little Linden before she left le Chambon sur Lignon. *Sleep well, my child.*

Aware only vaguely of the night sounds outside, Kate attuned the ear of her heart. And gradually, like a candle flame growing, the answer arrived, though she couldn't have explained how.

"My father, *le Renard.* It was my father."

Maybe he tiptoed in before he and her mother, still working for an espionage unit after the war, caught their flight. Perhaps a tear trickled down his cheek.

All speculation, to be sure, but this small flicker of memory reignited her sense of wellbeing. With the hot mug warming her hands, she opened herself to this other warmth. *Memories are like roses in December...* where had she heard that saying?

"My father loved me. This tells me, and so did Monsieur le Blanc." What if she could find someone else who worked at the front with her parents? And what if she discovered where and why they had to take that post-war trip? Nothing was impossible.

"Some things I cannot know, but this, I can hold dear. This is my rose in December."

The transmitter stole her attention until she returned the cup to the kitchen, recognizable by a single low fire. Wreathed in smoke, several partisans murmured there, and one of them nodded in her direction. His low-slung beret reminded her of the faint image of her father in Monsieur le Blanc's photograph.

How could she have known there was nothing to fear from Monsieur, or how meeting him in London would change her life? But his gift of her mother's graduation portrait and the faded image of her father led to so much more than she could ever have imagined.

Monsieur exposed an enticing remnant of truth, and as she awaited her baby's birth, her courage had grown. *The truth shall set you free* ... Exactly what Addie had experienced in her struggle with Harold.

For her, freedom led to embracing a new love. The cool night air caught Kate's question. "But what does freedom mean for me?"

Clouds blocked the moon, creating a misty darkness that shrouded the grounds. Along tents scattered upwind from the petrol's intense odor, she smelled fresh-dug potatoes, still encased in their own dirt, and recalled her first trip with Père in the ramshackle lorry to distribute vegetables to his parishioners.

Albert, Jean-Claude's son, hefted burlap bags of turnips and carrots into peasants' hands. By now, had those families who received the food fled the *Schutzstaffel*, too? That word signifying Hitler's notorious elite special services set Kate's teeth on edge, but her circuit of the camp revived her, giving her the energy she needed to face her three remaining transmissions.

Later, Père Gaspard poked his head in and beckoned her out to a fallen log. The camp seemed almost more awake by night than it was by day, with the sounds of partisans darting here and there through the trees. In hushed tones, Kate asked how Domingo could bear such great loss.

"We have *medicins homeopathique* here in France. Do you understand?"

"Homeopathic doctors who concoct herbal remedies?"

"It's a bit more complicated—they inject a tiny amount of the ailment into the solution. For an allergy to oak buds, they express part of the remedy from those very buds."

"Like an inoculation."

Père studied the shapes of some fast-moving clouds, dark against the moon. "Yes. I believe a similar principle works in our deep sorrows. Domingo has already lost his father and brother, as well as his betrothed. Those sufferings have expanded his capacity to bear this new grief."

After he left, Kate stared up at the sky. According to Père's logic, her childhood losses made losing Aunt Alvina and Alexandre easier, as if the first sorrow performed an initial cutting.

But when her baby died, she sank so very low. Thank goodness, Addie had already come to London. She had a way of making life more bearable, and now Mr. Tenney would have her beside him. That image brought a smile—and returned Kate to thoughts of Domingo. If only goodness traveled a swifter path.

TWENTY-SEVEN

Soaked through and shivering in the darkness, Domingo shuffled through a verdant thicket of saplings into a cave carved in a cliff. The worst he could do was disturb some fellow traveler holed up here for a few hours.

Springy branches brushed against his face and hands. He might have wished for a fuller moon or a cloudless night, but both would raise his chances of capture. Again, he wished Petra stalked these hills with him. Although his insistence that Domingo take this journey had been irritating, his powers of observation provided security. But anyone claiming this haven surely would have heard him by now and made their presence known.

He set down his pack, fashioned a nest in a bed of dry needles, and as he was about to lower himself to the earth, heard something stir. Then a single question reached him from the darkness. "Partisan?"

Domingo's heart played *pelota* with his rib cage. The peculiar twang of this voice belonged to a Frenchman, probably a city-dweller. In spite of the cave's relative warmth, a chill fingered Domingo's back as the stranger spoke again.

"You wear espadrilles, so you're not SS, and neither am I. Why do you travel alone?"

Domingo found his voice. "I might ask you the same."

"Reconnaissance. My team couldn't afford to send anyone along. You?"

Heat raced up Domingo's neck—his quest seemed selfish, despite what Petra said. He opted not to reply and prayed this stranger would soon fall asleep.

"I'll be gone in a couple of hours, but I've been thinking about my grandfather. He was one of the Hautefaye men who tortured an aristocrat, Alain de Moneys, during the Franco-Prussian War. The foolish fellow shouted, '*Vive le République!*' at a local fair."

Torture—just what Domingo needed to hear. Gradually, the outlines of the small space came into focus, and he scolded himself. Petra would have sensed this stranger's presence.

"*Oui*, Moneys's cousin, a Republican, came to visit, but fled when the mob, loyal to Napoleon, attacked. But the drunken crowd misinterpreted Moneys' declaration, and later, he was proven a patriot."

Surely Domingo's sigh reached the storyteller—why repeat these old stories? But the stranger seemed intent on completing his tale.

"A priest attempted in vain to reason with them. The mayor realized things had gotten out of hand, and, not much of a leader, said something like, 'Go ahead, eat him!' So they tortured Moneys for two hours with cudgels and pitchforks, destroyed one of his eyes and nailed horseshoes to his feet before burning him. Some say they sat around the fire, seasoning their *tartines* with his dripping fat."

Domingo gave a silent moan. Why, like Giriotte, did this fellow feel compelled to voice his every thought? Why rehearse these old tales? He tried to shut out the discordant image of burning flesh, but the aristocrat's fate had entered his soul.

"My grandfather retold this account to his dying day, and it came to me a short while before you came. Perhaps it has meaning for you."

Domingo feigned sleep, but the man continued. "You have great weariness of heart, to which I am no stranger. News arrived today of yet another commune ransacked by the SS, and I almost screamed at the messenger, 'Go away—enough!'

"But I heard him out. These stories must surface, or wreak mayhem inside us. And my grandfather's account, though gruesome, instructs me. Though misled about Moneys, the men of Hautefaye acted on their passion. The Huns have shown their furor, so now we act on our passion, as well."

He paused, and Domingo gave a sigh of relief. But then his fallen comrade Giriotte seemed to stand before him whispering, "Have patience."

"You have heard the fame of our *Maquis* that first formed in the north of Limousin?"

Of course—how could Domingo have failed to hear their exploits? They presaged the growth of the Correze group and even the partisans of Lot.

"Edmond Michelet performed the first *Résistance* act in '40 when he distributed tracts urging us to fight, regardless of France's capitulation and Petain's ascendance. One of those tracts appeared in our mailbox, close to Brive-la-Gaillarde. My father scrutinized the message and formed a meeting of six or seven locals that night.

"After they left, he told my grandfather's story, and said, 'We will make some mistakes, as they did, but better to be found in passionate error than to stand by in fear.' That sentiment sustains me, and tonight, perhaps this story strengthens you, as well."

Burying his head in the crook of his arm, Domingo welcomed the silence. He put every energy into focusing on hopeful thoughts—and they centered on Katarin. That remarkable American girl—even when her feet hurt her terribly on the trail, she had maintained silence.

~

To Domingo's surprise, a renegade shaft of sunshine wakened him. Birds twittered as if the war had ended. In a pile of last autumn's leaves, the indentation of the stranger still showed—he must have tiptoed out. Between there and Domingo's pack lay a hand sewn fabric bag tied with twine string.

What would Petra do right now? Domingo half-chuckled. His empty stomach rumbled as he held the bag in his palm. He hadn't touched anything of this soft texture since those dreaded Nazi tanks attacked the Resistance farm at Gaubadet. That name choked him— yes, that night he gave Sancha's scarf to a bewildered woman holding her wounded child. Hopefully, the girl still lived.

Worn drawstrings released without effort, revealing a small loaf of barley bread and a quarter-round of cheese. The meal heartened him. Had the stranger dropped the bag in error? Perhaps not, since he was one to share.

Sunlight dappled the cave. When had he slept this many hours in a row? Domingo eased down to a nearby creek, where cool water brought him to full consciousness. When he looked up, full sun blazed overhead.

"I should have asked him for directions." But even so, the man's boot prints still showed in moist earth, to guide Domingo to the camp. Maybe Petra had been right about this journey, for Providence provided both sustenance and a clear path, in spite of the stranger's grim tale now lurking in Domingo's memory.

~

When Kate asked the cook, hard at work over a mound of potatoes and onions, if he'd seen Père Gaspard, he gave her a frown and a brisk headshake, so she wandered toward the tents. She had yet to rouse a friendly word from him, but determined to prevail.

Even when she offered to help cut vegetables the other day, his surly glance bade her keep her distance. But who knew what he had suffered? Père had no idea if his family lived or died—maybe the cook dealt with a similar situation.

She continued up the slope—Père had to be here somewhere. Beyond the cook's tent a few ragged partisans flopped on the ground to recover from their latest missions, and a wary rat scurried from the brush.

From the north, a low buzz of human murmurings drifted like an incoming tide. Over the ridge, people blended together, young and old.

So many displaced, brought together by terror, peopling temporary shelters that circled a meadow. Kate skirted the gaggle of peasants, townsfolk, and children. By now, the camp in Lot surely contained the same profusion of refugees.

Years ago, Aunt Alvina said no two voices on earth sound exactly alike. "No one has your particular tone, Kathryn, or your precise fingerprints. In all the world, you were created unique."

But in this teeming mass, individuals blurred into one enormous cry for help. All distinctions faded, and clearly, that cry thrummed through Père Gaspard's very soul.

Before turning back, she scanned the camp one more time and

finally spotted him. On the far side of the expanse, he stood listening to an individual addressing a small crowd. One young man held his stomach and ran off into the woods. Kate steeled herself and drew within hearing distance.

"In Tulle, they hanged around a hundred men right in the streets, from balconies and lampposts. They used a weapons factory as a torture chamber, beat people with blackjacks and poured acid on their wounds. The *Milice* sent dozens of men off for deportation."

"How do you know this?"

"My uncle, my grandfather's brother, sent me to tell whomever I found. Much of the information comes from a priest who bears witness."

"What is his name?" Père Gaspard's question rose above the crowd.

The lad shrugged. "I'm not sure..." Someone brought him water, so he drank and wiped his mouth with his dirty shirtsleeve.

"You say they used the school?"

"The girls' school, yes, and the one at Souillac, too."

"The children..."

"I heard nothing about them, but they sent many men away."

Père Gaspard dropped his head into his hands. Others peppered the young messenger with questions.

"I know someone who lives near Oradour. Did the tanks trouble people outside the village?"

"And our own gendarmes do not rise up against them even now?"

"These German swine cannot be human, surely not. They have been possessed."

Tiptoeing forward, Kate touched Père's shoulder. He twisted, and the stunned look in his eyes sickened her. "Will you come away?" she asked.

"Away?"

"For a walk. A person can bear only so much."

"One of the priests in Tulle was my classmate." He stood with his shoulders slumped.

"Tell me about him." She led him away toward the foliage.

"I should not jump to conclusions, perhaps it was someone else. But this friend—oh his fervor! None of us could keep up with him."

The stream's melodic gurgle had a calming effect on them both. On him. But then, as they approached the tents again, a hunched old peasant accosted them. He grabbed Père's sleeve and pulled him closer.

"*Aidez-moi*! Père, only you can help..."

The man's forehead reflected midday sun. Hoarse from running, he scraped out his story. "My granddaughter Vivianne, you must help her, Père."

Père took the fellow's scabby hands and looked into his eyes. "What would you have me do, friend?"

"Not only my granddaughter. You see, there is a woman..."

Père addressed Kate. "Ask the cook for bread and cheese at my request—you will come along?" Without waiting, he turned to the man. "We'll meet you at the edge of camp in a few minutes."

"Of course." Thankfully, she'd finished her work until the next courier appeared.

The cook provided Kate with food for the journey. When she approached Père and the peasant, they sat on a fallen log, deep in conversation, but rose when they saw her.

"Off we go then." The cheer in Père's voice aroused her curiosity.

Green swathed every inch of the path, and wildflowers perked their heads along the way. The old peasant's crooked legs lacked nothing in swiftness, and Père's gait quickened to match his lead.

Kate fell into their rhythm, becoming aware of her own sour odor on the wind. She would have to find a better way to wash than in the creek. What would the cook say if she asked him for a pot of boiling water?

A protruding root caught her toe and launched her into Père Gaspard's backside—it took a few moments to regain her equilibrium. Better pay closer attention. Past a wide rivulet, the route became even more difficult.

Along a hedgerow designed to discourage predators, their small parade came to an opening. Their leader disappeared down an earthen bank, and Père dipped his head to enter.

Like Alice in Wonderland vanishing into her rabbit hole, Kate followed. How long had it been since she thought of that book, the first Aunt Alvina read to her? The two of them spent many evenings before the fireplace, and Alice's adventures accompanied Kate to her bedroom. The characters, so real and sometimes frightening, initiated several visits from Aunt Alvina before sleep came.

In contrast, this dense mass of vines, brambles, chestnuts and blackberries provided a sense of safety. Surely, German soldiers with their heavy boots and packs would find it impenetrable.

TWENTY-EIGHT

"Are we veering toward Argentat?" Père panted his inquiry. "I've lost all sense of direction, though I was born not so far south of here."

A memory from the day her instructor pulled out a map of France came to Kate. He told the agents to memorize all twenty-one regions, focusing on the Auvergne, the Limousin, and the Midi-Pyrénées.

"Picture the Department of Limousin and the Auvergne as a peasant's straw hat. The Midi-Pyrénées, taken with the Auvergne, resembles the American state of Kentucky, but conjure your own image."

The instructor pointed to the Department of Lot and let his wooden pointer linger there. "The Gestapo has difficulty navigating such high country, but not the Maquis—a camp between the Lot the Cantal is impenetrable to the Nazis.

Kate's word picture had come to her in a flash. Taken together, the Auvergne and the Limousin resembled the straw hat Addie plopped on her garden scarecrow a couple of summers ago, and her crooked kitchen stovepipe modeled the elevated Midi-Pyrénées perfectly.

Their guide chose a cow path to the right, crossed over a meadow and plunged almost straight up, following a vine-enclosed path.

The wizened man attempted to encourage Kate and Père "This way takes less time."

"If we live through it." Père muttered.

Steps away, their guide plunged through a ravine, where a hidden stream soaked Kate's espadrilles. The threesome formed a shadowy line through chestnut shadows, making progress across a pebbled expanse. Soon, a homestead appeared, and their leader paused at a small barn. A scrape answered his hesitant taps.

Kate braced herself. Then someone struck a match and a dim lantern glow revealed a face. Little more than a girl, in normal times she would be in pigtails and a school uniform.

But fear lined her darting eyes, and the old man rasped something to her. Then he added, "Père Gaspard, this is my granddaughter."

Père nodded to the girl. "*Bonjour,* my child."

In the deepest shadow behind an upturned wheelbarrow, something stirred. Then came a catlike hiss and a shuffle. Under a black coat, glistening feral eyes shone below a halo of graying hair.

The man continued, "Viviane found this woman in our chicken coop this morning. She'd killed one of the hens and was trying to pluck it. Something has sent her off into another world."

He motioned to Viviane. "Come, child. You have done well." He lifted his grizzled chin toward Père Gaspard.

Viviane reached her hand toward the woman. "Indeed, Madame Lamouette, they can work miracles. I have seen..."

The woman gave a shriek and sprang at Père. Little Viviane leaped back in terror. The woman's thin fingers stretched out like claws.

"May you rot in hell, priest!"

Her spittle hit Kate's cheek. Viviane shushed the woman and pulled at her arm. "Her name is Lamouette."

The woman shoved Viviane aside and stepped into the light from the open door.

"Because of a priest like you, I live, though my family perished. A priest in Saint Jouvent sent word—my mother was dying, and begged for me to come. How could I say no?"

As though putting words to her story strengthened her, she began to pace. "For three days she struggled for every breath while the priest fluttered about, hoping to pry one or two more sous from us.

"*Maman* was wealthy before the German vipers descended. By the time she breathed her last, the priest had vanished, so *Maman* died without last rites." She paused inches from Père and thrust her forefinger in his face. "He stole that consolation from her."

Père's silent stance seemed to quiet her.

"That, I can forgive. What I cannot forgive..." She fell to her knees and dug at the floor.

Kate knelt and wrapped her arms around the miserable woman. She thrashed, but Kate held tight. And then the story tumbled out in sobs and howls.

"The Germans separated the men from the women and children, took the men to barns, and the others to the church—hundreds of them. They told the children to sing as they marched. My son Henri would have obeyed ... such an obedient lad." For a moment her tone softened.

"I can picture the scene—the young men surely helped my blind husband to the barn, into the trap those swine had set."

"They killed them *all!* Machine gunned them, torched the buildings ... my sweet little Henri..."

She broke free and charged Père again. "Where was God then?"

Père reached for her, but she shrank back and turned on Kate. "You resistors—that is why they murder everyone. *Merde!* Their blood be upon you!" Finally, she pitched forward in a faint.

The grandfather held Viviane close. "Thank heaven." He turned to Père. "What shall we do with her?"

He could not wait for a reply. "Perhaps we find a safe place for Viviane, lock Madame in this shed and return for her..."

Père nodded. "*Oui*, a safe place..."

And idea occurred to Kate. "I can go with him and Viviane, Père."

The old peasant studied her. "About a kilometer away, a *maison de la Résistance* has sheltered others in need."

"Yes, this is where I belong." Père sank to the earth beside Madame Lamoutte, and the grandfather wasted no time starting out with his granddaughter and Kate on a different path from the one that led them here. Near a stone house, he gestured to Kate and Vivianne to wait and went ahead, but soon returned and lifted the little girl.

A diminutive woman welcomed them, brought warm milk and bread, and whispered something to a younger woman who disappeared into another room.

When Viviane's grandfather finished his portion, he rose. "I must return to Père and Madame, but we will come back for you."

After he left, Viviane ate, too, and soon slept. The woman beckoned Kate through a short door into a room cloaked in steam.

"*Ici, vous prenez un bain, Mademoiselle.*"

Here, you may bathe. The words swam in Kate's head as the woman bade her remove her filthy clothes. She left with them over her arm, and in a trance, Kate immersed herself—real soap, a scrubbing brush, and the sweet smell of lavender.

Half an hour later, in a pair of trousers and flannel shirt the woman had left on a trunk, Kate studied her face in a misty mirror.

"Yes, I do recognize you." She pulled a brush through her hair, fashioned a single braid, and entered the kitchen to ask after Viviane.

"Still, she sleeps. Perhaps you would like to join her?"

A bed with a fresh-smelling coverlet—how could this be true? Thinking she could never fall asleep, Kate sank into the luxury, and a quote from one of her instructors entered her thoughts. "If you recall your Roman history, you may remember the playwright Plautus. He wrote, 'consider the little mouse, how sagacious an amimal it is which never entrusts his life to one hole only.'"

Ah...so many holes she'd visited. She wakened only when Viviane's grandfather entered the house.

The woman roused Viviane, and Kate quickly dressed in her own clothes, now clean and dry. She accepted a food bag and thanked the woman for her kindness.

"Such is the way of war. One comes, another goes, and we do what we can."

When she inquired about Madame, Père shook his head. "We could only listen to her again before she ran off." He held up his palms. "Sometimes my training does me no good at all."

All the way back to camp, Kate luxuriated in the feel of the breeze against her skin. But the camp buzzed with news of Oradour—tales wrapped the place like fog and partisans spoke in hushed voices.

"It happened yesterday, but the smoke still rises ..."

"A few children escaped and one or two adults. Only charred buildings remain."

The words seared Kate's heart. She had clung to the hope that Madame Lamoutte, in her feverish grief, had been mistaken.

Père Gaspard fell in with a group they passed, but Kate continued on to her cave. Would this unthinkable news have reached London yet by the hand of some other operator?

The British had faced such horrors—her days of joining Mrs. Tenney in her air warden duties, with bombs falling in the night, came to mind. The citizens had cursed the Germans, yet banded together, as she pictured them doing even now, with V-1 rockets killing hundreds more.

The War Ministry once again posted warnings and notices in the tube stations, as people descended on them late each day, hoping for a safe night huddled together underground. And the Prime Minister continued to address his people—another speech to sustain them through the second Blitz. Through all its history, the English always summoned words.

But for this face-to face slaughter of women and children in Oradour, Kate could find none.

~

Just when Domingo thought he must be near the camp, sounds of a struggle wafted from some brambly growth staggering a rise. His ears told him only one person writhed a few meters beyond. Panting, moaning, wriggling against metal, then silence. He continued in that direction.

Then he spied an airplane wing stuck three-quarters of the way up some saplings. He traced the plane's track all the way back through the woods and waited, his heart in his throat.

When sounds came again, he climbed a sturdy chestnut sapling. Ander taught him well—always seek the highest place. June sunshine amplified the foliage, making it difficult to gain a clear view, but what showed through dappled leaves left Domingo breathless.

The airplane had crashed some time ago, the only sign of life a shivering blood-soaked arm. Mangled aluminum trapped the rest of a man's body.

Deathly pale against his brown leather jacket, the hapless flyer seemed to aim his hand for a rectangular black box, perhaps a motor. A short scope and long silver bolts stuck out from dark protrusions on the mechanism's side. Domingo shinnied down and knelt as close as he could to the injured fellow.

Blood-matted hair, hazel eyes, and a fist-sized bruise from temple to jawbone. But those eyes still radiated purpose.

Only one English word occurred to Domingo. "American?"

The soldier blinked and gestured toward the black box. "Bombardier ... have to destroy..."

Intent on keeping him alive, Domingo paid no attention. He'd never witnessed such severe trembling, and opened the man's leather jacket to a puddle of flesh, blood, and bone. He tore off his shirt to cover the poor fellow.

"I will... get you out." The English words sounded stilted, but the man understood.

"Too late..." He hooked Domingo's arm with his hand and strained his eyes toward the black box. Seconds later, they rolled back in his head.

Domingo supported his neck. "Here. Let me..."

The man gasped. "Top ... secret.... destroy ..."

For a moment, his final breath hovered in the airy warmth. Then, with a shudder, the bombardier slipped away in Domingo's arms.

Salt filled Domingo's throat and tears stung his eyes. From the land of Katarin's birth, this fellow offered himself for *la France*, for him, grandson of Aitaita Ibarra of the Basque regions near the Pyrenees.

For his cantankerous people, conquered and divided between countries throughout the ages, for France, split into political regions and departments and now ruled by malicious oppressors, this American gave his life. Domingo bowed his head. *Greater love has no man than this ...*

He closed the bombardier's eyes, as Père Gaspard would do and made the sign of the cross. *Les inconnus...*Pere spoke of common French citizens, but this American, too, qualified. Perhaps his family would never know the story of his sacrifice.

No one ought to die like this way, an ocean away from his birthplace. But the brave fellow wore no identification—strange. Domingo carefully positioned the bombardier's head in the rubble and crawled through the sharp metal mess.

He eyed the object that held the American's attention to his last breath. Cast iron.

It weighed far more than any radio or ammunition crate he'd hauled away from a parachute drop, more than that heisted pack of gold bars. He braced his feet and brought the box to his waist. Panting, he hoisted the box from the wreckage and hauled it a few meters beyond the airplane.

A vague recollection of an invention Père Gaspard described surfaced then, something about the need to level a bomber and measure the wind. The alignment of gages and lenses intrigued Domingo, but how to destroy them with only his knife and small pistol, an M1911? Petra said its bullets would fell a Nazi with one shot, but what good would bullets do now?

Besides, a shot might alert the *Milice* or Gestapo to the crash site, and that would not do. The partisans must get here first.

Destroy—twice the bombardier used that word. There was a small shed about five minutes down the trail—maybe a tool lay in there. Domingo ran full force and returned with a sledgehammer. His first blow crushed the eyepiece on top, his second, a recorder at the lower right.

The impact reverberated up his arms, but he imagined the American smiling. With no deep water nearby to drown the box, Domingo rummaged through the rubble and found a piece of metal to dig a hole behind a large rock. Every few minutes, he paused to listen, until finally, he half rolled, half carried the apparatus and shoved it in. Dripping with sweat, he shoveled earth and green moss over the depression before hefting more large rocks over the area.

For a moment, then, he hesitated, looking back at the American. "I buried your secret, and I will bury you, too..."

With vultures already circling and no way to remove the body, he wrangled a large piece of steel from the other end of the debris to cover the fallen warrior. As he pushed it in place, something metal glinted up from the earth, and Domingo retrieved it—the impact must have blown this small rectangle from its chain. *Calvin R. Pierce* Numbers then, and *Catholic*.

"Had you grown up here, you might have attended my parish."

Domingo bit his lip. "I'll bring some men to help, and the enemy will never find a trace of you."

For once, speaking his thoughts aloud brought Domingo a measure of comfort. One more set of human eyes would accompany him now—hazel eyes. But at least this man had not died alone. If only he could pool all the losses of this war into one and bury it as he had that bombsight.

At the camp, he enlisted the cook and two others. Back at the crash site, they entombed much of the charred bomber, along with the bombardier and two other crewmembers.

Gathered around the grave, someone whispered, "*Repose en paix.*" They stood in the afternoon stillness for a full minute. Then someone made a move, and they returned to the trail. Domingo brought up the rear, relieved that no one engaged him in small talk.

Rest in peace ... In Katarin's native tongue, the bombardier's farewell would sound like this. But peace seemed otherworldly now, entirely at odds with this confused earth. Her smile flitted through Domingo's consciousness, but the bombardier's final pleading expression overwhelmed all else.

Heaviness of heart slowed Domingo's pace. How much more suffering could his country embrace? The Great War, the horrible fighting in Spain, and now this present endless debacle drenched the land in blood. Graves everywhere, and the news from the northern beaches listed tens of thousands more.

Eventually he caught up with the rest, and twilight followed them into camp. One of the men showed Domingo to a tent. He collapsed in sleep, but the bombardier's countenance still accompanied him. Perhaps these eyes would take the place of the American pilot he had left behind under that rotting carcass so many months ago.

The pilot's comrade had said, "You can come back for him later— otherwise, we'll all die." But even so, had he made the right choice?

Once, Domingo startled awake, hardly aware of his location. After he oriented himself and settled back under his blanket, a lone star peeked at him from the heavens. Then a newfound realization gripped him. The peculiar essence burrowed deep inside, a fresh yearning he had heard others voice, but never before entertained.

Yet certainty rode this unexpected new longing. He wanted to go to the far-away land of America.

TWENTY-NINE

After stopping to refuel in Mexico, the small aircraft soared on to land in lush Peruvian high country. Benjamin announced each location, and said they'd make another stop in Santiago. They sailed on above mountains and lakes so beautiful they made Kathryn gasp. Benjamin chatted with the pilot, and from time to time, brought word of their present location.

As if the biting air had stunned her senses, Kathryn lost track of landings and takeoffs. She couldn't still be tired, and yet she slept. Anything was better than warding off Benjamin's attempts at conversation. He seemed bent on forcing her to find joy in this circumstance. Let him try—she wanted only to complete the task and go home.

What day was it? What date? Fatigue enfeebled her mind and her thoughts ran aimlessly. The rodeo—what about Mara's rodeo? Worse, she conjured the look on that precious child's face if Grandma failed to appear.

"Don't worry," Benjamin intoned more than once. "We're ahead of schedule. As soon as you identify our man, we're back in this plane."

Easy for him to say, when she had no control over anything. The only time she'd experienced this sense of utter helplessness was during the winter months before D-Day when Eugene forced the dissolution of her circuit. Half the time, she'd awakened not knowing where she was. But back then, she'd been younger and better able to cope with uncertainty.

Now, she'd forgotten how to manage the ambivalence that threatened her. She'd made the right choice in coming, surely she had. And yet, her aching body declared the opposite. How could she have endangered herself like this, after all she'd been through these past weeks?

Benjamin's odd accent was mildly British, but with something else added. "Do you want to visit Israel? You would marvel at the greening of our country and life on a *kibbutz*."

All I want for the rest of my life is to stay at home—Idaho's plenty beautiful for me.

Stubbornness reared up in Kathryn, and she determined not to answer him. Why should she, when he'd stolen even more priceless time from her? As if losing six whole weeks of her life from the accident weren't enough. That scene replayed endlessly, still full of mystery: the strange fall, the veiled reference to Klaus Barbie.

And then, as Benjamin announced that they finally approached Argentina's border, something inside Kathryn snapped. A moment before, she'd sat in this filthy airplane seat with only questions, but all of a sudden, she knew. As surely as he wore brown tweed, this man had pushed her in the church balcony.

Gall rose in her throat, and she stared him down as he launched some stupid pleasantry her way. Something in his eyes changed. He understood.

"You are to bring up old memories, but not *that* memory, Kathryn."

She turned toward the window. How dare he pretend friendliness? True, he may only have meant to alert her to his presence, but why sneak up on her in the first place?

Cold chills ran up her arm when he touched her wrist, and she pulled away. She might have agreed to meet this present need, but that didn't mean she did it for him, or that she had to put on a friendly act.

The lack of a timepiece made this horrid ride even worse. One hour ran into the next, and today fused with tomorrow, with such a tentative hope of escape.

"Only one more refueling. Trust me."

When ewes grow antlers. Benjamin—or whoever he was—turned to his comrade behind them, suddenly businesslike.

"All right, let's go over the plan again. A taxi takes us into the city, and we stake out near the school. Perfect timing. He visits on Wednesdays and walks his grandchild home. All we need is one good look at him."

Kathryn turned his last words into a prayer. "One good look at him—please, let it happen right away."

~

Domingo awakened to a gritty mud smell, the same endless miry earth that had slowed him and the other partisans as they'd sifted through the mangled bomber and buried the bodies yesterday. But another scent enticed him, rough and inviting.

He opened his eyes fully to a steaming tin mug perched on a tree stump. Not far beyond the cup, creating a dark, textured backdrop, sat Père Gaspard. Domingo shook his head. He must be dreaming.

But indeed, Père leaned against a tent pole, asleep. His legs sprawled out under his soutane, the bottoms of his espadrilles worn thin. It must be afternoon, for that singular mottled effect created by a late-day sun colored the tent canvas and created a scarlet halo of Père's impossibly snarled hair.

Soundlessly, Domingo sat up and stretched his arms. But when he reached for the cup, Père's blue-sky eyes surveyed him with an impossible-to-read expression. As Domingo sipped the hot elixir, a flood of recent memories nearly strangled him.

The bombardier. The black box. The burial, and then that long, hard climb through slippery mud. He and the others toted everything recognizable that was left at the site. No question, they must hide as much as possible from the enemy, even though the Bosche might never range this high.

Partisans lost their footholds and slid into each other on the path, cursing the rain and the mud. But that had been hours ago. Now, Domingo stretched briefly, having relished the luxury of sleep, and waking on his own.

"What?"

Père's artless inquiry roused untamed emotion, but Domingo gathered his wits. The hot chicory opened his sinuses, and a deep breath cleared his mind. Could that really be Père Gaspard? At last, he trusted his voice to respond.

"Père."

"*Oui*. What is it?"

Some minutes passed. This most recent incident, like all the rest, lingered unspeakable. Why rehearse it? Yet the look in Père's eyes invited Domingo to speak, and drew out the pain like a compress on a sprain.

"We ... I met an American. He died for us, Père, a bombardier. He never had a chance. Do you remember that invention you told me about, that gauges the winds and balances an airplane? He wanted it destroyed, so I..." He gulped.

A hint of emotion passed over Père's face, and suddenly Domingo remembered the truffle hunter who told him that the SS tanks hit Terrou. He must ask after Père's family.

"What do you hear of Terrou?"

Père rubbed his nose between his thumb and forefinger. He closed his eyes and gave his head a slight shake.

"Later, my son. You have slept long and hard. You must be ravenous. I'll get you something to eat. Drink your coffee while I fetch you some food. Then we'll take a walk."

~

After hours at the radio, Kate fell asleep. But a vivid memory blasted her back into consciousness. It was months ago, when she'd acclimated to her courier duties and begun to feel at home in the Clermont-Ferrand circuit.

The city's towering black steeples had beckoned her when she'd returned from an assignment. She pedaled her bicycle along the tree-lined road until all of a sudden, the two outstanding landmarks appeared. Only that brief figment, but why should she recall those dark steeples right now? True, they comprised a landmark *extraordinaire*, but had always seemed more sinister than comforting.

With no idea what time of day it was, she stepped outside her cave and found the sun risen and well on its way across the sky. Better take a walk to clear her head. She wandered to the refugee area, hoping to see Père Gaspard. These days, he flitted in and out of camp like a nervous bird—who knew how many people sought him?

Ah, there he sat at the far edge of the camp, speaking with someone. Of course, wasn't he always? The man sat with his back to her. Kate looked again, and the thickness of the listener's neck stopped her in her tracks.

Domingo's name slipped from her lips, part-question, part cry. Across the distance, Père Gaspard spotted her, then re-focused on Domingo. Though she longed to rush through the makeshift tents, Kate backed away and hurried to her den.

At the entrance, she stilled her wild heartbeat. Père knew what he was about, and he knew Domingo. The almost imperceptible movement of his head instructed her to pray. This was no time to consider her desires.

Père was telling Domingo about Madame Ibarra and Gabirel. That alone mattered. The rest, she must leave to fate.

At the thought that she might not see Domingo, she clutched her throat, but in the hushed coolness of the cave, Kate held out her hands. With a groan, she let go her tenacious longings.

In that act, a fresh, profound sense of serenity arose, as though her whole future had been pressing in on her, the future she could not know. She'd held on to it as if she maintained control, as if things yet to come would yield to her wishes even before they occurred.

All foolishness—how well she knew. But in this moment, she stopped wrestling and knelt at her makeshift bed. Before her closed eyes, a sky full of stars appeared. They shone as real as though she looked up into the great bowl of the heavens.

Their glitter, so strong and close, called up tears and drew her lifetime out before her as if each twinkle signified an experience. At the same time, she understood that each experience rested in the hands of a loving God, the victorious champion sculpted on Saint Pierre's tymphanum.

No meek and mild Deity, this, and far more than the capricious fate that mere humans conjured. No, far more than that, because through each sorrow, a twinkle in this vast heaven evidenced the Almighty's presence. The pain of losing her parents, her aunt, Alexandre, their baby, the wrench of leaving Addie behind in London, and then Monsieur le Blanc's passing paraded before her mind's eye.

But somehow, here in this dank, solitary space, compassion encompassed all these memories. Such a great loving concern enfolded her, at one with the guidance that brought her here, and with the call back to London that allowed her to witness Addie's wedding.

Her whisper floated out. "I am never alone. No matter what happens, I never will be. And though I've felt so lost, You have always been with me. You brought me to Aunt Alvina and Addie. You gave me Alexandre and brought Monsieur le Blanc to me, and with him, my father."

Her words circled in the cavern like friendly fireflies in an Iowa cornfield. As Père Gaspard had said, even in the midst of his own weighty losses, all was well. That truth filled Kate afresh. She knew it in her soul, and spoke the sentiment aloud.

"All is well."

She gave herself to her work. Some time later, she peered outdoors again. Late afternoon closed in on the camp. Morning had always been her favorite part of the day, but she lingered at the opening to allow evening shadows to lengthen over her.

Oh, how lovely the growing dusk seemed right now— a time to pause the day's occupation. Morning, afternoon, dusk, evening, and night. Come what may, this constant rhythm endured.

Still no sign of Domingo, but quiet acceptance cloaked Kate. Grief required time and space, and his needs mattered more than anything else. "Please, even in the midst of the dreadful pain that lies ahead, give him peace."

~

"My son, we have received word about your family. First through a courier on the Causse de Gramat, and then again early this morning."

Domingo's ears rang, not unlike the bonging in the belfry at Tulle when he hung on the rope to warn the village. He and Père might be meeting on a deserted island instead of within earshot of the refugee camp.

Maybe Père chose this place because he surmised Domingo's legs could take him nowhere else. Whatever his reasons, Domingo surmised the truth before they sat on a fallen log. Then tears coursed Père's lean face.

"I harangued the courier, though he had no reason to lie to us." A pang crossed Domingo's chest. *So Katarin knows, too.*

Père read his thoughts. "She heard the first report, but not this second witness. She bears you in her heart, Domingo—your mother and Gabirel, as well. When I heard today's confirmation, I waited to tell her so she could hear the news from you."

Domingo's heart throbbed against his rib cage.

"No partisan rides the train to Montauban, meets a peasant boy named Gabirel grieving his mother's recent death, and flees to this particular camp to tell the story unless God deigns it.

He told the tale with a mournful heart."

"Tell me what he said."

"Your mother stayed brave to the end, when she suffered a heart attack being transferred between train cars. She passed in an instant, Gabirel told him. Your brother was right there with her when she passed."

"If only I had been home when those vermin came ... why would they bother with an old woman?" Domingo bowed his head and Père embraced him. When Domingo could speak again, a single question surfaced.

"*Maman* knew no pain?"

"Perhaps at first, but only for a short period."

"I want to meet this fellow who spoke with Gabirel."

"He left hours ago, bound for parts north." Père leaned his elbow on his knee and peered into Domingo's eyes. "Your mother did not suffer long, but surely poor Gabirel still does. And suffering means hope."

More than once, Domingo had heard Père say this. *To live means to suffer. Therefore, in suffering, we find hope. And when we die, we rest in the hands of our merciful God, with all of our hopes fulfilled at last.*

"But if I had been there, at least I could have fought them. How can I...?" Domingo's cry faded into a groan. "Now, what will they do with Gabirel? How will he survive?"

"No amount of regret alters the past and no amount of anxiety has power to change the future. We can only manage the present—believe me, these recent weeks have shown me how poorly I do that. But still the Almighty deals patiently with me."

So like Père, conveying eternal truths, yet as practical as potatoes.

"What would you like to do?"

Domingo shrugged. Follow the rail line to Germany? Sheer folly, though the race itself might heal him. No, he must fight, and after the war, return home to wait. Perhaps one day when the rails had been repaired, the train would roar into Figeac from the east, bearing his little brother.

If not, he could seek Gabirel Martino Ibarra, his last living family member, in Germany. But in the meantime, he would fight like a wild bull. Strangely, that desire tamed his pain.

"Walk with me some more."

They wove through people, sleeping, eating, crying and laughing—alive. Then Père chose a trail past water gliding over tumbled rocks. They sat, silent in the sound.

Finally, Père asked again. "What will you do, Domingo?"

"Fight."

"And what else lies in your heart?"

Today had shown Domingo that his heart told him the truth. Even Petra's insights and superhuman perception on the trail lacked Domingo's own instinctive wisdom concerning *Maman*. From now on, he would rely on that intuition, yet what his heart contained at this moment, he surely must keep hidden. To speak of Katarin would be presumption.

Instead, he asked a question, as Petra taught him. "What do you think?"

Père shrugged. "What I think means nothing." Meaning passed between them, yet Domingo still hesitated.

"Where is…"

"She's here, transmitting. She carries you and your family—holds you up for mercy. Whom do you carry, Domingo?"

Hoarse as dry bones, Domingo murmured "Katarin" under the water's babble. But Père read the name on his lips as if he'd shouted it for all the world to hear. This priest, who'd baptized and confirmed him, knew him through and through.

"Ah. So it is, love in the midst of hatred." Père stared out over the water. A long minute passed, then another. In this quietness, what might he be thinking?

Better yet, what would he be praying? Their many talks ran through Domingo's mind. Ever since the news came of Papa and Ander's deaths, Père Gaspard had been his rock. Especially after Sancha's death, Père's perspective sustained him.

Finally, Père repeated himself. "What will you do?"

"It would not be fair to her to … I'll find Petra and join the fight now. Besides, London may call her back at any moment."

"Actually, they already did. But yes, they could again—and so?"

"This would add one more puzzle for her."

"Do you claim to know our Creator's mind?"

Domingo gulped. "But if I die…"

"What then?"

"She's already lost her husband."

"You presume God cannot care for her?"

"But what if…"

"She does not return your love? Every man takes such a risk, as you did with Sancha. Do you regret obeying your heart with her?"

"No." The answer came strong, like the sizzle of fish frying over a campfire.

"And do you feel any less for Kate than you did for Sancha?"

This time Père's question seemed nonsensical. How could one measure such things?

"If you die, our American friend will know you loved her, and love makes all things bearable. Her husband's death led her here, after all. But a lifetime of not knowing you cared for her would amount to torture."

In silence, Père rose. They walked until they approached a woman hunched over an iron skillet.

"You will stay the night?"

"*Oui.* Where do you sleep?"

"Over there." Père pointed to a tarp. "Always room for one more."

"Where...?"

"In a bunker behind the cook's tent. I can take you there." Neither of them spoke her name, but Domingo pictured Katarin like that woman cooking by her campfire, only Katarin huddled over her transmitter.

Père turned toward the refugees, while Domingo took a roundabout route into the forest. Two truths transfixed him: his life had changed forever, yet his inner perception prepared him for hearing about *Maman*. He began to grieve her back in Lot, when he tasted that apple in her kitchen.

Gabirel's destiny remained a vast question mark, but an inner sense, fibrous and lithe, strengthened Domingo for the wait. *Waiting on the war.* Maybe Giriotte or another partisan-turned-comrade had used that phrase. A shaggy willow offered its shade, and Domingo sank against it as afternoon waned. Around him, mice or other small animals foraged before seeking shelter for the night.

He must let *Maman* go now, here in this place, with no service in their small church and no burial place to visit. This was war's way, harsh and swift. And he must pray for Gabirel. He must believe he would survive. Gabirel would feel his prayers, surely. He must live, for how could Domingo carry on the Ibarra name alone?

His chest hurt when he thought of *Maman,* a hurt that might never release. But in offering her up, the pressure at the back of his neck lessened.

And then came this other thing, what bound him to Katarin, an American who would return to her homeland when this was all over. Domingo circled the camp. He could leave now and allow Providence to write the future. But Père thought otherwise, and Aitaita's voice instructed him, too.

If you love someone, do not rush to proclaim your feelings. Wait until all seems right.

With Sancha, that had been possible, yet now, nothing seemed right. Certainty had become a dream, the present a nightmare, and the future a jumble of pending battles. *Right* had collapsed into a meaningless syllable. Yet Père pointed him to the present.

By the time they met again, Domingo knew he could not leave

without seeing Katarin. He would tell her about *Maman,* that was all. But when he rounded the tents and saw Père walking to meet him, he knew he would say more, for Père's eyes reflected courage and conviction.

"You are ready?"

"*Oui.*"

Père's long stride led around the cook's tent, where they armed themselves with hot chicory. Then Père led the way. An odd calmness attended Domingo as dusk deepened into twilight.

"There." He followed Père's gesture, took the extra steaming cup from him, and walked on alone.

THIRTY

Kathryn had done what she promised, and stood stunned at the enormity of her act. Vaguely aware of the sun's warmth on her shoulders and a minor afternoon breeze against her legs, she allowed the past and future to slip away. All that mattered was this moment.

It turned out, after all, that the man they wanted her to identify was not Barbie—they'd located him elsewhere. But high in this Andes village, seemingly at the end of the known earth, they'd cornered one of the henchmen who had facilitated his brutality.

A streak of bitterness rode Kathryn's throat—nice of them to conceal that fact until the very last instant. But now she finally knew how Maurice had met his death—at the hands of this scar-faced servant of the Reich.

On a sunny street a few minutes before school let out, an older man approached the entrance. Stooped now, it was easy to see that he'd been a giant in his day.

Benjamin hissed at Kathryn, "Go back to the day you saw Barbie. We assume you also observed his guard?"

"Yes."

"At close range?"

"Close enough to remember. He aimed a gun our way." The moment outside Clermont-Ferrand with its dark steeples returned as if it recurred right now. "He had a jagged scar on the right side of his face."

Benjamin's foot jitterbugged against the car's floorboard. He sounded breathless. "Look carefully at that man waiting over there. Is that who you saw that day?"

Before Kathryn could answer, a teacher opened the school door and children flowed out. One little girl ran toward the man they watched, and he scooped her up in his arms.

As he did, he turned toward the car, revealing the exact scar Kathryn recalled. At the same time, Benjamin's cohort bent to his camera sight.

Snap. Snap.

Such a crisp sound on this windless day—what if the exiled German had heard? Kathryn bit her lip. But the grandfather set the girl down and ambled from the schoolyard toward a steep descent. The innocent child clutched his hand and chattered.

The cameraman put away his apparatus and took the driver's seat. When Benjamin poked him in the shoulder, he turned the key and gunned the engine. They sped down a street.

"So, that's finished. We've got him." The cameraman careened around city corners as he addressed Benjamin. "The locals deny it, but he's not the only one they harbor here."

He twisted toward Kathryn. "At long last, we have secured our evidence. Our nation owes you a debt of gratitude."

The sight of that former Nazi, calmly awaiting the blonde, curly-haired sprite after her school day, had yet to leave Kathryn. But the scene Benjamin had described to her, of this very man pulling Maurice by his ankles down flights of granite stairs until he bled from the ears juxtaposed with this one.

How could this monster live here in safety, well fed, dressed in a fine suit and enjoying his family? After what he'd stolen from so many during the war, how could he put it all behind him and live out his life here in these beautiful mountains? What enabled him to slip into a fog of forgetfulness about such dire events? Could he sleep at night?

At least she had absolutely no doubt he was the one. How could she ever forget his image from that day when she'd sought to deliver a message to Eugene?

Benjamin's shadow partner waited for her response, but Kathryn was in no mood. She only wanted to get back to Idaho, whatever it took. A little girl waited for her too, a bright, bubbly treasure with her own grandfather's inky eyes—intelligent eyes, measuring the world around her, but also kind and always ready to help.

Benjamin's ragged sigh left her unfazed. She'd done her duty and owed him nothing. Now the responsibility fell to him to keep his promise.

As if he read her mind, he mumbled. "Don't worry. We'll get you back in time. I swear it. You'll be the worse for wear, true, but delivered to your family."

His eyes looked gray all around—perhaps he nursed an ailment unknown to Kathryn. Perhaps he suffered from more than his eternal determination to find the Nazis who disappeared after the war.

The thought of suffering brought Addie to mind. Kathryn simply couldn't get used to the idea that her illness might take her before her time. That letter she sent from London at Christmastime had painted such a positive picture—Charles and their two adult children were getting along fine.

But in her next letter, Addie described her visit to a doctor. Kathryn had to read the careful handwriting over and over in order to take in the meaning. Tumor...possible surgery ... questionable outcome ... loss of motor skills ...

What did it all mean? Might Addie become paralyzed?

Benjamin rubbed his left temple, and something about his posture touched Kathryn. Did he have a family of his own? Driven as he was for justice, it might be better if he traversed this world alone. They parked in a large lot, left the car, and he hustled her to the airplane.

Only as she settled into the uncomfortable seat did she realize how sore she was. Her shoulders, her neck, her back. But at least the long return trip had begun. She swallowed a pain pill without water and realized the gift of this moment—she could once again sleep.

~

At the cook's tent, Kate listened to word about increased V1 attacks in London. "In Grove Road, Hackney, they killed six last week, and then on Sunday they struck the Hungerford Rail Bridge and Guards Chapel, St. James—Wellington Barracks. The service had just started, the church was packed with guardsmen and their families, and more than a hundred and thirty were killed.

"We once laughed at Hitler's 'secret weapon'—thought it was a joke. After all, what else could he do to us that he hadn't already tried? But as I took off two days ago, we flew near the church. Total destruction—they were still searching the rubble for bodies."

She'd come hoping for a bowl of stew, but the news dissolved Kate's appetite. Addie and Charles said their vows farther north in the city, but still—London was London, and these new attacks meant even more suffering.

Back in her cave, she checked for messages, but Domingo's face rose before her, along with others. They came to her so often in memory, their portraits might have hung along the walls of this refuge. Mrs. Tenney in her air warden garb, Madame at the Presbytery in Le-Chambon, Maurice and Eugene, that woman she called Auntie outside Clermont-Ferrand, the pastor who'd hidden her overnight, Monsieur le Blanc, Gabirel, Madame Ibarra ...

Her very existence depended on each of these people for certain periods of time, yet they entered and exited her life so quickly. With no way of knowing their fates, she could only hold them up to the Almighty.

An hour or two later, a courier brought messages of more drop locations, so Kate lit the oil lantern and continued her work. Remembering Mother Helene's warning, she gave the transmitter a rest, even though the Gestapo had failed to penetrate to this isolated camp.

When she emerged from her shelter, a pale moon shone over temporary refugee tents, lending a placid air to this corner of the world. But the Gestapo might even now be shutting off electricity to every town in the region, one by one, so it would be easy to detect where a transmitter still worked.

True, they were unable to detect battery transmissions, but why not stay on the safe side? Leave it to the Germans to have invented yet an even more versatile device. She pulled out the miniature receiving set, also run by batteries, and tuned in to the BBC, flooded with personal messages and war music.

Tonight, they featured Vera Lynn's *There'll be Bluebirds Over the White Cliffs of Dover.* "We bring you that timely gift from American lyricists Walter Kent and Nat Burton. Oh, how this tune uplifted our spirits during those early years when we fought alone!

"Back then, ugly manmade birds with horrendous bombs flew over Dover. As most Brits knew, bluebirds, native to the United States, would likely never fly over those white cliffs. But still, the image brought hope to every British heart. That hope remains steadfast as new birds descend, complete with a complementary buzzing sound."

A postlude followed the song. "As to what I said earlier, mates. Knowing the ingenuity of our Allies across the Atlantic, who am I to say bluebirds will never fly here? This war has brought a multitude of innovations, so why not bluebirds over those white cliffs?"

Heaviness descended on Kate. Back in the winter of '42, when she first arrived in Great Britain, she'd witnessed the aftermath of the Blitz, and then far more destruction by the Luftwaffe. The announcer intended to cheer his listeners, noting that all the ingenuity of the United States, England, Canada, Australia, Poland, and so many other countries amassed in one great effort on the beaches north of here.

Surely the Allies would win—how could they not, when so much had been sacrificed? But Domingo's sorrow weighed on Kate.

For the hundredth time, she sent up a prayer for him. Miss G, eyes blazing, came to mind then. During training, she broached the subject of romance more than once with the female agents.

"Your mission comes before all else. If you do become entangled, be discreet, and then put the relationship out of your head. Concentrate on your work. Lives depend on you."

Put it out of your head. At the time, Kate assumed that would be the easiest part of her task, since grief for Alexandre and their baby still consumed her. Now, time had brought healing, but she certainly hadn't meant for her heart to become linked to Domingo.

After she ate a little supper, she walked her plate back to the kitchen. Mellow eveningtide quieted her spirit, and back in her cavern, she lighted her lantern and tackled her work again. But Domingo's image persisted—his heart must be broken.

"Help him, and help me concentrate."

The camp quieted until only a low murmur, like the hum of insects, wafted from the refugee area, along with the smell of humanity massed together. At the same time, Kate caught of whiff of herself. The effects of that wonderful bath out in the countryside had faded completely. If Domingo did come, she'd have another good reason to keep her distance.

And if he didn't ... well, she'd learned a lot about herself. She was no heroine like Madame Dreyfus, and no Nancy Wake. At best, she'd come here in good faith, but in her darkest moments, wondered if she only pretended to risk all for the Allied cause. If she allowed for utter truthfulness, her longing to discover her family roots, lost so long ago, might have equaled that selfless desire.

For a few seconds, she toyed with a cowardly possibility. She could leave the camp and vanish into the Auvergne. In so doing, she would drop from the history of the S.O.E. Eventually, the records would report her as missing in action. Maybe after the war, they would send someone to search for her, but most likely not. Hadn't they warned new recruits that they would enjoy no protection under British law?

Even if they searched for her, they'd find no trace, because she'd have wended her way northeast, to the Great War front. With so many refugees on the move, how hard could that be? There, she'd visit Chaumont, where her parents began their life together. She'd track down their history and maybe even discover where her mother worked. Père believed this was possible, so why shouldn't she?

And then? Perhaps she'd live the rest of her life as the French woman she might have been, had her parents chosen to live here instead of in the States. But the next minute, she shook off these speculations. Why couldn't she simply remain in the present and live into the outcome of her questions? Why must she forever analyze memories and clues?

Listening to the BBC often brought release from her ponderings. Maybe something significant would ride the airwaves tonight.

Sometime after full dark, a shuffle sounded at the entrance. Ah, probably Père Gaspard, who had not come all day. Kate switched off the machine and stretched. The aroma of hot chicory invaded the cave as she turned toward the shadows.

But the step belonged to someone else—a wayfarer laced with the scent of decayed leaves, mud, and intensity. Then the breadth of Domingo's shoulders, even in this dim light, startled Kate into recognition.

He hesitated before dragging a wooden crate near. He held out the cup to her and sat on the crate as if he'd entered like this often. Kate sank back into her chair and grasped the handle as the anguish written on Domingo's face smote her. Unbidden, a strange sound rasped from her throat.

The angular planes of Domingo's face dipped in hollows. His eyes were two bright glimmers in the lantern light. A shiver passed over Kate's shoulders at the low tenor of his voice.

"So, you are here."

Fullness swamped her throat. Silence pulsed between them until Domingo said, "I wanted to..."

But Kate spoke at the same time. "Père Gaspard told you about...?"

She waited, and Domingo answered her question. "*Oui.* And about *Maman's* stalwart courage up to the end."

The cup trembled in Kate's hand.

"She died in Montauban, with Gabirel beside her. Père heard the news this morning from someone who met Gabirel after she passed."

Kate's hot chicory spilled, and she stared at the glistening splash of liquid on packed earth, a dark comma in the lantern light.

Domingo touched her shoulder, and his arm blurred the space between them. "I knew it before, in my heart, but hearing the details helps. Likely, *crise cardiaque* took *Maman*, and she passed quickly. No one could have done anything to save her."

A heart attack, but brought on by the S.S. Kate closed her eyes as if to blot out the scene. When she opened them, something besides tears smoldered in Domingo's eyes, something serene and strong, quiet yet fluid. She held onto that essence, even as she choked on her words.

"I am so sorry."

"At least *Maman* died with Gabirel beside her."

She covered her lips with her fingers, but her cry still came forth, and Domingo embraced her with such concern, Kate could scarcely bear it. She drew back. "Forgive me."

"Why?"

"You comfort me in your loss."

Domingo swept the shadows with his hand. "The loss belongs to both of us. But perhaps, in spite of everything, this will become my time for joy." His eyes flamed in the undulating light. He let out a long breath and dropped his arms. "Katarin Isaacs."

His tender tone froze her in place.

"Away from you these weeks, I ..."

The walls closed in. A suffocating sensation threatened to smother her.

"I have found that..." His intense gaze pierced her. "*J'ai besoin de toi.*"

"You ... you need me?"

He pressed his lips together. So close she felt his breath on her forehead, he grazed her jawline with his forefinger, igniting fire down her spine.

"I do not want to leave you, *jamais*... never. And though I must, you will stay in my heart."

Kate's cheeks burned. At the same time, goose bumps covered her arms. Thick worry lines razed Domingo's brow, so she reached for him with a single word. "Domingo..."

He stroked her hair, reminding her of the incredible comfort she experienced when he broke into a lullaby after Monsieur le Blanc's passing. She let him pull her close until her tears spilled over.

When she could speak again, she whispered, "You have my heart, Domingo Ibarra. *Toujours.*"

Always. His breath wisped her cheek and his lips brushed hers. The roar in Kate's ears replaced all thought. So far from everything she had ever known, in the midst of such bitter reality, a new assurance of *home* laid claim on her.

THIRTY-ONE

Drifting from a faraway place where *Maman* attended him, Domingo tried to open his eyes. The copper smell permeating this place, he knew all too well. Someone had been injured.

"Keep administering the morphine—same dosage every four hours. And change that bandage during this lull."

"Yes, doctor."

But before he could take in his surroundings, Domingo slipped back into the welcome shelter of his family. The utter comfort in *Maman's* eyes assured him without a doubt that she experienced peace.

Aitaita appeared, jovial yet intent at the same time. As always, he had a word for his middle grandson. "Remember who you are, Domingo. Always keep in mind your heritage and what our name stands for."

Meadow ... such a simple meaning, but oh the meadows he'd trod during the past few years! Beautiful, most of them, but some, full of welcoming committees for drops from London, also housed treachery. Meadows had seen too many men die, nameless to him but known to God—*les inconnus*.

A list of given names—cousins, mostly—filtered through Domingo's mind. Igancio, Ramon, Mariano, Filiberto, all those who joined the great migration across the Atlantic Ocean along with Castor and Estebon. With each name came a story or several, a host of tales in all.

In his vision, Ander joined Aitaita, with an easy glimmer of mischief in his glance. Papa also visited Domingo in this quiet world, his voice deep and strong. "You must live, my son. You must carry on our name."

But Domingo wanted only to bask in their familiarity. He eased into the warmth of that place, so serene and safe compared to this present world. Then, like a tardy shadow, that storyteller Giriotte appeared. A faint young woman hovered in the background, and finally, an American—a pilot.

Some time later, a searing pain in Domingo's knee drew him back to vibrant voices. "He's strong and young, he'll make it. They brought him here so quickly that he lost little blood. I would hate to take that leg, but..."

"Let's give it more time—no signs of gangrene or septicemia yet, and some penicillin is on the way, they tell me."

"That miraculous cure did wonders for so many wounded in the landings. You're certain the shipment is coming?"

"We'll see. The local doctor has been known to pull strings before.

In and out, in and out, from that land to this, Domingo traveled. This one he failed to understand. Nothing made sense here, and no particular voice piqued his interest. Yet each communication told him these people were trying to save his leg.

Why then, did he long to join his loved ones in that other place? But they kept urging him back here, to an odor that smelled of something awful, worse than pigs, worse than onions. Gradually, he identified the focused scent of suffering.

A bit later, he woke again. All around him men groaned and cried out, though his eyes still refused to open. And in the background, always the sounds of fighting, like thunder and trains rumbling in the night. But those trains never arrived at their destination.

These distractions returned him to the fighting again, with Petra leading the way, of course. But this time, Petra's intuition failed them, for the Germans attacked from behind. Domingo heard them first, before Petra turned, understood the danger, and howled a battle cry. But he yelled too late to keep one of them from bludgeoning Domingo's knee.

Next, a rifle aimed at his nose, but Petra screamed a wild, "No!" and took to the air. Then a heavy *whack* split bone, and Petra panted, "Are you all right?"

In the next instant, Domingo's world went dark.

~

Rumors ranged the camp like late July's testy heat, and Kate heard them all, since the cook had finally softened to her offers of help. He even told her his name—Bernardo. Peeling potatoes and stirring porridge brought a certain satisfaction, but she missed Père. One day, he'd gathered his things to accompany the last partisans, leaving her some instructions.

"Keep your eyes and ears open. Pray that I can find Domingo. Remember the ultimate triumph, and that we'll return for you."

Ultimate triumph, a fitting motto, like the theme of Saint Perre's tymphanum. Her location remained perfect for transmitting, and the messages showed no sign of lessening as drops from London continued.

Neither did the rampant speculations in camp. Bernardo gleaned news from every partisan who passed through, and made spreading the word his personal task.

"Have you heard the Allies have badly wounded Field Marshal Rommel? Our boys strafed his car from the air." The clatter of tin spoons against dishes mixed with more information as the eater took his meal standing.

"The German troops, mostly veterans from the Eastern Front, still call the area of Limousin "Little Russia," because of so many attacks. We have done ourselves proud. They may have slaughtered our people at Oradour and at Tulle, but our liberation lies very near."

Whenever hungry partisans approached for food, Bernardo's eyes gleamed with their stories, and the comers never seemed to tire of his ministrations. Gallons of porridge, cauldrons of stew—always something for the hungry.

Today, Bernardo disappeared in the early August dawn to hunt partridges and rabbits. Always, starving men appeared with empty stomachs, and he received his payment in stories.

"The *Moyenne-Correze*, undeterred by the atrocities at Tulle, have risen again and are on the prowl."

"The Allies have taken St. Lo—have you heard? They've broken out from Normandy's hedgerow country and will soon reach Paris.

They've taken Livorno, Italy, too. Won't be long before they attack the last German position in the north."

Between her messages and Bernardo's consistent stream of announcements, Kate felt well informed on the Allies' progress.

"When the Germans withdrew from Southern Italy in the face of our advancing forces, they took a million dollars in Italian gold, and looted more millions from Belgium, Austria, Hungary, and the Netherlands, to force everyone to use Reich marks for currency.

"Now we have re-taken much of that gold. Those bars marked with RB for Reich bank represent the gold rings, teeth, crystal and silver of the Chosen who were taken captive. Some justice, eh? We arm ourselves with the money the Bosche stole from God's people."

With no way of discerning truth from falsehood, Kate continued her work and spent the rest of her time assisting Bernardo. One day, a woman she'd befriended followed her husband to the fight. They had developed a routine of searching for herbs in the afternoons, and Kate missed her companionship

A few days later, on a hot afternoon as she looked up from scrubbing a pile of plates, Kate almost fell off her wooden stool. A cheery voice prompted her. "So, they've turned you on the dirty dishes?"

She rushed into long arms extending from a filthy soutane. Fiery auburn hair scratched her cheek. "Oh, Père, I'm so glad to see you. You're looking as bedraggled as ever."

"Why, thank you. I make that my business, *Madame*." He addressed Bernardo.

"*Monsieur*, would you mind if I took this girl away for a short while?"

The surly cook grunted and resumed stirring his massive pot. Actually far less grumpy than he let on, a week ago he even shared a little about his family with Kate.

Père grabbed her hand and pulled her past her den. She couldn't wait to ply him with questions.

"Now I can find out what's true and what's not. Did Rommel's car really get strafed?"

"Yes. We mustn't rejoice when someone suffers, but I admit that I did when I heard that. I only wish one of the attempts on Hitler's life had given us even more cause for rejoicing."

"Whispers about Operation Dragoon range the camp, and word of the Allies landing on the south coast. Have you heard anything about that, or what's going on near Paris?"

"Umm ..." Père veered down a shady path. "What's happened around here since I've been gone? Have you seen anything of Madame Lamoutte or little Viviane's grandfather?"

He must know something unrepeatable as yet.

"No, hopefully that poor woman found some peace. But one other survivor stayed here for a few days, a child someone found out in a field."

Père shook his head as they entered a shaded area with ample fallen logs. He sank on one of them, as weary as he was dirty.

"Have you been back to Lot?"

He gave no clear reply. "At least the S.S. left, but ... Oh, my. I doubt we'll ever fully recover."

The murmur from a small waterfall backed idle midsummer bird chirps and animal sounds, and also insulated their conversation from eavesdroppers. Kate itched to ask about Domingo, but Père surely knew how she longed for news. Silence stretched between them, but he leaned back against a tree and offered nothing.

Finally, she launched a safe inquiry. "Have you written any outstanding sermons in the past few weeks?"

"I have been remiss in my priestly duties, I'm afraid, enough to lose my position. It's a good thing my people demonstrate the soul of patience—of course, so many have gone into hiding, we probably couldn't fill one pew if we did meet."

He munched on a squeaky weed. "But that does bring to mind something I promised to tell you a long time ago."

"About the tymphanum?"

"How did you know?"

"I figured you'd eventually remember."

"Sorry to disappoint you, but I'm still chewing on that concept ... I may never finish, not in this life. It's something about the juxtaposition of seeming defeat and victory. The Cross and the Crown right there together. Do you see?"

"I think so." Kate shed her new espadrilles, a gift from Bernardo, to give her feet some air while Père rested. His bony wrists, scratched and raw, extended from his over-sized sleeves. "You traveled a long distance?"

"Not so far. Have your transmissions slowed down?"

"The activity has been monumental, but I feel it building toward some grand finale."

"Umm ... just between us, the *Résistance* under Colonel Rol plans an uprising in Paris. Charles de Gaulle is pleading with General Eisenhower to send aid. If that happens, there's bound to be a bloody battle with Dietrich von Choltitz, the military governor in charge of the city."

And Domingo, what of Domingo? Miss G had been so right about Kate's weakest point. Waiting was the worst, and she always had to wait—for word, for assignments, for confirmation.

At long last, Père released her. "Domingo and I parted when he left for the Limousin, but we met again."

Kate leaned toward him. *Come on, Père. Why are you taking so long?* And then the sun filtered through the foliage, lighted his face and exposed the glints in his eyes.

"I could never have imagined him so exhausted. But he's with a good man, an older fellow named Petra. They take care of each other, and when Domingo and I found a moment alone, he gave me a message for you. 'Tell Kate to stay strong. Assure her that I will find her.'"

~

That voice repeating his name ... From the depths of slumber, the low, understated tone called Domingo back. Puffs of air hit his face as though someone aimed words at him.

"Listen to me, my brother. It's August fifteenth. We've liberated Brive-la-Gaillarde, the first French city to be freed. Soon Paris will be released, and then all the rest. Wake up, Domingo. This is our time, when everything we've worked for comes to pass."

Far down in his being, something stirred, stifling Domingo's desire to rest forever. When he opened his eyes, a rascally face hovered over him, eyes alight with expectation, body rank with trail odors.

"Can't believe you took all this time off—never knew you to be lazy."

"Pe ... Petra?"

"Who else? I've been out there without my partner. That's no good. But we've come a long way, and freed…"

"Brive…"

"Brive-la-Gaillarde, yes. We've got the Huns on the run, heading for a last-ditch fight with the Allies on the Maginau Line. The fighting has all but ended here, so it's safe for you to get out of bed, my friend."

Petra flashed a grin and Domingo shifted his weight, but a bolt of pain coursed through his thigh. In a daze, he saw a woman hold up her hand.

"Oh, no. You can't run out on us just because you're finally conscious. You must build up your endurance." She crossed her arms and looked from Domingo to Petra. "Maybe now, one of you will tell us whose leg we saved."

Petra made a gallant bow. "*Merci, Madame.* Meet *La Foudre,* the soul of *La Résistance.* Long may he live."

~

"We ate our fill and brought some home." A partisan dumped his pack at Kate's feet, and she could hardly fathom her good fortune. Apples and small pears—she couldn't do apple pie the justice Addie could, but set her mind to making a cobbler after devouring a dripping pear.

The aftertaste satisfied her longing, so she found a bowl and a knife. The camp, almost deserted except for a few men like these who just passed through, still held women and children living in tents. They could use a treat like this.

Excited for the opportunity to brighten their stark lives, she washed the fruit. Little by little, she'd gotten to know some of these women, so now they greeted her on her morning and evening strolls. Everyone used only first names here, probably false, but knowing her neighbors helped Kate's state of mind.

Her new comradeship with Bernardo also filled some of the void whenever she switched off the transmitter. Gradually, her transmissions waned until only a few messages arrived during the last three days. What would she do when London no longer needed her here?

Would they still ask her to travel to Lyon at that point? If Domingo hadn't come before then, how could she leave without knowing his fate? *So exhausted...* Père's description belied the energetic Domingo she knew.

Only prayer abated her constant questions, so she prayed more and more. Domingo and his partner entered her thoughts a thousand times a day, along with Père, who had left again.

"Calm down. Remember how you were sent back from London, and how Père found you right on the trail. Don't forget that Domingo promised to come for you."

A youth ran through the camp shouting, "They've liberated Paris, have you heard? Charles de Gaulle led a victory parade through the city yesterday, under *L'Arc de Triomphe!*"

By the time Kate removed a bubbling cobbler from Bernardo's makeshift oven, the glorious news spread through camp. Such a perfect time to distribute this treat. She savored a small piece so hot and sweet she almost cried. With portions in a big basket lined with a towel, she set out to hand them to the women and children.

Bernardo returned from his hunting and set her to work on tonight's stew. She prayed while she worked, so lost in her thoughts and longings that a partisan slipped up unseen. But his words brought her to attention.

"Light hair and dark eyes, came here with Père Gaspard."

"Right over there." Bernardo hailed Kate. "Someone wants to see you."

She'd noted many dirty berets, but never one this worn-out. The muscled partisan pushed it back and stood before her. "You know Domingo Ibarra?"

Kate's spoon clattered against the pot. *Oh no, please. Don't let him say...*

"*Mademoiselle,* I am Petra, bringing word from Domingo. He ... ran out of strength. He must see you."

Kate could only gape, so Bernardo intervened in his gruff manner. "Well, do you want to see this Domingo or not?"

Tears streamed her cheeks and her throat clogged, so he continued. "Go with him."

Petra spun into motion. "Is there a stretcher around here? I need another man to..."

Bernardo pointed out a lone partisan slumped under a tree, so Petra started toward him. Soon Kate followed the two of them down a path.

So many trails since she'd arrived here, so many kilometers. Following, always following. Now she fell into the routine. *Ran out of strength* ... Domingo? Impossible. What could this mean?

She soon saw. Eyes closed, Domingo sprawled on the earth with a man fanning his flushed face. Kate knelt beside him, whispered his name. Finally, Domingo's eyes cracked open, but his grimace shouted his pain.

"You're hurt ... we'll get you home."

He shook his head. "I ... am ...home."

"What?"

"You ... are my ... home." The men slid the stretcher under him and Domingo reached for Kate as he whispered, "America ... good land ... for sheep?"

Kate searched her geography lessons. "Why, yes, in Idaho."

"Idaho..." He reached for her. "We can start over there?"

"We...yes. But what about Gabirel?"

Light tinged Domingo's face even as he groaned. "We...will... find ... him."

~

Striped canvas awnings stood watch over food tables, show calves mooed from individual barn stalls, and a cacophony of excited voices streamed in every direction. But one in particular struck Kathryn's ears like a melody. Precious Mara, all rigged out in her cowgirl boots and riding gear, tore through the crowd.

"You're back, Grandma—you came!" She slammed into Kathryn with a storm's force.

"Of course I did, honey." Kathryn caught her breath after the onslaught. Catching up with Mara, Gabby enveloped them both in her arms.

"Mom—oh, you're home." She wiped away sudden tears. "Darlene said you were in Denver, but … Oh, this has been so frustrating—where did they take you?"

"It's about time for Mara's group, hon. We'll have to save all this for later. Anyway, I'm finally home, and so glad to be."

Linking arms with the two of them, Kathryn gave thanks for their sturdiness. After insane flights zigzagging northward, and so many takeoffs and landings, she craved solid ground and a long, long rest.

At the grandstand, Gabby paused before going with Mara. "One thing I know you'll be happy to hear—a letter came from Charles Tenney. He said Addie came through her surgery and is on the mend."

"Oh my…thank you for telling me." Kathryn stumbled a little, and Gabby led her to the grandstand railing.

"You look so pale, Mom. Are you sure you're all right?"

"Sure. Go on now—this is Mara's big moment, honey." Kathryn sank into the nearest empty spot on the bleachers. A wave of homesickness for Domingo almost overwhelmed her—if only he would come home early, but she knew better. The men always kept the sheep in the high country for at least another few weeks.

Oh, this heat—what a change from the South American winter she'd just left, and that freezing airplane. She could sure use something to drink from one of those food stands, but queasiness told her to stay right where she dropped. Her head swirled with all the sudden changes, landing during the night in Denver, the crazy drive back to Idaho, and coming to a screeching halt just outside the fairgrounds only a short time ago.

Benjamin had opened her door for her and grabbed her suitcase from the trunk. "Thank you." That was all he said, and Kathryn rummaged in her repertoire for something to give him—a gift of words.

"You succeeded. I'm glad for you."

He swallowed. "We couldn't have done it without you." In the same brown tweed as always, he re-entered the car. Just before he pulled his door shut, he looked her in the eyes. "You don't believe me, but I truly did not mean to send you flying out of that balcony. I..."

The racket from the rodeo grounds called to Kathryn, and she could think of nothing to say. Benjamin shrugged, closed his door and the driver drove away.

Just one more scene to analyze in the years to come. But for now, she must put that experience out of her mind. It certainly wouldn't be the first time. Every spring when Domingo left for the Sawtooth high country with the sheep, Kathryn steeled herself to be strong, to take care of everything until he came home without allowing her longing for him to hold sway over her.

The announcer called out a list of names starting with the youngest riders. Now, what set did Gabby say Mara would ride in? Kathryn thought the second, but dizziness threatened her again.

Can't end up in the hospital again. Hang on until she rides ... just hang on. Then Gabby will take you home and you can rest. By the time Domingo comes home, you'll be back to normal.

Sunlight blended with the shadow of a tall cowboy sitting behind her ... wasn't that the story of her life? Light and darkness, easy and tough, all dappled together like a forest scene. But that word *home*—oh, how it enticed her. She could barely wait to enter her house, sit at the kitchen table, and lie on her own bed.

The bleachers vibrated with people finding seats, and that constant tremor melded with the weakness that coursed through Kathryn. *Hold on—you made it back, you can't fail Mara now.*

And then, someone strong squeezed in beside her, put a cool glass in her hand, and commanded, "Drink."

She obeyed. Lemonade, just the ticket. The ice-cold tartness cleared Kathryn's mind, and then the scent of wool on the hoof and a worn shirt claimed her. That someone leaned closer.

Domingo? Disbelief flooded her. No, it couldn't be. He was always the last one to come down before winter. But there was no denying those eyes.

Tender and dark as onyx under his stained hat, they found hers. Then the roughness of his face brushed her skin, and her eyes burned against his chest.

"How did you...?"

"I learned long ago to listen to my heart. You taught me that, Katarin. My heart's been saying something's wrong down here, that you need me. So here I am."

"But the flock..."

"Remember, we have a son—two of them. They've learned well—they urged me to leave and seemed pleased to shoulder the responsibility. Besides, Gabirel is up there with his flock, too. Remember?"

He held her even closer and wiped her tears away with his stumpy little finger. "Your face is awfully white. You've been sick."

"Yes. Oh, I do need you so much right now—and somehow, you knew it."

"Père Gaspard would have something to say about that—he called us *les inconnus*, but always maintained we were known by God. And guided by Him."

Hearing Père's name, Kathryn sighed and leaned even closer, if that were possible. So many agents returned to their lives alone after the war—what a gift to share these memories with Domingo.

"Look out there, Katarin. Little Mara's riding into the arena, just like her mother did years ago. She flies along as if she were born to ride."

He whispered low then, so only she could hear. "And like her grandmother, who fell right out of the sky, almost into my arms."

ABOUT THE AUTHOR

Words have always been comfort food for Gail Kittleson. After instructing expository writing and English as a Second Language, she began writing memoir. Now, intrigued by the World War II era, Gail creates women's historical fiction from her northern Iowa home and also facilitates writing workshops/retreats.

She and her husband, a retired Army chaplain, enjoy their grandchildren and in winter, Arizona's Mogollon Rim Country. You can count on Gail's heroines to ask honest questions, act with integrity, grow in faith, and face hardships with spunk.

Visit Gail online at: GailKittleson.com